POKéMON™
ADVENTURES

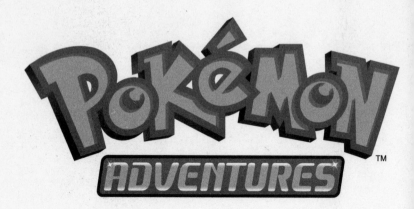

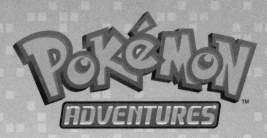

Pokémon ADVENTURES
Volume 4
Perfect Square Edition

Story by **HIDENORI KUSAKA**
Art by **MATO**

© 2009 Pokémon.
© 1995-2009 Nintendo/Creatures Inc./GAME FREAK inc.
TM, ®, and character names are trademarks of Nintendo.
POCKET MONSTERS SPECIAL Vol. 4
by Hidenori KUSAKA, MATO
© 1997 Hidenori KUSAKA, MATO
All rights reserved.
Original Japanese edition published by SHOGAKUKAN.
English translation rights in the United States of America, Canada, the
United Kingdom and Ireland arranged with SHOGAKUKAN.

English Adaptation/Gerard Jones
Translation/Kaori Inoue
Miscellaneous Text Adaptation/Ben Costa
Touch-up & Lettering/Wayne Truman
Design/Sam Elzway
Editor, 1st Edition/William Flanagan
Editor, Perfect Square Edition/Jann Jones

Printed in the U.S.A.

Published by VIZ Media, LLC
P.O. Box 77010
San Francisco, CA 94107

10 9 8
First printing, December 2009
Eighth printing, March 2016

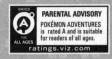

www.perfectsquare.com   www.viz.com

Pokémon™ Adventures

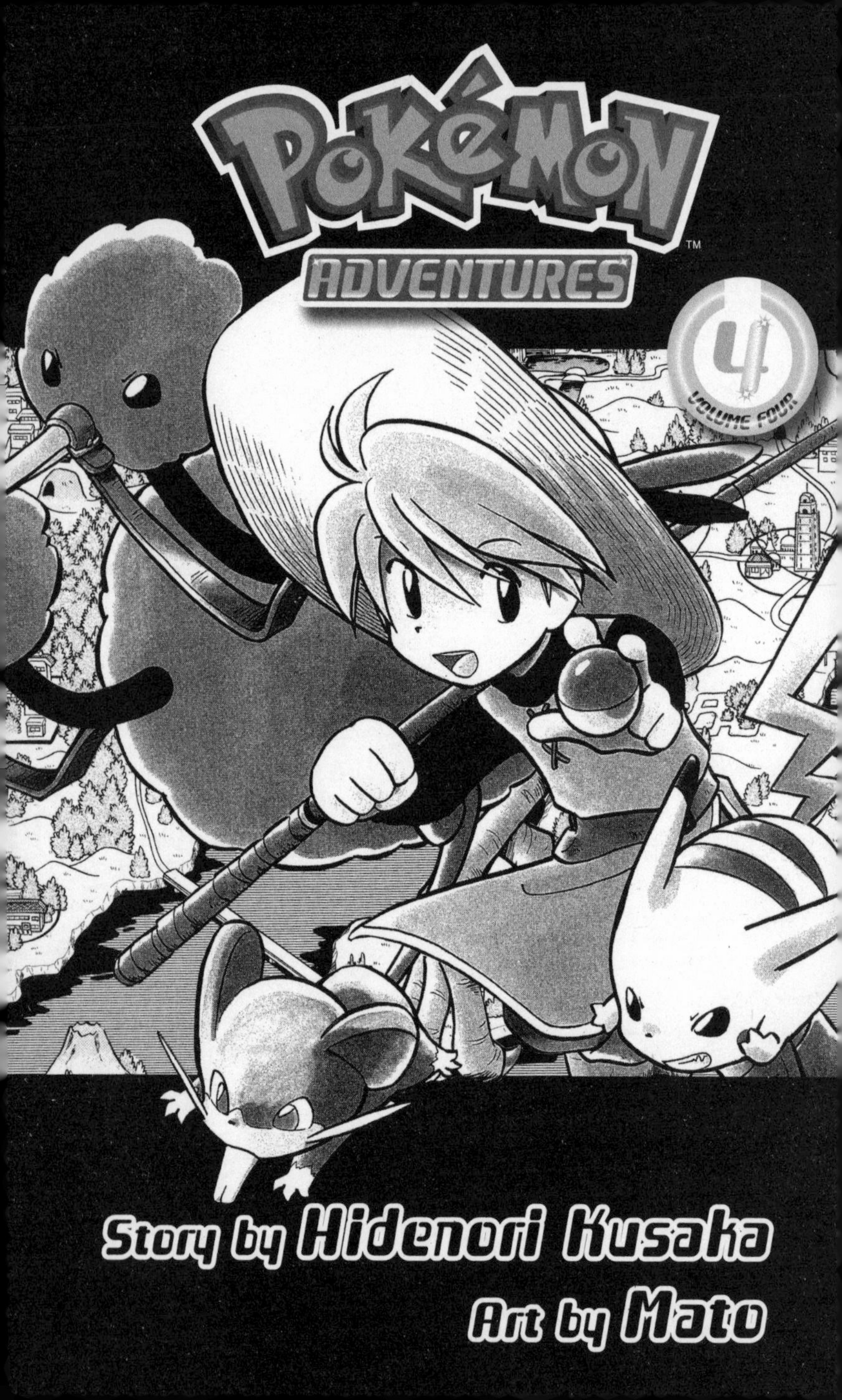

4
VOLUME FOUR

Story by Hidenori Kusaka

Art by Mato

CHARACTERS

THUS FAR...

Over the course of their adventures, Red and his Pokémon friends have really matured, surmounting many life-and-death situations.

A YOUNG BOY WITH A YELLOW STRAW HAT

A mysterious trainer suddenly arrives in Pallet Town. What could this trainer's purpose possibly be...?!

GYM LEADERS OF THE VARIOUS CITIES:

VIRIDIAN CITY GYM LEADER	SAFFRON CITY GYM LEADER	FUCHSIA CITY GYM LEADER	VERMILION CITY GYM LEADER
GIOVANNI	SABRINA	KOGA	LT. SURGE

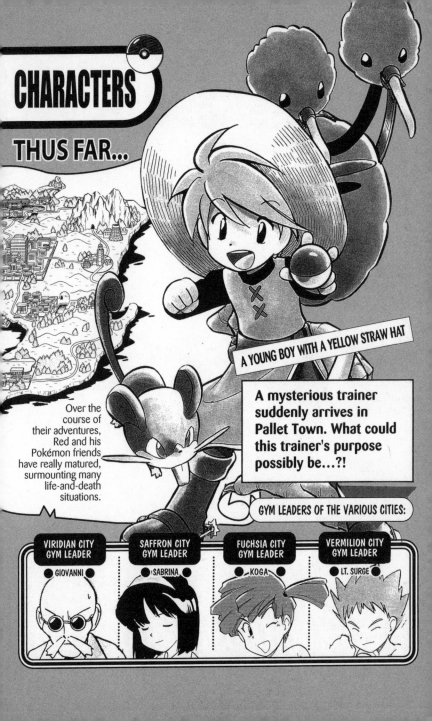

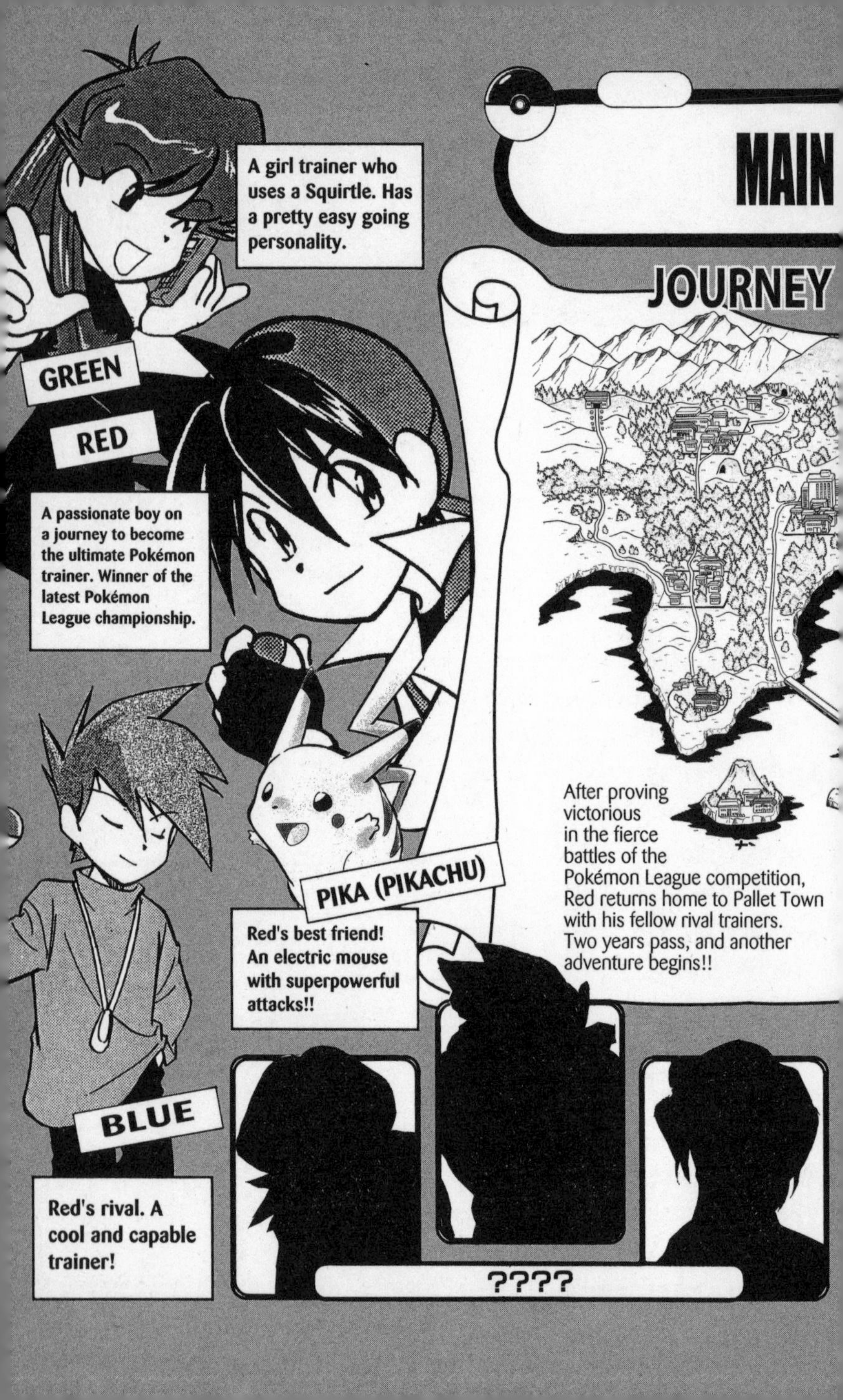

MAIN
JOURNEY
After proving victorious in the fierce battles of the Pokémon League competition, Red returns home to Pallet Town with his fellow rival trainers. Two years pass, and another adventure begins!!
A girl trainer who uses a Squirtle. Has a pretty easy going personality.
GREEN
RED
A passionate boy on a journey to become the ultimate Pokémon trainer. Winner of the latest Pokémon League championship.
PIKA (PIKACHU)
Red's best friend! An electric mouse with superpowerful attacks!!
BLUE
Red's rival. A cool and capable trainer!
????

CONTENTS

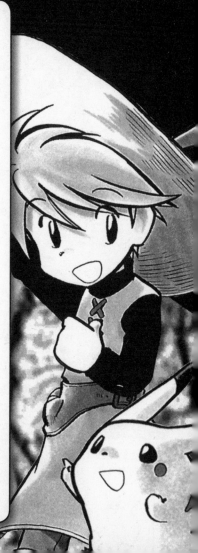

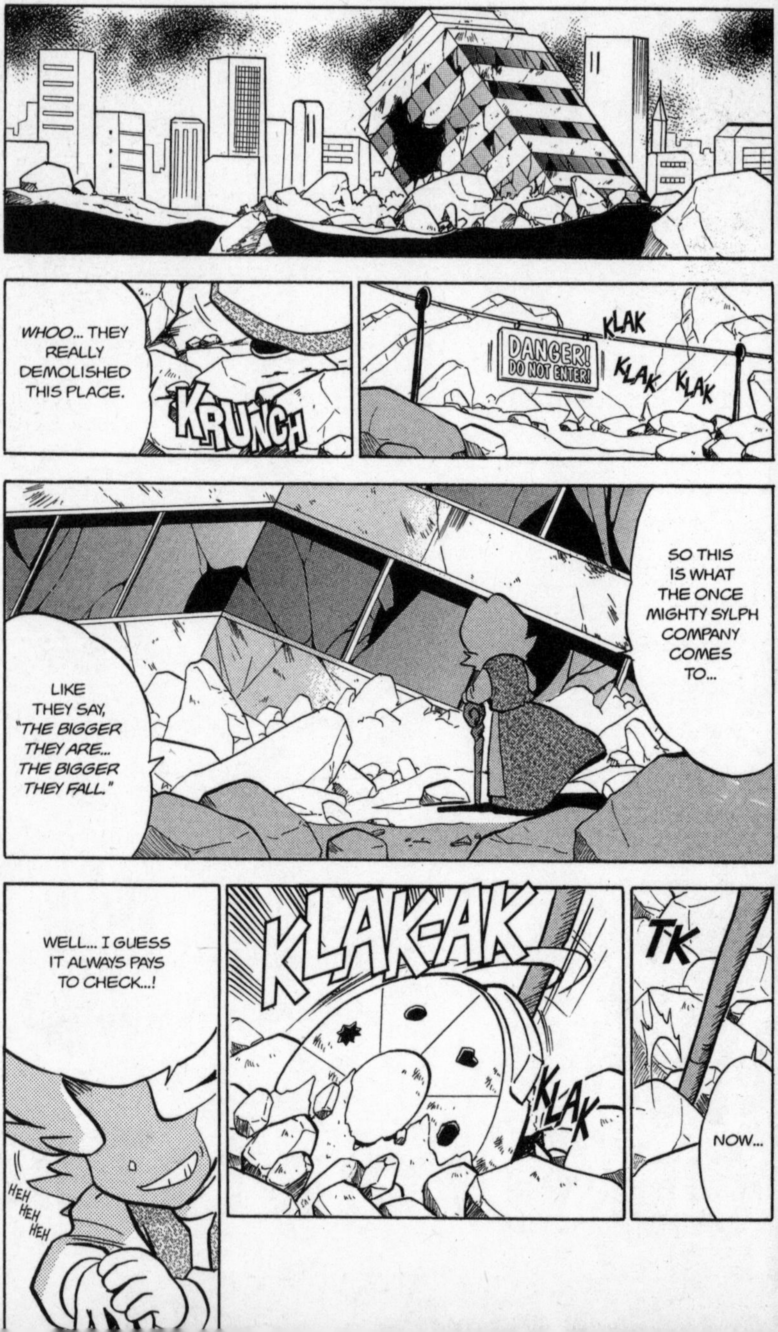

DANGER! DO NOT ENTER!
KLAK
KLAK
KLAK
WHOO... THEY REALLY DEMOLISHED THIS PLACE.
KRUNCH
SO THIS IS WHAT THE ONCE MIGHTY SYLPH COMPANY COMES TO...
LIKE THEY SAY, "THE BIGGER THEY ARE... THE BIGGER THEY FALL."
TK
NOW...
KLAK-AK
KLAK
WELL... I GUESS IT ALWAYS PAYS TO CHECK...!
HEH HEH HEH

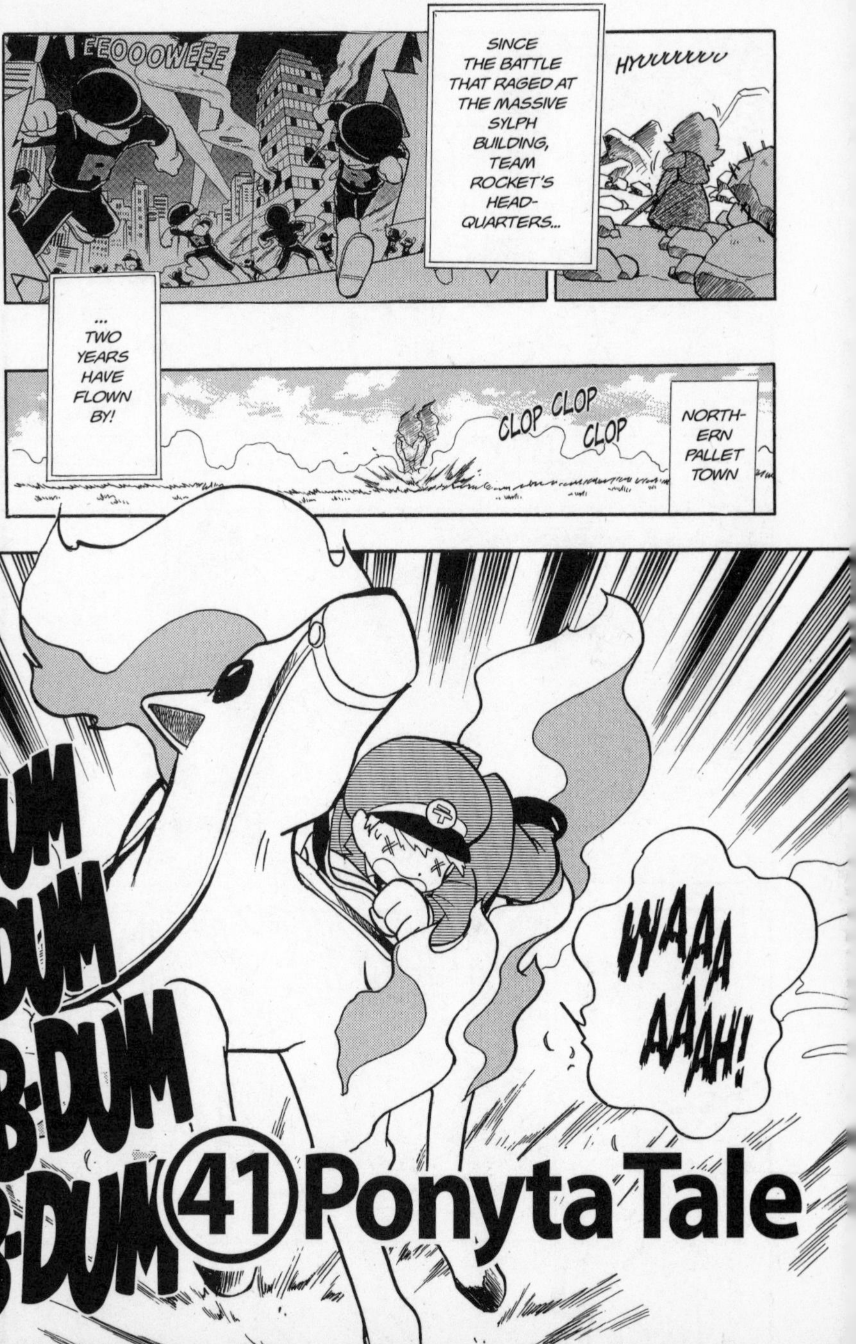
HYUUUUUU
SINCE THE BATTLE THAT RAGED AT THE MASSIVE SYLPH BUILDING, TEAM ROCKET'S HEAD-QUARTERS...
EEOOOWEEE
... TWO YEARS HAVE FLOWN BY!
NORTH-ERN PALLET TOWN
CLOP CLOP CLOP
WAAAAAAH!
DUM DUM B-DUM B-DUM
41 Ponyta Tale

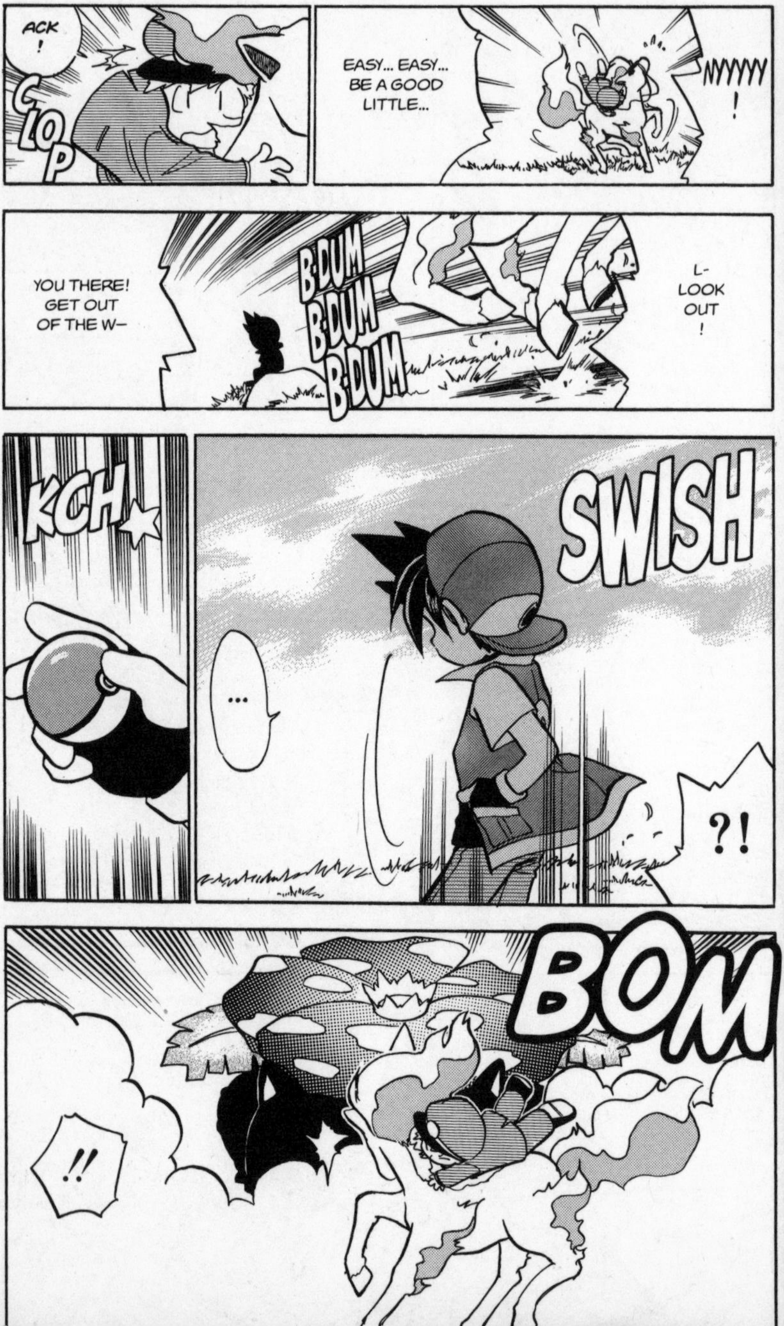
NYYYYY!
EASY... EASY... BE A GOOD LITTLE...
ACK!
CLOP
L-LOOK OUT!
B-DUM B-DUM B-DUM
YOU THERE! GET OUT OF THE W—
SWISH
?!
...
KCH
BOM
!!

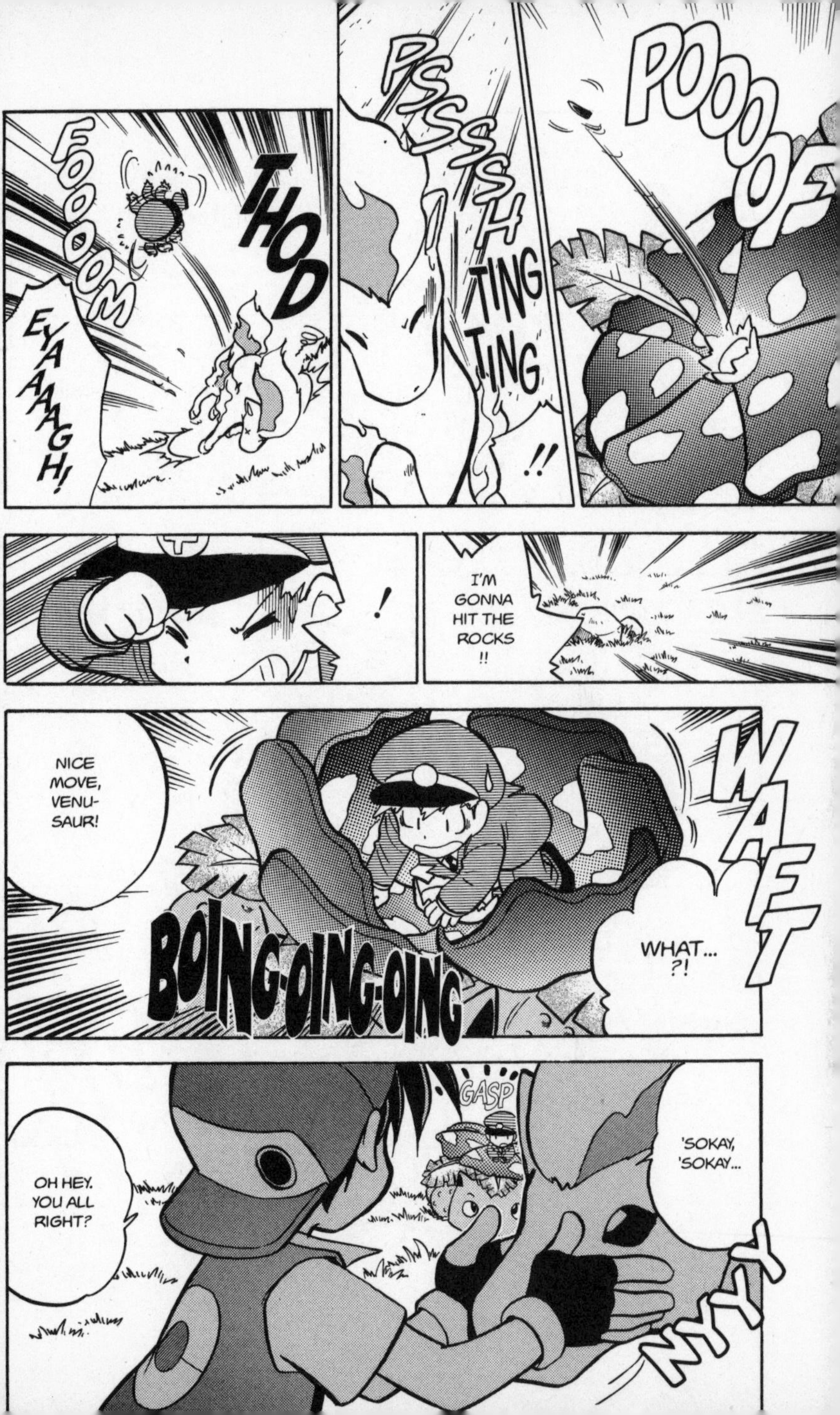
POOOOF
PSSSSH
TING
TING
!!
FOOOOM
THOD
EYAAAAGH!
I'M GONNA HIT THE ROCKS !!
!
WAFT
WHAT... ?!
BOING-OING-OING
NICE MOVE, VENU-SAUR!
'SOKAY, 'SOKAY...
NYYY
GASP
OH HEY. YOU ALL RIGHT?

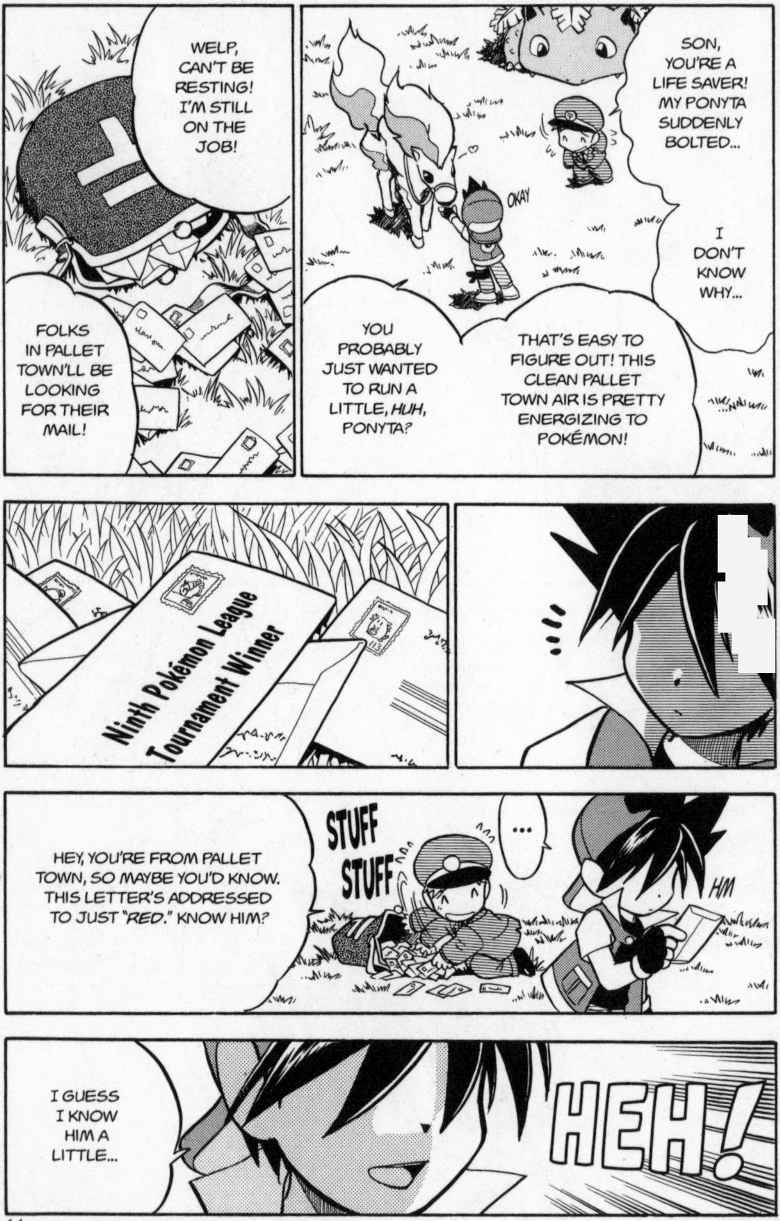
SON, YOU'RE A LIFE SAVER! MY PONYTA SUDDENLY BOLTED...
I DON'T KNOW WHY...
OKAY
THAT'S EASY TO FIGURE OUT! THIS CLEAN PALLET TOWN AIR IS PRETTY ENERGIZING TO POKÉMON!
YOU PROBABLY JUST WANTED TO RUN A LITTLE, *HUH*, PONYTA?
WELP, CAN'T BE RESTING! I'M STILL ON THE JOB!
FOLKS IN PALLET TOWN'LL BE LOOKING FOR THEIR MAIL!
Ninth Pokémon League Tournament Winner
HM
...
STUFF STUFF
HEY, YOU'RE FROM PALLET TOWN, SO MAYBE YOU'D KNOW. THIS LETTER'S ADDRESSED TO JUST "*RED*." KNOW HIM?
HEH!
I GUESS I KNOW HIM A LITTLE...

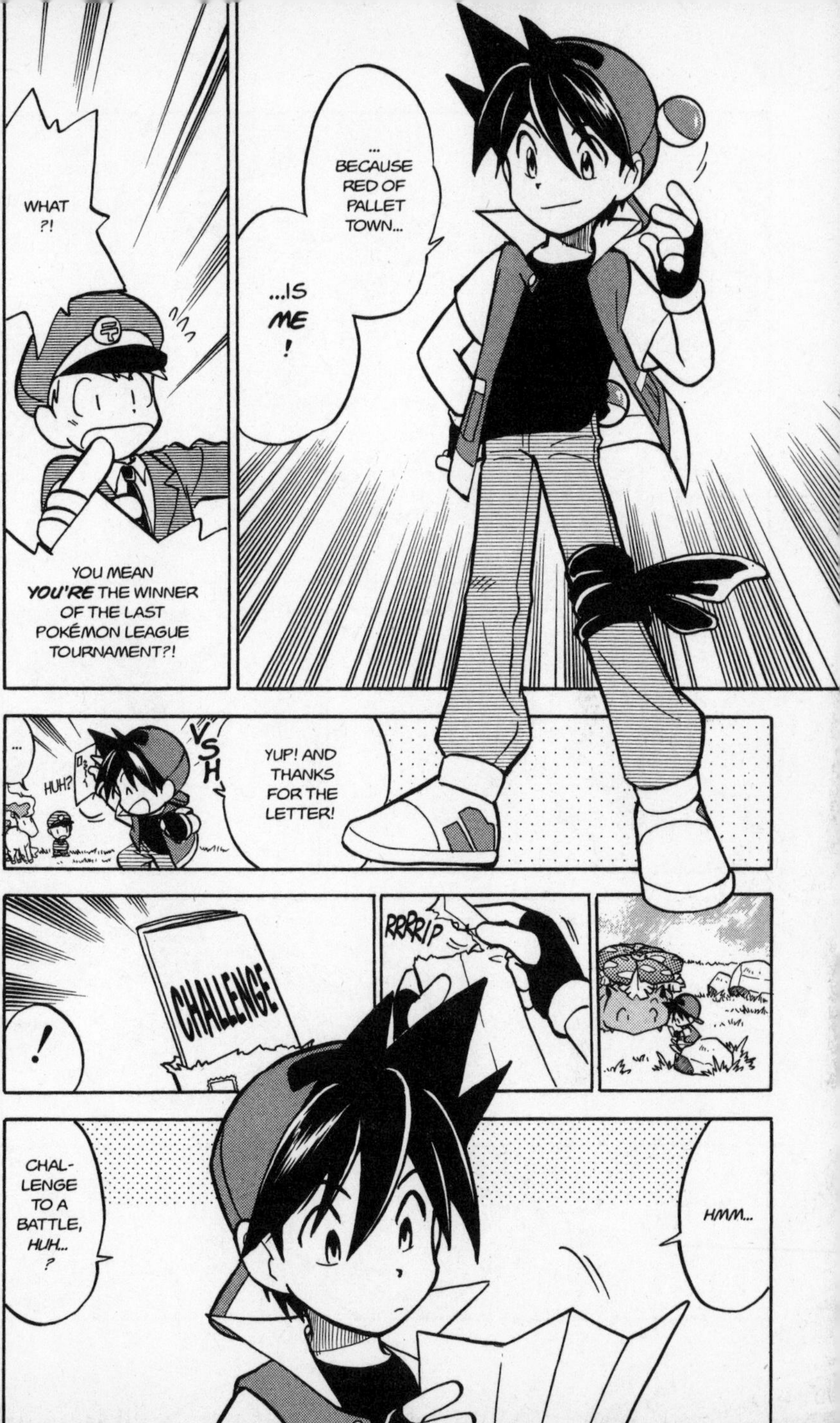
... BECAUSE RED OF PALLET TOWN...
...IS ME!
WHAT ?!
YOU MEAN YOU'RE THE WINNER OF THE LAST POKÉMON LEAGUE TOURNAMENT?!
YUP! AND THANKS FOR THE LETTER!
VSH
HUH?
...
RRRRIP
CHALLENGE
!
HMM...
CHALLENGE TO A BATTLE, HUH...?

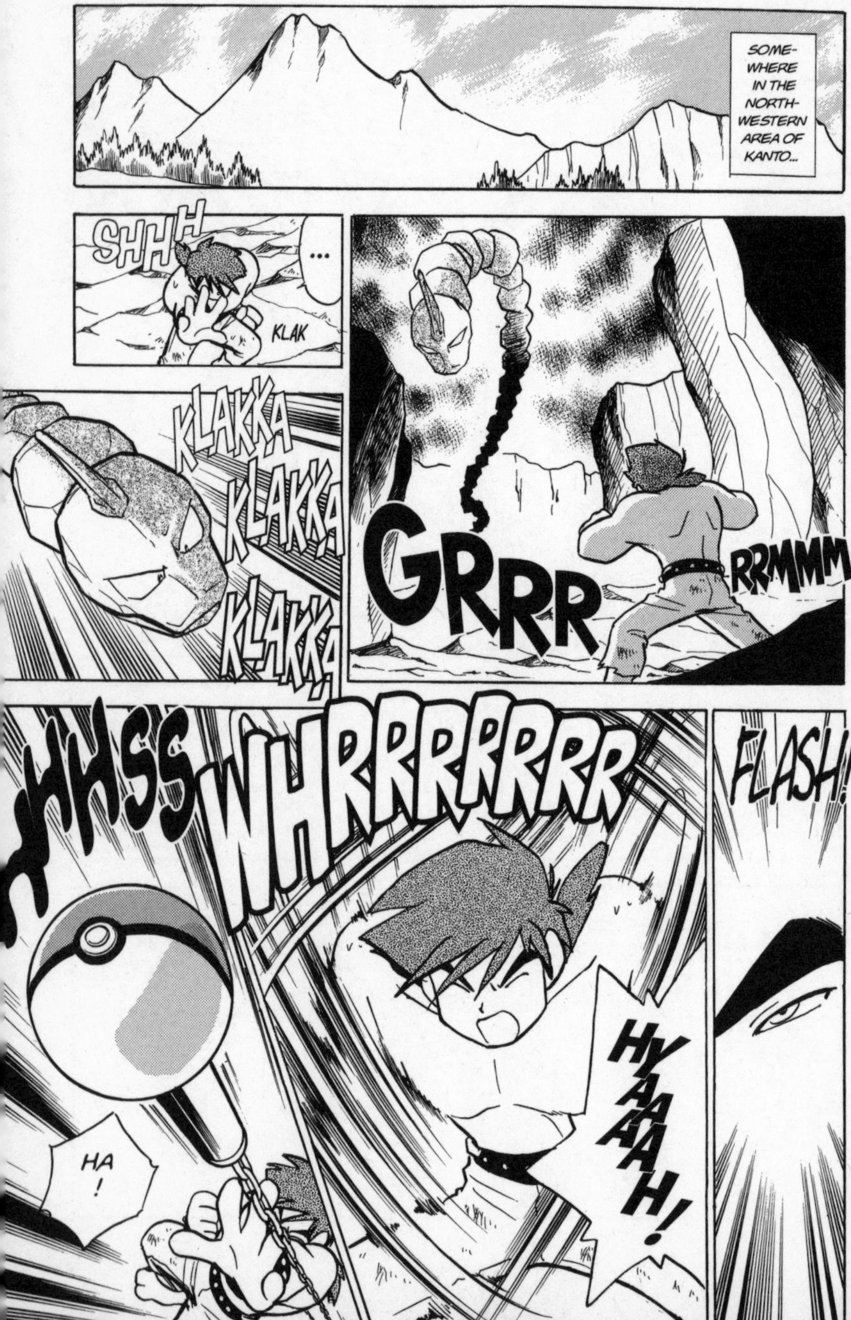

SOME-WHERE IN THE NORTH-WESTERN AREA OF KANTO...
GRRRR
RRMMM
SHHH
...
KLAK
KLAKKA KLAKKA KLAKKA
FLASH!
WHRRRRRRR
SHHSS
HYAAAAAH!
HA!

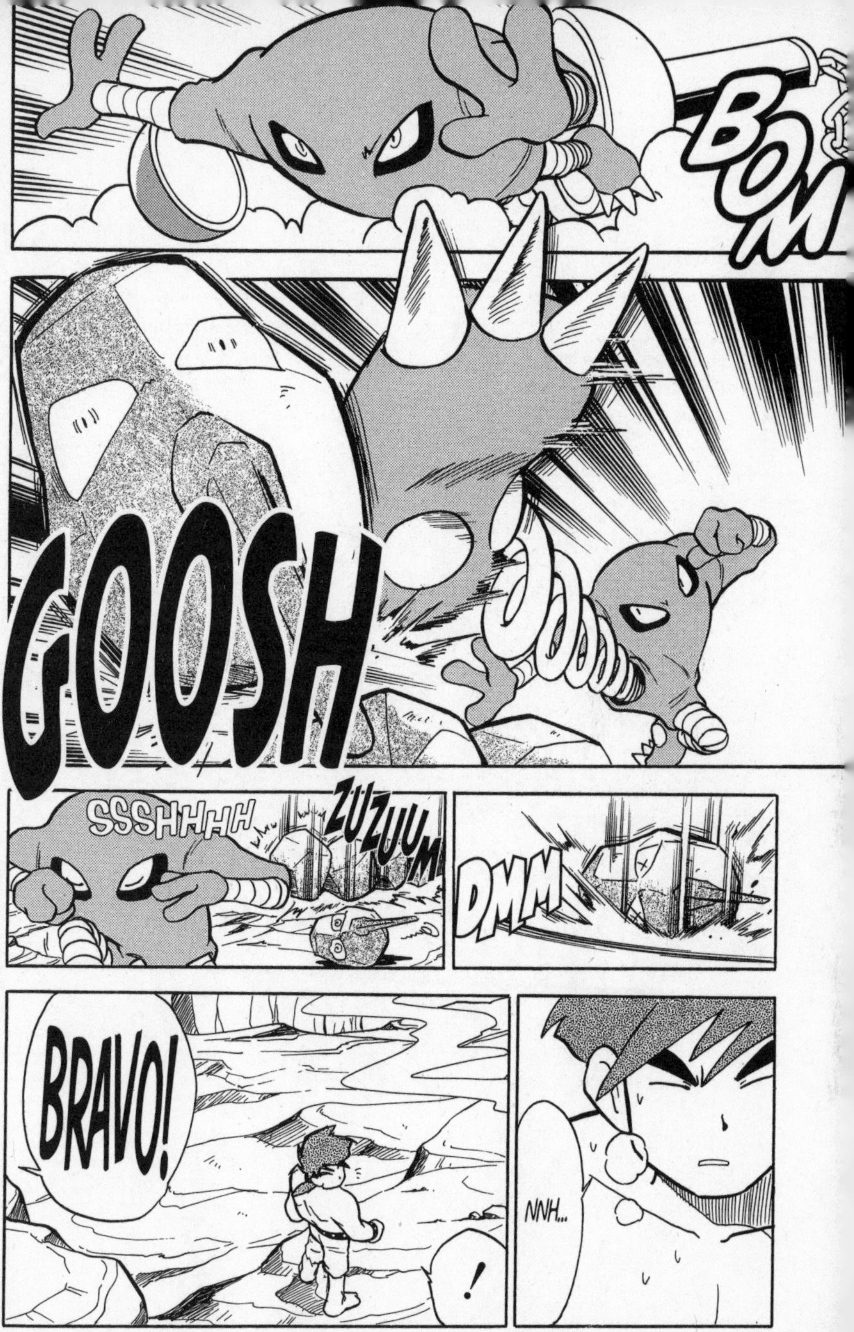
BOM
GOOSH
DMM
ZUZUUM
SSSHHHH
NNH...
BRAVO!
!

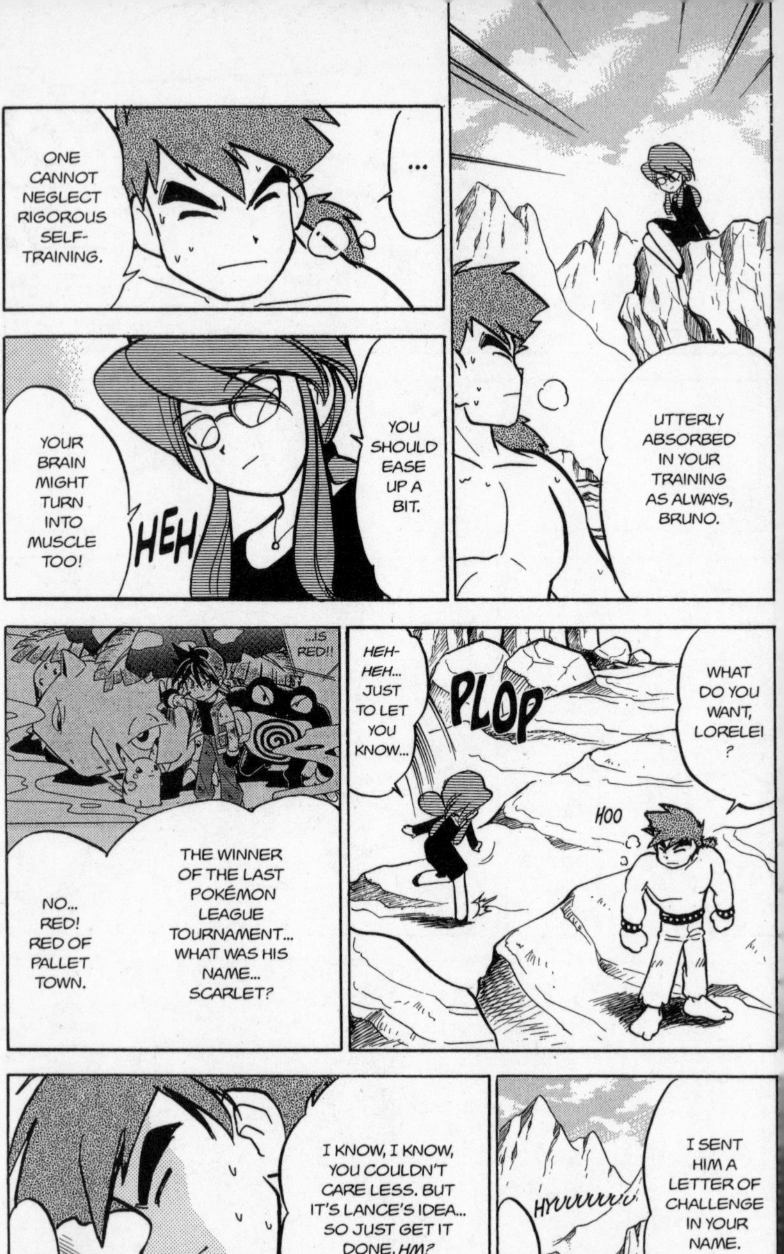
UTTERLY ABSORBED IN YOUR TRAINING AS ALWAYS, BRUNO.
...
ONE CANNOT NEGLECT RIGOROUS SELF-TRAINING.
YOU SHOULD EASE UP A BIT.
HEH
YOUR BRAIN MIGHT TURN INTO MUSCLE TOO!
WHAT DO YOU WANT, LORELEI?
HOO
PLOP
HEH-HEH... JUST TO LET YOU KNOW...
...IS RED!!
THE WINNER OF THE LAST POKÉMON LEAGUE TOURNAMENT... WHAT WAS HIS NAME... SCARLET?
NO... RED! RED OF PALLET TOWN.
I SENT HIM A LETTER OF CHALLENGE IN YOUR NAME.
HYUUUUUU
...
I KNOW, I KNOW, YOU COULDN'T CARE LESS. BUT IT'S LANCE'S IDEA... SO JUST GET IT DONE, *HM?*
...

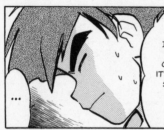

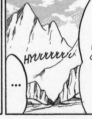

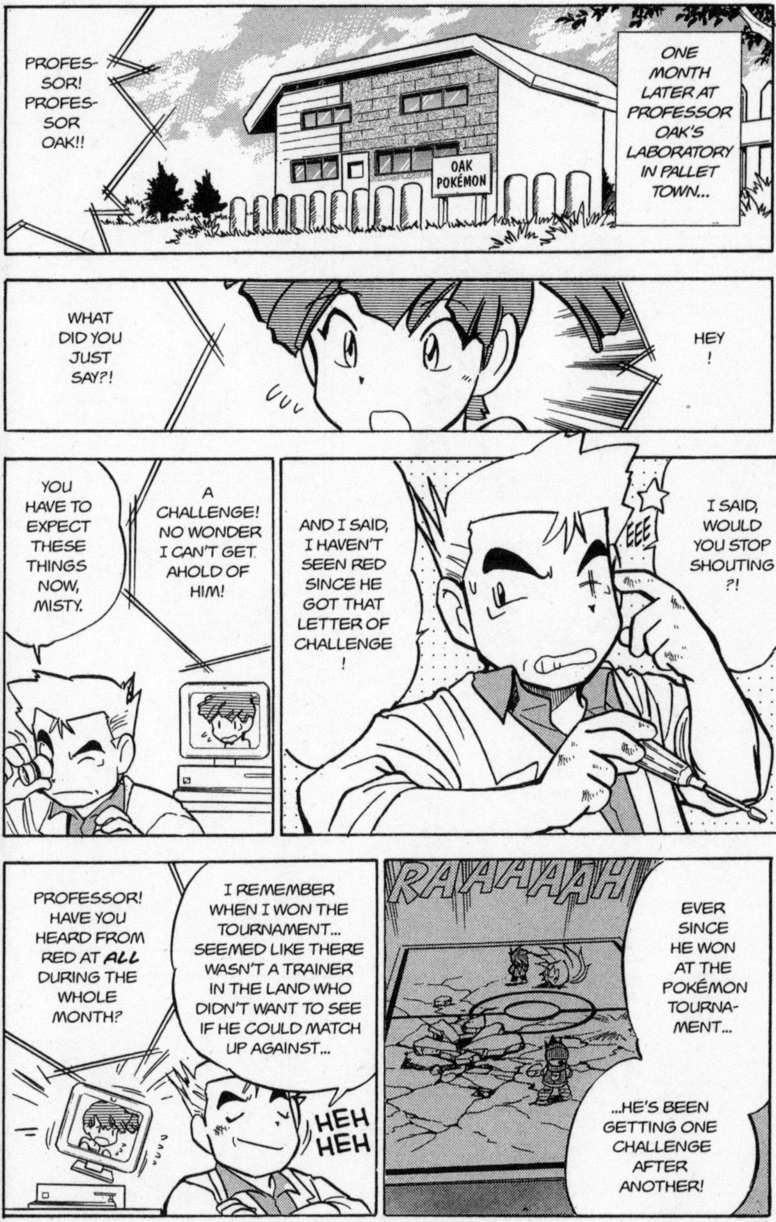
ONE MONTH LATER AT PROFESSOR OAK'S LABORATORY IN PALLET TOWN...
OAK POKÉMON
PROFES-SOR! PROFES-SOR OAK!!
HEY!
WHAT DID YOU JUST SAY?!
I SAID, WOULD YOU STOP SHOUTING?!
EEE
AND I SAID, I HAVEN'T SEEN RED SINCE HE GOT THAT LETTER OF CHALLENGE!
A CHALLENGE! NO WONDER I CAN'T GET AHOLD OF HIM!
YOU HAVE TO EXPECT THESE THINGS NOW, MISTY.
RAAAAAH
EVER SINCE HE WON AT THE POKÉMON TOURNA-MENT...
...HE'S BEEN GETTING ONE CHALLENGE AFTER ANOTHER!
I REMEMBER WHEN I WON THE TOURNAMENT... SEEMED LIKE THERE WASN'T A TRAINER IN THE LAND WHO DIDN'T WANT TO SEE IF HE COULD MATCH UP AGAINST...
PROFESSOR! HAVE YOU HEARD FROM RED AT ***ALL*** DURING THE WHOLE MONTH?
HEH HEH

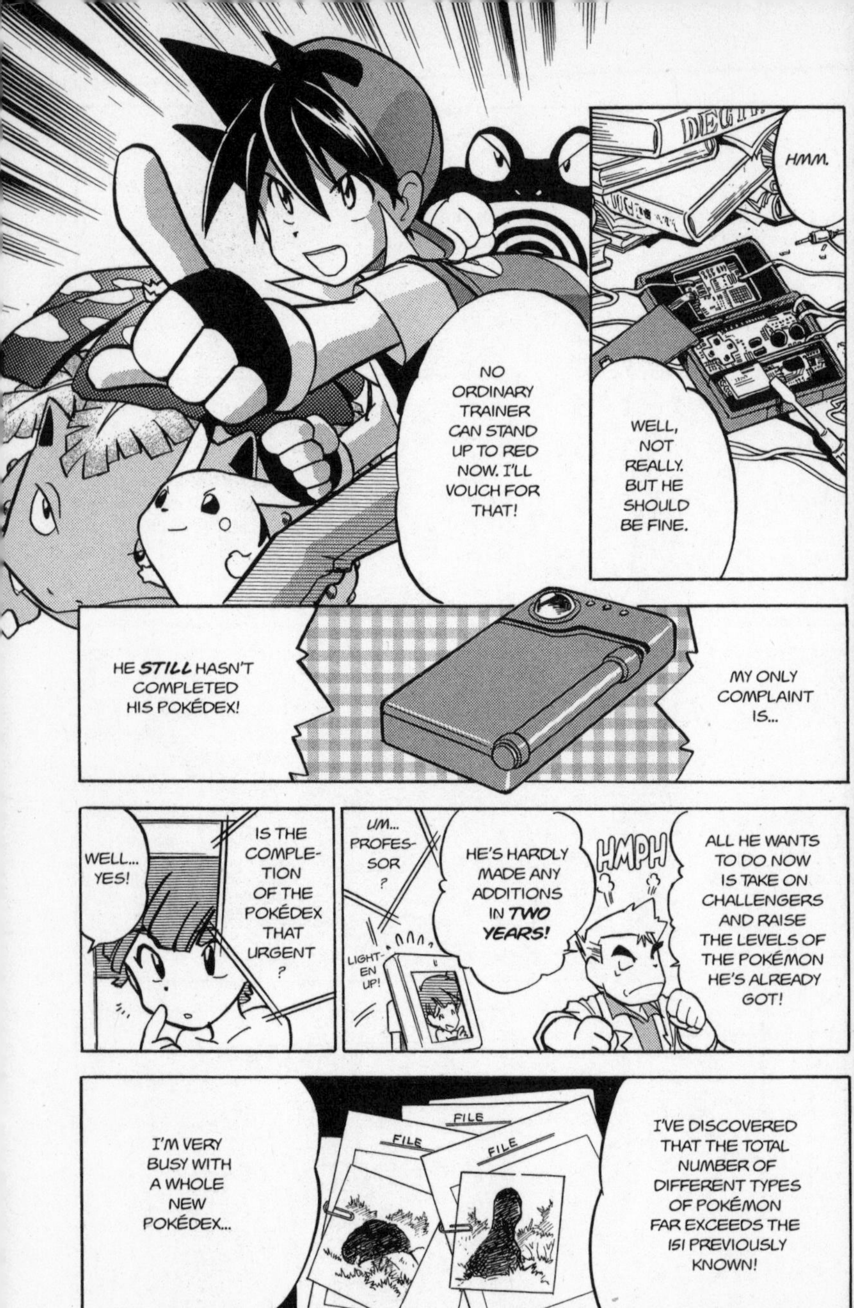
HMM.
WELL, NOT REALLY. BUT HE SHOULD BE FINE.
NO ORDINARY TRAINER CAN STAND UP TO RED NOW. I'LL VOUCH FOR THAT!
MY ONLY COMPLAINT IS...
HE STILL HASN'T COMPLETED HIS POKÉDEX!
ALL HE WANTS TO DO NOW IS TAKE ON CHALLENGERS AND RAISE THE LEVELS OF THE POKÉMON HE'S ALREADY GOT!
HMPH
HE'S HARDLY MADE ANY ADDITIONS IN TWO YEARS!
UM... PROFESSOR?
LIGHTEN UP!
IS THE COMPLETION OF THE POKÉDEX THAT URGENT?
WELL... YES!
I'VE DISCOVERED THAT THE TOTAL NUMBER OF DIFFERENT TYPES OF POKÉMON FAR EXCEEDS THE 151 PREVIOUSLY KNOWN!
FILE
FILE
FILE
I'M VERY BUSY WITH A WHOLE NEW POKÉDEX...

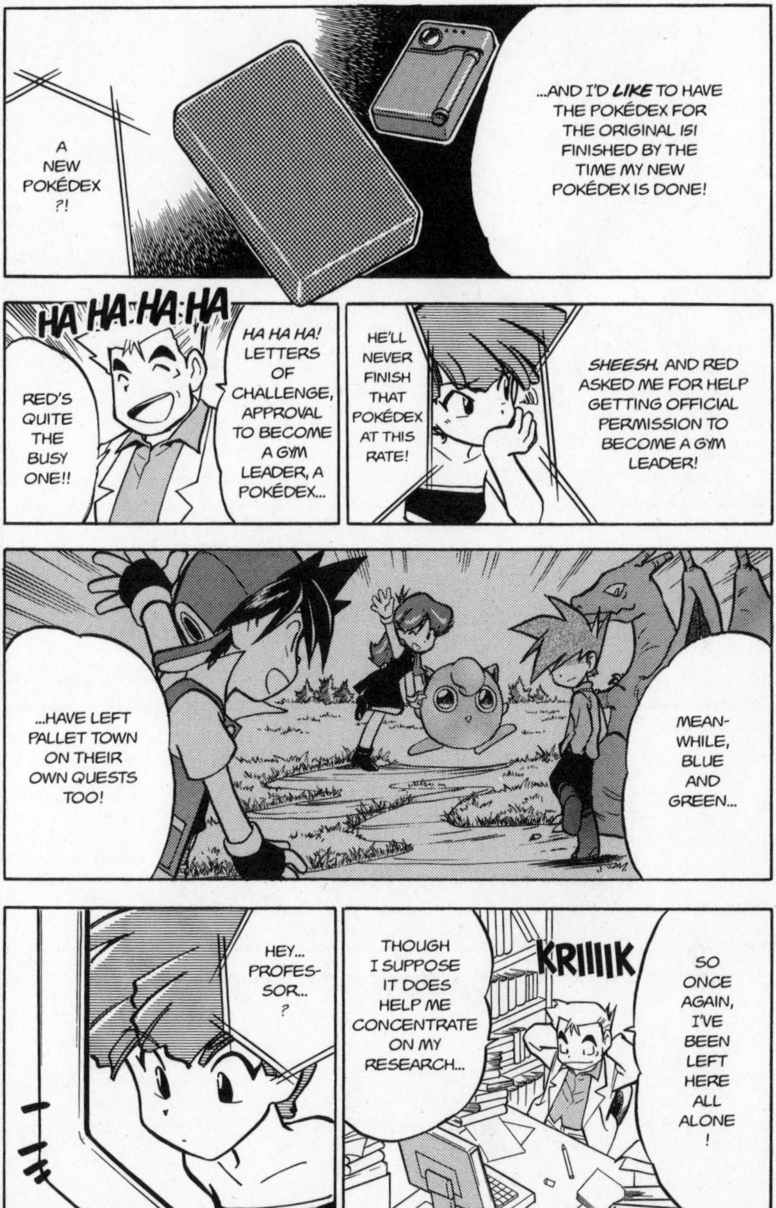
...AND I'D ***LIKE*** TO HAVE THE POKÉDEX FOR THE ORIGINAL 151 FINISHED BY THE TIME MY NEW POKÉDEX IS DONE!
A NEW POKÉDEX ?!
SHEESH. AND RED ASKED ME FOR HELP GETTING OFFICIAL PERMISSION TO BECOME A GYM LEADER!
HE'LL NEVER FINISH THAT POKÉDEX AT THIS RATE!
HA HA HA HA
HA HA HA! LETTERS OF CHALLENGE, APPROVAL TO BECOME A GYM LEADER, A POKÉDEX...
RED'S QUITE THE BUSY ONE!!
MEAN-WHILE, BLUE AND GREEN...
...HAVE LEFT PALLET TOWN ON THEIR OWN QUESTS TOO!
SO ONCE AGAIN, I'VE BEEN LEFT HERE ALL ALONE!
KRIIIIK
THOUGH I SUPPOSE IT DOES HELP ME CONCENTRATE ON MY RESEARCH...
HEY... PROFES-SOR... ?

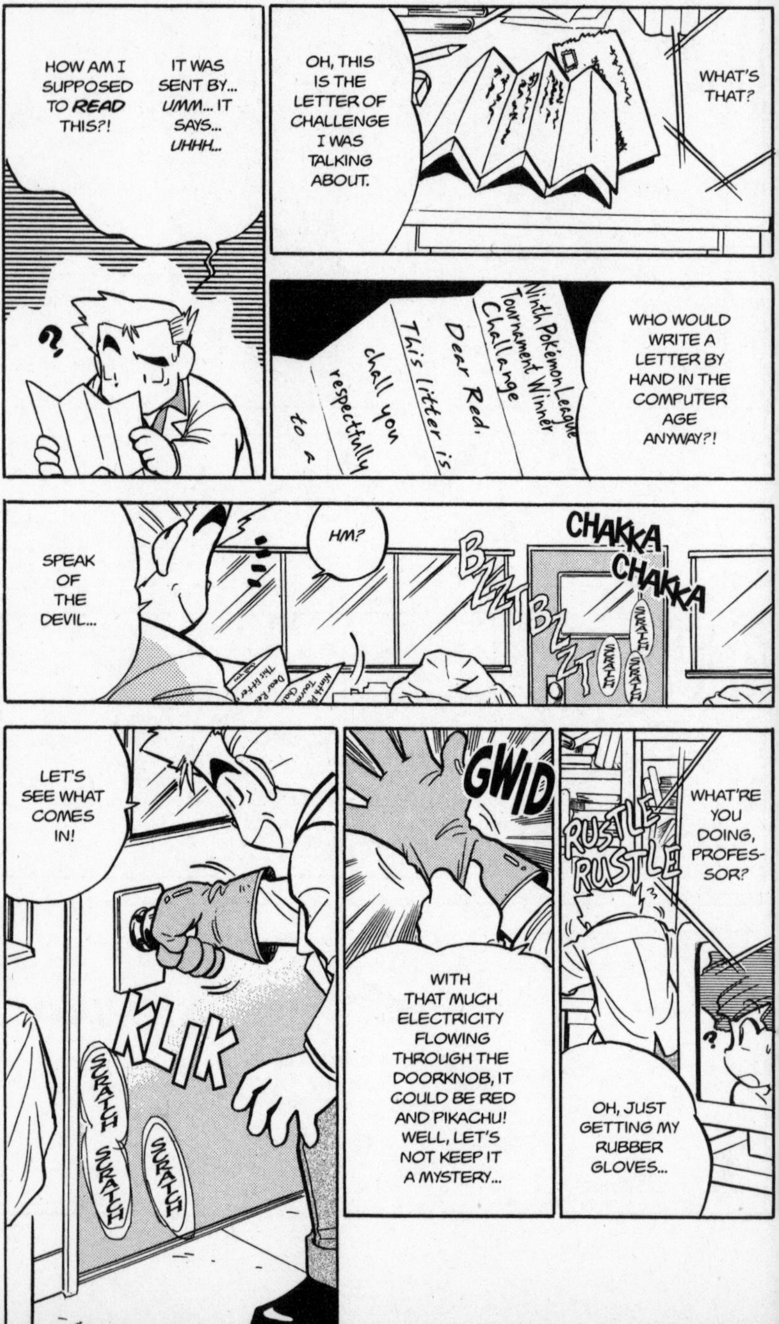
WHAT'S THAT?
OH, THIS IS THE LETTER OF CHALLENGE I WAS TALKING ABOUT.
Ninth Pokémon League Tournament Winner Challenge
Dear Red,
This litter is
chall you
respectfully
to a
WHO WOULD WRITE A LETTER BY HAND IN THE COMPUTER AGE ANYWAY?!
IT WAS SENT BY... UMM... IT SAYS... UHHH...
HOW AM I SUPPOSED TO READ THIS?!
CHAKKA CHAKKA
BZZTBZZT
SCRATCH SCRATCH SCRATCH SCRATCH
HM?
SPEAK OF THE DEVIL...
WHAT'RE YOU DOING, PROFESSOR?
RUSTLE RUSTLE
OH, JUST GETTING MY RUBBER GLOVES...
GWID
WITH THAT MUCH ELECTRICITY FLOWING THROUGH THE DOORKNOB, IT COULD BE RED AND PIKACHU! WELL, LET'S NOT KEEP IT A MYSTERY...
LET'S SEE WHAT COMES IN!
KLIK
SCRATCH SCRATCH SCRATCH

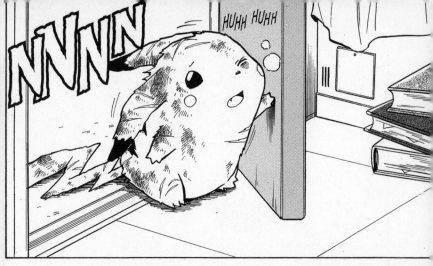

HUHH HUHH

NNNN

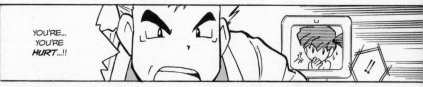

YOU'RE... YOU'RE *HURT*...!!

!!

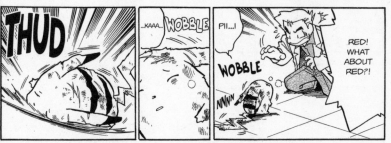

THUD

...KAAA... WOBBLE

PII...I

WOBBLE

NNNN

RED! WHAT ABOUT RED?!

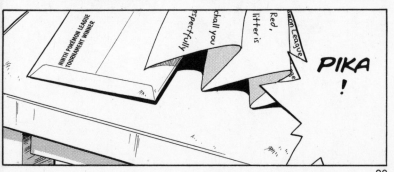

NINTH POKÉMON LEAGUE TOURNAMENT WINNER

respectfully

chall you

Red, litter is

mon League

PIKA !

20

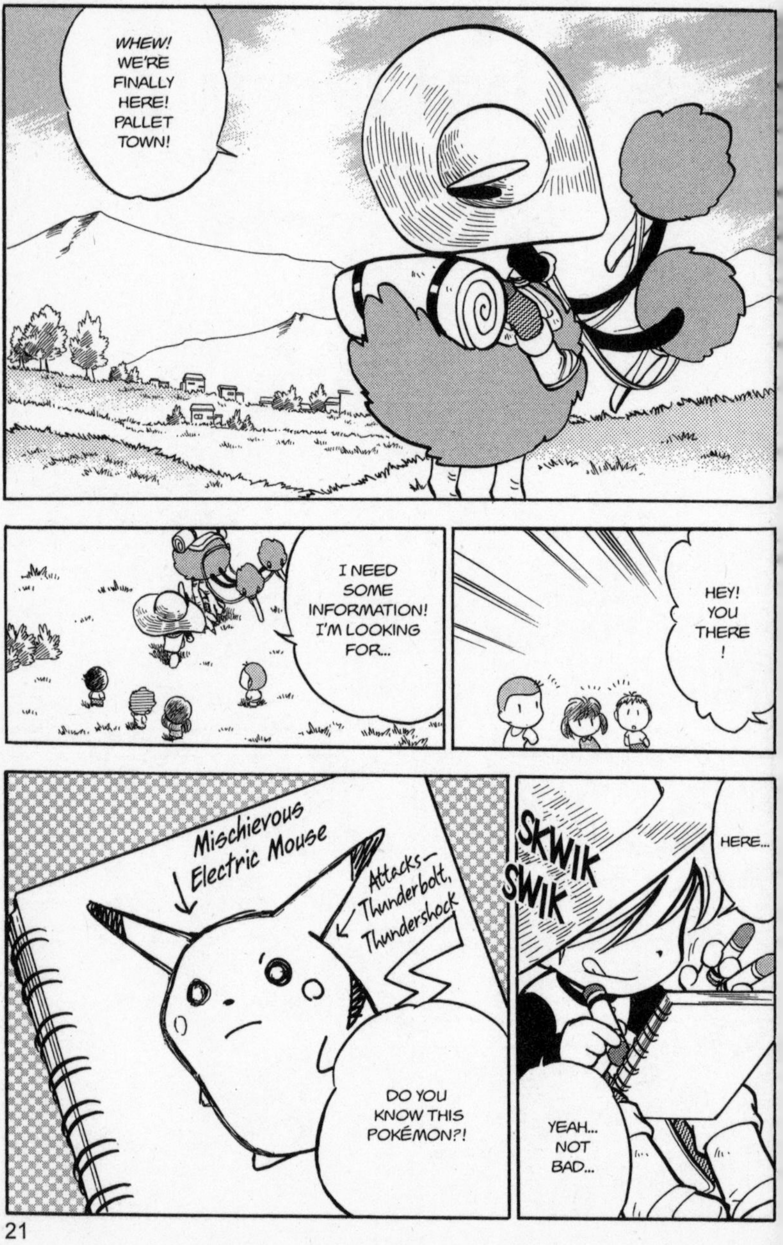
WHEW! WE'RE FINALLY HERE! PALLET TOWN!
HEY! YOU THERE!
I NEED SOME INFORMATION! I'M LOOKING FOR...
HERE...
SKWIK SWIK
YEAH... NOT BAD...
Mischievous Electric Mouse
Attacks— Thunderbolt, Thundershock
DO YOU KNOW THIS POKÉMON?!

42 Do Do That Doduo

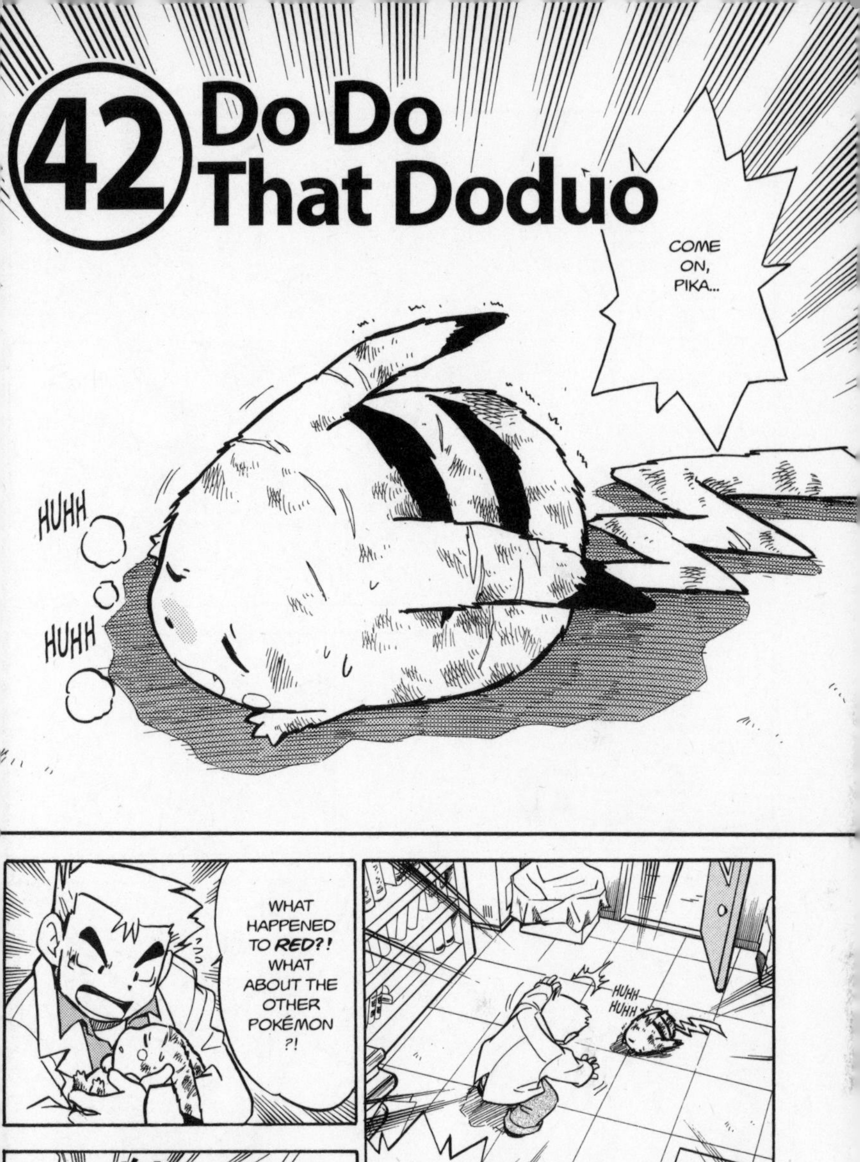
COME ON, PIKA...
HUHH
HUHH
HUHH HUHH
HANG ON!
WHAT HAPPENED TO RED?! WHAT ABOUT THE OTHER POKÉMON ?!
PROFES-SOR! TAKE CARE OF PIKA FIRST!
KSSH
RIGHT, RIGHT !!

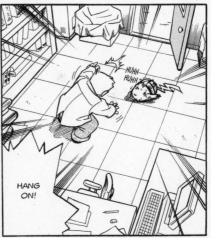

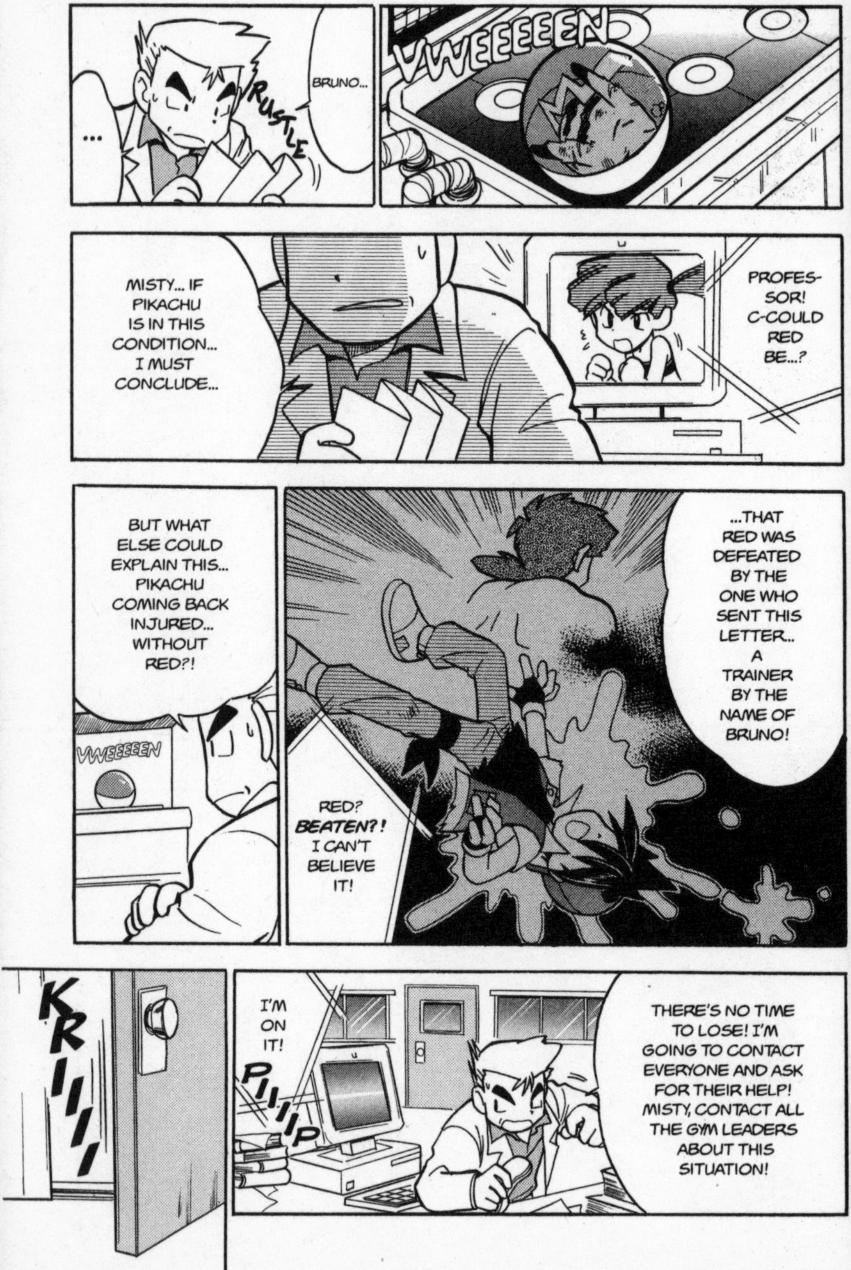
VWEEEEEN
BRUNO...
RUSTLE
...
PROFES-SOR! C-COULD RED BE...?
MISTY... IF PIKACHU IS IN THIS CONDITION... I MUST CONCLUDE...
...THAT RED WAS DEFEATED BY THE ONE WHO SENT THIS LETTER... A TRAINER BY THE NAME OF BRUNO!
RED? ***BEATEN?!*** I CAN'T BELIEVE IT!
BUT WHAT ELSE COULD EXPLAIN THIS... PIKACHU COMING BACK INJURED... WITHOUT RED?!
VWEEEEEN
THERE'S NO TIME TO LOSE! I'M GOING TO CONTACT EVERYONE AND ASK FOR THEIR HELP! MISTY, CONTACT ALL THE GYM LEADERS ABOUT THIS SITUATION!
I'M ON IT!
PIIIIP
KRIIIII

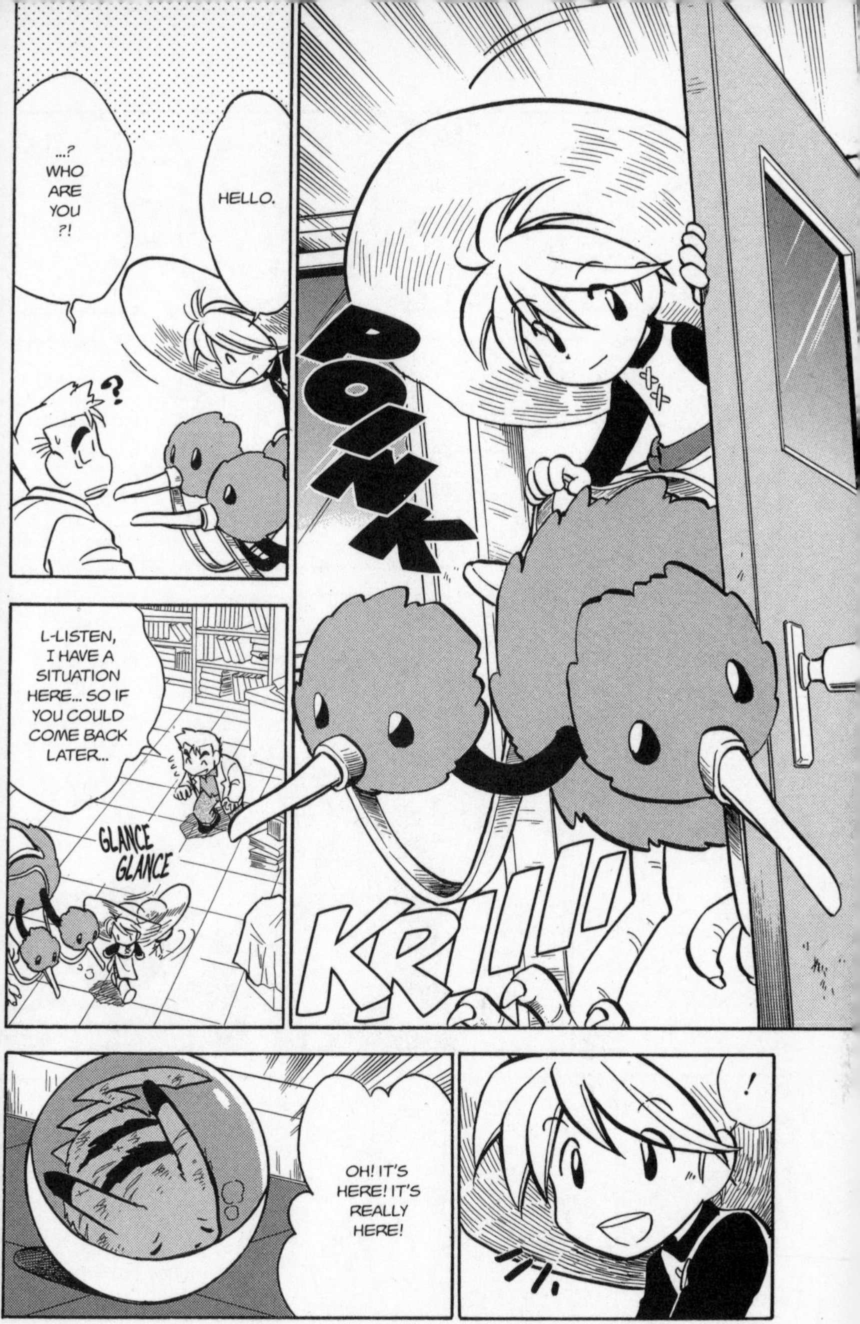
POINK
KRII
HELLO.
...? WHO ARE YOU ?!
L-LISTEN, I HAVE A SITUATION HERE... SO IF YOU COULD COME BACK LATER...
GLANCE GLANCE
!
OH! IT'S HERE! IT'S REALLY HERE!

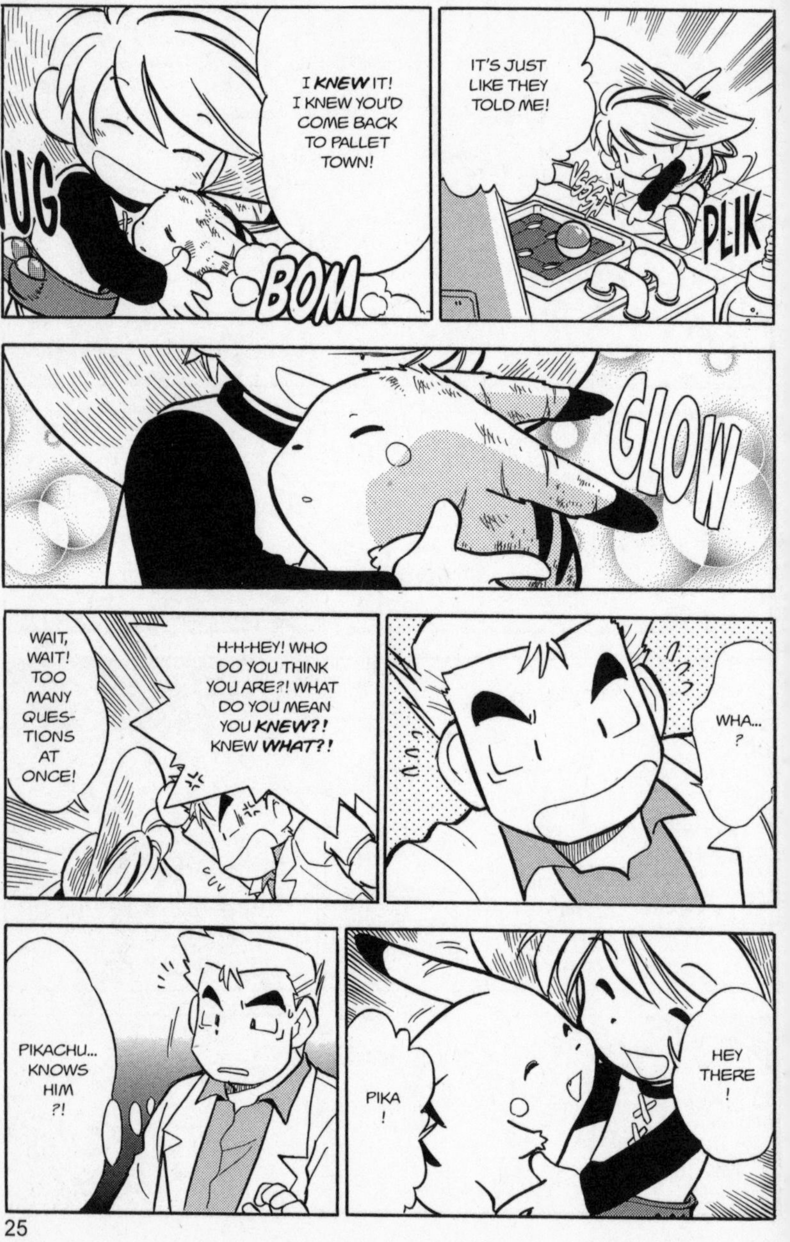
IT'S JUST LIKE THEY TOLD ME!
PLIK
I *KNEW* IT! I KNEW YOU'D COME BACK TO PALLET TOWN!
HUG
BOM
GLOW
WHA...?
H-H-HEY! WHO DO YOU THINK YOU ARE?! WHAT DO YOU MEAN YOU *KNEW?!* KNEW *WHAT?!*
WAIT, WAIT! TOO MANY QUES-TIONS AT ONCE!
HEY THERE!
PIKA!
PIKACHU... KNOWS HIM?!

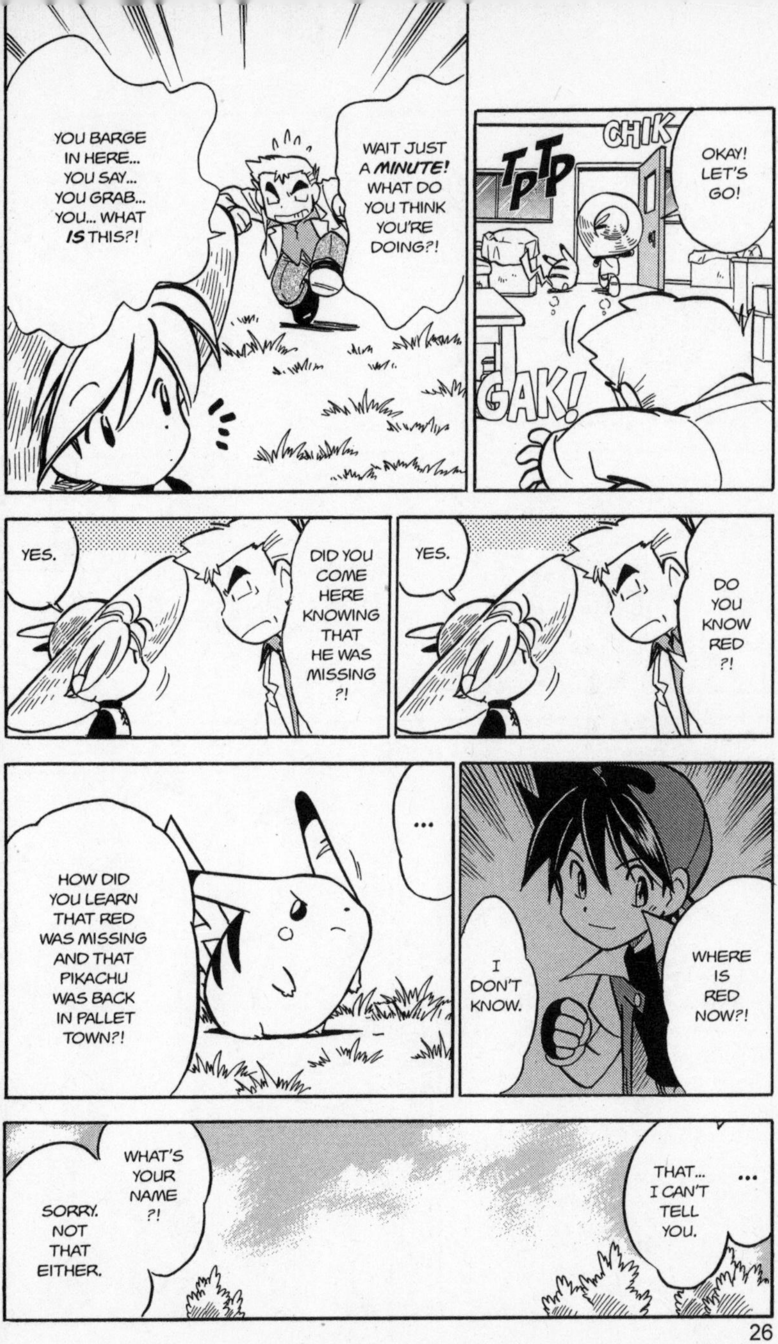
CHIK
OKAY! LET'S GO!
TPTP
GAK!
WAIT JUST A ***MINUTE!*** WHAT DO YOU THINK YOU'RE DOING?!
YOU BARGE IN HERE... YOU SAY... YOU GRAB... YOU... WHAT ***IS*** THIS?!
DO YOU KNOW RED ?!
YES.
DID YOU COME HERE KNOWING THAT HE WAS MISSING ?!
YES.
WHERE IS RED NOW?!
I DON'T KNOW.
...
HOW DID YOU LEARN THAT RED WAS MISSING AND THAT PIKACHU WAS BACK IN PALLET TOWN?!
...
THAT... I CAN'T TELL YOU.
WHAT'S YOUR NAME ?!
SORRY. NOT THAT EITHER.

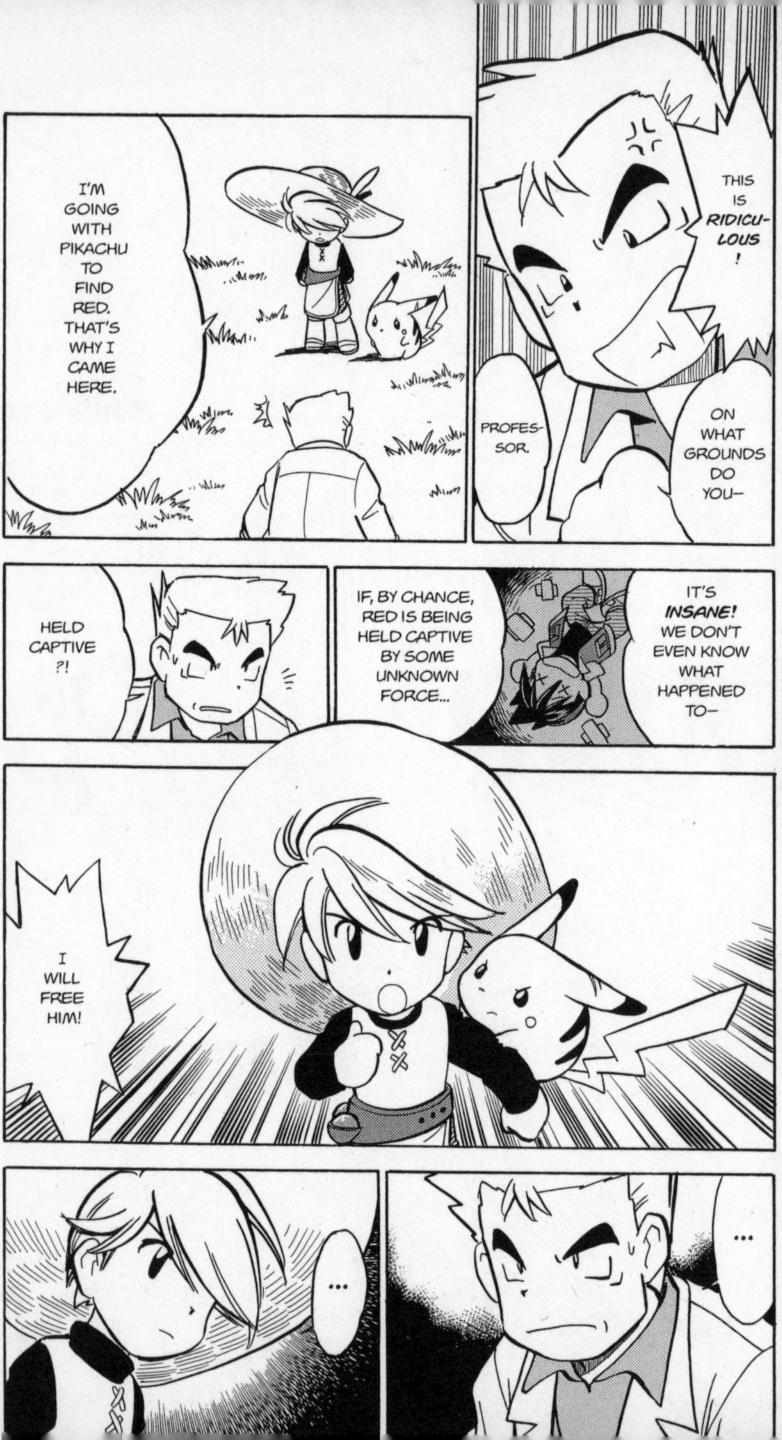
THIS IS RIDICULOUS!
ON WHAT GROUNDS DO YOU—
PROFESSOR.
I'M GOING WITH PIKACHU TO FIND RED. THAT'S WHY I CAME HERE.
IT'S INSANE! WE DON'T EVEN KNOW WHAT HAPPENED TO—
IF, BY CHANCE, RED IS BEING HELD CAPTIVE BY SOME UNKNOWN FORCE...
HELD CAPTIVE?!
I WILL FREE HIM!
...
...

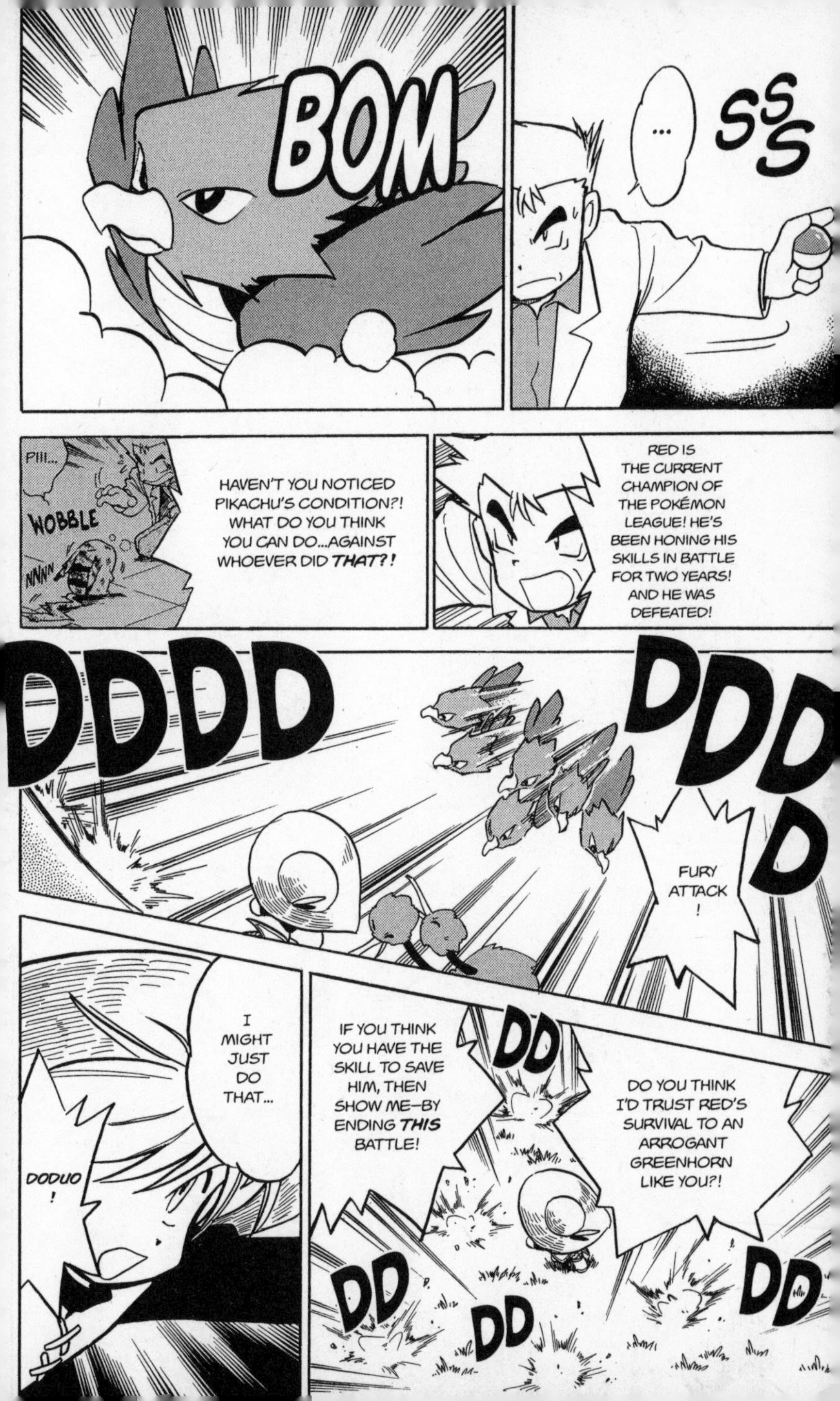

...
SSS
BOM
RED IS THE CURRENT CHAMPION OF THE POKÉMON LEAGUE! HE'S BEEN HONING HIS SKILLS IN BATTLE FOR TWO YEARS! AND HE WAS DEFEATED!
HAVEN'T YOU NOTICED PIKACHU'S CONDITION?! WHAT DO YOU THINK YOU CAN DO...AGAINST WHOEVER DID ***THAT?!***
PIII...
WOBBLE
NNNN
DDDD
FURY ATTACK !
DDDD
DD
DO YOU THINK I'D TRUST RED'S SURVIVAL TO AN ARROGANT GREENHORN LIKE YOU?!
IF YOU THINK YOU HAVE THE SKILL TO SAVE HIM, THEN SHOW ME—BY ENDING **THIS** BATTLE!
DD
DD
DD
I MIGHT JUST DO THAT...
DODUO !

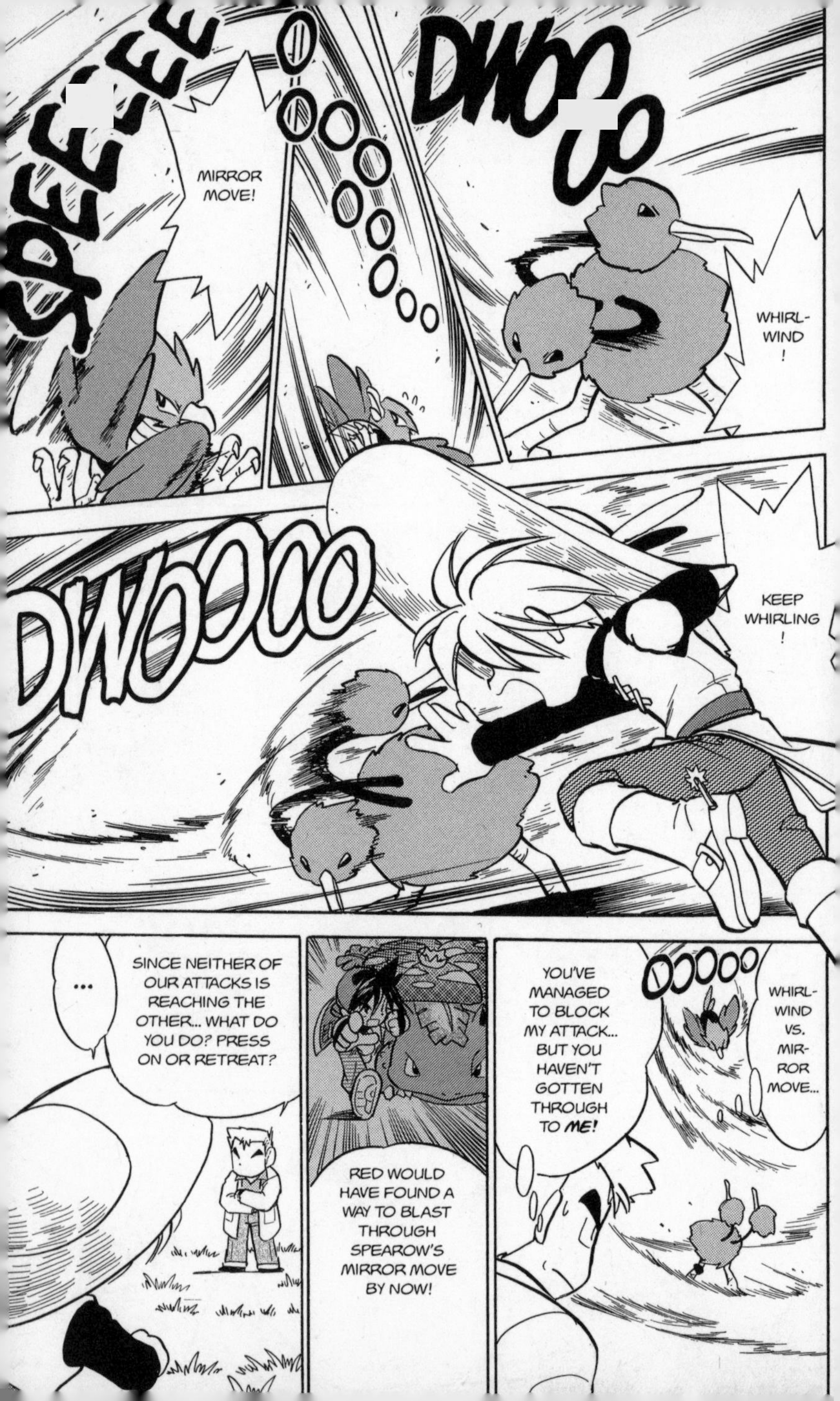
WHIRL-WIND!
MIRROR MOVE!
KEEP WHIRLING!
DWOOOO
WHIRL-WIND VS. MIR-ROR MOVE...
YOU'VE MANAGED TO BLOCK MY ATTACK... BUT YOU HAVEN'T GOTTEN THROUGH TO ME!
RED WOULD HAVE FOUND A WAY TO BLAST THROUGH SPEAROW'S MIRROR MOVE BY NOW!
SINCE NEITHER OF OUR ATTACKS IS REACHING THE OTHER... WHAT DO YOU DO? PRESS ON OR RETREAT?
...

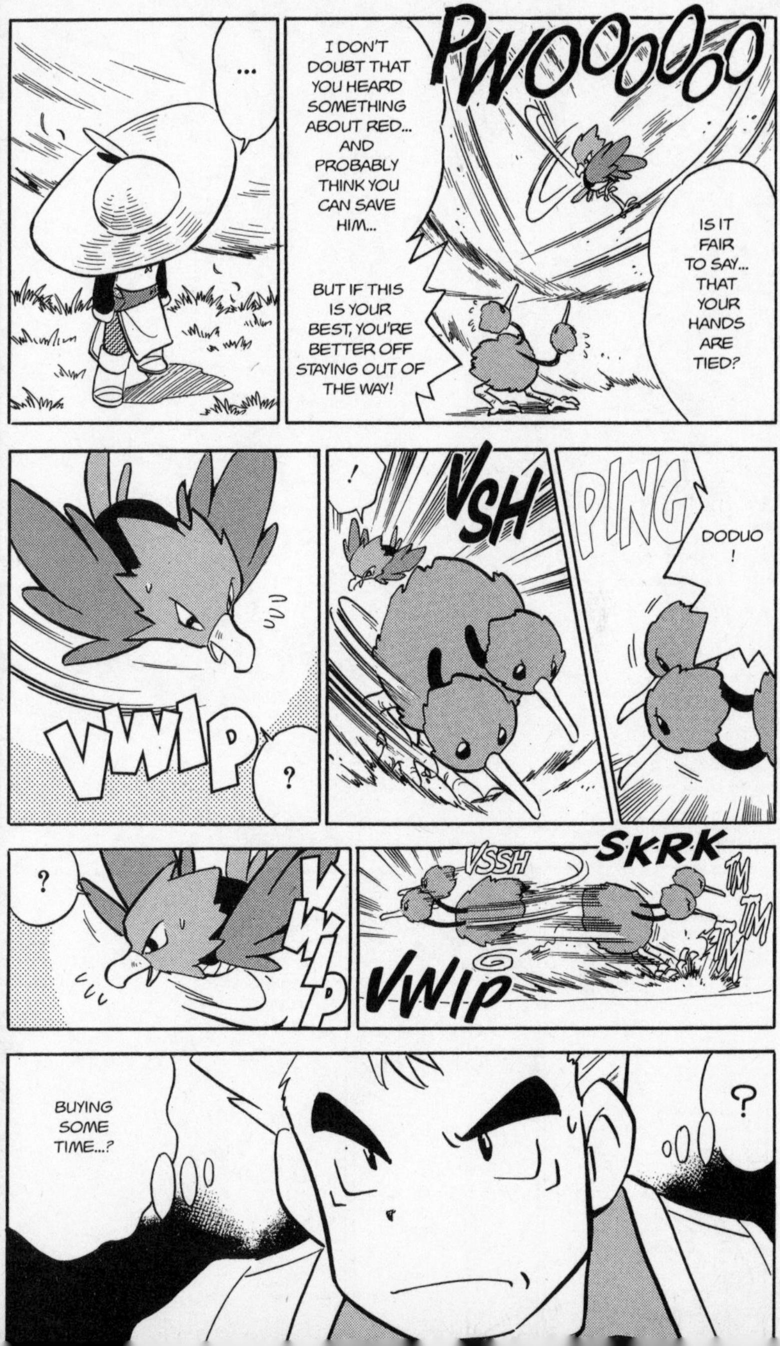
PWOOOOOO
I DON'T DOUBT THAT YOU HEARD SOMETHING ABOUT RED... AND PROBABLY THINK YOU CAN SAVE HIM...
BUT IF THIS IS YOUR BEST, YOU'RE BETTER OFF STAYING OUT OF THE WAY!
IS IT FAIR TO SAY... THAT YOUR HANDS ARE TIED?
...
PING
DODUO!
VSH
!
VWIP
?
S-K-R-K
VSSH
TM TM TM TM
V-W-I-P
VWIP
?
?
BUYING SOME TIME...?

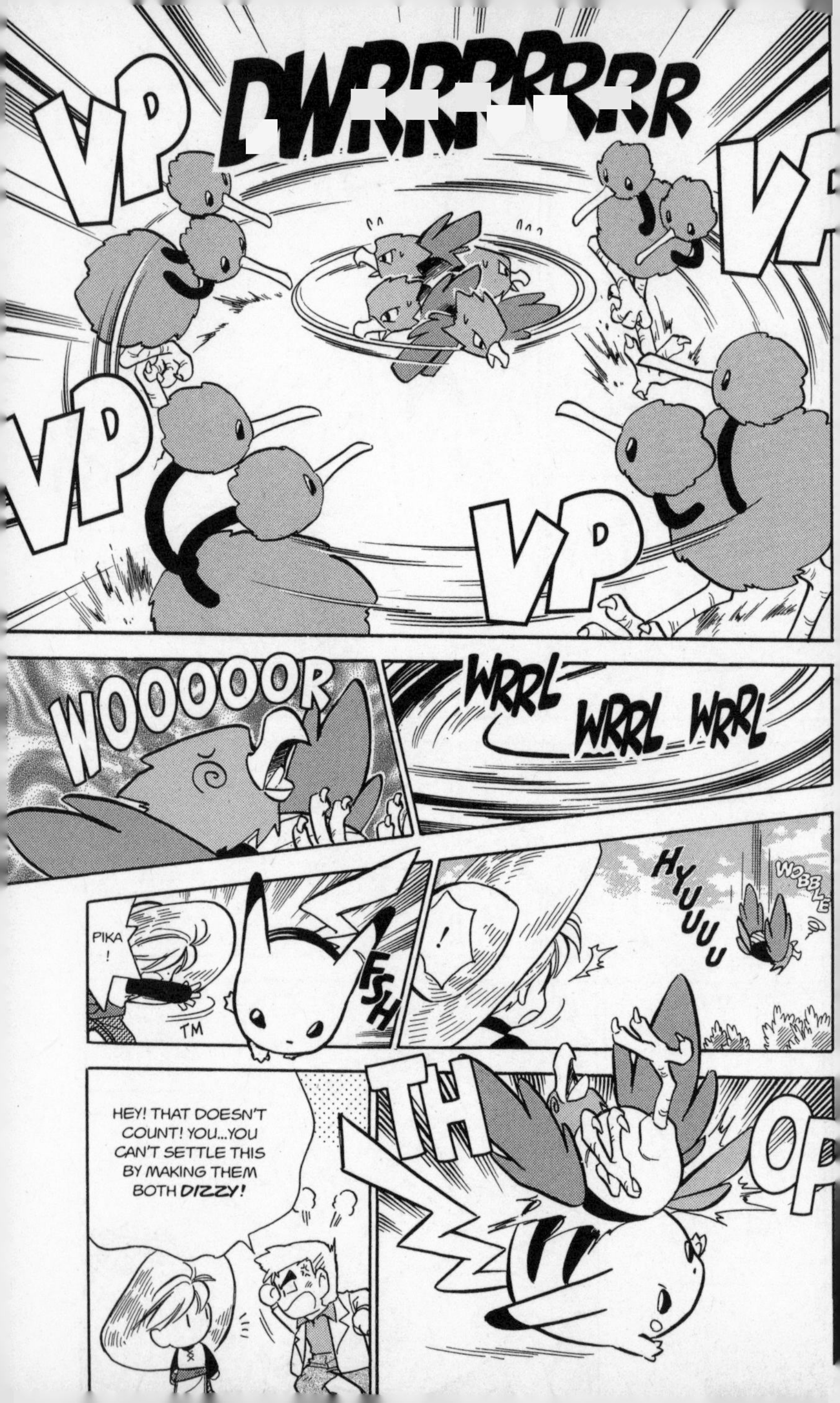
VP
DWRRRRRRR
VP
VP
VP
WRRL WRRL WRRL
WOOOOOR
HYUUUU
WOBBLE
!
FSH
PIKA !
TM
TH
OP
HEY! THAT DOESN'T COUNT! YOU...YOU CAN'T SETTLE THIS BY MAKING THEM BOTH *DIZZY*!

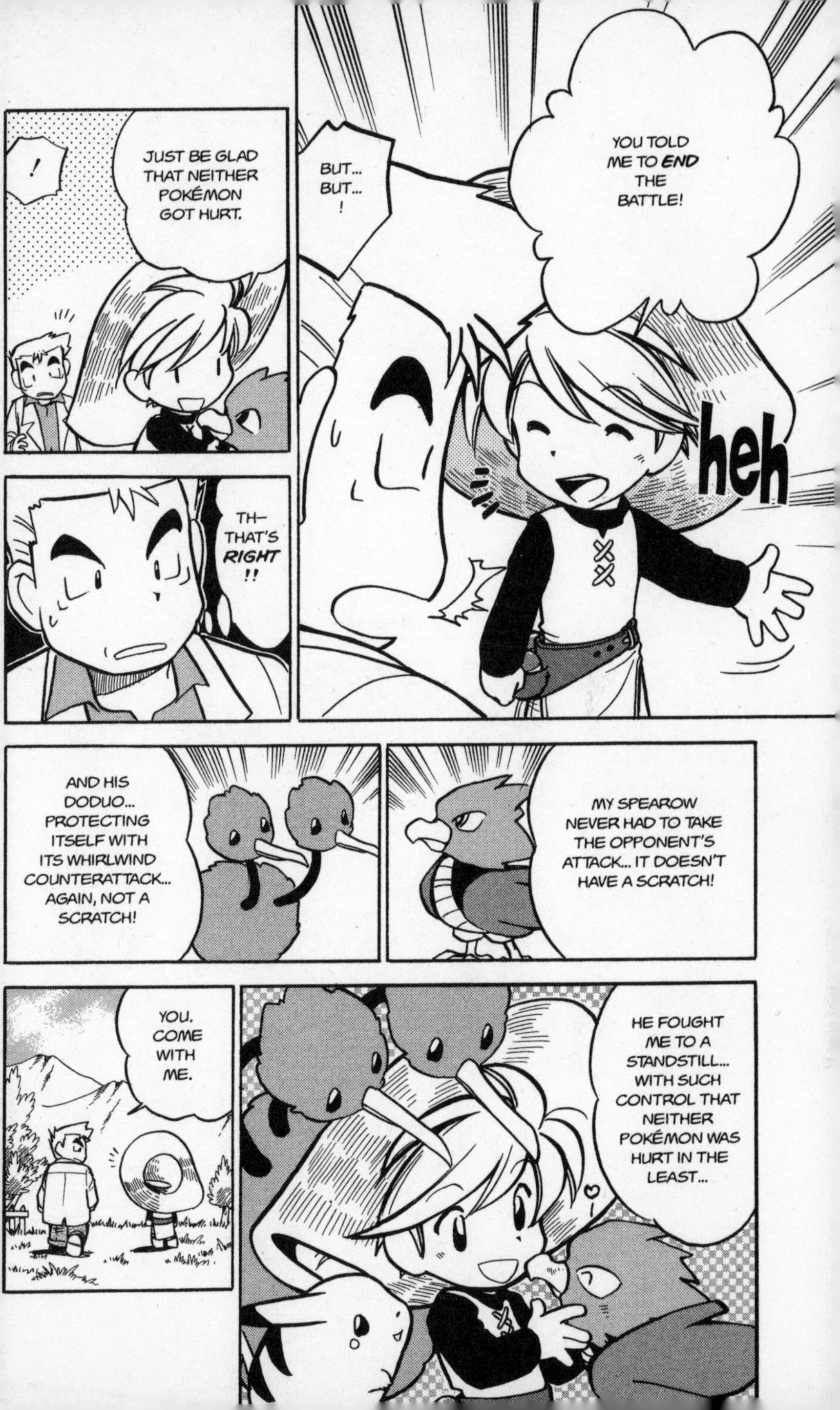
YOU TOLD ME TO END THE BATTLE!
BUT... BUT... !
heh
!
JUST BE GLAD THAT NEITHER POKÉMON GOT HURT.
TH— THAT'S RIGHT !!
MY SPEAROW NEVER HAD TO TAKE THE OPPONENT'S ATTACK... IT DOESN'T HAVE A SCRATCH!
AND HIS DODUO... PROTECTING ITSELF WITH ITS WHIRLWIND COUNTERATTACK... AGAIN, NOT A SCRATCH!
HE FOUGHT ME TO A STANDSTILL... WITH SUCH CONTROL THAT NEITHER POKÉMON WAS HURT IN THE LEAST...
YOU. COME WITH ME.

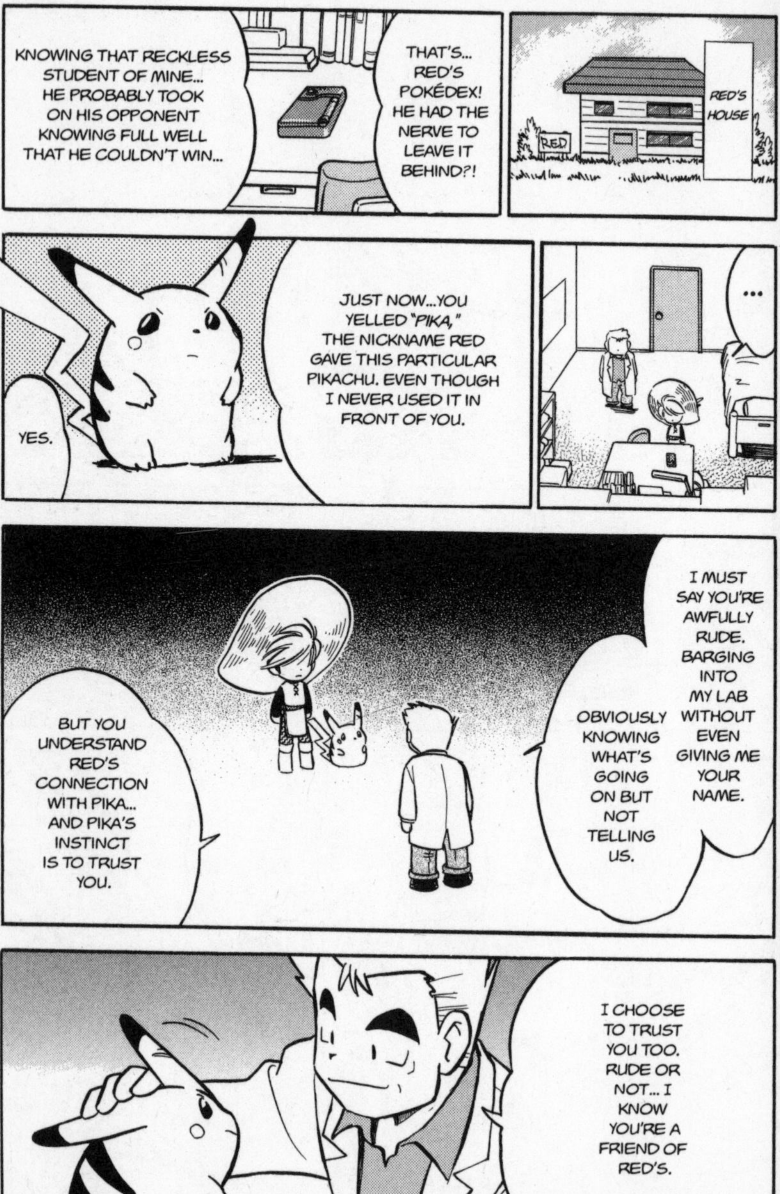
RED'S HOUSE
RED
THAT'S... RED'S POKÉDEX! HE HAD THE NERVE TO LEAVE IT BEHIND?!
KNOWING THAT RECKLESS STUDENT OF MINE... HE PROBABLY TOOK ON HIS OPPONENT KNOWING FULL WELL THAT HE COULDN'T WIN...
...
JUST NOW...YOU YELLED "PIKA," THE NICKNAME RED GAVE THIS PARTICULAR PIKACHU. EVEN THOUGH I NEVER USED IT IN FRONT OF YOU.
YES.
I MUST SAY YOU'RE AWFULLY RUDE. BARGING INTO MY LAB WITHOUT EVEN GIVING ME YOUR NAME.
OBVIOUSLY KNOWING WHAT'S GOING ON BUT NOT TELLING US.
BUT YOU UNDERSTAND RED'S CONNECTION WITH PIKA... AND PIKA'S INSTINCT IS TO TRUST YOU.
I CHOOSE TO TRUST YOU TOO. RUDE OR NOT... I KNOW YOU'RE A FRIEND OF RED'S.

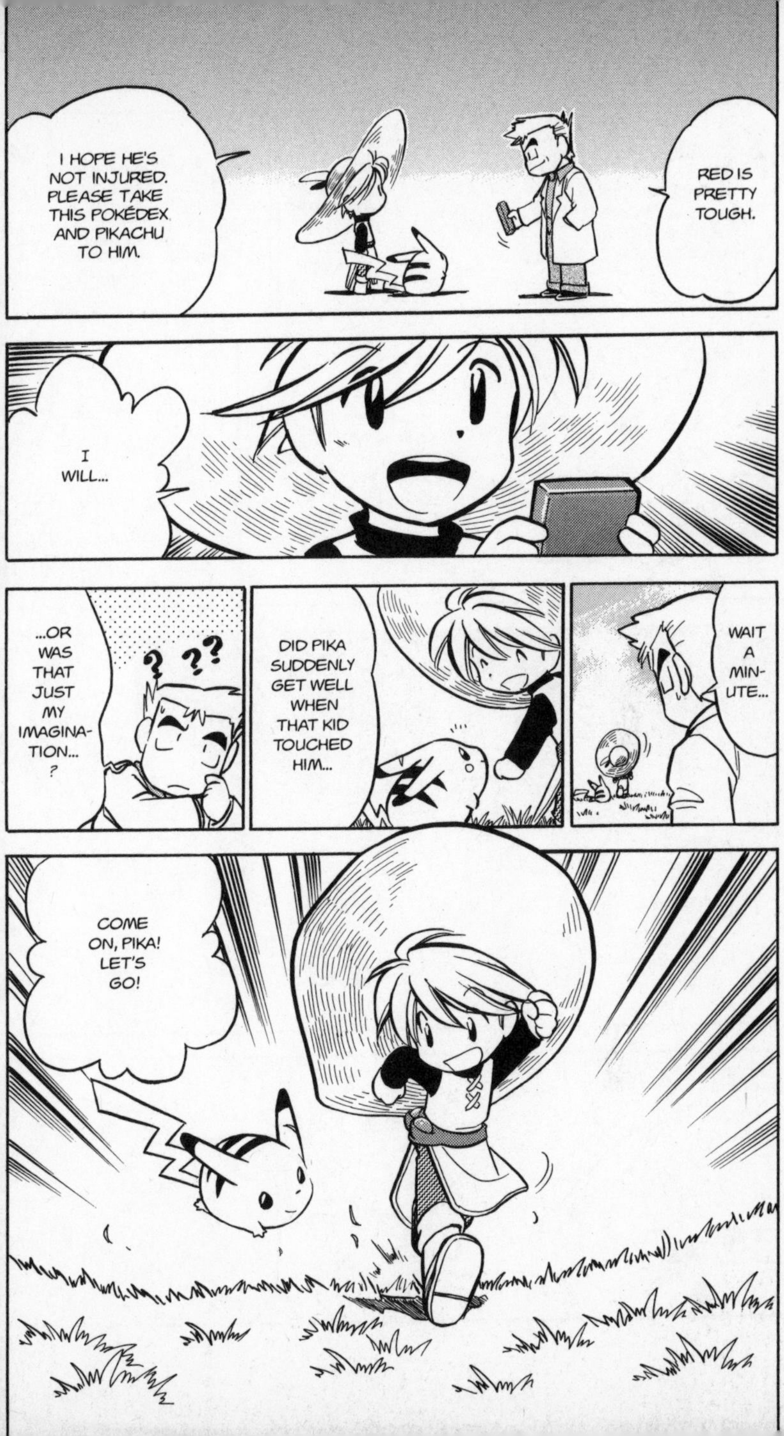
RED IS PRETTY TOUGH.
I HOPE HE'S NOT INJURED. PLEASE TAKE THIS POKÉDEX AND PIKACHU TO HIM.
I WILL...
WAIT A MIN-UTE...
DID PIKA SUDDENLY GET WELL WHEN THAT KID TOUCHED HIM...
...OR WAS THAT JUST MY IMAGINA-TION...?
COME ON, PIKA! LET'S GO!

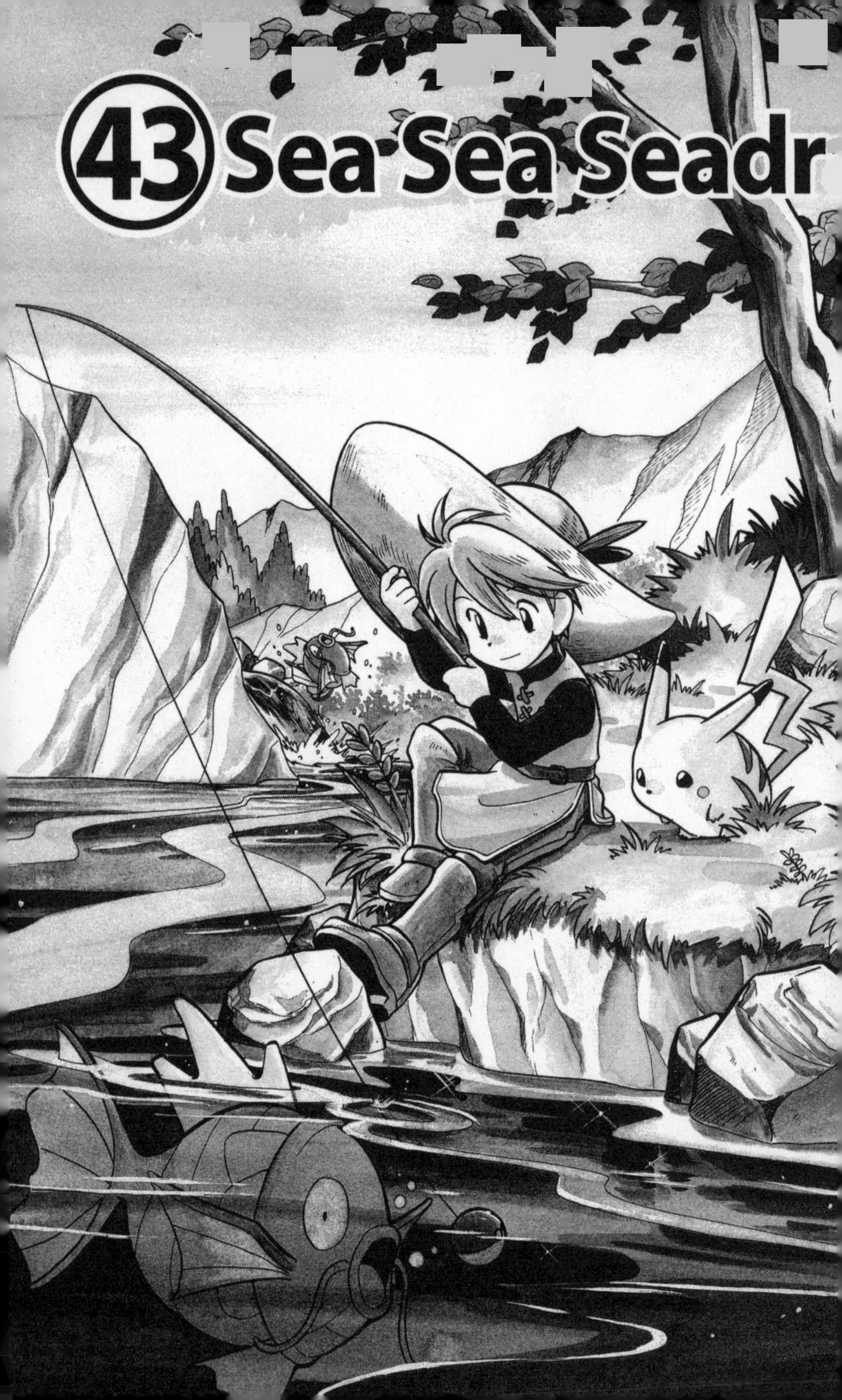
43 Sea Sea Seadr

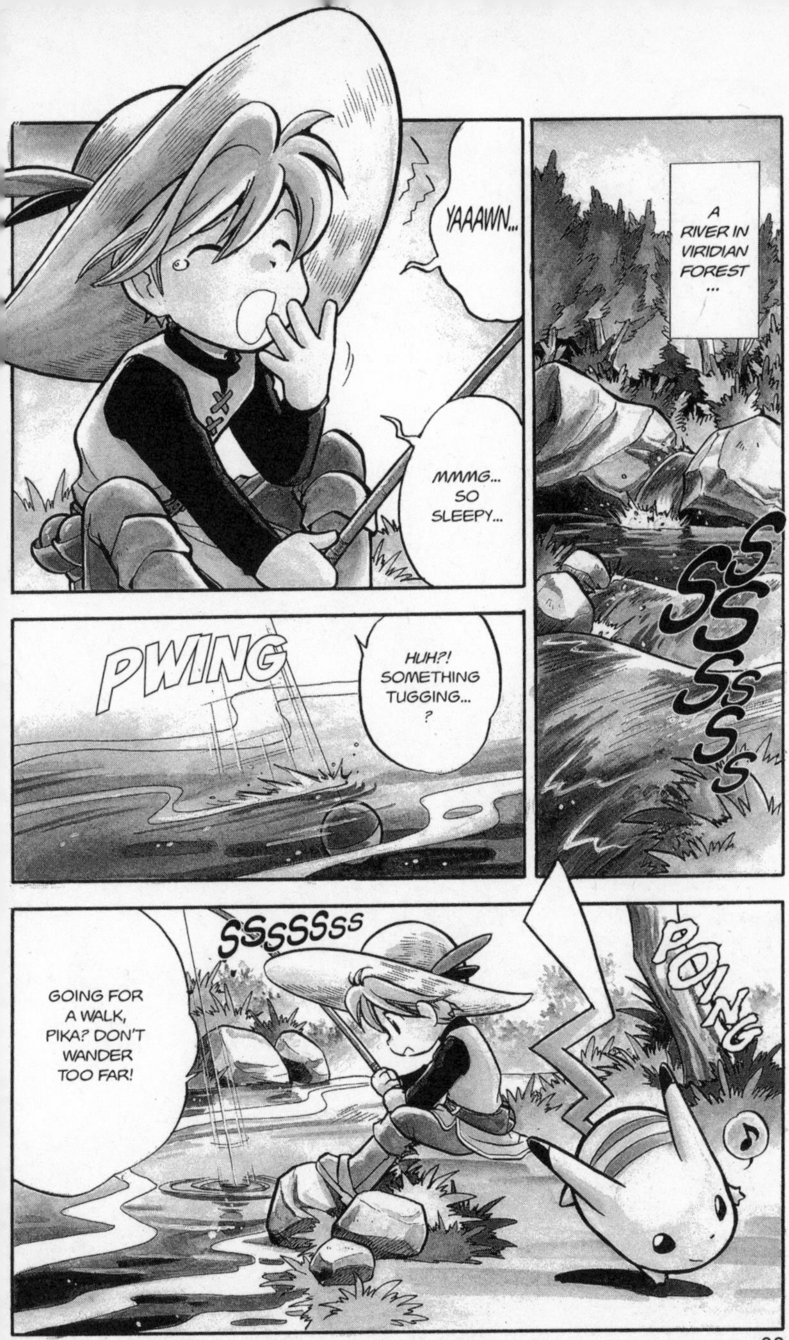
A RIVER IN VIRIDIAN FOREST ...
SSSSSSSS
YAAAWN...
MMMG... SO SLEEPY...
PWING
HUH?! SOMETHING TUGGING... ?
POING
SSSSSSS
GOING FOR A WALK, PIKA? DON'T WANDER TOO FAR!

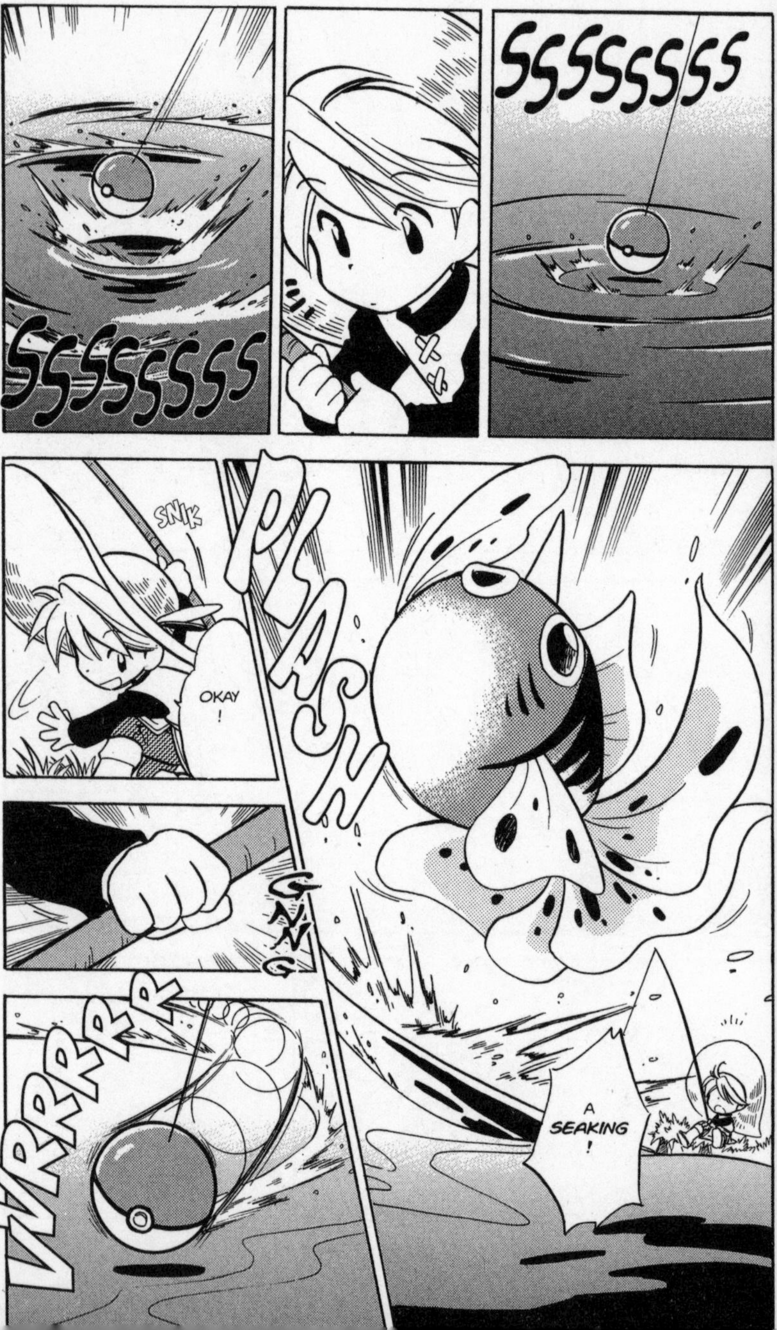
SSSSSSSSS
SSSSSSSSS
PLASH
A SEAKING!
SNIK
OKAY!
GNNG
VRRRRR

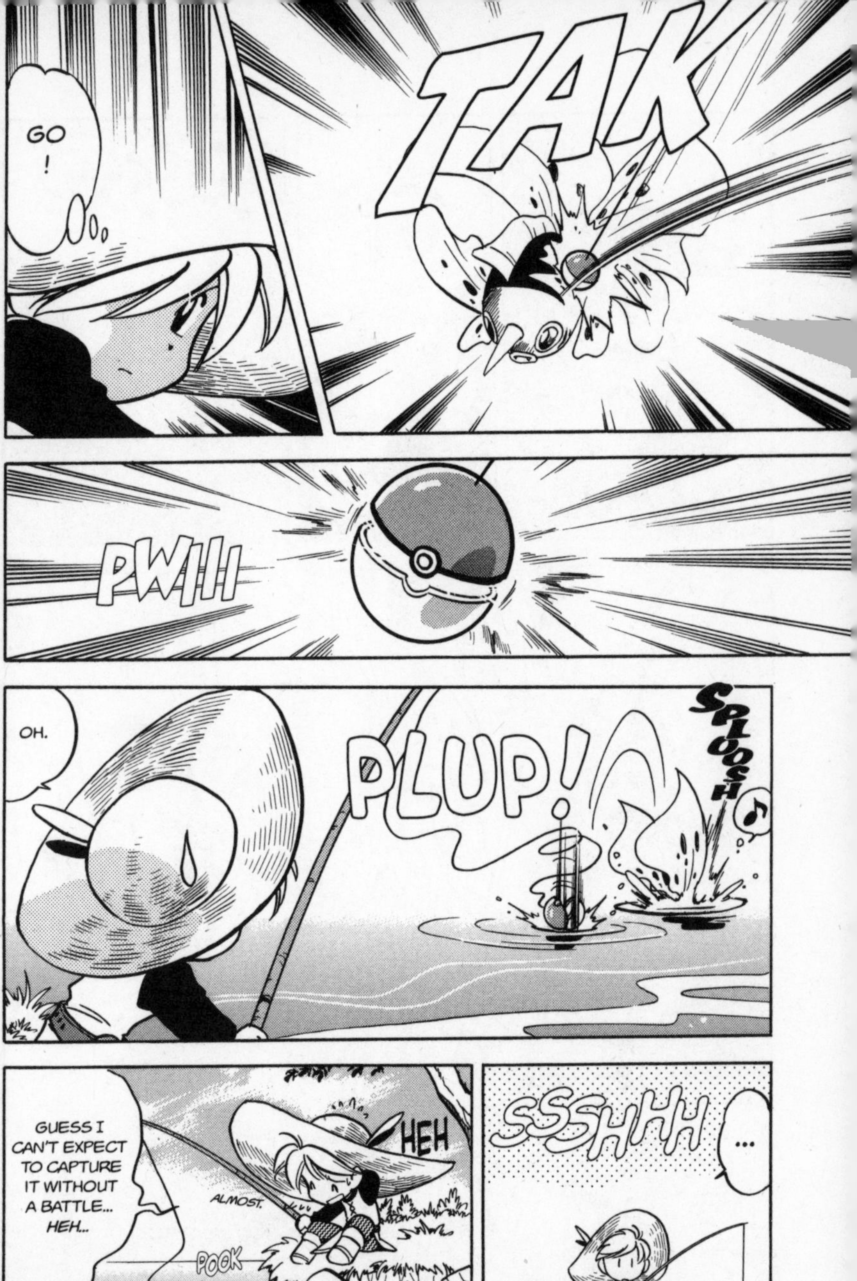
TAK
GO !
PWIII
SPLOOSH
♪
PLUP!
OH.
SSSHHH
...
HEH
GUESS I CAN'T EXPECT TO CAPTURE IT WITHOUT A BATTLE... HEH...
ALMOST.
POOK

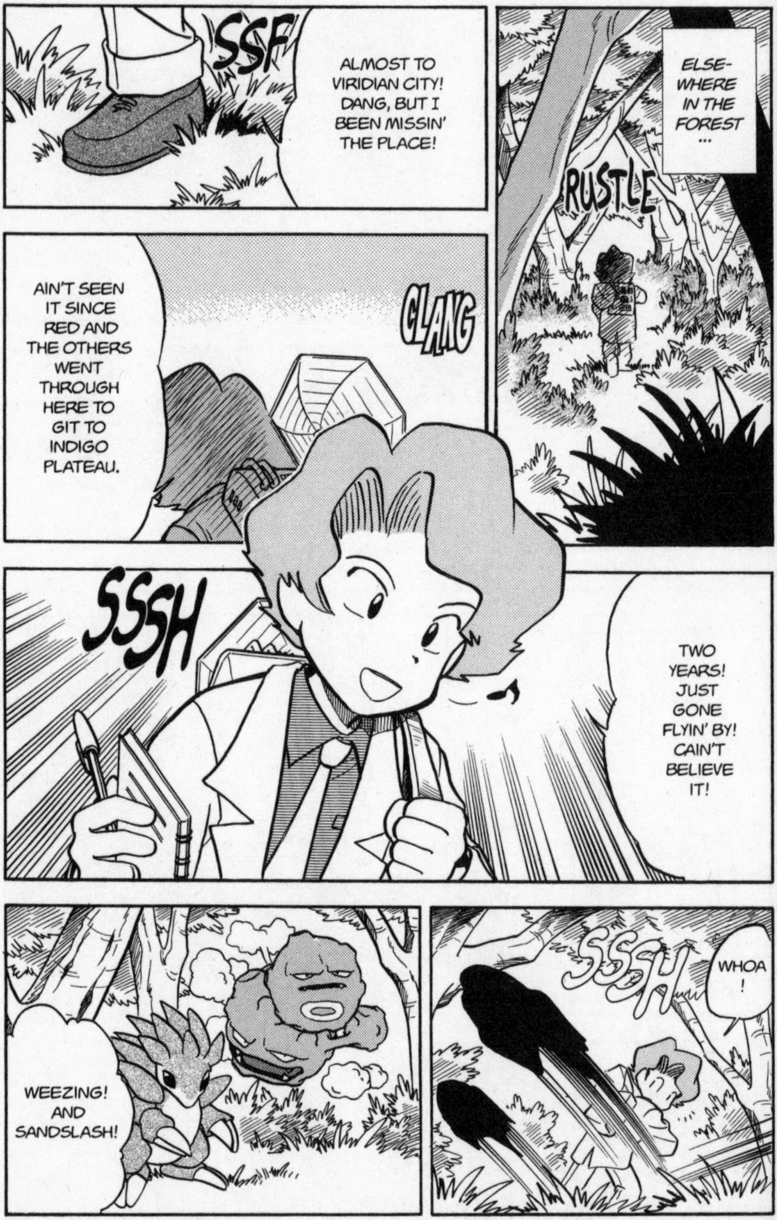
ELSE-WHERE IN THE FOREST ...
RUSTLE
ALMOST TO VIRIDIAN CITY! DANG, BUT I BEEN MISSIN' THE PLACE!
SSF
CLANG
AIN'T SEEN IT SINCE RED AND THE OTHERS WENT THROUGH HERE TO GIT TO INDIGO PLATEAU.
TWO YEARS! JUST GONE FLYIN' BY! CAIN'T BELIEVE IT!
SSSH
WHOA!
SSSH
WEEZING! AND SANDSLASH!

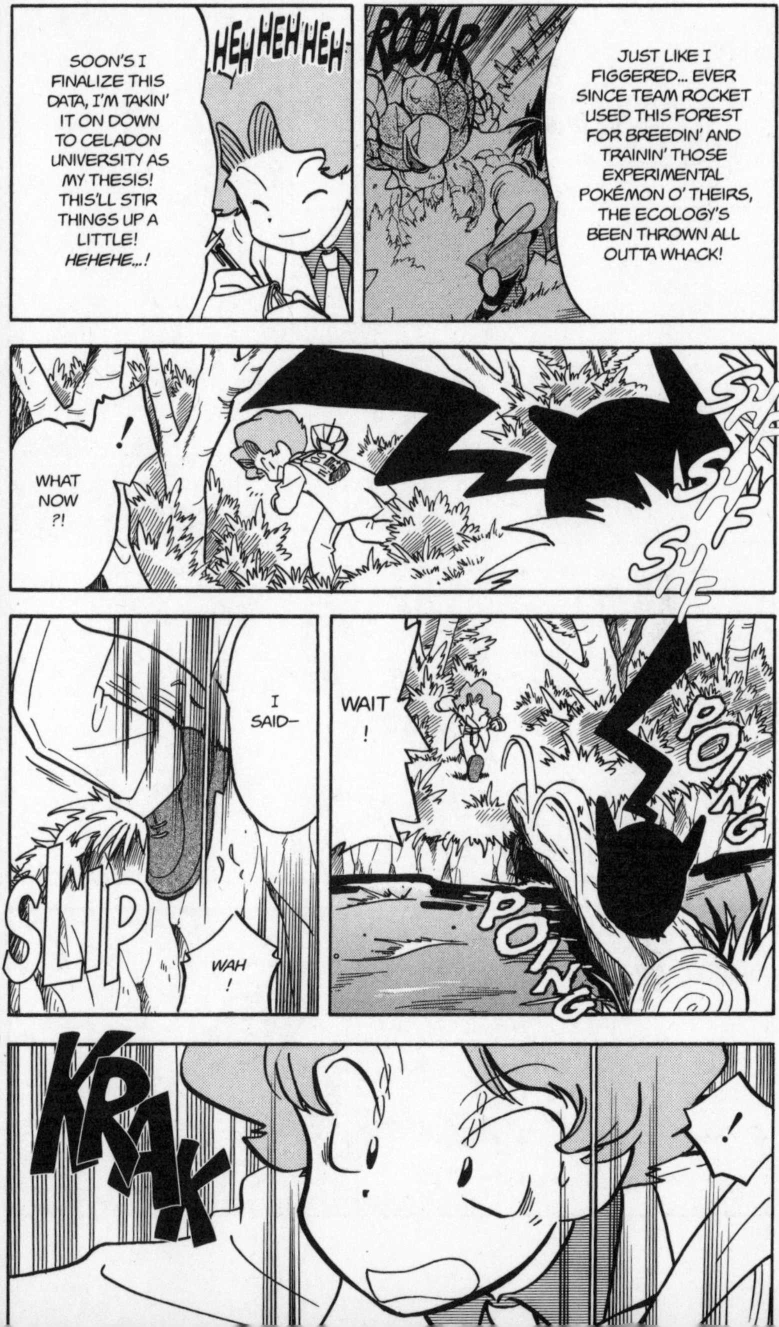
ROOAR
JUST LIKE I FIGGERED... EVER SINCE TEAM ROCKET USED THIS FOREST FOR BREEDIN' AND TRAININ' THOSE EXPERIMENTAL POKÉMON O' THEIRS, THE ECOLOGY'S BEEN THROWN ALL OUTTA WHACK!
HEH HEH HEH
SOON'S I FINALIZE THIS DATA, I'M TAKIN' IT ON DOWN TO CELADON UNIVERSITY AS MY THESIS! THIS'LL STIR THINGS UP A LITTLE! *HEHEHE...!*
SHF SHF SHF
!
WHAT NOW ?!
POING
WAIT !
POING
I SAID—
SLIP
WAH !
KRAK
!

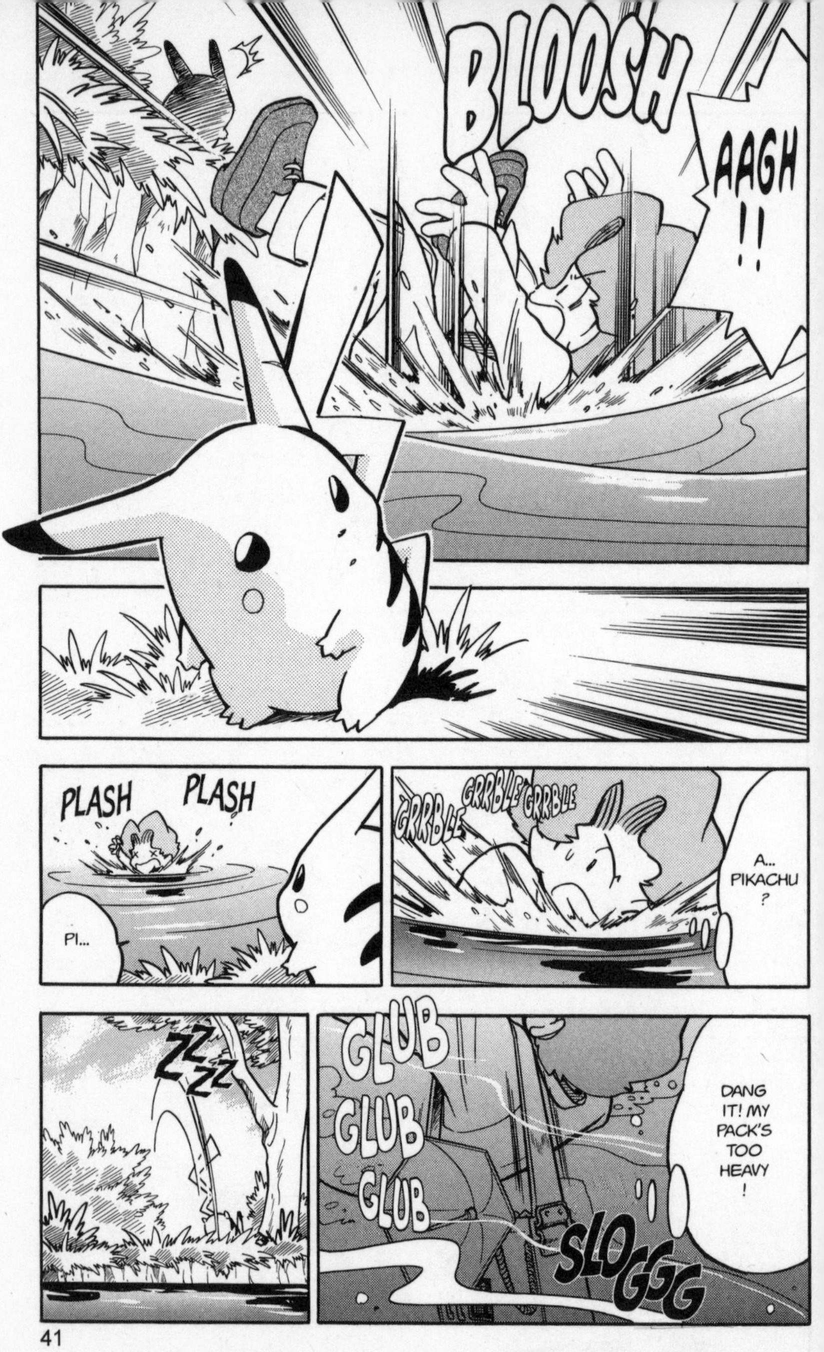
AAGH!!
BLOOSH
A... PIKACHU?
GRRBLE GRRBLE GRRBLE
PLASH PLASH
PI...
DANG IT! MY PACK'S TOO HEAVY!
GLUB GLUB GLUB
SLOGGG
ZZZZ

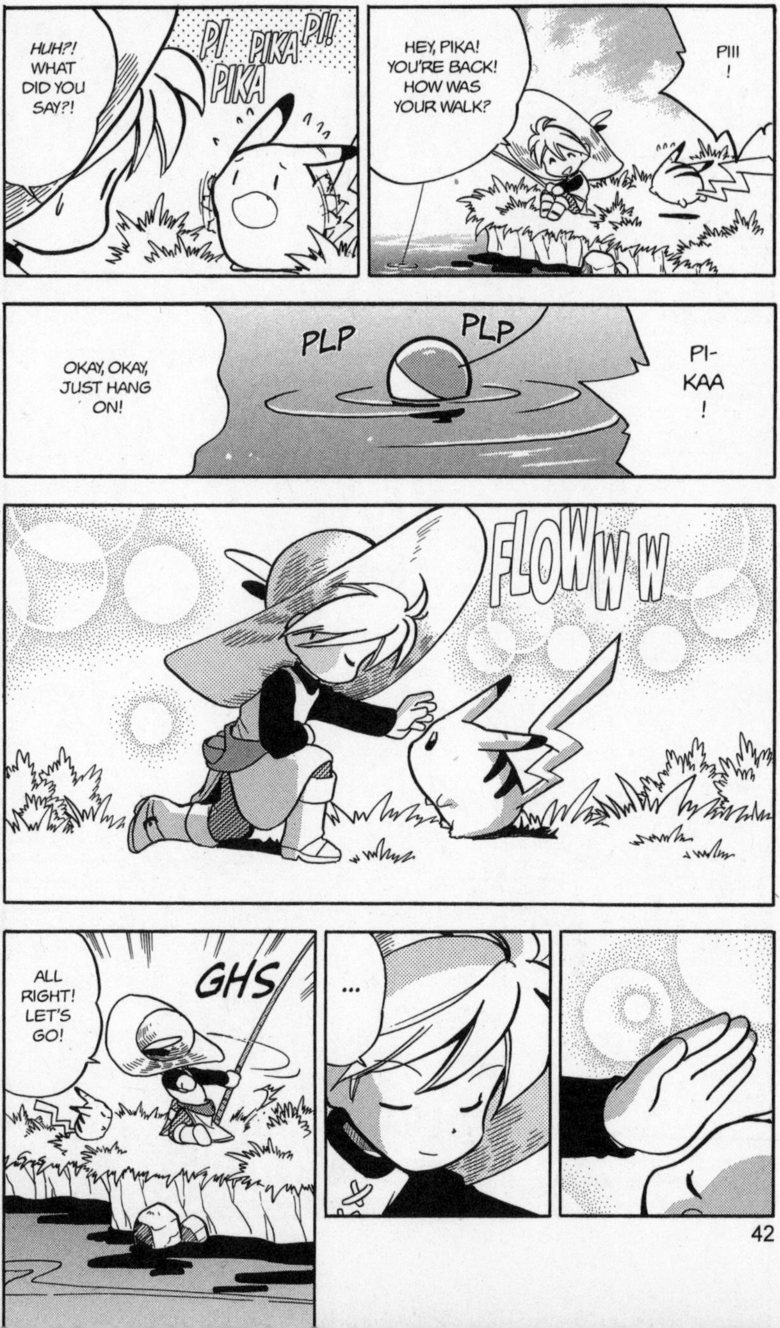
HEY, PIKA! YOU'RE BACK! HOW WAS YOUR WALK?
PIII !
PI PIKA PIKA PI!!
HUH?! WHAT DID YOU SAY?!
PI- KAA !
PLP
PLP
OKAY, OKAY, JUST HANG ON!
FLOWWW W
...
GHS
ALL RIGHT! LET'S GO!

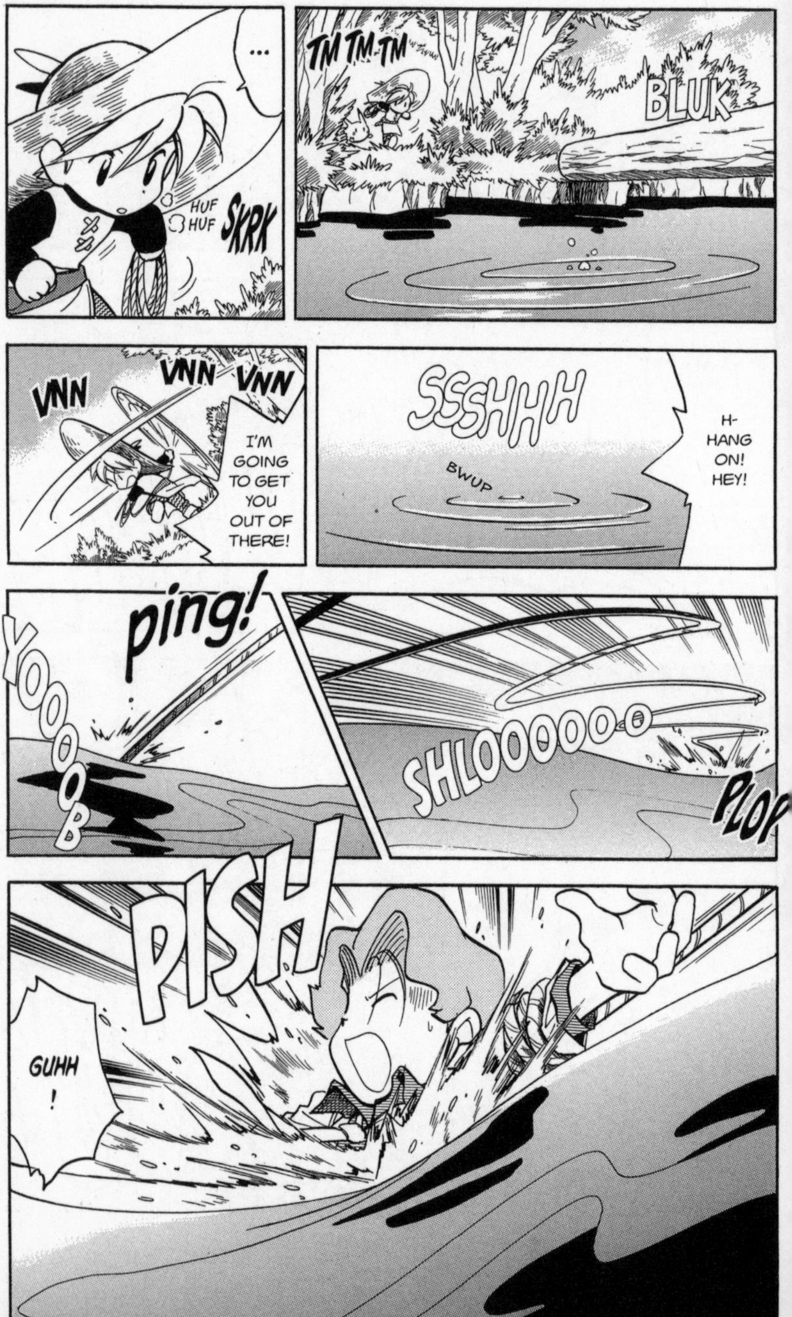
TM TM TM
BLUK
...
HUF HUF
SKRK
SSSHHHH
BWUP
H- HANG ON! HEY!
VNN VNN VNN
I'M GOING TO GET YOU OUT OF THERE!
SHLOOOOOO-O
PLOP
ping!
YOOOOB
PISH
GUHH !

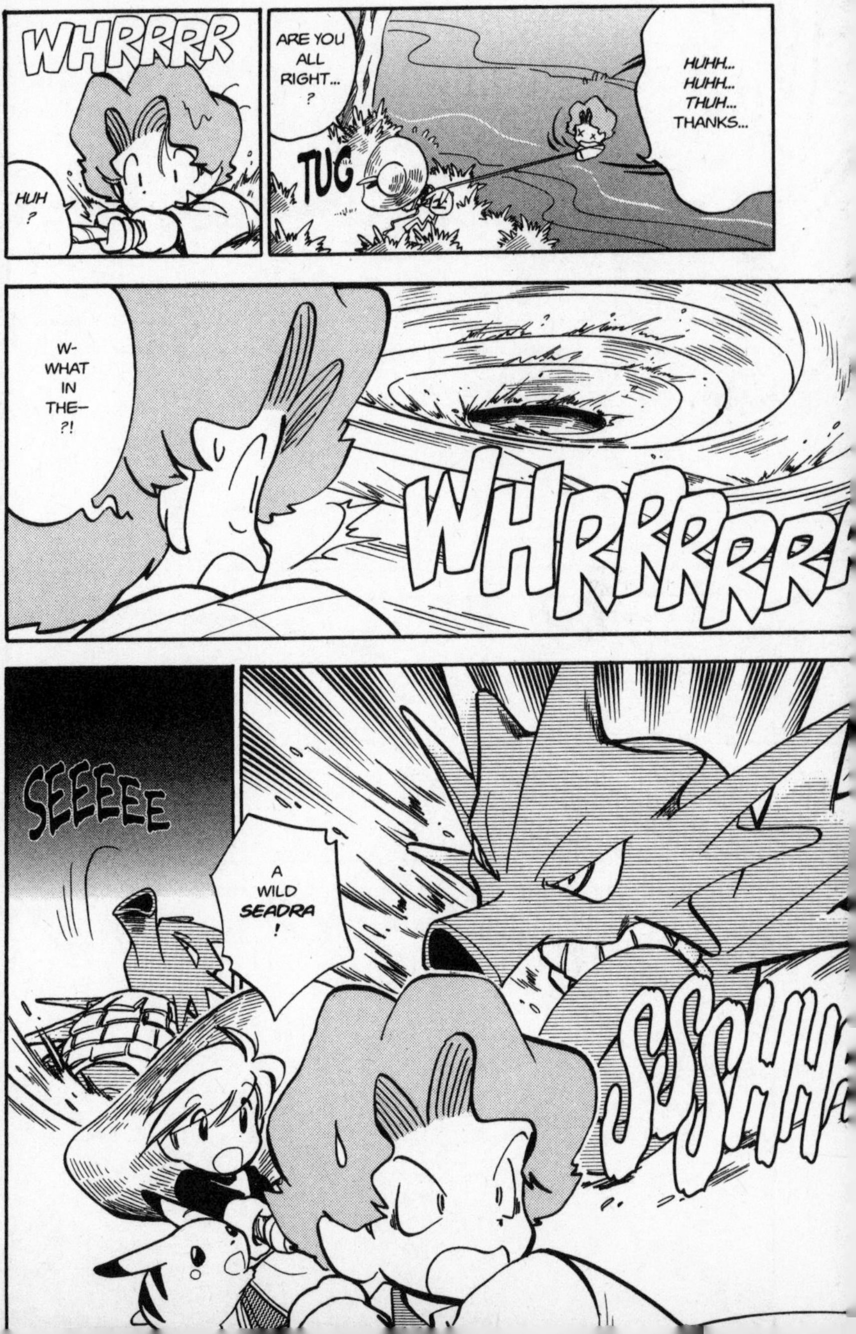

ARE YOU ALL RIGHT... ?
TUG
HUHH... HUHH... THUH... THANKS...
WHRRRR
HUH ?
WHRRRRRR
W- WHAT IN THE— ?!
SSSHH
A WILD SEADRA !
SEEEEEE

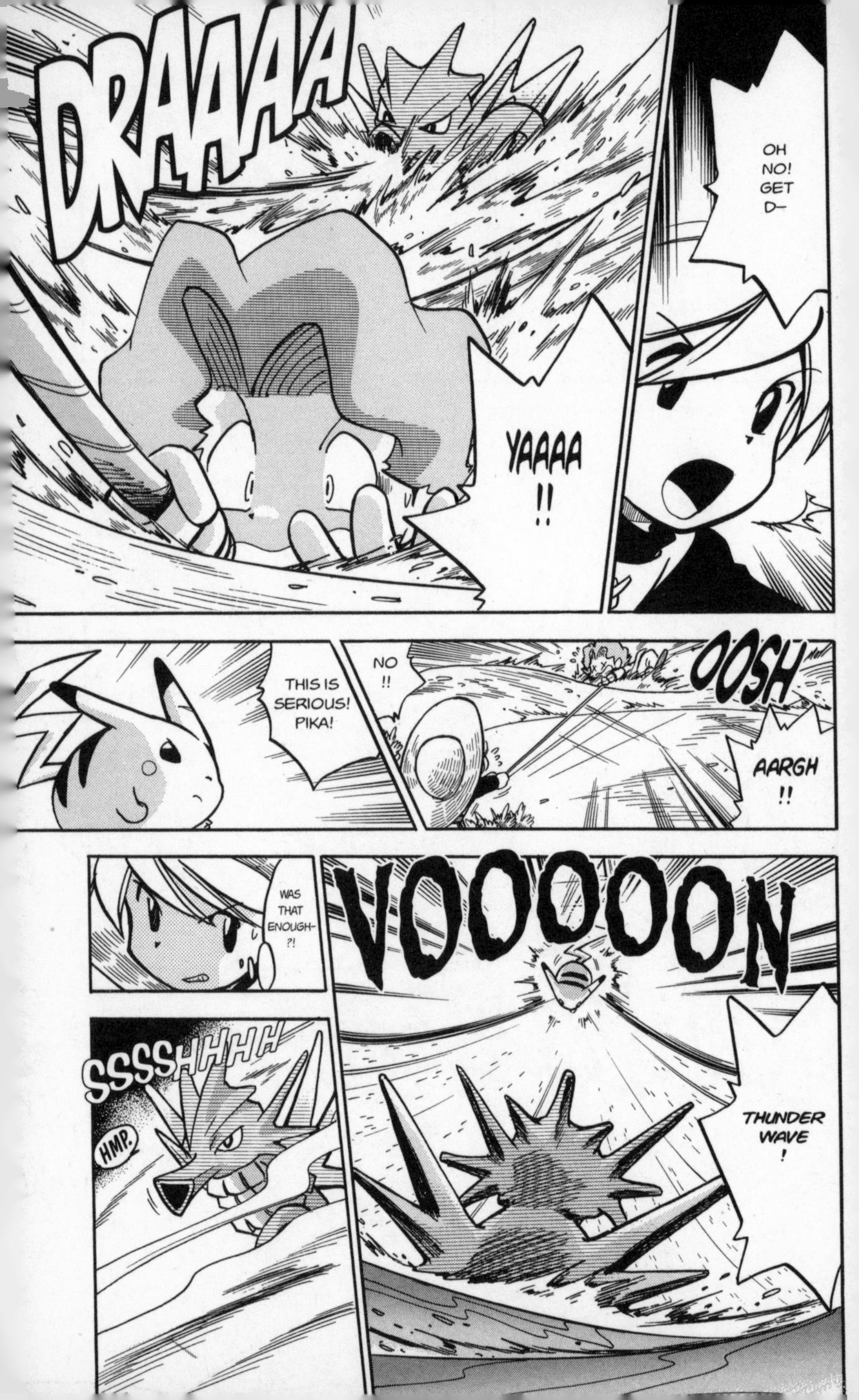
OH NO! GET D—
DRAAAA
YAAAA!!
OOSH
NO!!
AARGH!!
THIS IS SERIOUS! PIKA!
VOOOOON
THUNDER WAVE!
WAS THAT ENOUGH—?!
SSSSHHHH
HMP.

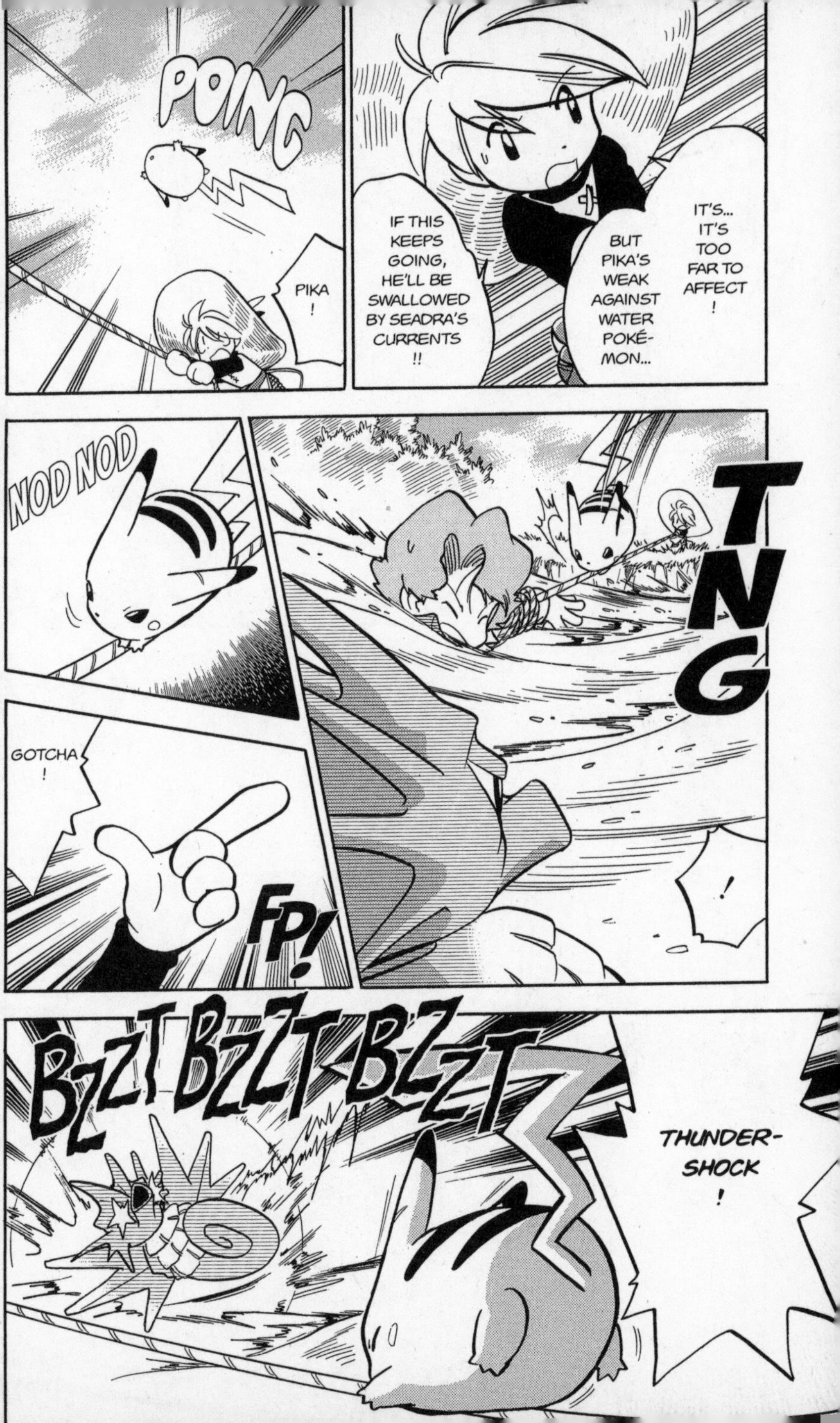

IT'S... IT'S TOO FAR TO AFFECT!
BUT PIKA'S WEAK AGAINST WATER POKÉMON...
IF THIS KEEPS GOING, HE'LL BE SWALLOWED BY SEADRA'S CURRENTS!!
POING
PIKA!
TNG
!
NOD NOD
GOTCHA!
FP!
BZZT BZZT BZZT
THUNDER-SHOCK!

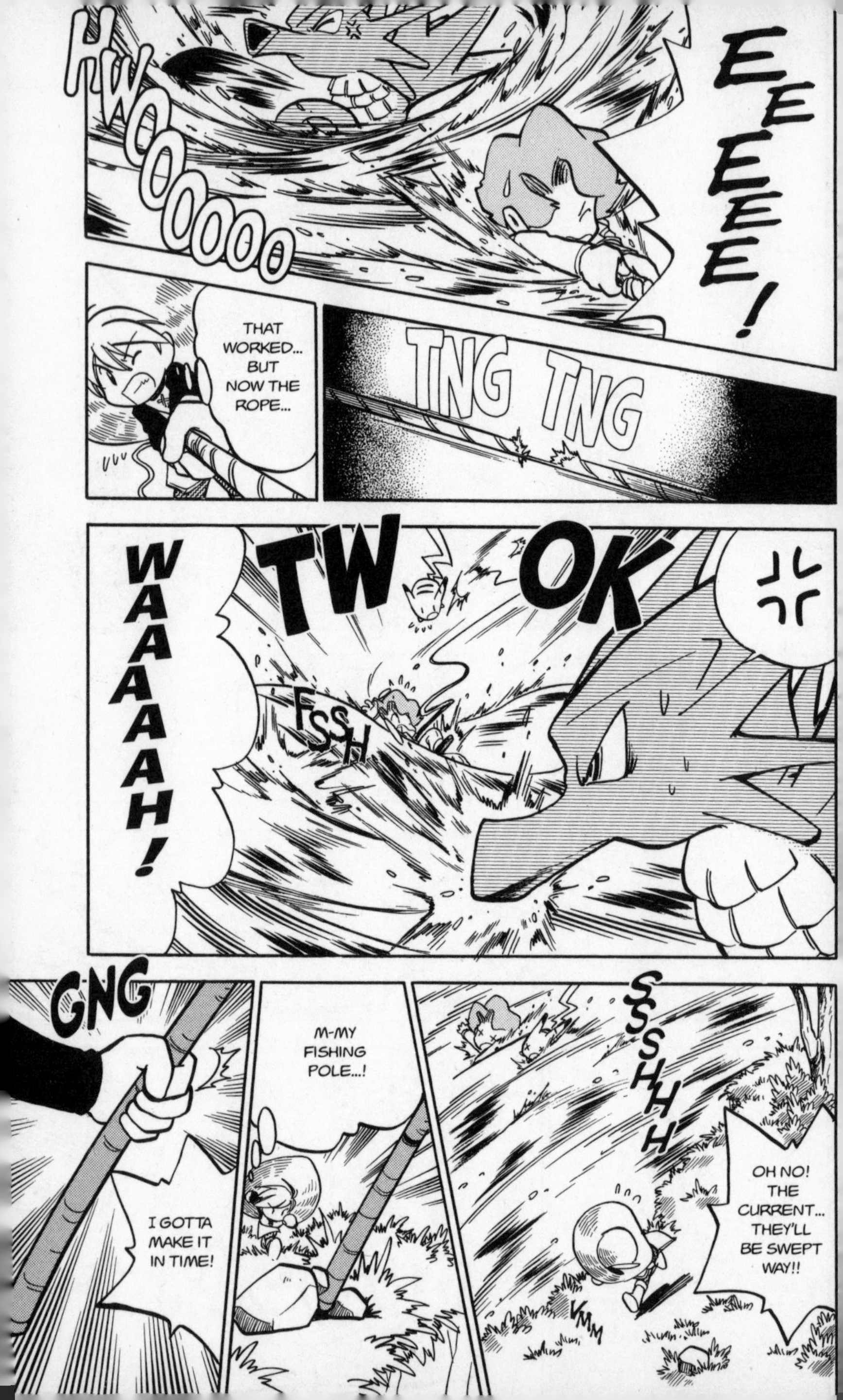
EEEEEE!
HWOOOOOO
TNG TNG
THAT WORKED... BUT NOW THE ROPE...
TWOK
FSSH
WAAAAAAH!
SSSHHHH
OH NO! THE CURRENT... THEY'LL BE SWEPT WAY!!
VMM
M-MY FISHING POLE...!
GNG
I GOTTA MAKE IT IN TIME!

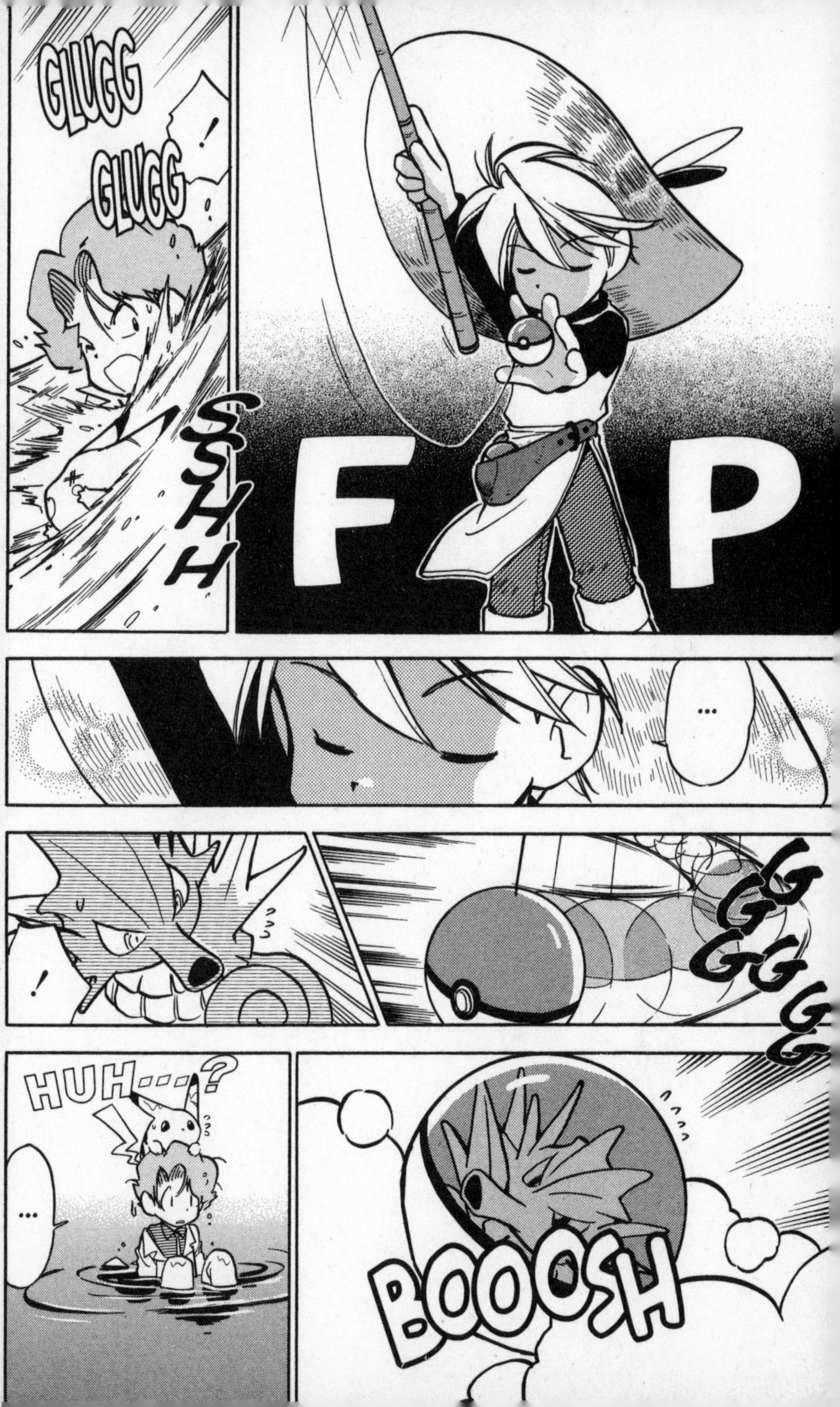
F P
GLUGG
GLUGG
!
SSHHH
...
GGGGGG
!
BOOOSH
HUH...?
...

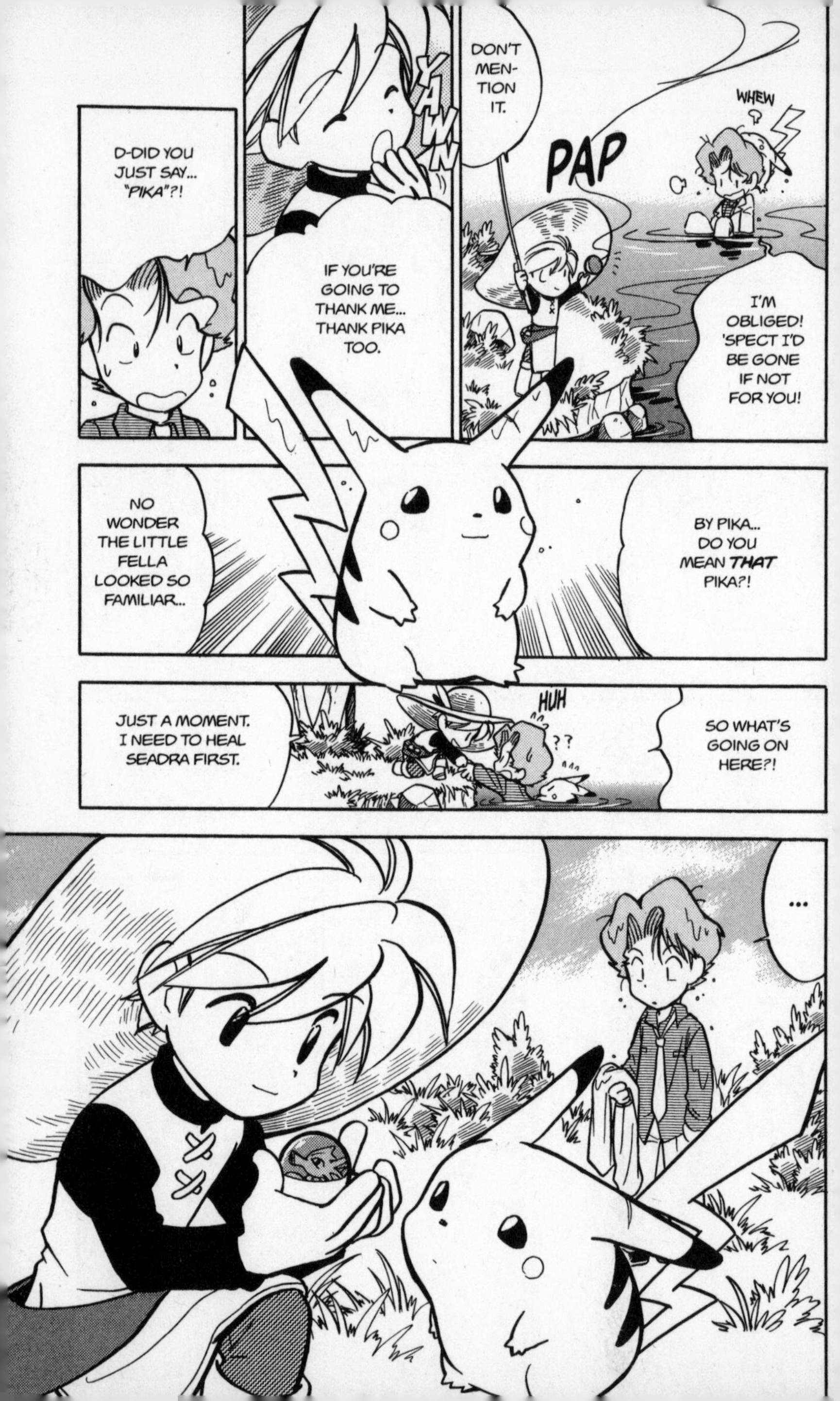
WHEW
PAP
I'M OBLIGED! 'SPECT I'D BE GONE IF NOT FOR YOU!
DON'T MEN-TION IT.
YAWN
IF YOU'RE GOING TO THANK ME... THANK PIKA TOO.
D-DID YOU JUST SAY... "PIKA"?!
BY PIKA... DO YOU MEAN *THAT* PIKA?!
NO WONDER THE LITTLE FELLA LOOKED SO FAMILIAR...
SO WHAT'S GOING ON HERE?!
HUH
??
JUST A MOMENT. I NEED TO HEAL SEADRA FIRST.
...

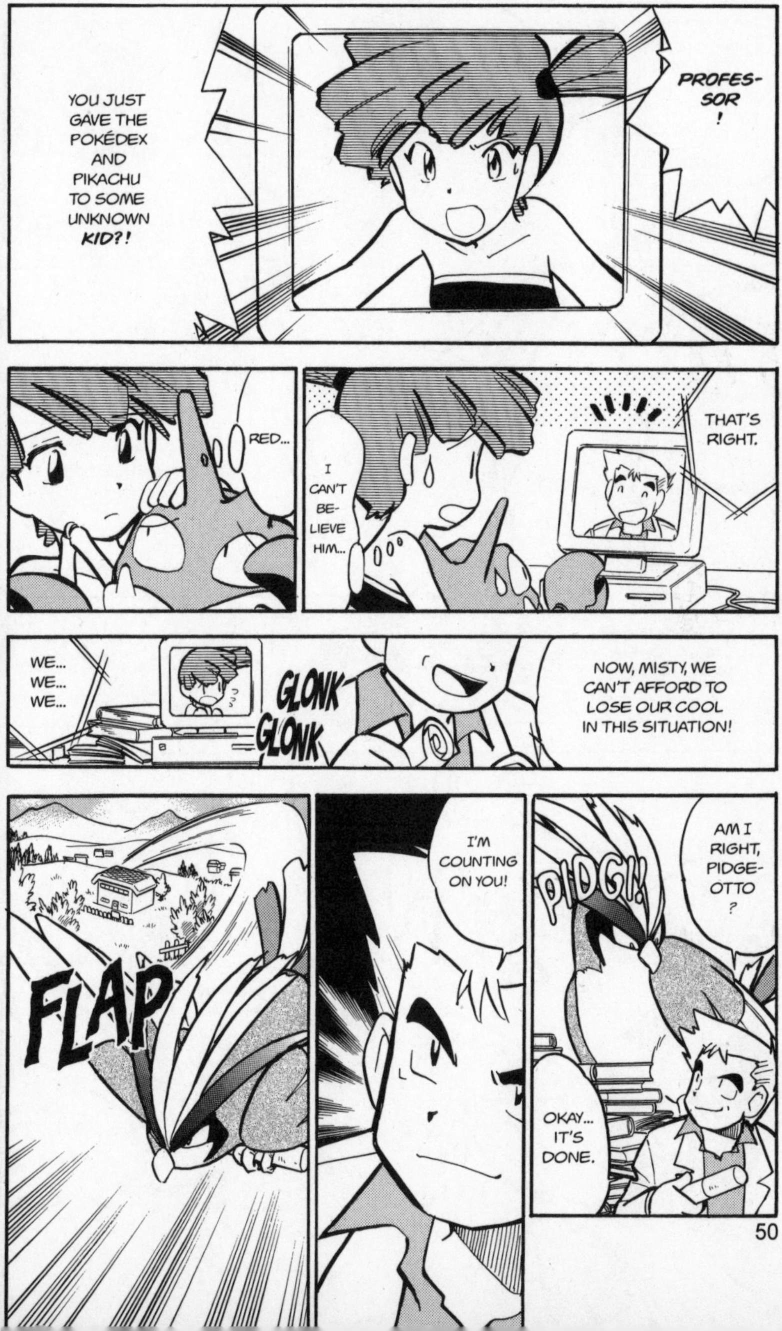
PROFES-SOR!
YOU JUST GAVE THE POKÉDEX AND PIKACHU TO SOME UNKNOWN KID?!
THAT'S RIGHT.
I CAN'T BE-LIEVE HIM...
RED...
NOW, MISTY, WE CAN'T AFFORD TO LOSE OUR COOL IN THIS SITUATION!
GLONK GLONK
WE... WE... WE...
AM I RIGHT, PIDGE-OTTO?
PIDG!!
OKAY... IT'S DONE.
I'M COUNTING ON YOU!
FLAP

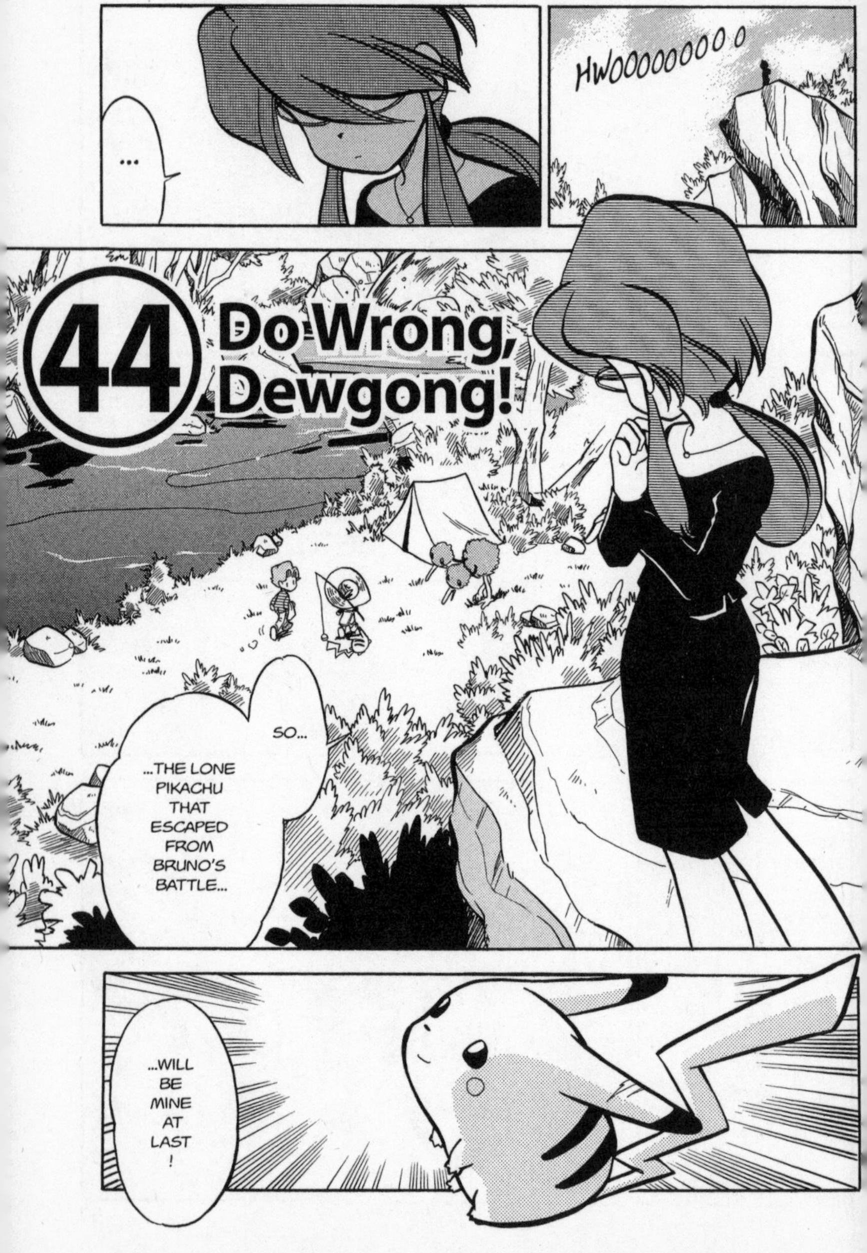
HWOOOOOOOO O
...
44 Do Wrong, Dewgong!
SO...
...THE LONE PIKACHU THAT ESCAPED FROM BRUNO'S BATTLE...
...WILL BE MINE AT LAST!

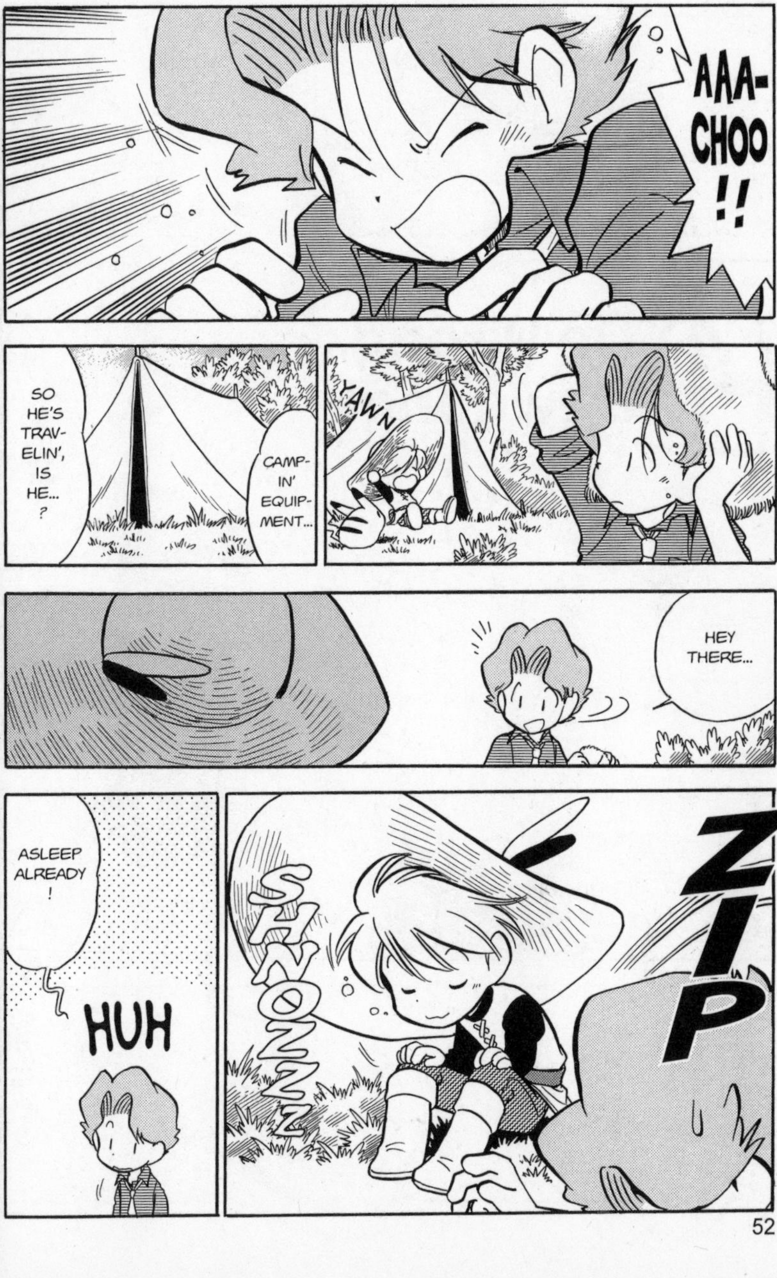
AAA-CHOO!!
YAWN
CAMP-IN' EQUIP-MENT...
SO HE'S TRAV-ELIN', IS HE...?
HEY THERE...
ZIP
SHNOZZZ
ASLEEP ALREADY!
HUH

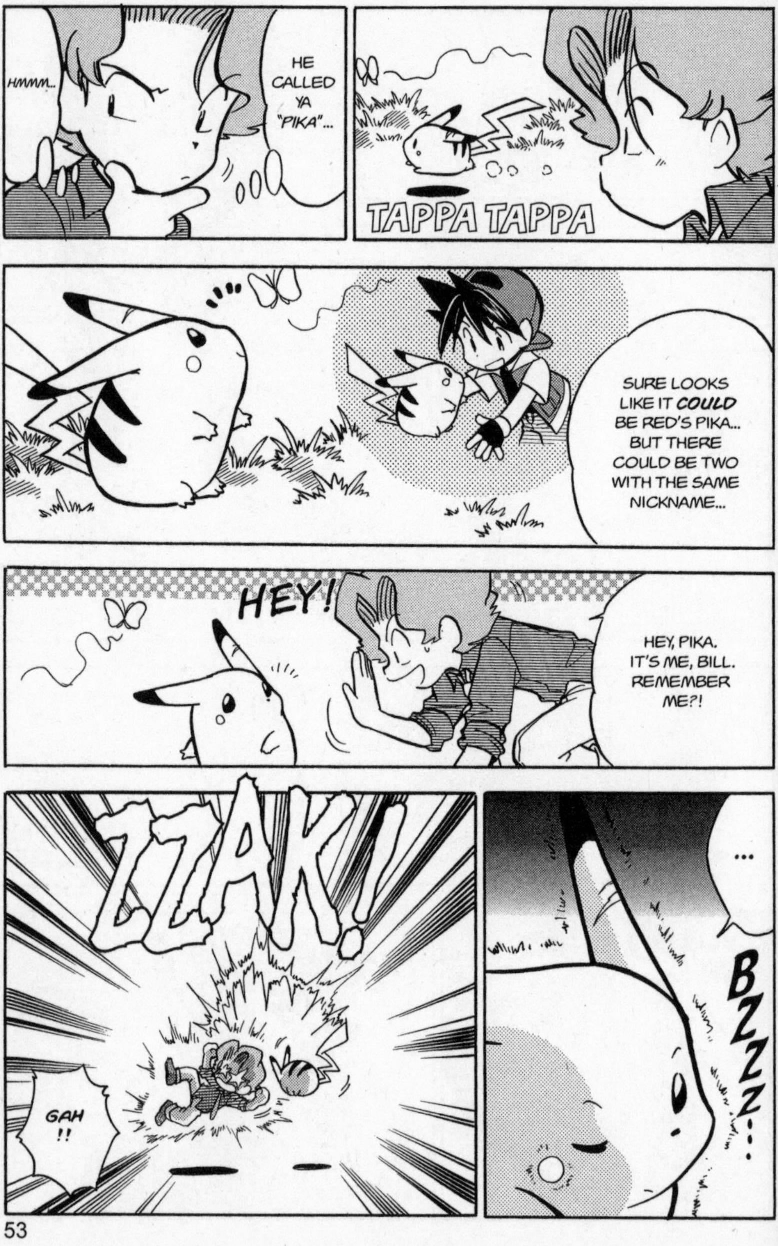
TAPPA TAPPA
HE CALLED YA "PIKA"...
HMMM..
SURE LOOKS LIKE IT COULD BE RED'S PIKA... BUT THERE COULD BE TWO WITH THE SAME NICKNAME...
HEY, PIKA. IT'S ME, BILL. REMEMBER ME?!
HEY!
...
BZZZ...
ZZAK!
GAH!!

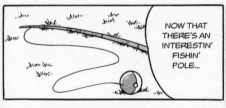

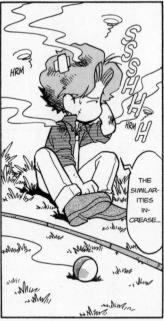

HRM
SSSHHH
HRM
THE SIMILAR-ITIES IN-CREASE...
NOW THAT THERE'S AN INTERESTIN' FISHIN' POLE...
SEEMED LIKE THAT BALL MOVED ON ITS OWN... AGAINST THE CURRENT! RECKON I COULD BE DREAMIN...
...OR IT COULD BE SOME NEW GADGET THAT...
?
HMM
HMM
HUH?! WELL HOWDY-DO! JES' A REG'LAR POKÉ BALL ATTACHED TO A STRING!
CLATTER CLATTER
CLATTERCLATTER

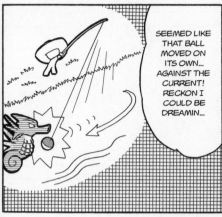

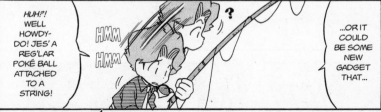

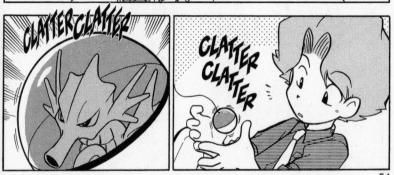

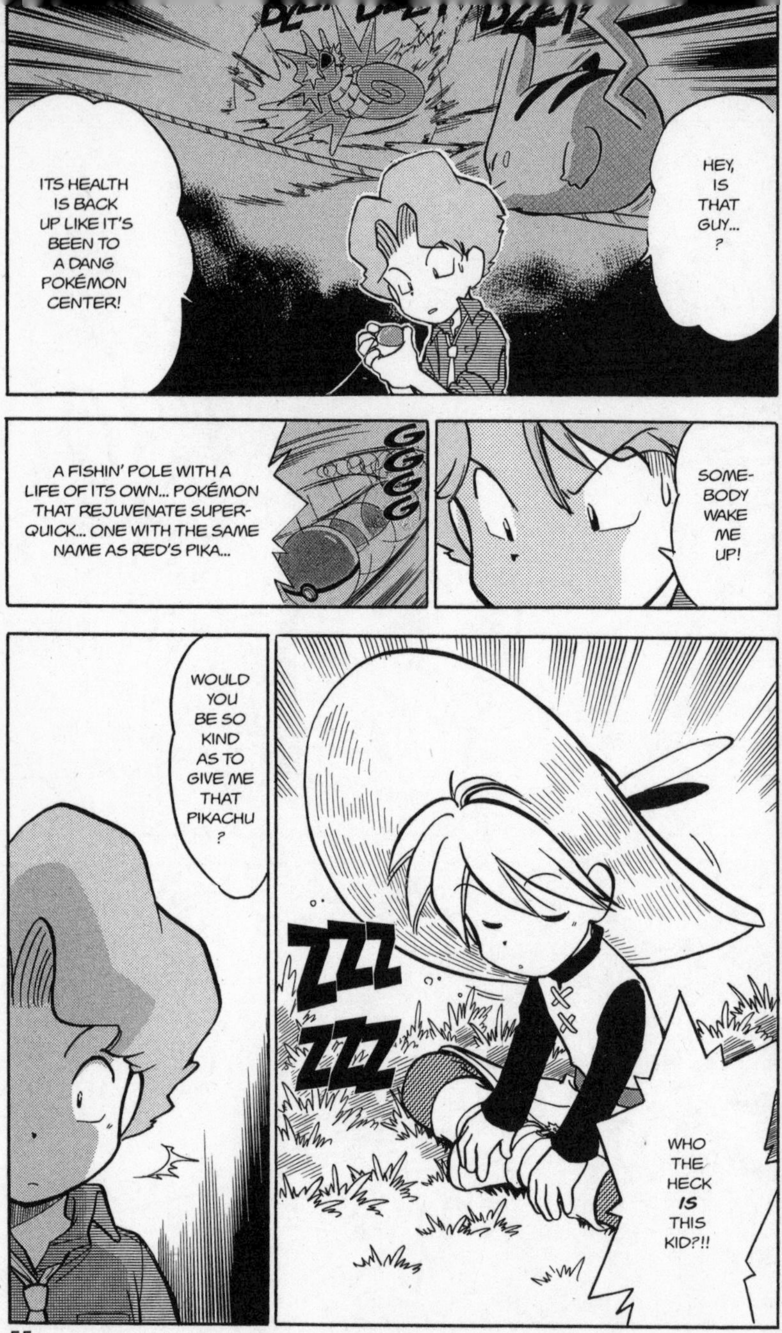
HEY, IS THAT GUY...?
ITS HEALTH IS BACK UP LIKE IT'S BEEN TO A DANG POKÉMON CENTER!
SOME-BODY WAKE ME UP!
GGGG
A FISHIN' POLE WITH A LIFE OF ITS OWN... POKÉMON THAT REJUVENATE SUPER-QUICK... ONE WITH THE SAME NAME AS RED'S PIKA...
ZZZ ZZZ
WHO THE HECK *IS* THIS KID?!!
WOULD YOU BE SO KIND AS TO GIVE ME THAT PIKACHU?

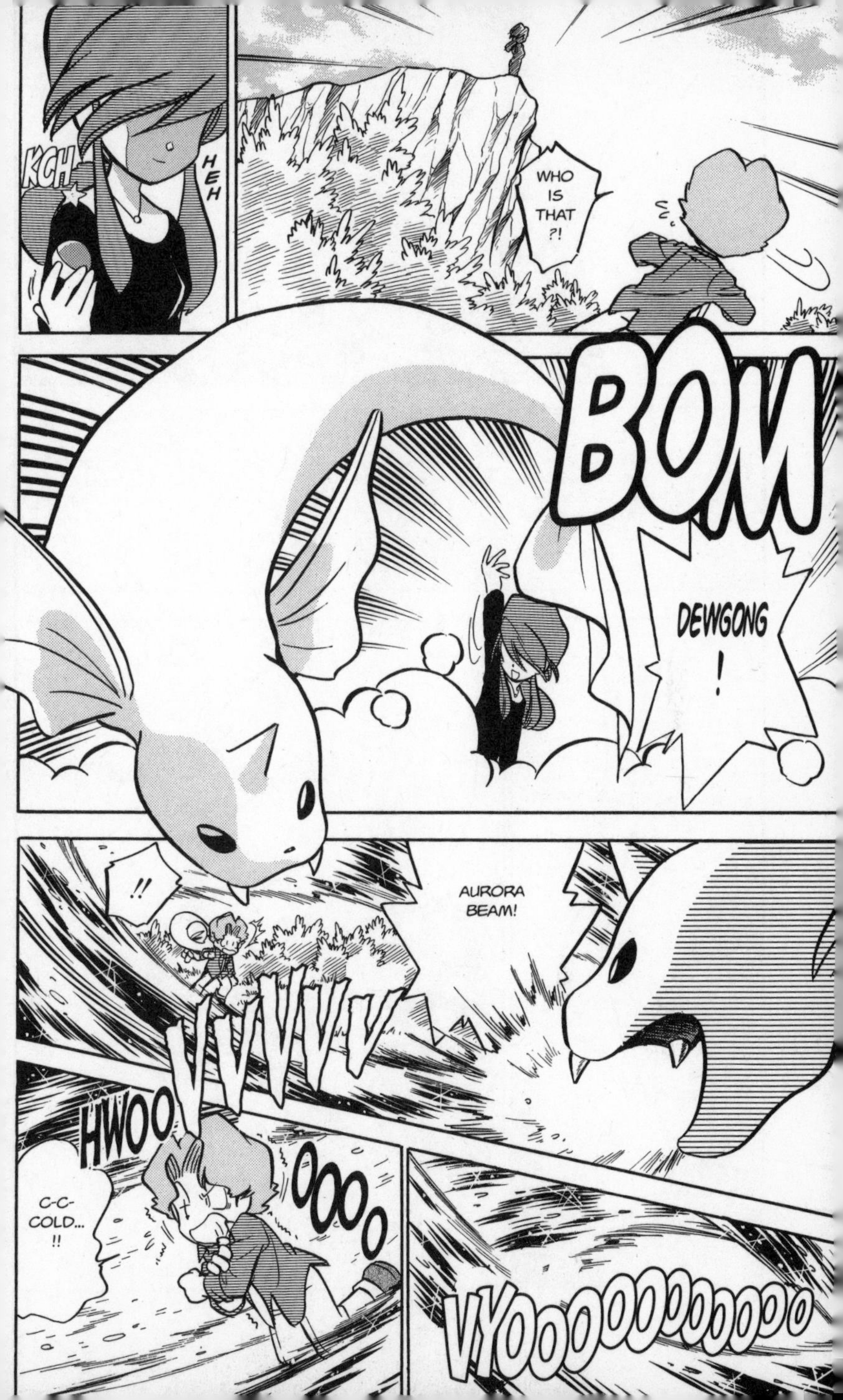
WHO IS THAT ?!
KCH
HEH
BOM
DEWGONG !
AURORA BEAM!
!!
VVVVV
VYOOOOOOOOOOO
HWOOOOOO
C-C-COLD... !!

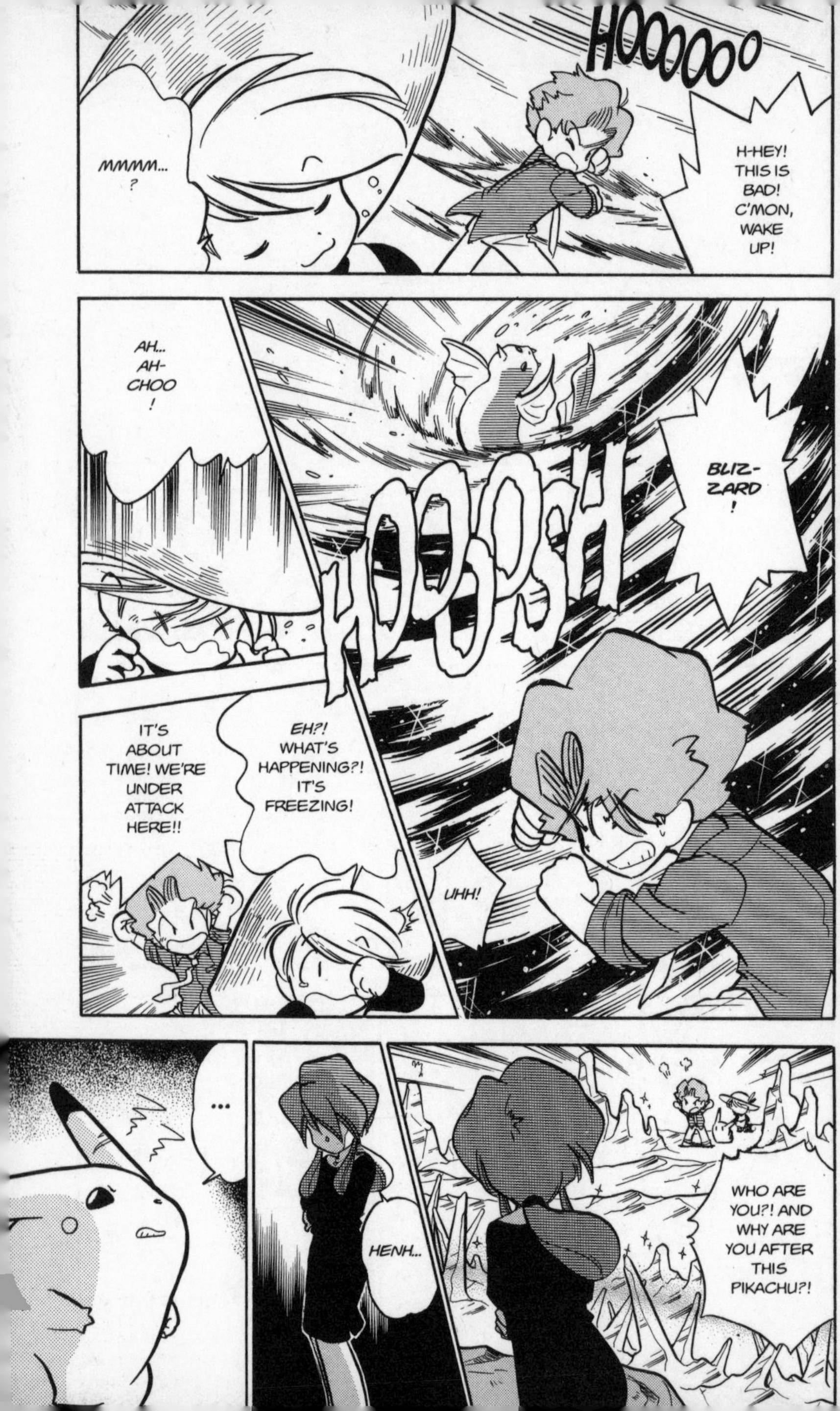
HOOOOOO
H-HEY! THIS IS BAD! C'MON, WAKE UP!
MMMM... ?
BLIZZARD!
WHOOSH
UHH!
AH... AH-CHOO!
EH?! WHAT'S HAPPENING?! IT'S FREEZING!
IT'S ABOUT TIME! WE'RE UNDER ATTACK HERE!!
WHO ARE YOU?! AND WHY ARE YOU AFTER THIS PIKACHU?!
HENH...
...

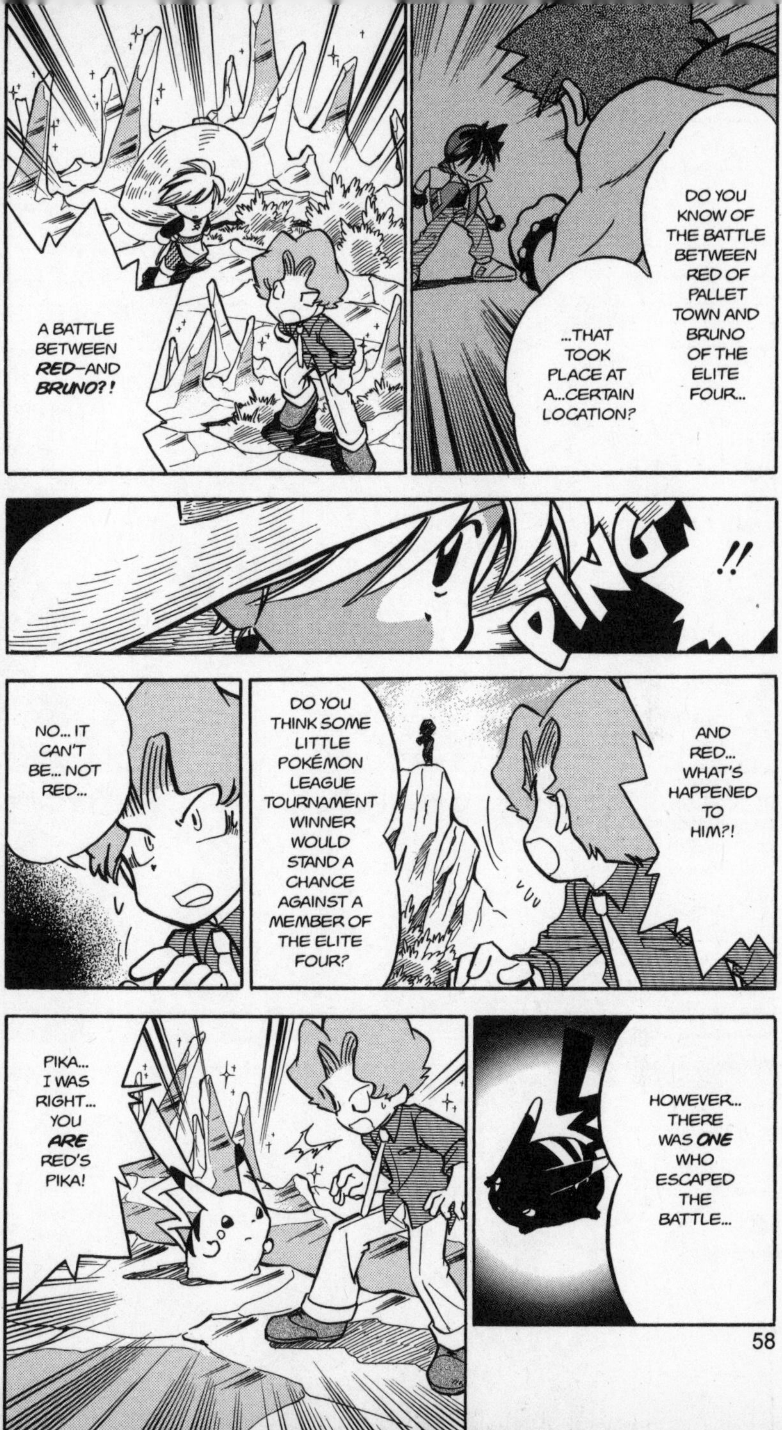
DO YOU KNOW OF THE BATTLE BETWEEN RED OF PALLET TOWN AND BRUNO OF THE ELITE FOUR...
...THAT TOOK PLACE AT A...CERTAIN LOCATION?
A BATTLE BETWEEN ***RED***—AND ***BRUNO?!***
PING
!!
AND RED... WHAT'S HAPPENED TO HIM?!
DO YOU THINK SOME LITTLE POKÉMON LEAGUE TOURNAMENT WINNER WOULD STAND A CHANCE AGAINST A MEMBER OF THE ELITE FOUR?
NO... IT CAN'T BE... NOT RED...
HOWEVER... THERE WAS ***ONE*** WHO ESCAPED THE BATTLE...
PIKA... I WAS RIGHT... YOU ***ARE*** RED'S PIKA!

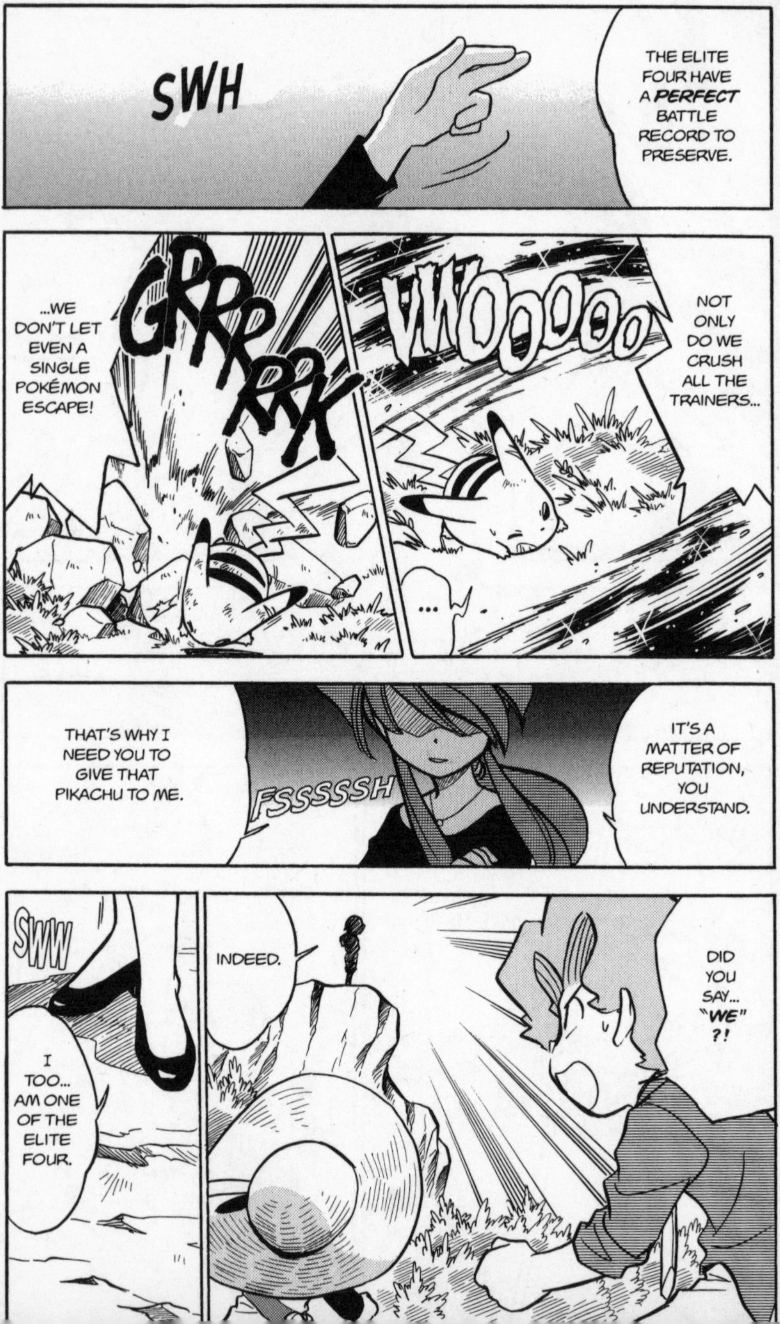
THE ELITE FOUR HAVE A **PERFECT** BATTLE RECORD TO PRESERVE.
SWH
VWOOOOO
NOT ONLY DO WE CRUSH ALL THE TRAINERS...
...
GRRRRRK
...WE DON'T LET EVEN A SINGLE POKÉMON ESCAPE!
IT'S A MATTER OF REPUTATION, YOU UNDERSTAND.
FSSSSSH
THAT'S WHY I NEED YOU TO GIVE THAT PIKACHU TO ME.
DID YOU SAY... "**WE**"?!
INDEED.
SWW
I TOO... AM ONE OF THE ELITE FOUR.

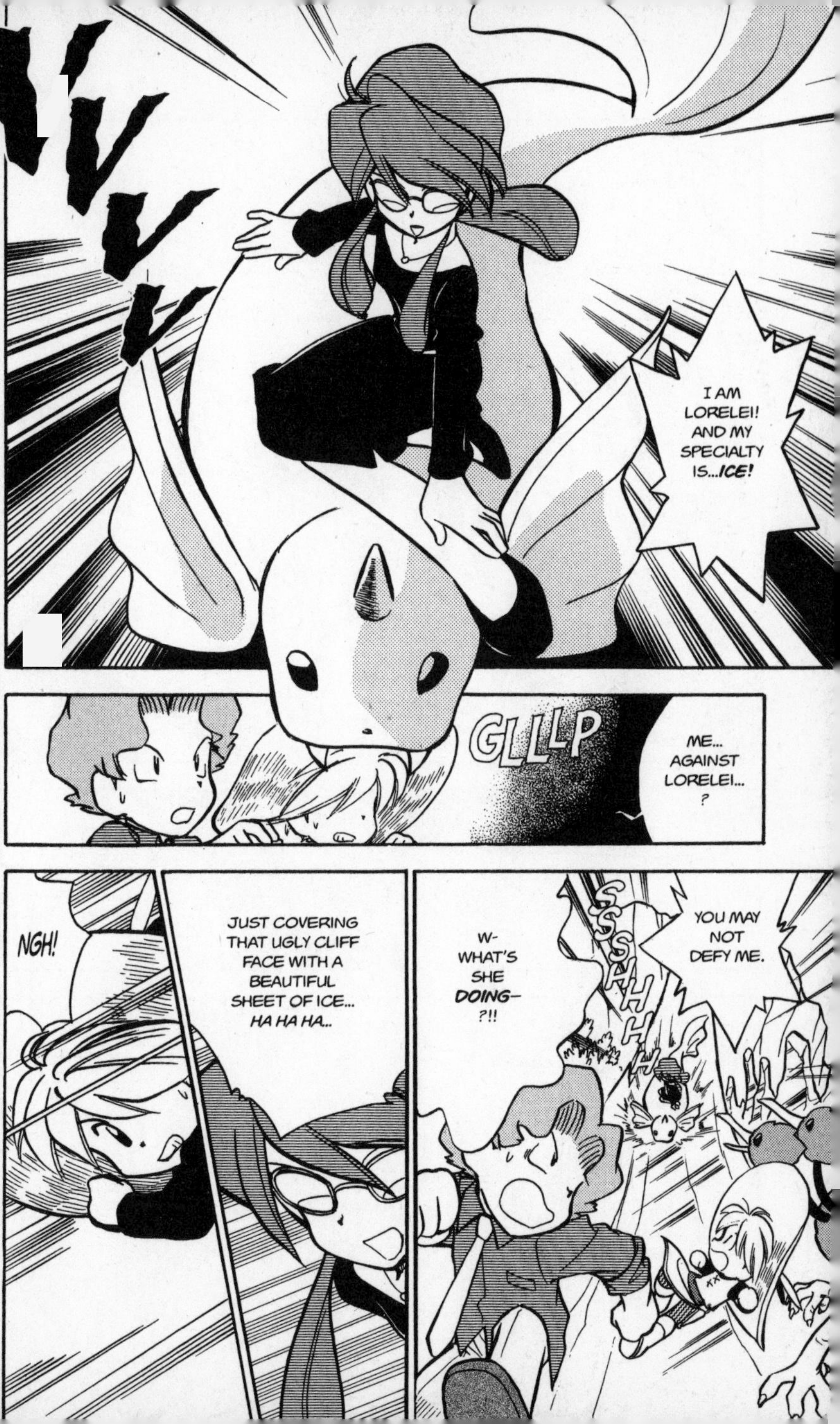
I AM LORELEI! AND MY SPECIALTY IS...**ICE!**
ME... AGAINST LORELEI... ?
GLLLP
YOU MAY NOT DEFY ME.
SSHHHH
W- WHAT'S SHE **DOING**— ?!!
JUST COVERING THAT UGLY CLIFF FACE WITH A BEAUTIFUL SHEET OF ICE... *HA HA HA...*
NGH!

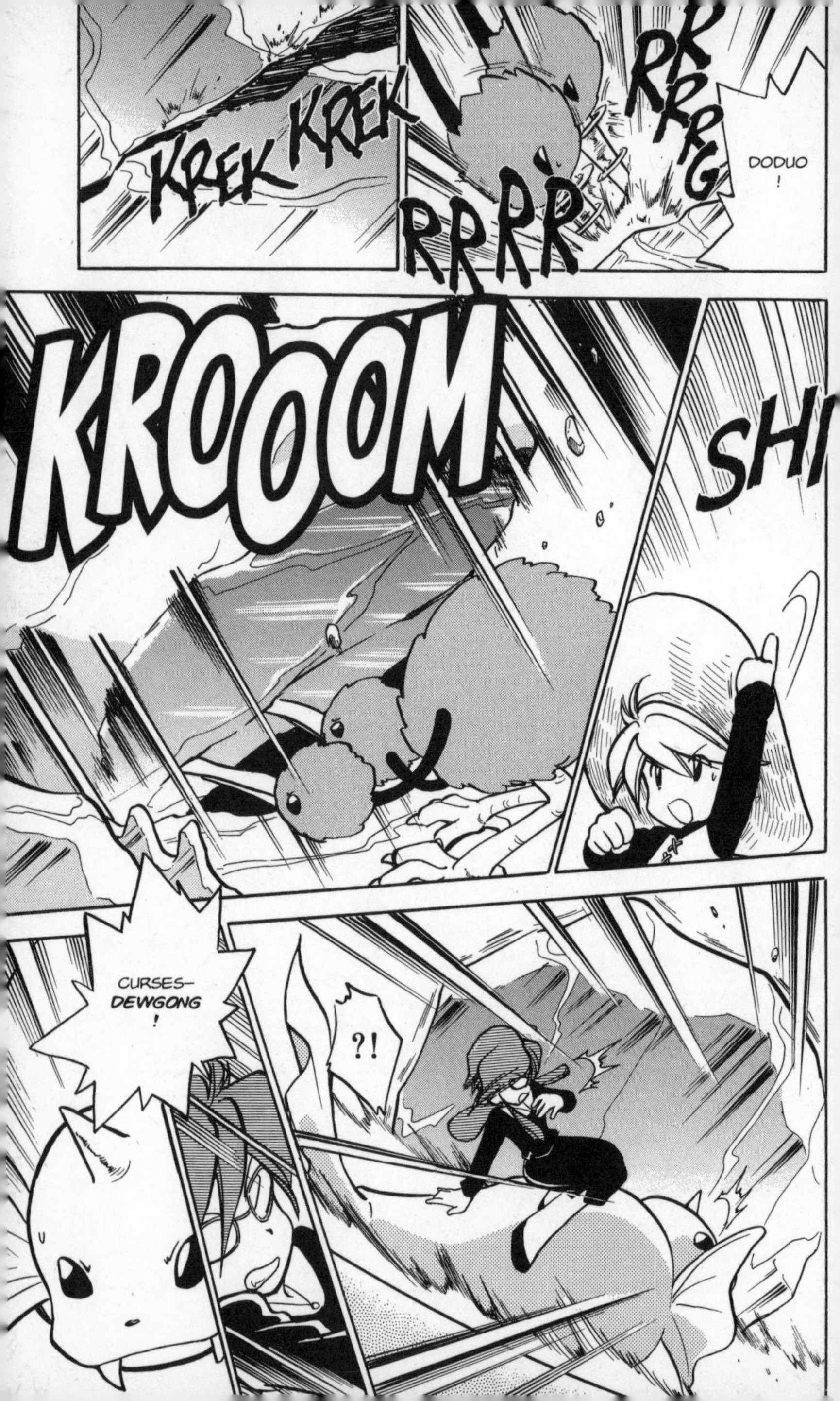
DODUO!
RRRR
KREK KREK
SHI
KROOOM
?!
CURSES—DEWGONG!

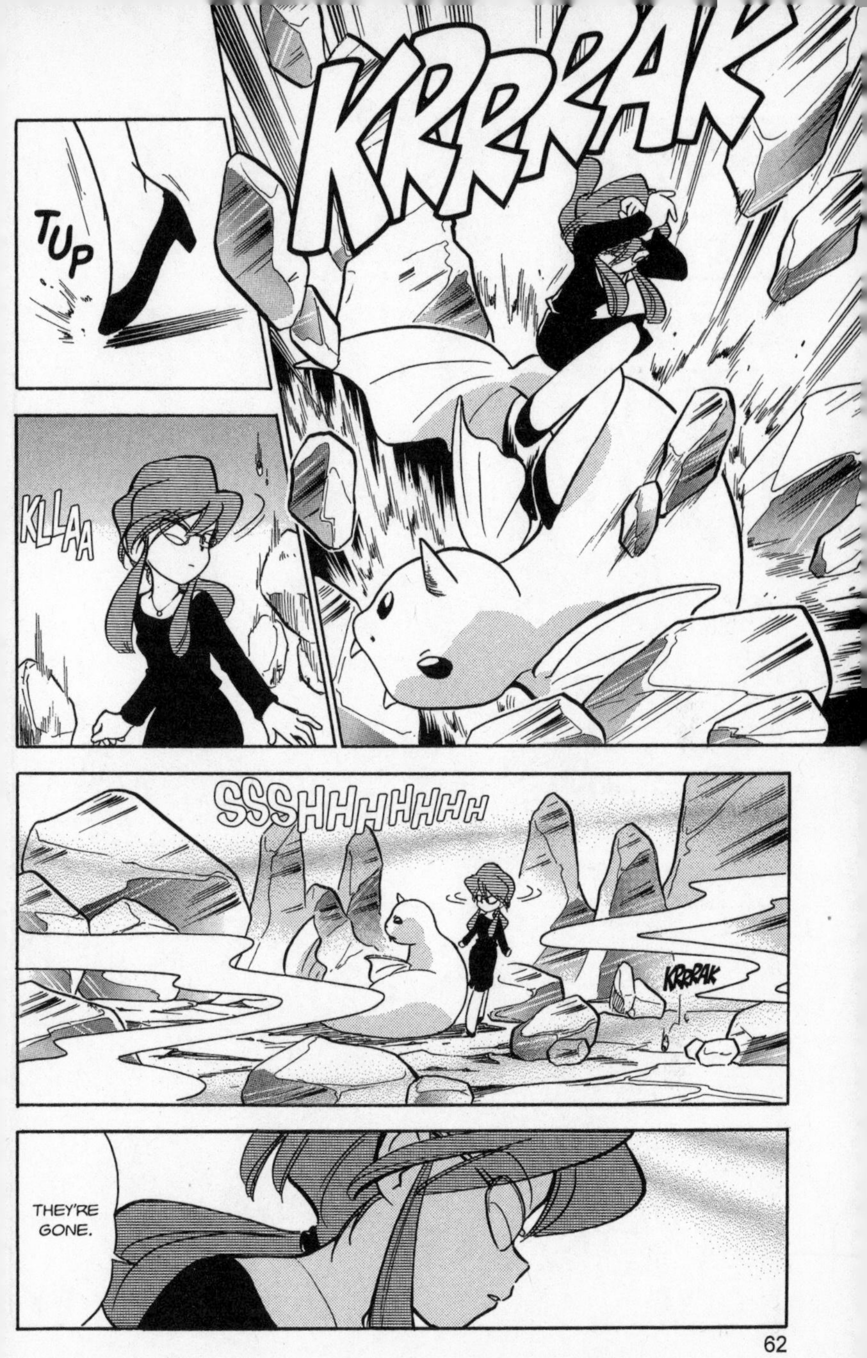
KRRRAK
TUP
KLLAA
SSSHHHHHHH
KRRRAK
THEY'RE GONE.

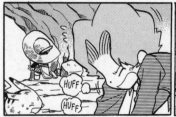

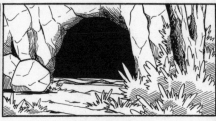

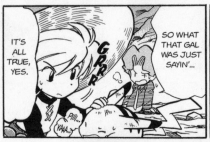

HUFF
HUFF
MAN, I HATE DAYS LIKE THIS...!
SO WHAT THAT GAL WAS JUST SAYIN'...
GRRR
IT'S ALL TRUE, YES.
PIII...
KAAA...
WHEN RED WAS LAST SEEN, HE WAS GOING OFF TO ANSWER A LETTER OF CHALLENGE. HE PROBABLY THOUGHT IT WAS FROM JUST ANOTHER TRAINER...
...BUT IT WAS REALLY FROM *THEM*...
SQUEEZE
...AND ONLY PIKA CAME BACK ALIVE...
I CAN'T BE-LIEVE IT!
THERE'S AN ENEMY NOT EVEN THE POKÉMON LEAGUE CHAMPION CAN BEAT...

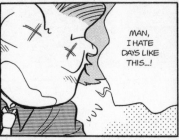

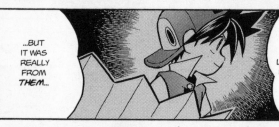

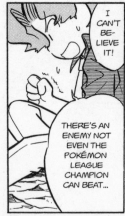

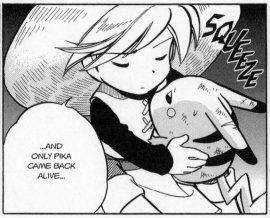

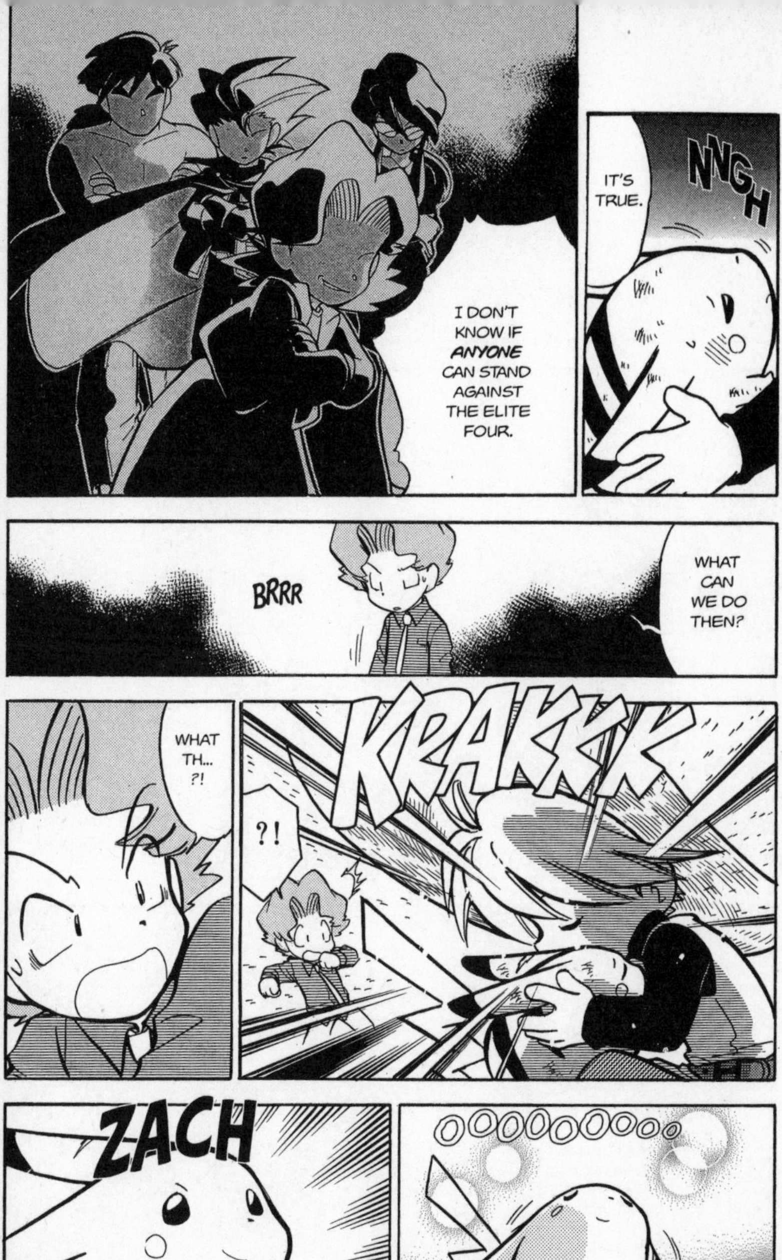
NNGH
IT'S TRUE.
I DON'T KNOW IF *ANYONE* CAN STAND AGAINST THE ELITE FOUR.
WHAT CAN WE DO THEN?
BRRR
KRAKKK
?!
WHAT TH... ?!
OOOOOOOOOO
ZACH

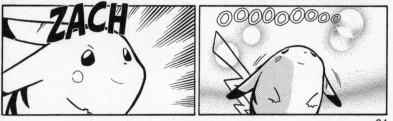

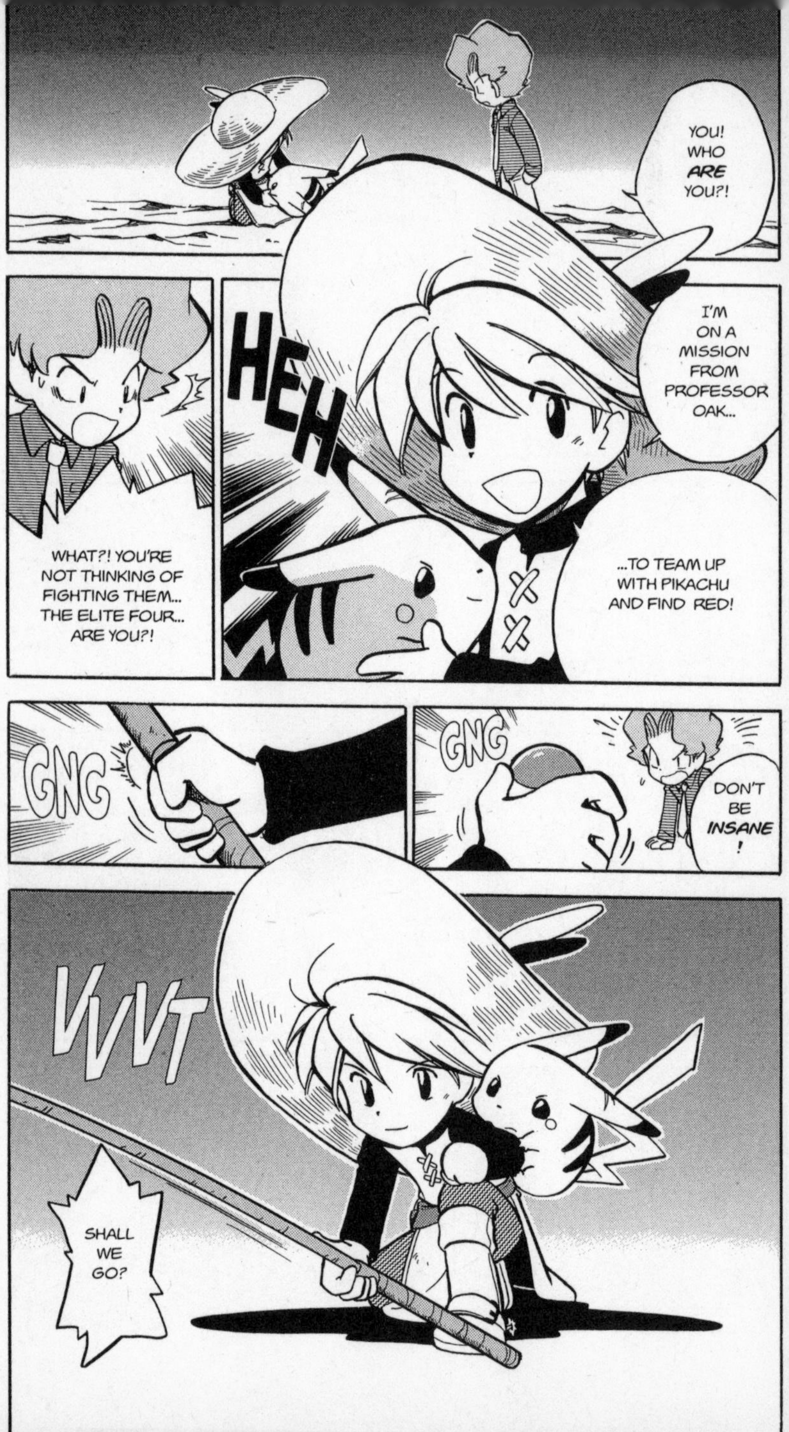
YOU! WHO ARE YOU?!
HEH
I'M ON A MISSION FROM PROFESSOR OAK...
...TO TEAM UP WITH PIKACHU AND FIND RED!
WHAT?! YOU'RE NOT THINKING OF FIGHTING THEM... THE ELITE FOUR... ARE YOU?!
GNG
DON'T BE INSANE!
GNG
VVVT
SHALL WE GO?

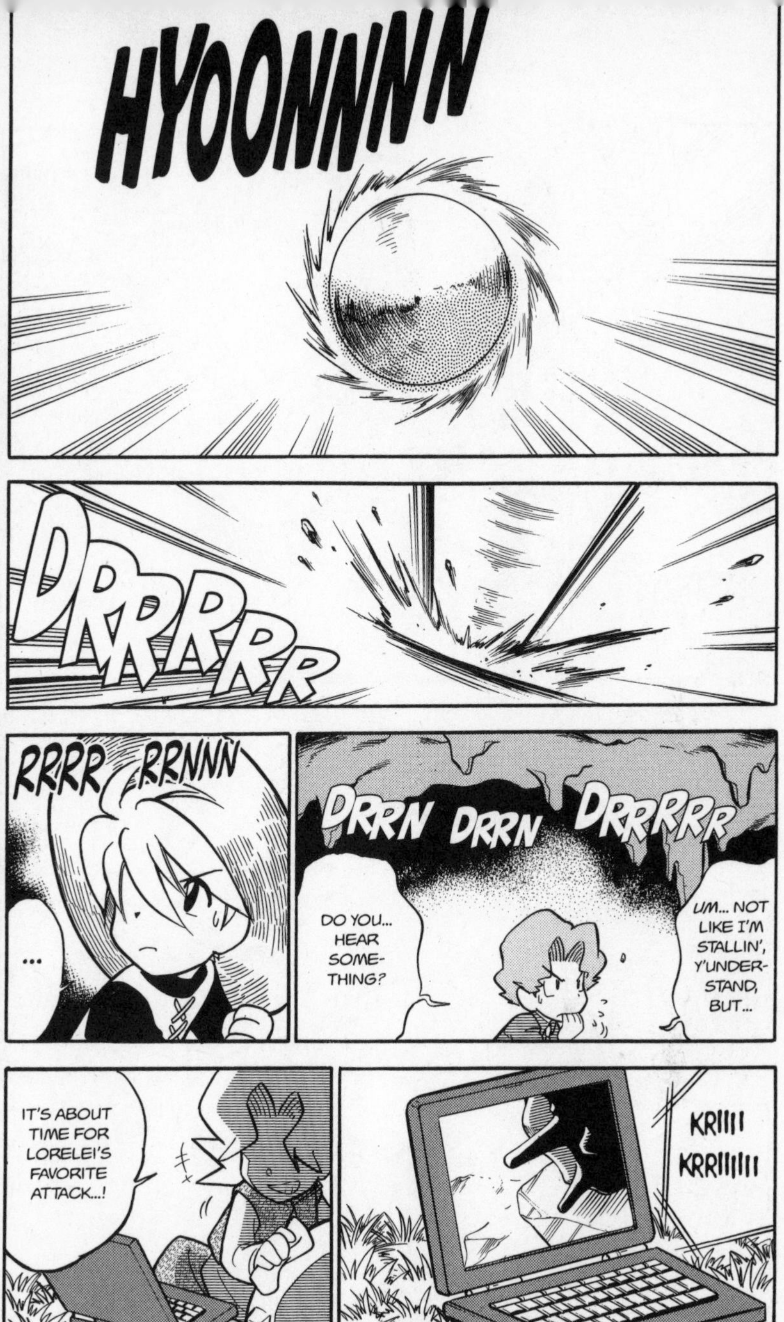
HYOONNNN
DRRRRRR
DRRN DRRN DRRRRR
UM... NOT LIKE I'M STALLIN', Y'UNDERSTAND, BUT...
DO YOU... HEAR SOMETHING?
RRRR RRNNN
...
KRIIII
KRRIIIIII
IT'S ABOUT TIME FOR LORELEI'S FAVORITE ATTACK...!

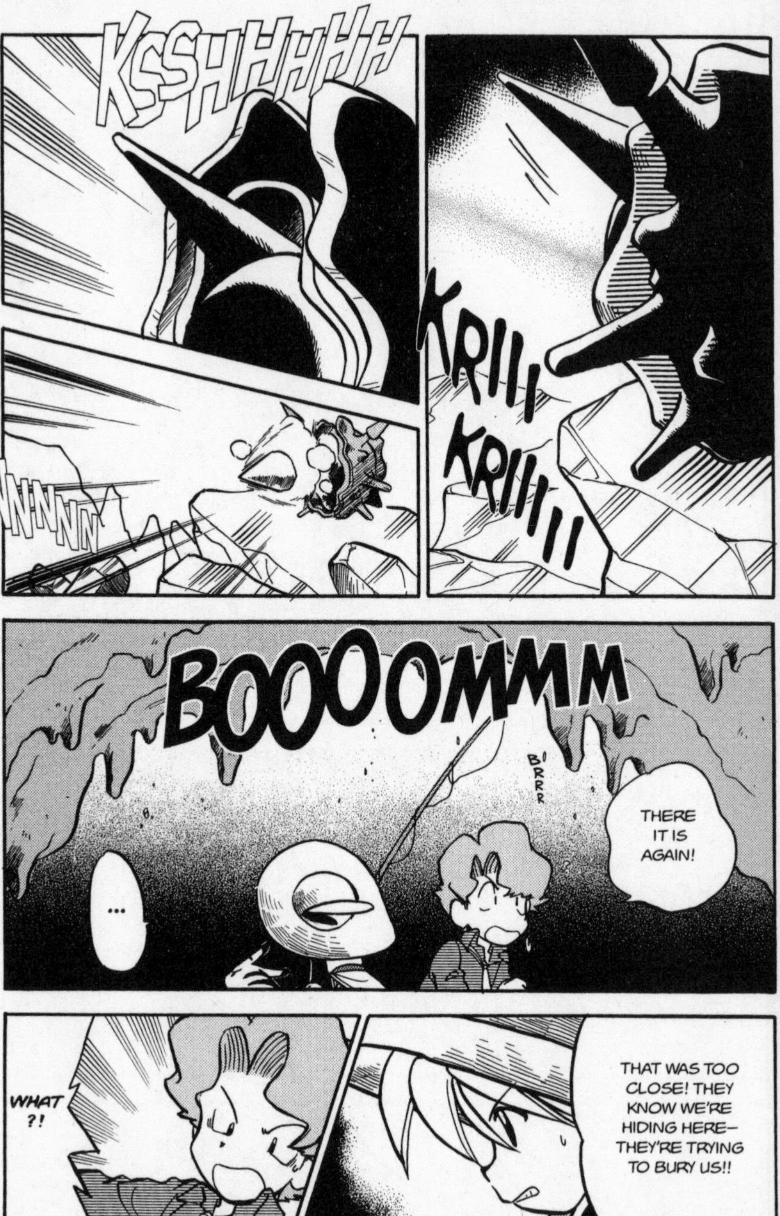
KRIII
KRIIIII
KSSHHHHHH
NNNNNN
BOOOOMMM
B'RRR
THERE IT IS AGAIN!
...
THAT WAS TOO CLOSE! THEY KNOW WE'RE HIDING HERE— THEY'RE TRYING TO BURY US!!
WHAT?!

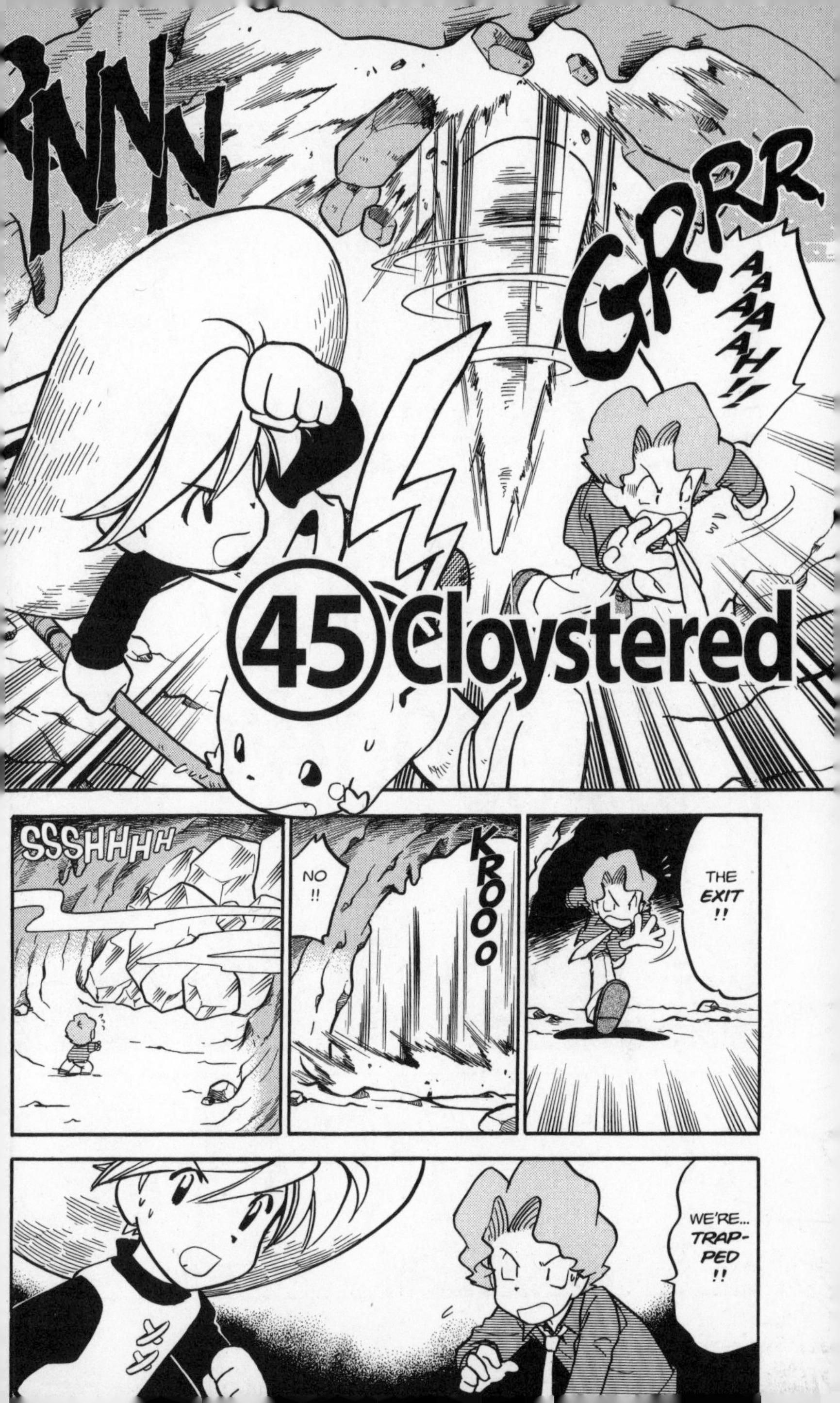
GRRR
AAAAAH!!
NN
45 Cloystered
THE EXIT!!
KROOO
NO!!
SSSHHHH
WE'RE... TRAP-PED!!

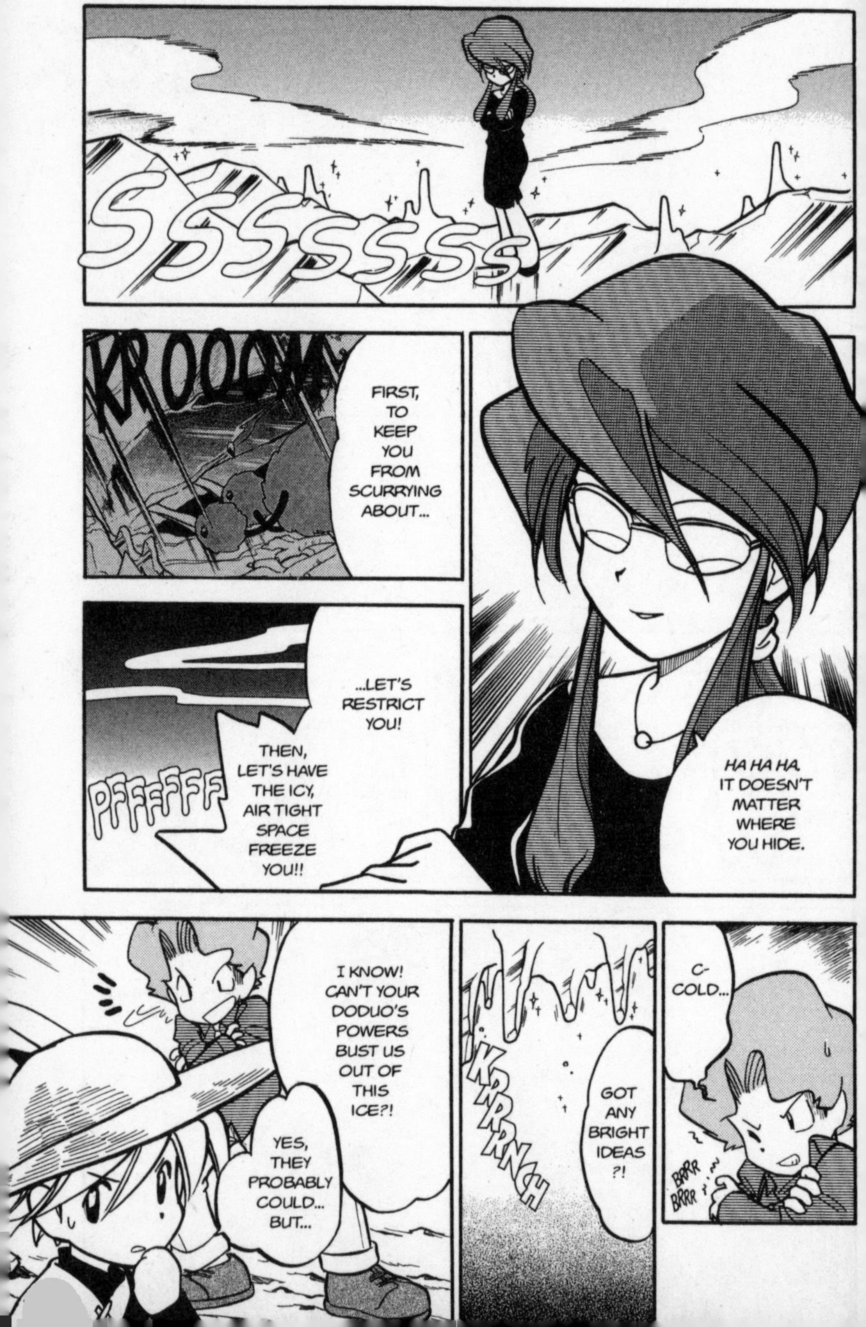
SSSSSSSS
HA HA HA. IT DOESN'T MATTER WHERE YOU HIDE.
FIRST, TO KEEP YOU FROM SCURRYING ABOUT...
KROOOM
...LET'S RESTRICT YOU!
THEN, LET'S HAVE THE ICY, AIR TIGHT SPACE FREEZE YOU!!
PFFFFFF
C-COLD...
BRRR BRRR
GOT ANY BRIGHT IDEAS?!
KRRRNCH
I KNOW! CAN'T YOUR DODUO'S POWERS BUST US OUT OF THIS ICE?!
YES, THEY PROBABLY COULD... BUT...

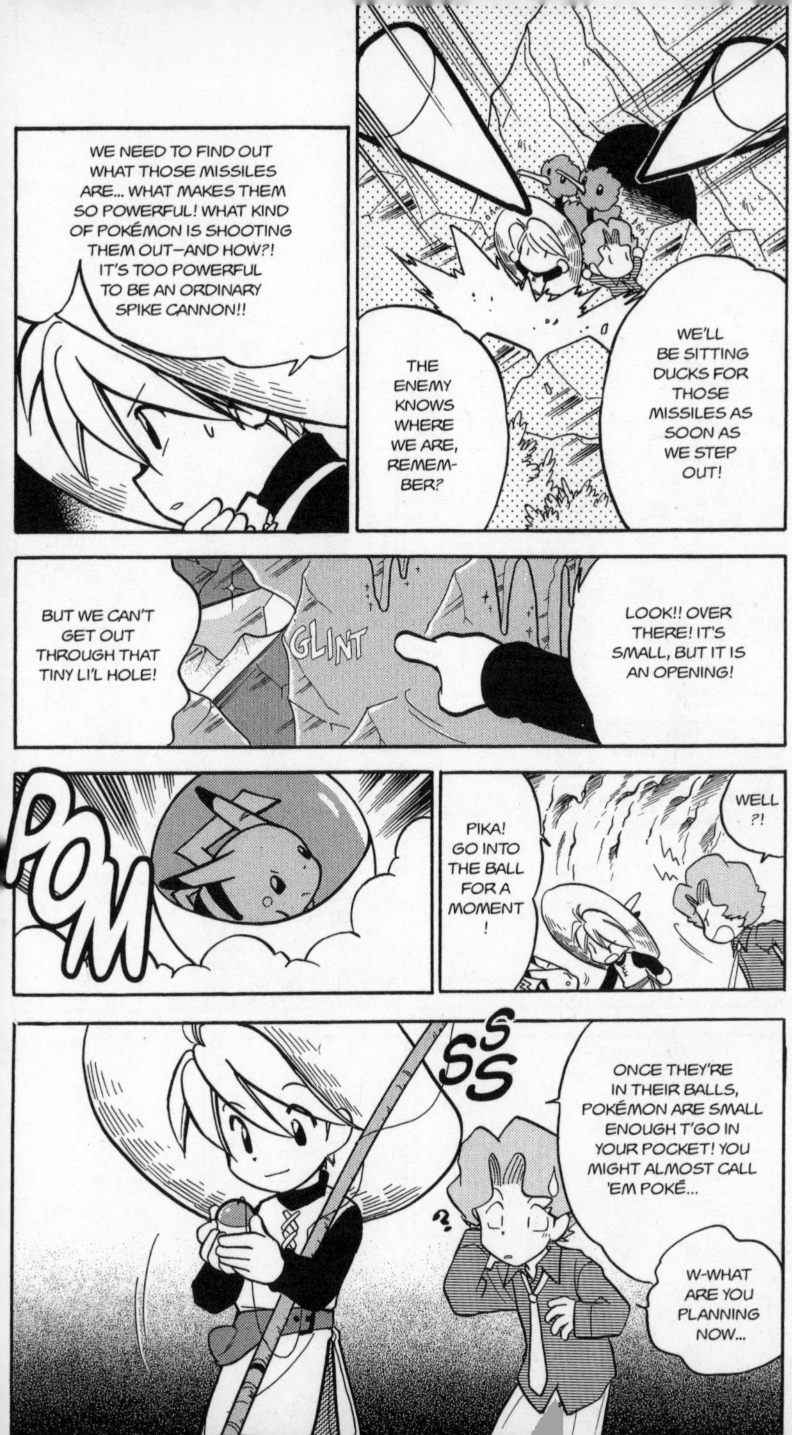
WE'LL BE SITTING DUCKS FOR THOSE MISSILES AS SOON AS WE STEP OUT!
THE ENEMY KNOWS WHERE WE ARE, REMEMBER?
WE NEED TO FIND OUT WHAT THOSE MISSILES ARE... WHAT MAKES THEM SO POWERFUL! WHAT KIND OF POKÉMON IS SHOOTING THEM OUT—AND HOW?! IT'S TOO POWERFUL TO BE AN ORDINARY SPIKE CANNON!!
LOOK!! OVER THERE! IT'S SMALL, BUT IT IS AN OPENING!
GLINT
BUT WE CAN'T GET OUT THROUGH THAT TINY LI'L HOLE!
WELL ?!
PIKA! GO INTO THE BALL FOR A MOMENT !
POM
ONCE THEY'RE IN THEIR BALLS, POKÉMON ARE SMALL ENOUGH T'GO IN YOUR POCKET! YOU MIGHT ALMOST CALL 'EM POKÉ...
SSS
W-WHAT ARE YOU PLANNING NOW...

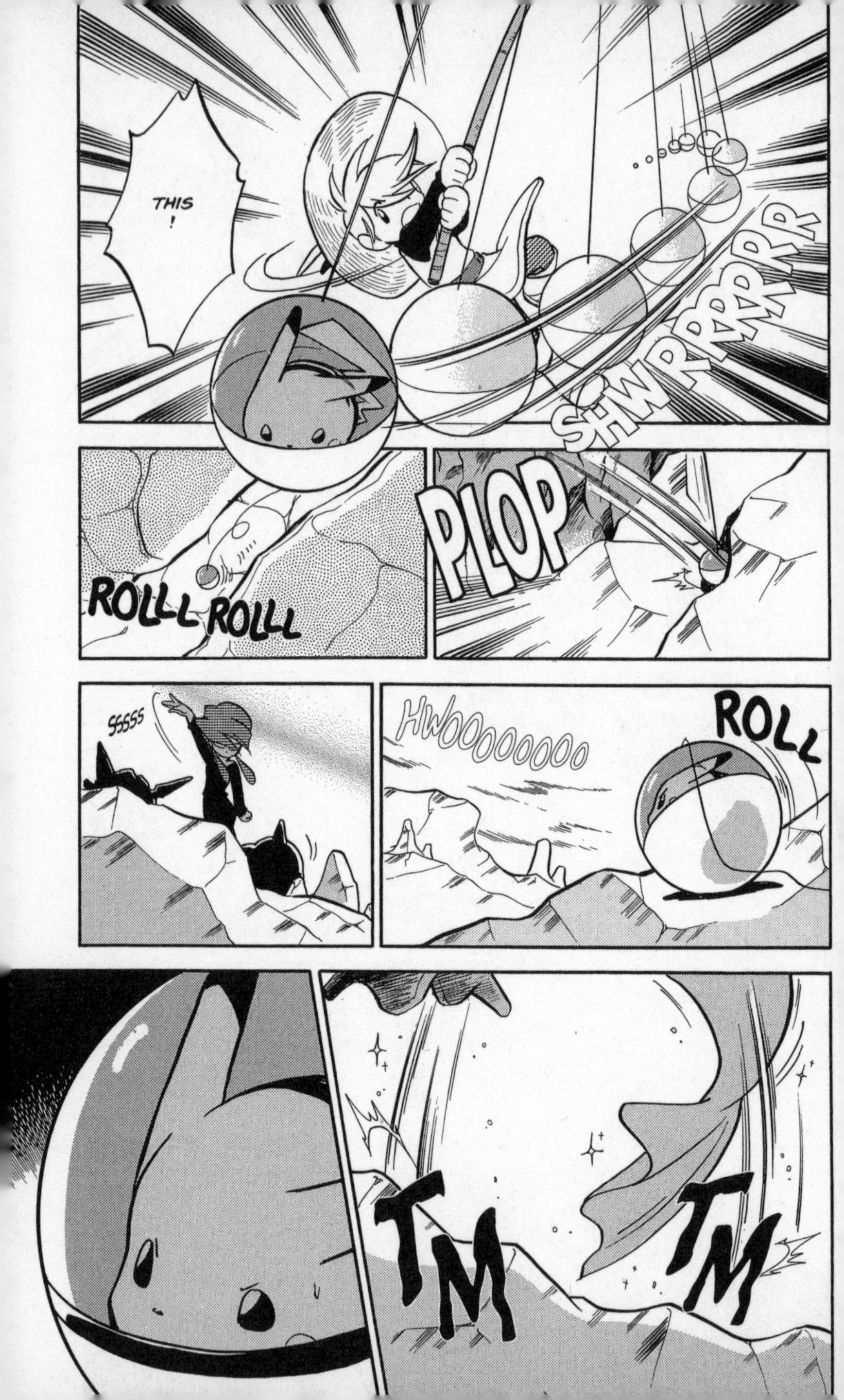
THIS!
SHWRRRRRR
PLOP
ROLLL ROLLL
HWOOOOOOOOO
ROLL
SSSSS
TM TM

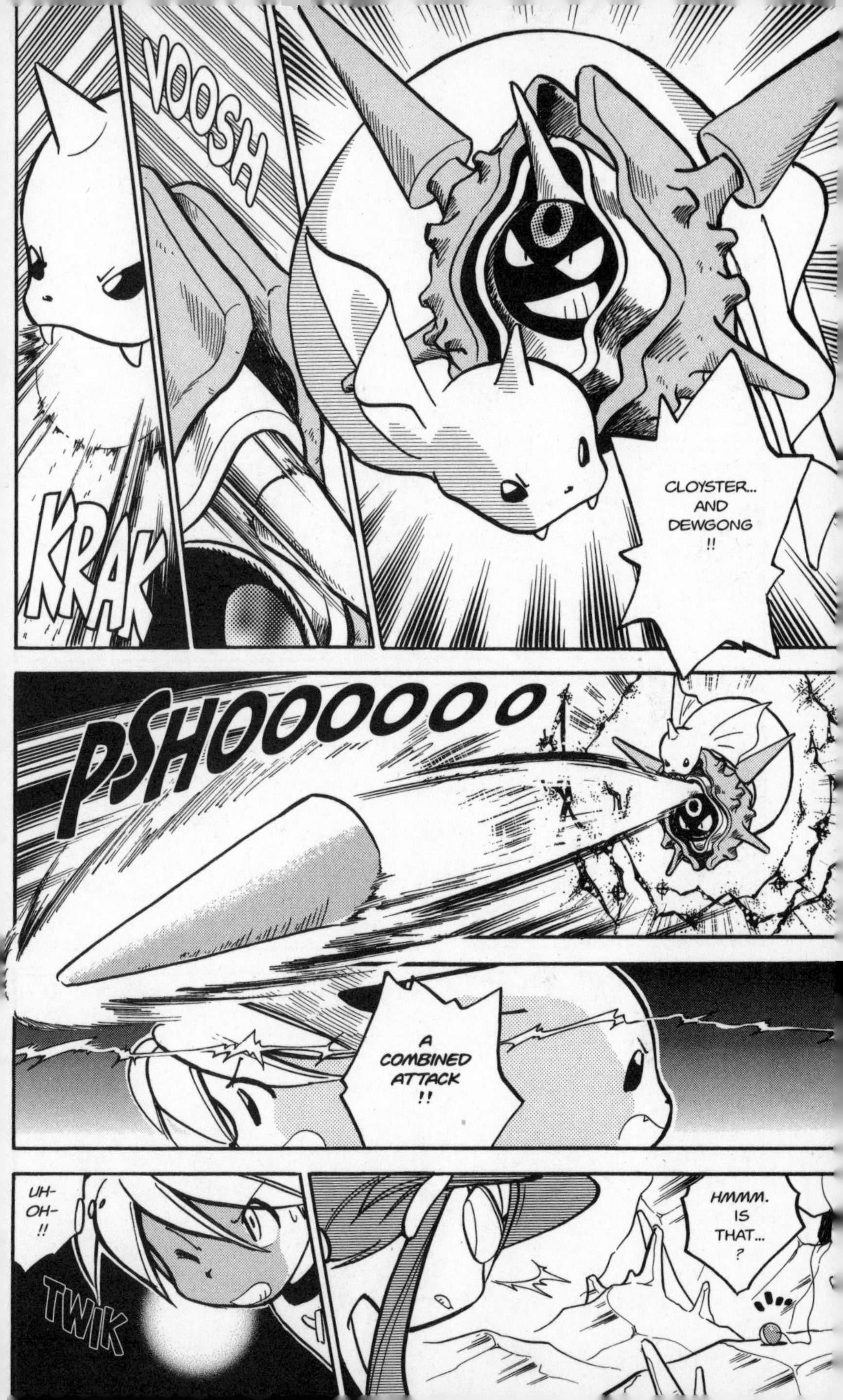
VOOSH
CLOYSTER... AND DEWGONG !!
KRAK
PSHOOOOOOO
A COMBINED ATTACK !!
HMMM. IS THAT... ?
UH-OH-!!
TWIK

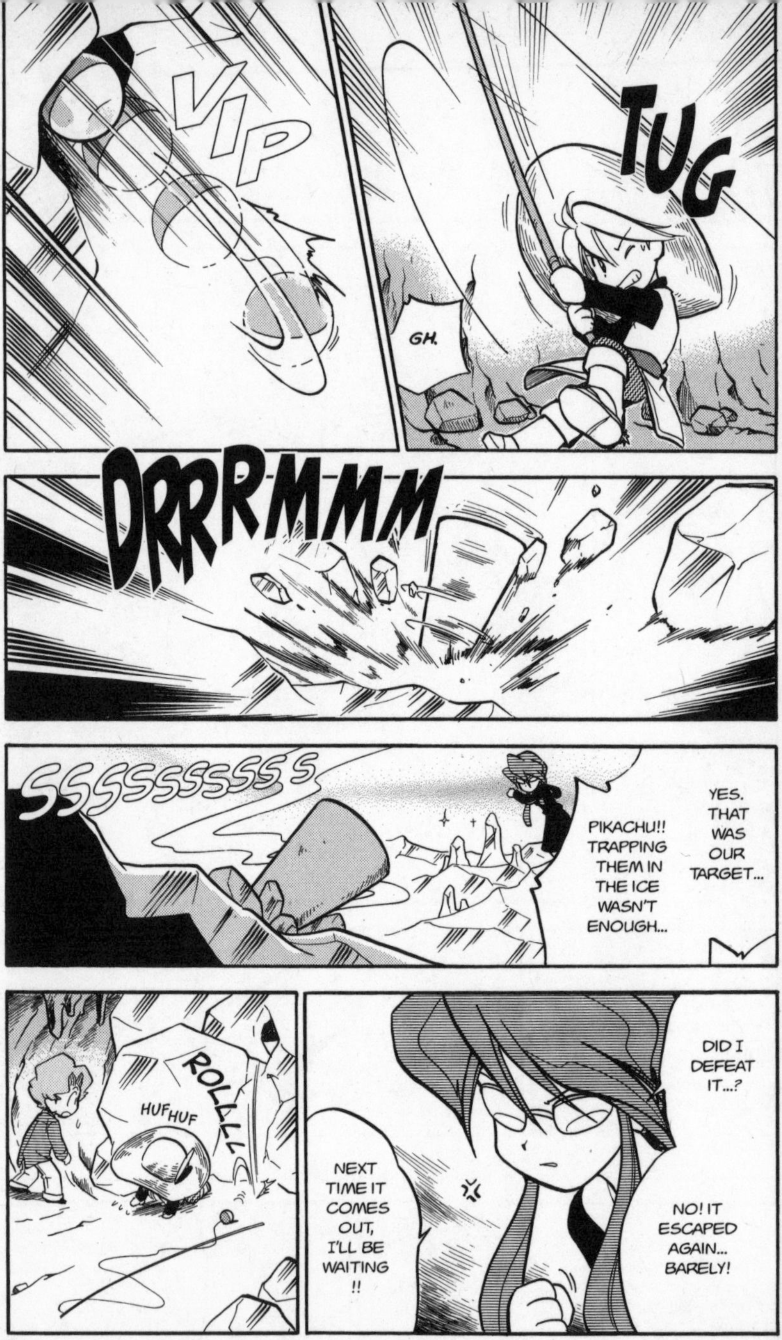

TUG
GH.
VIP
DRRRMMM
YES. THAT WAS OUR TARGET...
PIKACHU!! TRAPPING THEM IN THE ICE WASN'T ENOUGH...
SSSSSSSSSS
DID I DEFEAT IT...?
NO! IT ESCAPED AGAIN... BARELY!
NEXT TIME IT COMES OUT, I'LL BE WAITING!!
ROLLLL
HUF HUF

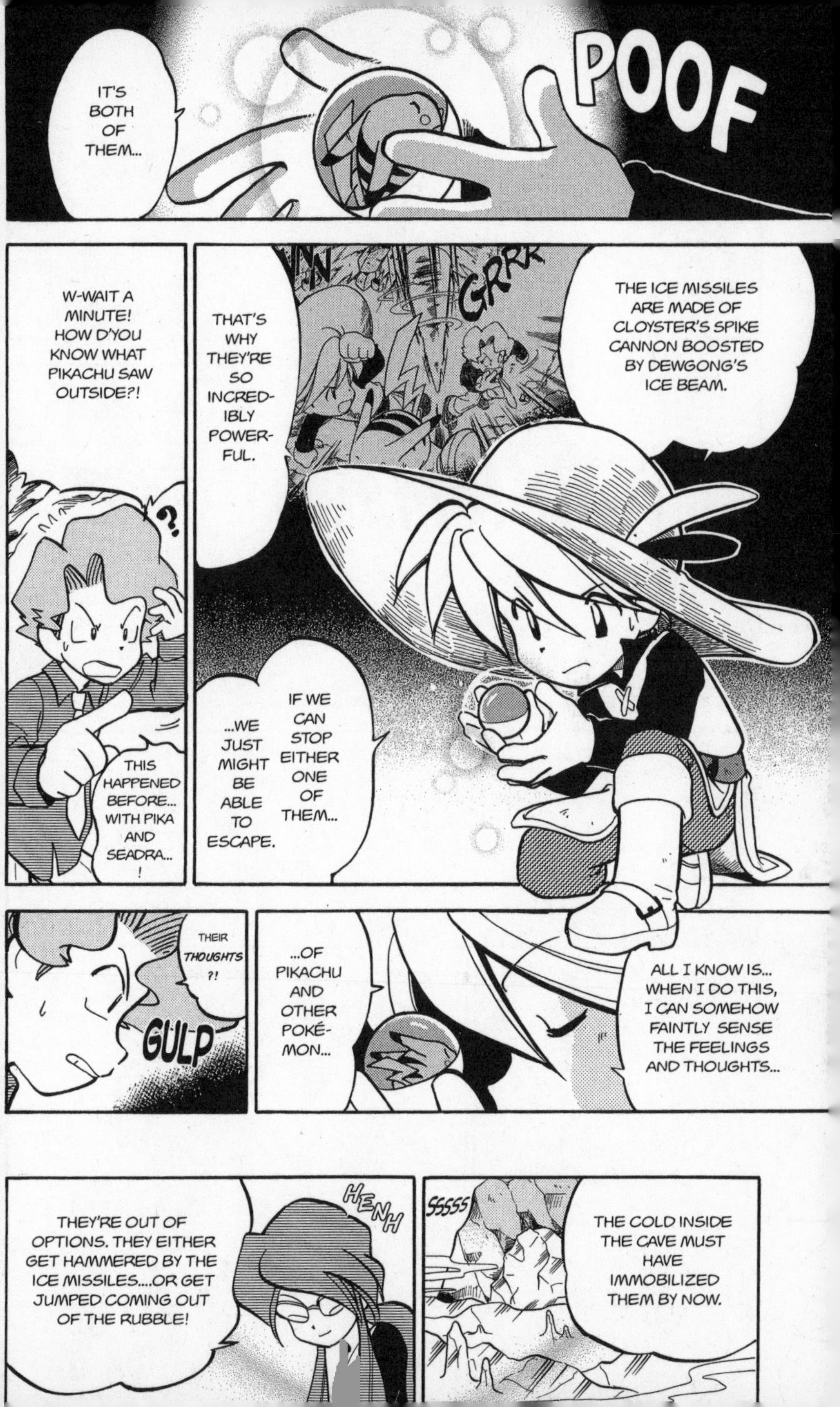
POOF
IT'S BOTH OF THEM...
THE ICE MISSILES ARE MADE OF CLOYSTER'S SPIKE CANNON BOOSTED BY DEWGONG'S ICE BEAM.
GRRR
THAT'S WHY THEY'RE SO INCRED-IBLY POWER-FUL.
IF WE CAN STOP EITHER ONE OF THEM...
...WE JUST MIGHT BE ABLE TO ESCAPE.
W-WAIT A MINUTE! HOW D'YOU KNOW WHAT PIKACHU SAW OUTSIDE?!
?
THIS HAPPENED BEFORE... WITH PIKA AND SEADRA... !
ALL I KNOW IS... WHEN I DO THIS, I CAN SOMEHOW FAINTLY SENSE THE FEELINGS AND THOUGHTS...
...OF PIKACHU AND OTHER POKÉ-MON...
THEIR *THOUGHTS* ?!
GULP
THE COLD INSIDE THE CAVE MUST HAVE IMMOBILIZED THEM BY NOW.
SSSSS
HENH
THEY'RE OUT OF OPTIONS. THEY EITHER GET HAMMERED BY THE ICE MISSILES....OR GET JUMPED COMING OUT OF THE RUBBLE!

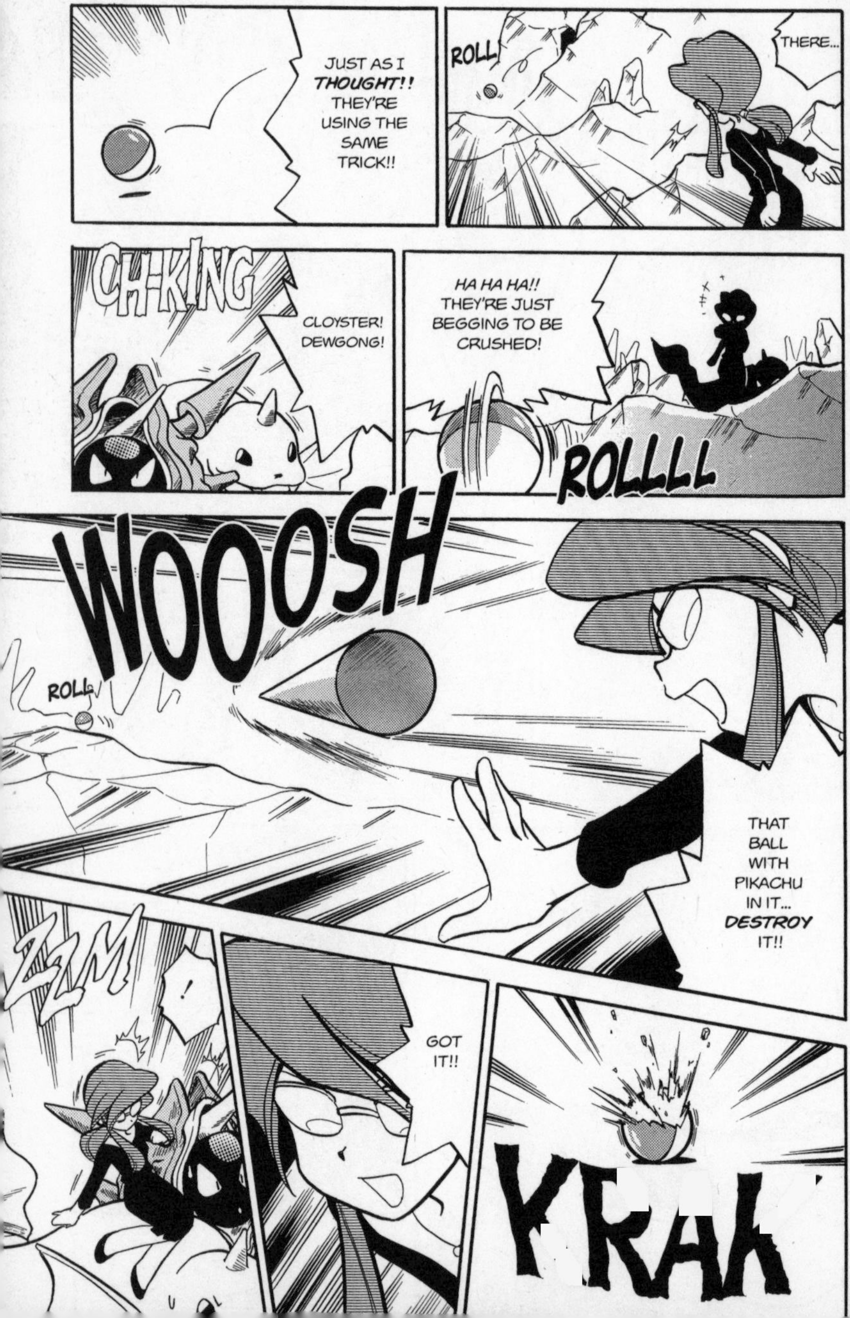
THERE...
ROLL
JUST AS I THOUGHT!! THEY'RE USING THE SAME TRICK!!
HA HA HA!! THEY'RE JUST BEGGING TO BE CRUSHED!
ROLLLL
CH-KING
CLOYSTER! DEWGONG!
WOOOSH
THAT BALL WITH PIKACHU IN IT... DESTROY IT!!
ROLL
KRAK
GOT IT!!
ZZM
!

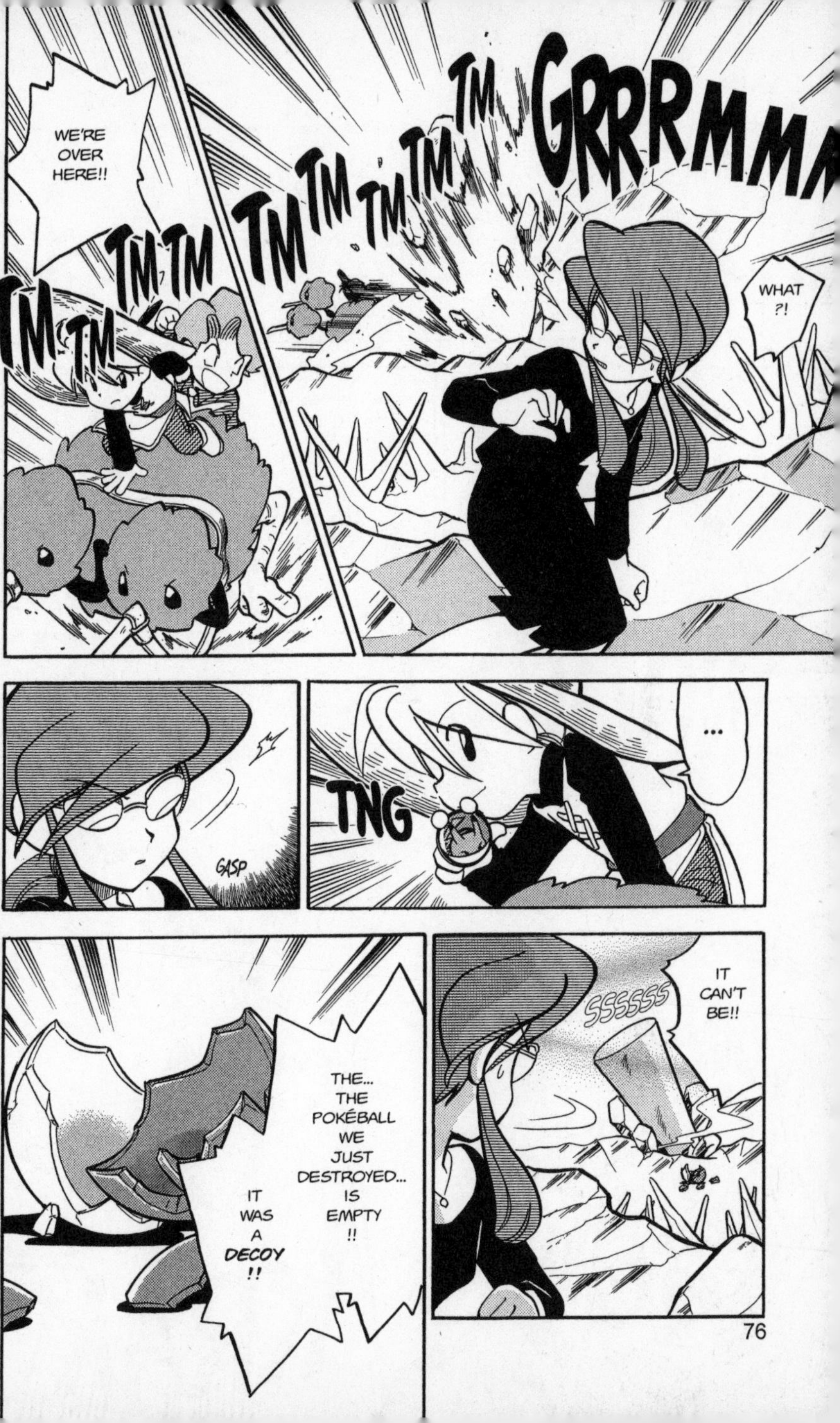
GRRRMMM
TM TM TM TM
WHAT ?!
WE'RE OVER HERE!!
TM TM TM TM TM
...
TNG
GASP
SSSSSS
IT CAN'T BE!!
THE... THE POKÉBALL WE JUST DESTROYED... IS EMPTY !!
IT WAS A DECOY !!

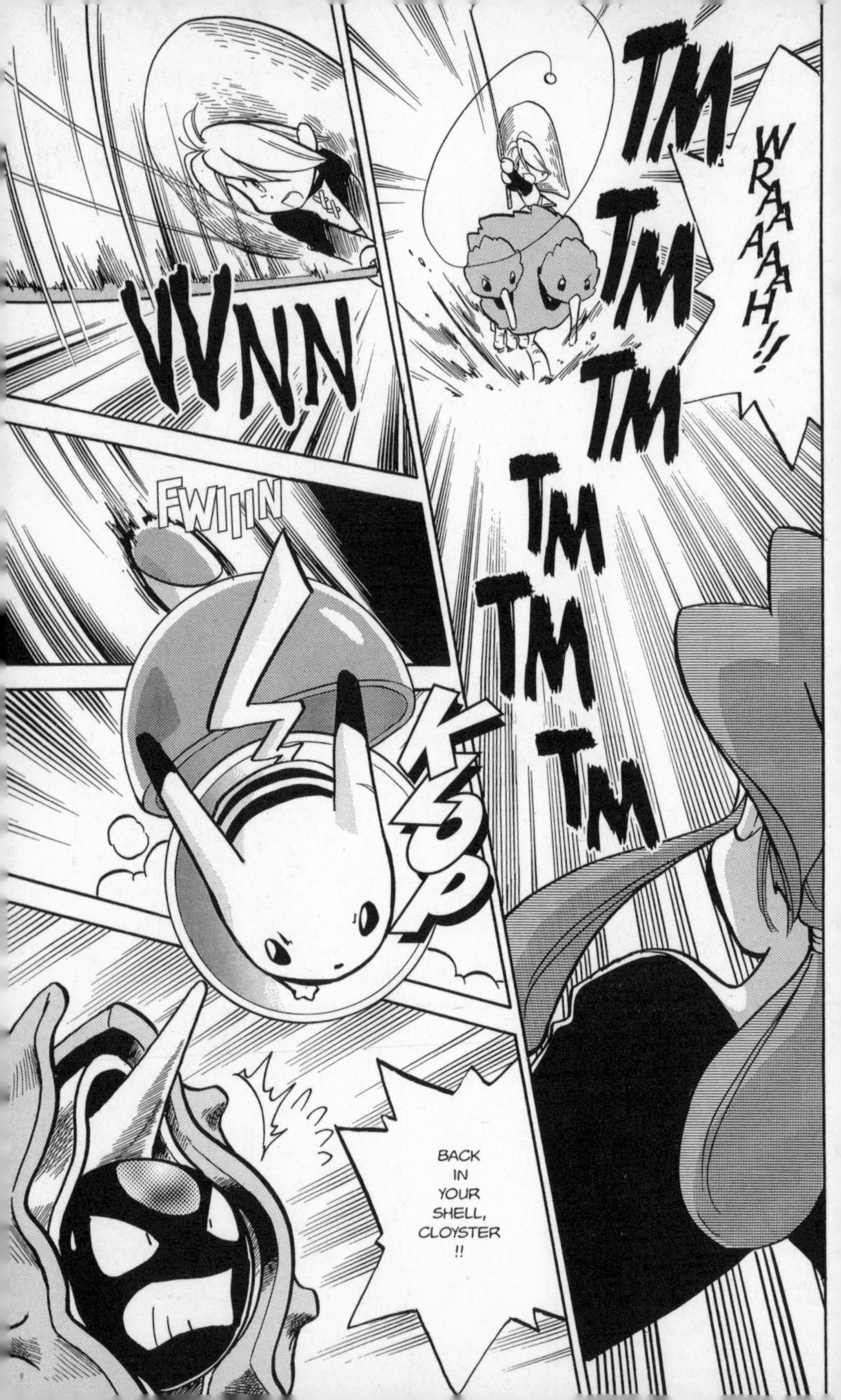
WRAAAAH!!
TM TM TM TM TM TM TM
VVNN
FWIIIN
KSP
BACK IN YOUR SHELL, CLOYSTER!!

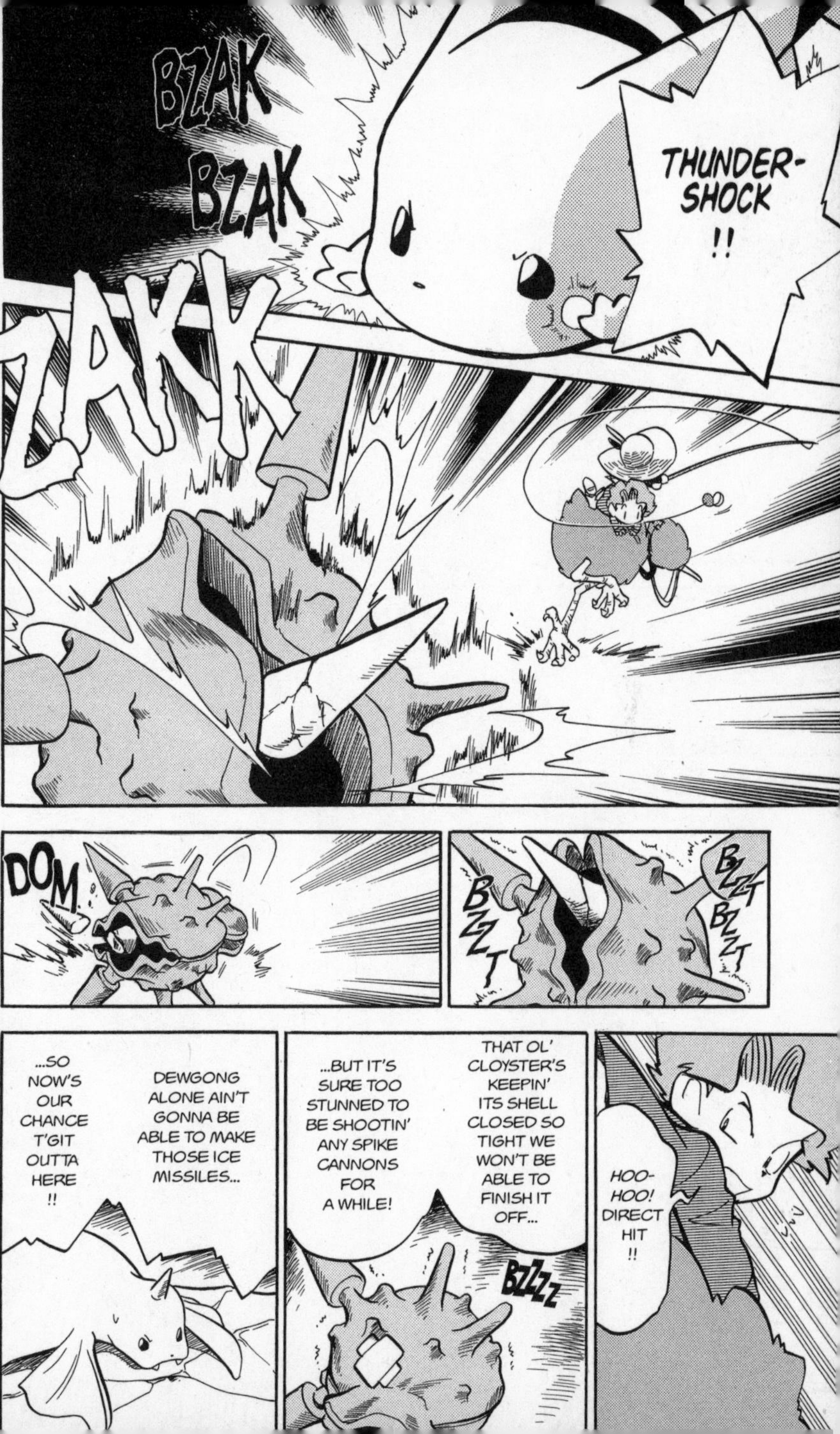
THUNDER-SHOCK !!
BZAK BZAK
ZAKK
BZZT BZZT
BZZT
DOM
HOO-HOO! DIRECT HIT !!
THAT OL' CLOYSTER'S KEEPIN' ITS SHELL CLOSED SO TIGHT WE WON'T BE ABLE TO FINISH IT OFF...
...BUT IT'S SURE TOO STUNNED TO BE SHOOTIN' ANY SPIKE CANNONS FOR A WHILE!
BZZZZ
DEWGONG ALONE AIN'T GONNA BE ABLE TO MAKE THOSE ICE MISSILES...
...SO NOW'S OUR CHANCE T'GIT OUTTA HERE !!

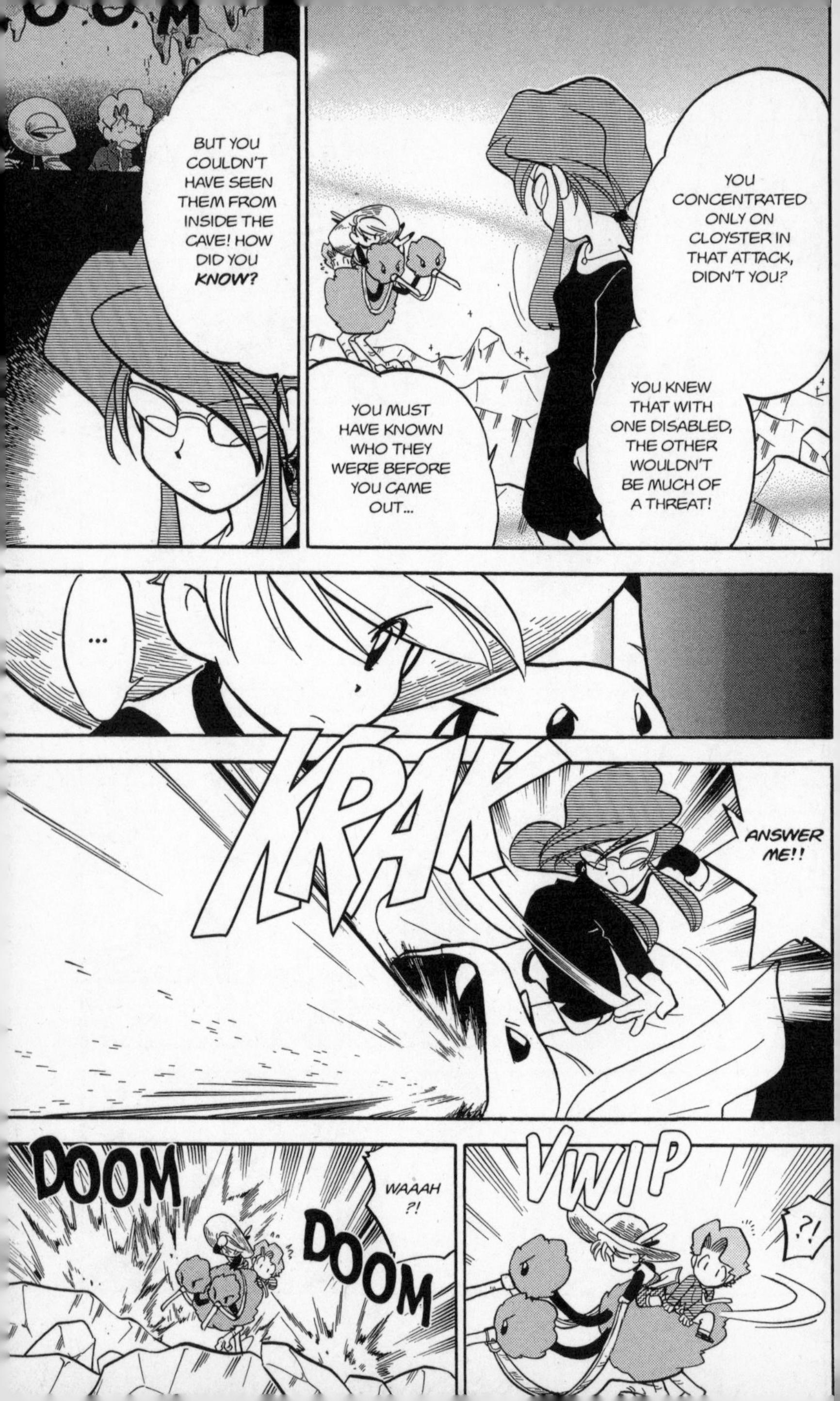
YOU CONCENTRATED ONLY ON CLOYSTER IN THAT ATTACK, DIDN'T YOU?
YOU KNEW THAT WITH ONE DISABLED, THE OTHER WOULDN'T BE MUCH OF A THREAT!
YOU MUST HAVE KNOWN WHO THEY WERE BEFORE YOU CAME OUT...
BUT YOU COULDN'T HAVE SEEN THEM FROM INSIDE THE CAVE! HOW DID YOU *KNOW?*
...
KRAK
ANSWER ME!!
VWIP
?!
DOOM
WAAAH ?!
DOOM

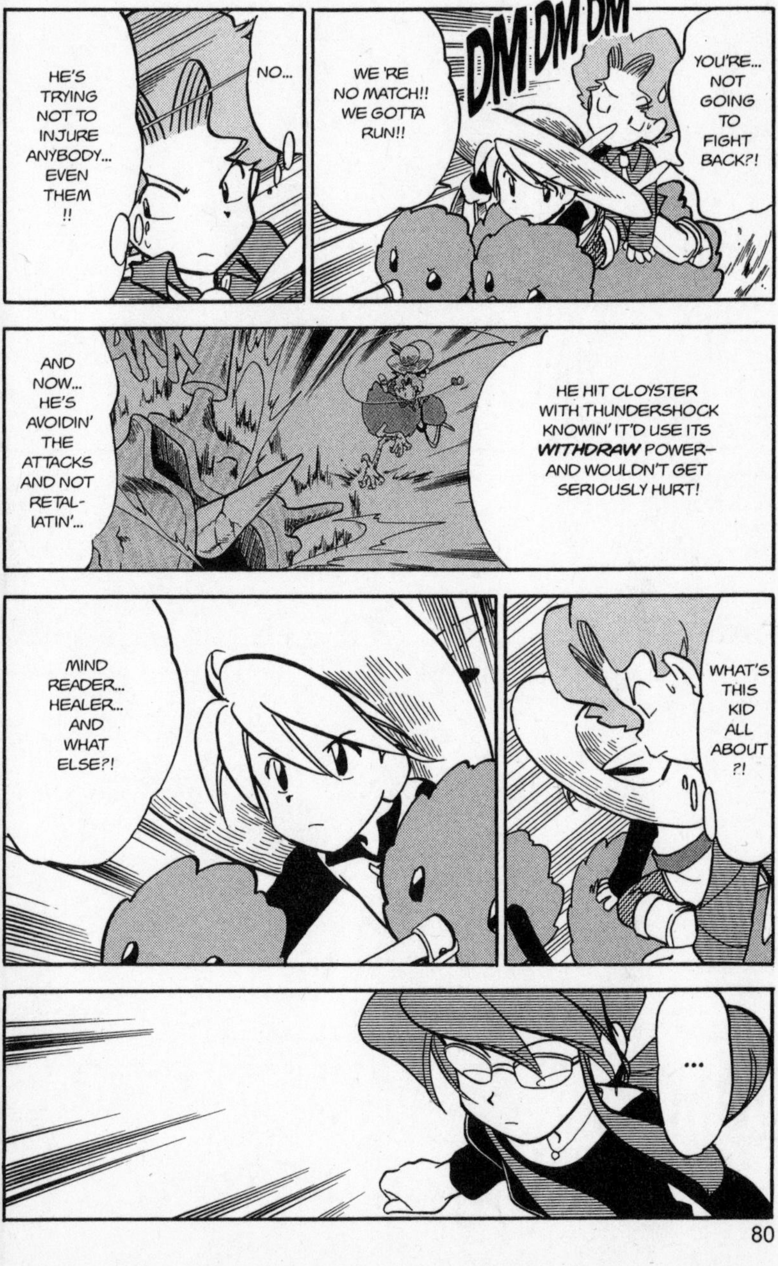

YOU'RE... NOT GOING TO FIGHT BACK?!
DM DM DM
WE 'RE NO MATCH!! WE GOTTA RUN!!
NO...
HE'S TRYING NOT TO INJURE ANYBODY... EVEN THEM!!
HE HIT CLOYSTER WITH THUNDERSHOCK KNOWIN' IT'D USE ITS *WITHDRAW* POWER—AND WOULDN'T GET SERIOUSLY HURT!
AND NOW... HE'S AVOIDIN' THE ATTACKS AND NOT RETAL-IATIN'...
WHAT'S THIS KID ALL ABOUT?!
MIND READER... HEALER... AND WHAT ELSE?!
...

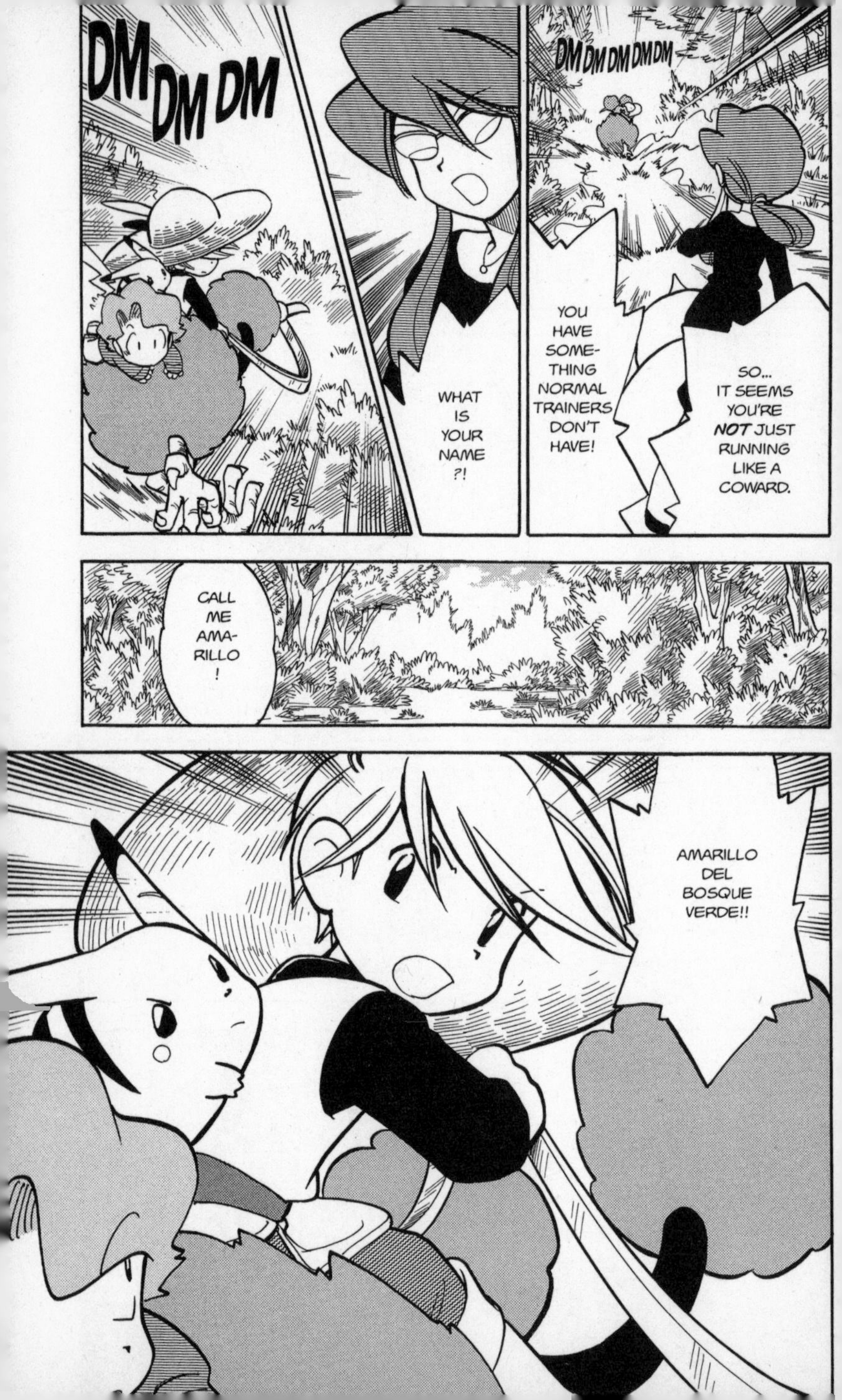
DM DM DM DM DM
SO... IT SEEMS YOU'RE NOT JUST RUNNING LIKE A COWARD.
YOU HAVE SOMETHING NORMAL TRAINERS DON'T HAVE!
WHAT IS YOUR NAME?!
DM DM DM
CALL ME AMARILLO!
AMARILLO DEL BOSQUE VERDE!!

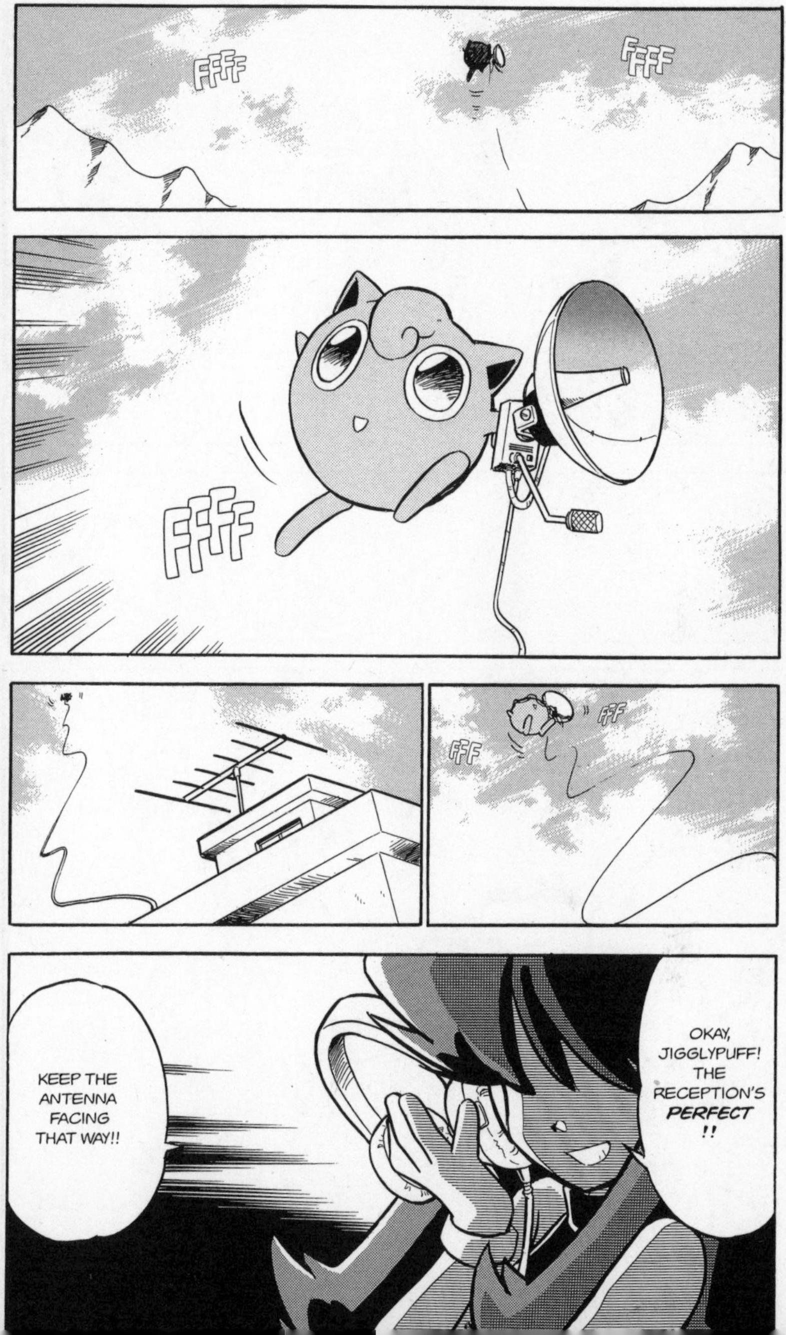
FFFF
FFFF
FFFF
FFF
FFF
OKAY, JIGGLYPUFF! THE RECEPTION'S **PERFECT**!!
KEEP THE ANTENNA FACING THAT WAY!!

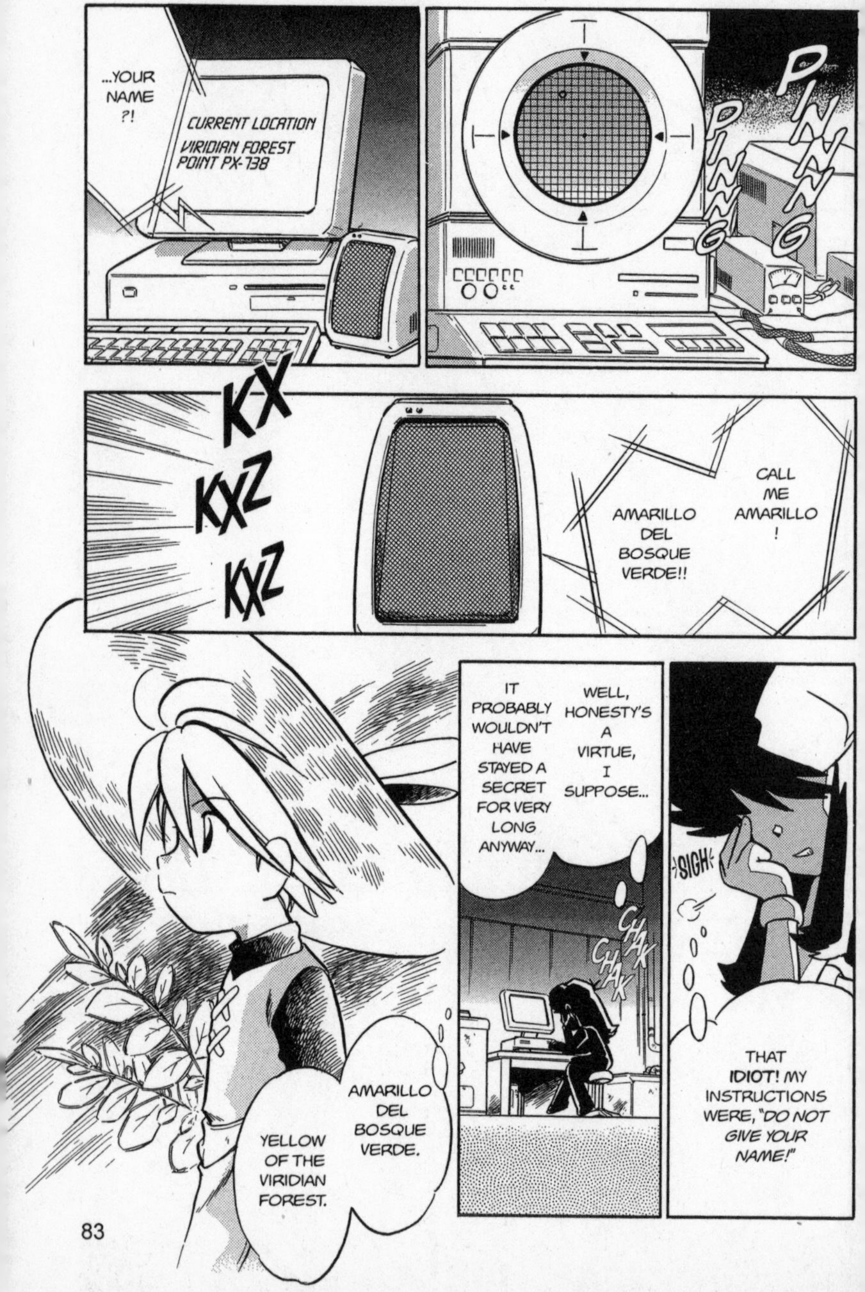
PINNNG
PINNNG
...YOUR NAME ?!
CURRENT LOCATION
VIRIDIAN FOREST POINT PX-738
CALL ME AMARILLO!
AMARILLO DEL BOSQUE VERDE!!
KX
KXZ
KXZ
SIGH
THAT IDIOT! MY INSTRUCTIONS WERE, "DO NOT GIVE YOUR NAME!"
WELL, HONESTY'S A VIRTUE, I SUPPOSE...
IT PROBABLY WOULDN'T HAVE STAYED A SECRET FOR VERY LONG ANYWAY...
CHAK
CHAK
AMARILLO DEL BOSQUE VERDE.
YELLOW OF THE VIRIDIAN FOREST.

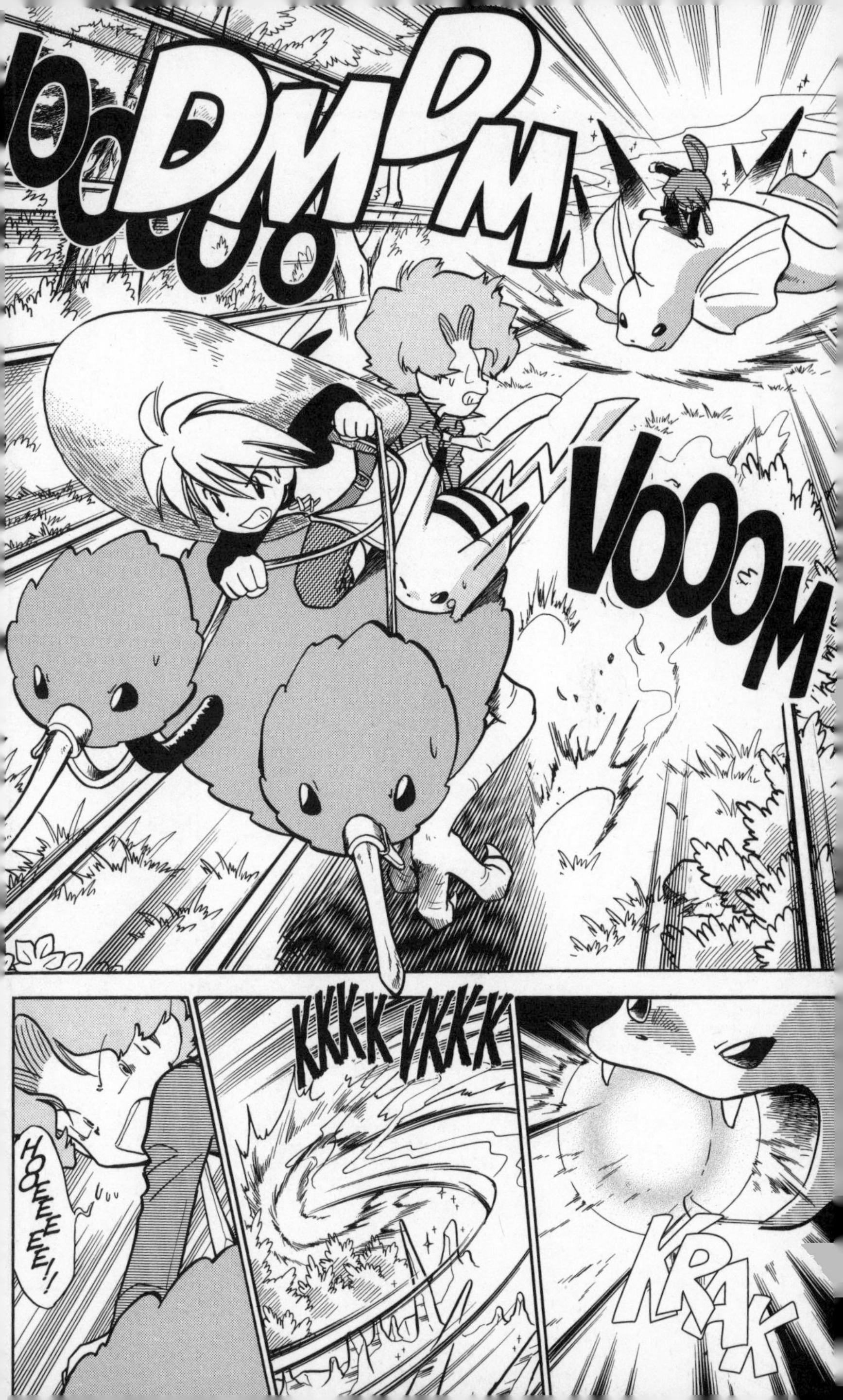
DMPM
VOOOM
KRAK
KKKK VKKK
HOOEEEEE!!

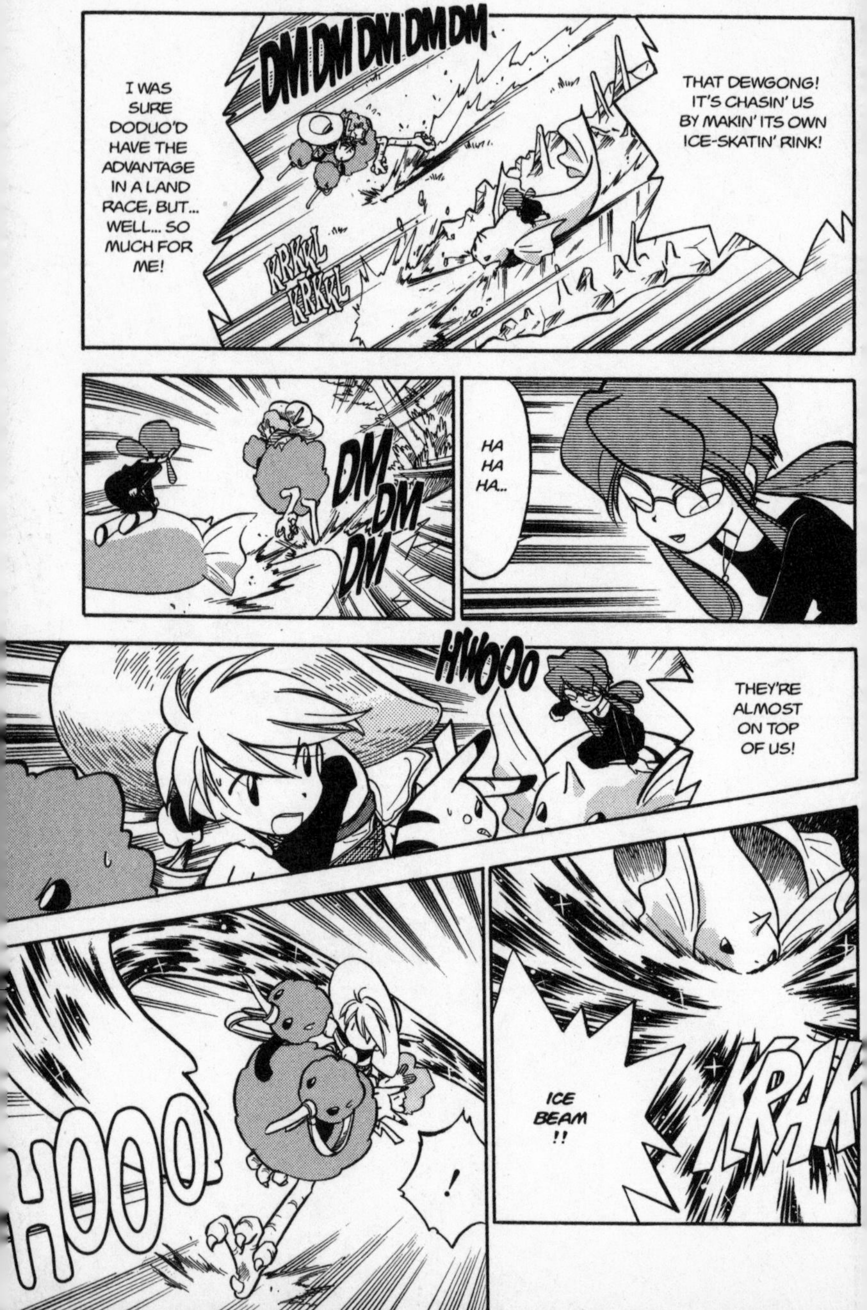
DM DM DM DM DM
THAT DEWGONG! IT'S CHASIN' US BY MAKIN' ITS OWN ICE-SKATIN' RINK!
I WAS SURE DODUO'D HAVE THE ADVANTAGE IN A LAND RACE, BUT... WELL... SO MUCH FOR ME!
KRKKRL KRKKRL
HA HA HA...
DM DM DM
HWOOO
THEY'RE ALMOST ON TOP OF US!
KRAK
ICE BEAM !!
HOOO
!

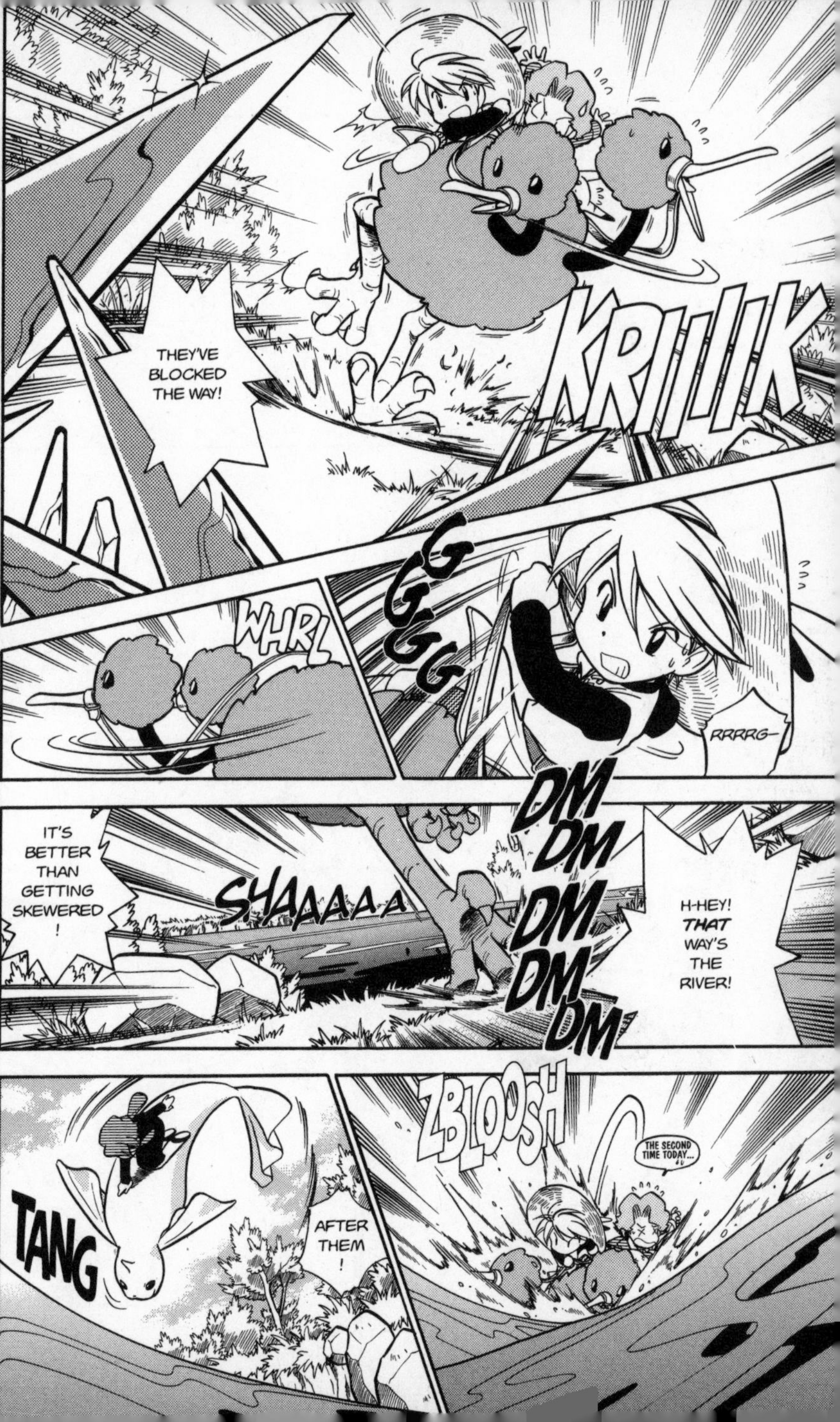
KRIIIK
THEY'VE BLOCKED THE WAY!
GGGG
RRRRG—
WHRL
DM DM DM DM DM DM
H-HEY! *THAT* WAY'S THE RIVER!
SHAAAAA
IT'S BETTER THAN GETTING SKEWERED!
ZBLOOSH
THE SECOND TIME TODAY...
TANG
AFTER THEM!

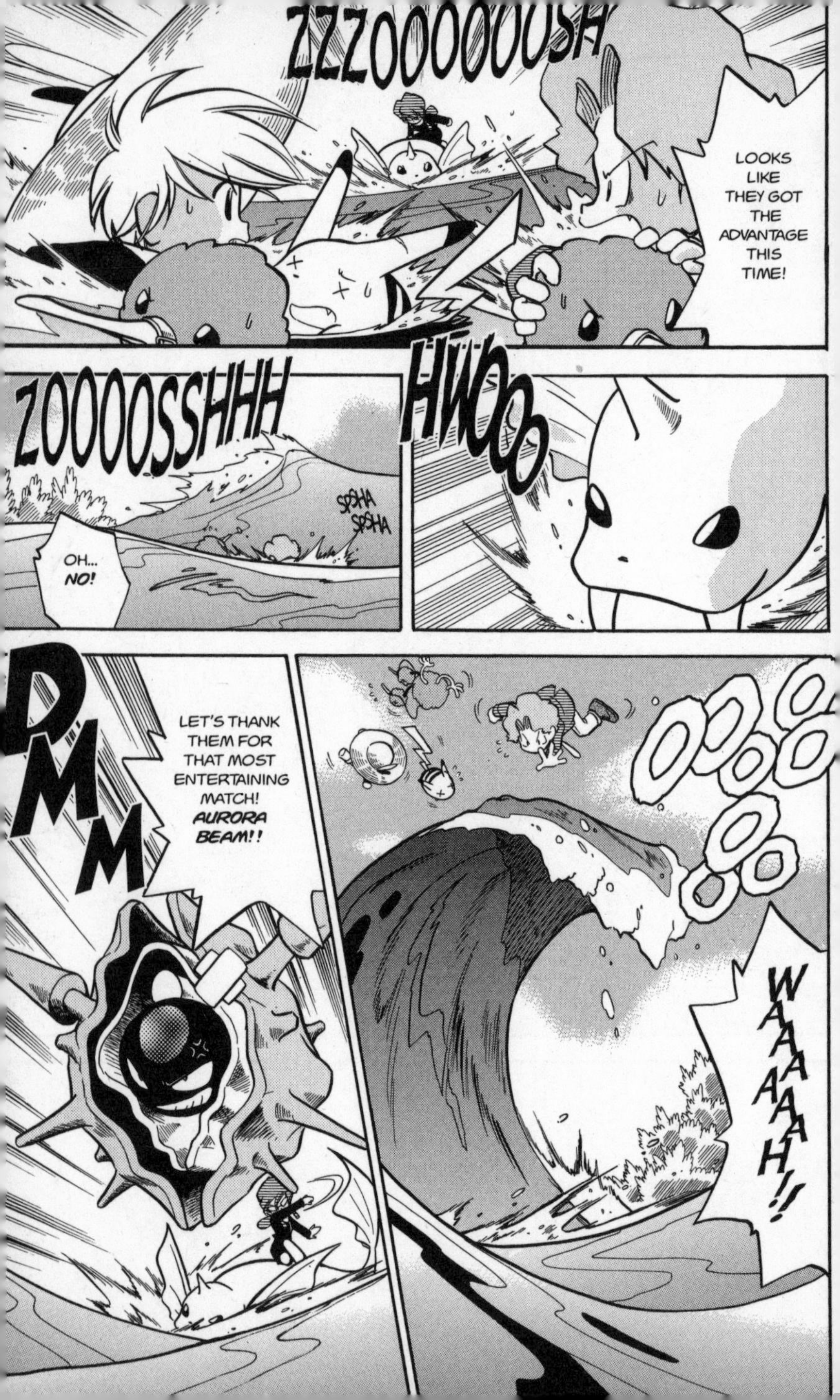
ZZZOOOOOUSH
LOOKS LIKE THEY GOT THE ADVANTAGE THIS TIME!
HWOOO
ZOOOOSSHHH
SPSHA SPSHA
OH... NO!
WAAAAAH!!
DMM
LET'S THANK THEM FOR THAT MOST ENTERTAINING MATCH! AURORA BEAM!!

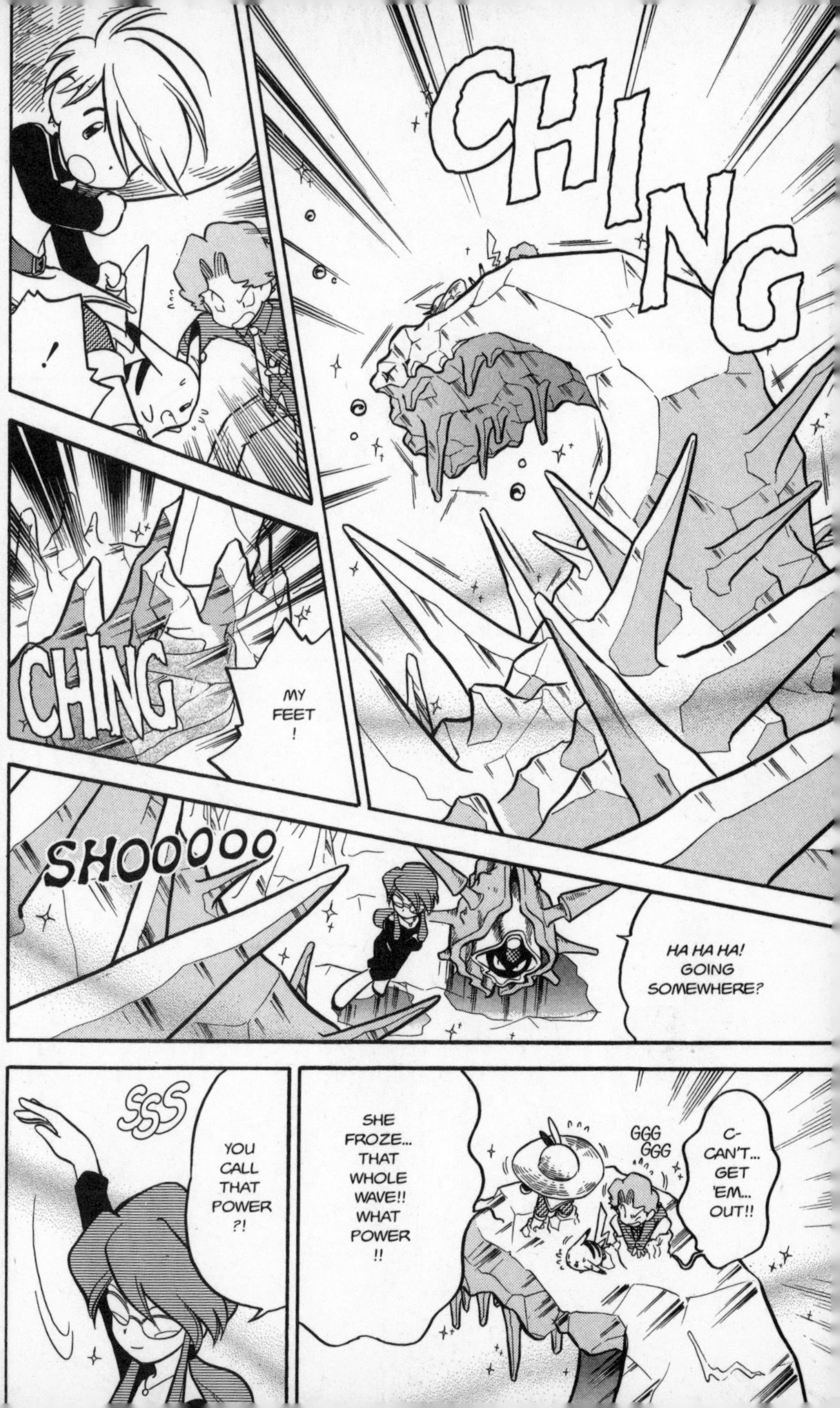
CHING
!
CHING
MY FEET!
HA HA HA! GOING SOMEWHERE?
SHOOOOO
C-CAN'T... GET 'EM... OUT!!
GGG GGG
SHE FROZE... THAT WHOLE WAVE!! WHAT POWER!!
SSS
YOU CALL THAT POWER?!

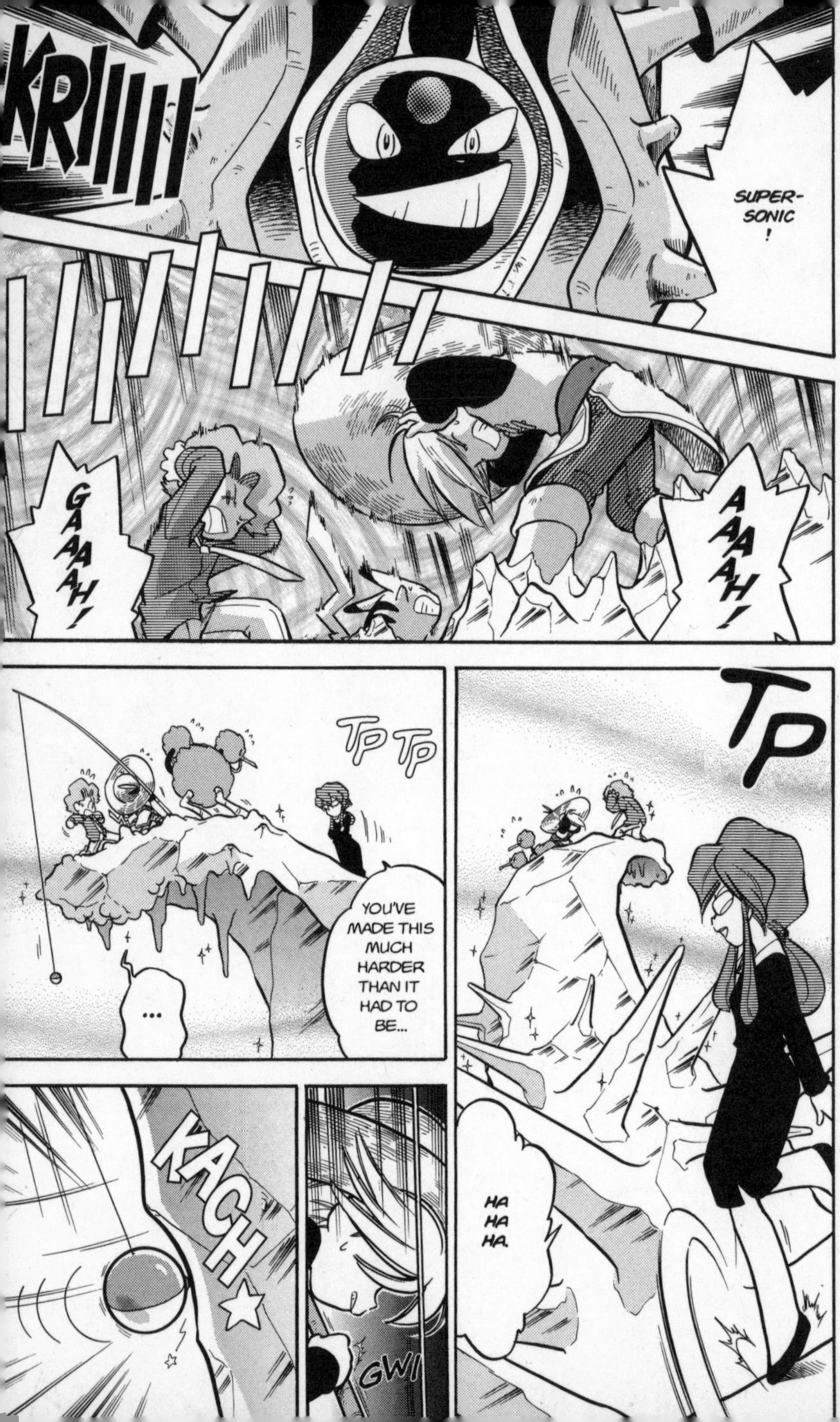
SUPER-SONIC!
KRIIIII
IIIIIIIII
AAAAH!
GAAAAH!
TP
HA HA HA.
TP TP
YOU'VE MADE THIS MUCH HARDER THAN IT HAD TO BE...
...
GWI
KACH

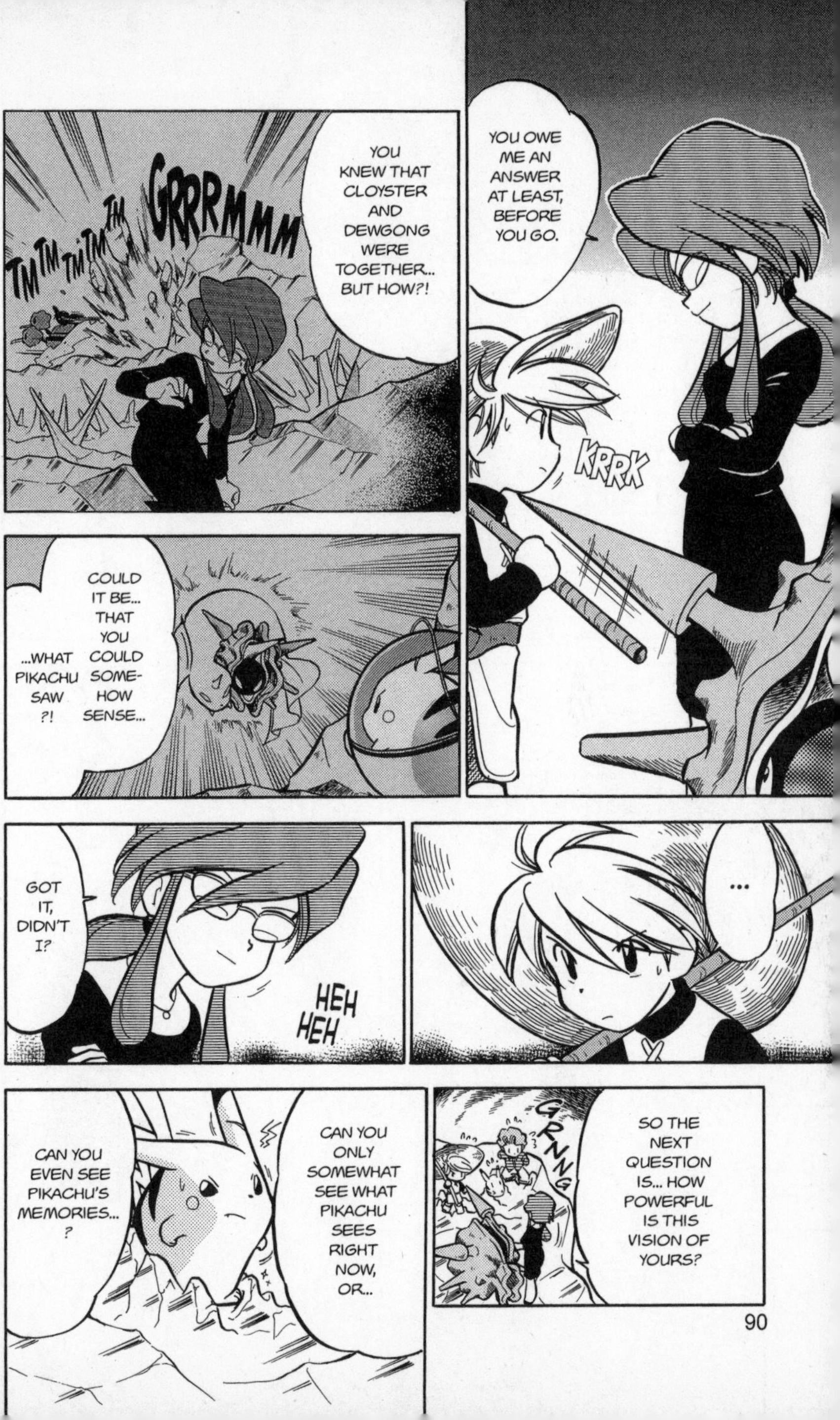
YOU OWE ME AN ANSWER AT LEAST, BEFORE YOU GO.
KRRK
YOU KNEW THAT CLOYSTER AND DEWGONG WERE TOGETHER... BUT HOW?!
GRRRMMM
TMTMTMTMTM
COULD IT BE... THAT YOU COULD SOME-HOW SENSE...
...WHAT PIKACHU SAW?!
...
GOT IT, DIDN'T I?
HEH HEH
SO THE NEXT QUESTION IS... HOW POWERFUL IS THIS VISION OF YOURS?
GRNNG
CAN YOU ONLY SOMEWHAT SEE WHAT PIKACHU SEES RIGHT NOW, OR...
CAN YOU EVEN SEE PIKACHU'S MEMORIES...?

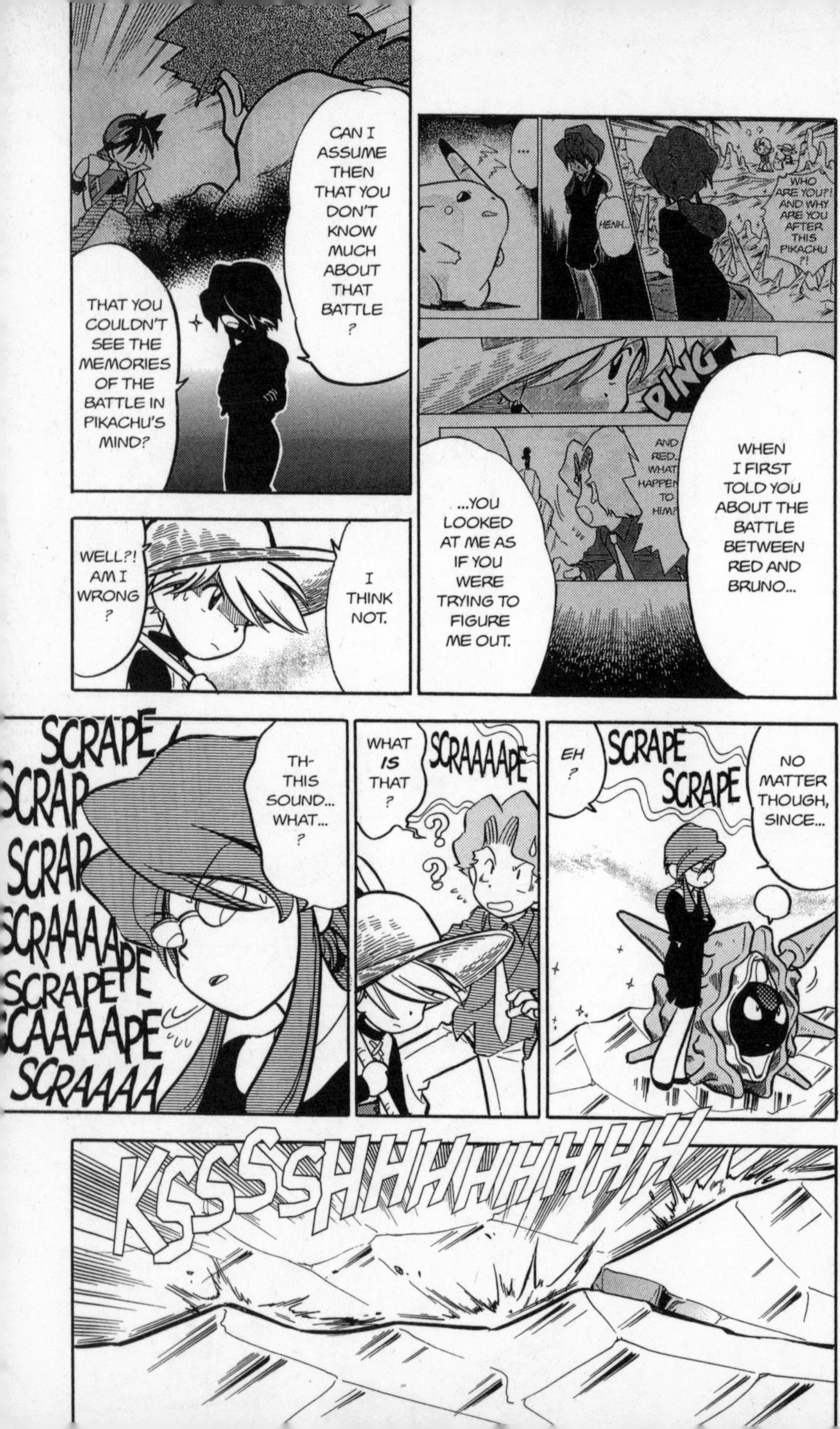
WHO ARE YOU?! AND WHY ARE YOU AFTER THIS PIKACHU?!
...
HENH...
PING
WHEN I FIRST TOLD YOU ABOUT THE BATTLE BETWEEN RED AND BRUNO...
AND RED... WHAT HAPPENED TO HIM?
...YOU LOOKED AT ME AS IF YOU WERE TRYING TO FIGURE ME OUT.
CAN I ASSUME THEN THAT YOU DON'T KNOW MUCH ABOUT THAT BATTLE?
THAT YOU COULDN'T SEE THE MEMORIES OF THE BATTLE IN PIKACHU'S MIND?
WELL?! AM I WRONG?
I THINK NOT.
NO MATTER THOUGH, SINCE...
SCRAPE SCRAPE
EH?
SCRAAAAPE
WHAT IS THAT?
TH-THIS SOUND... WHAT...?
SCRAPE SCRAP SCRAP SCRAAAAAPE SCRAPE SCAAAAPE SCRAAAA
KSSSSHHHHHHHHHH

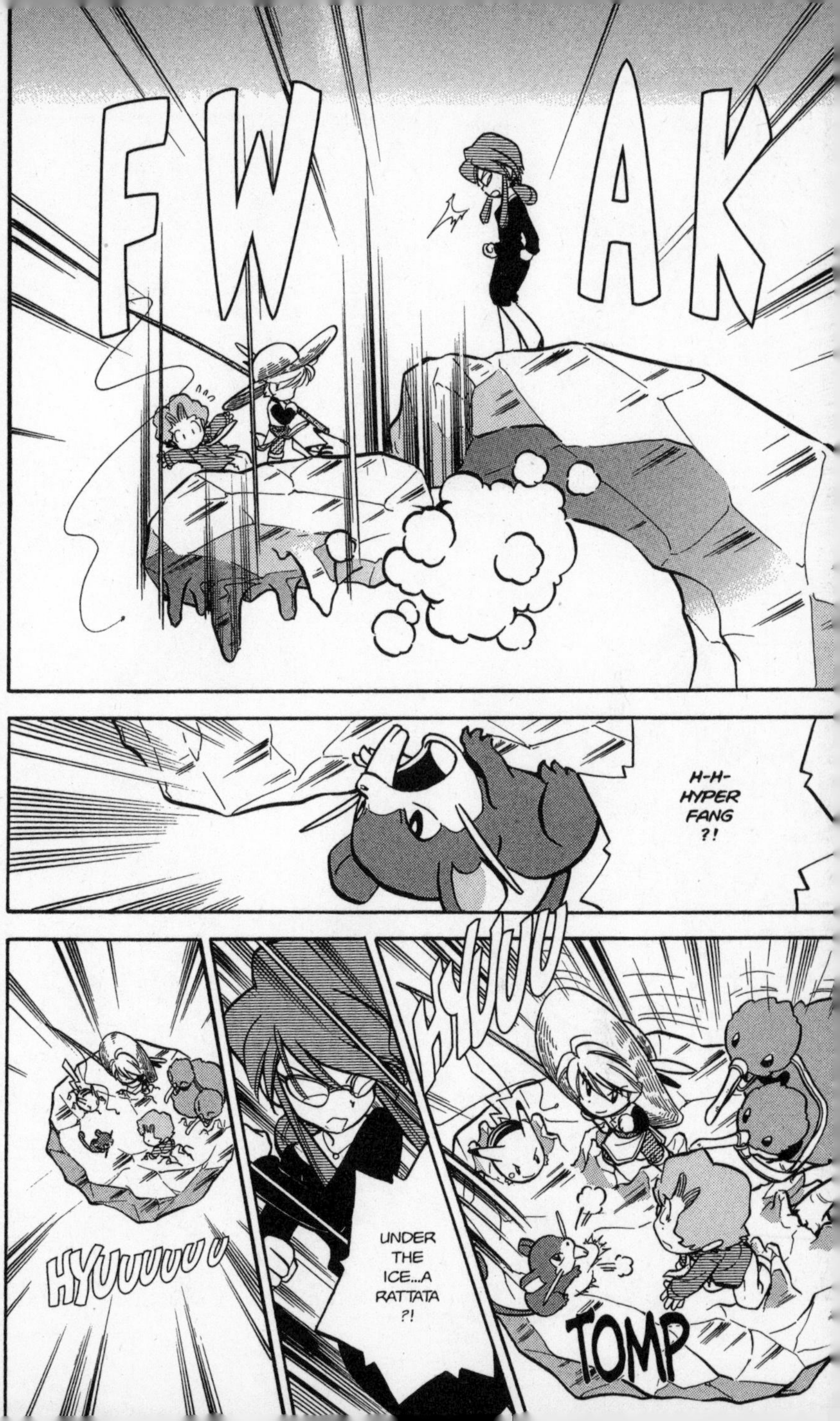
FWAK
H-H-HYPER FANG ?!
HYUUU
TOMP
UNDER THE ICE...A RATTATA ?!
HYUUUUUU

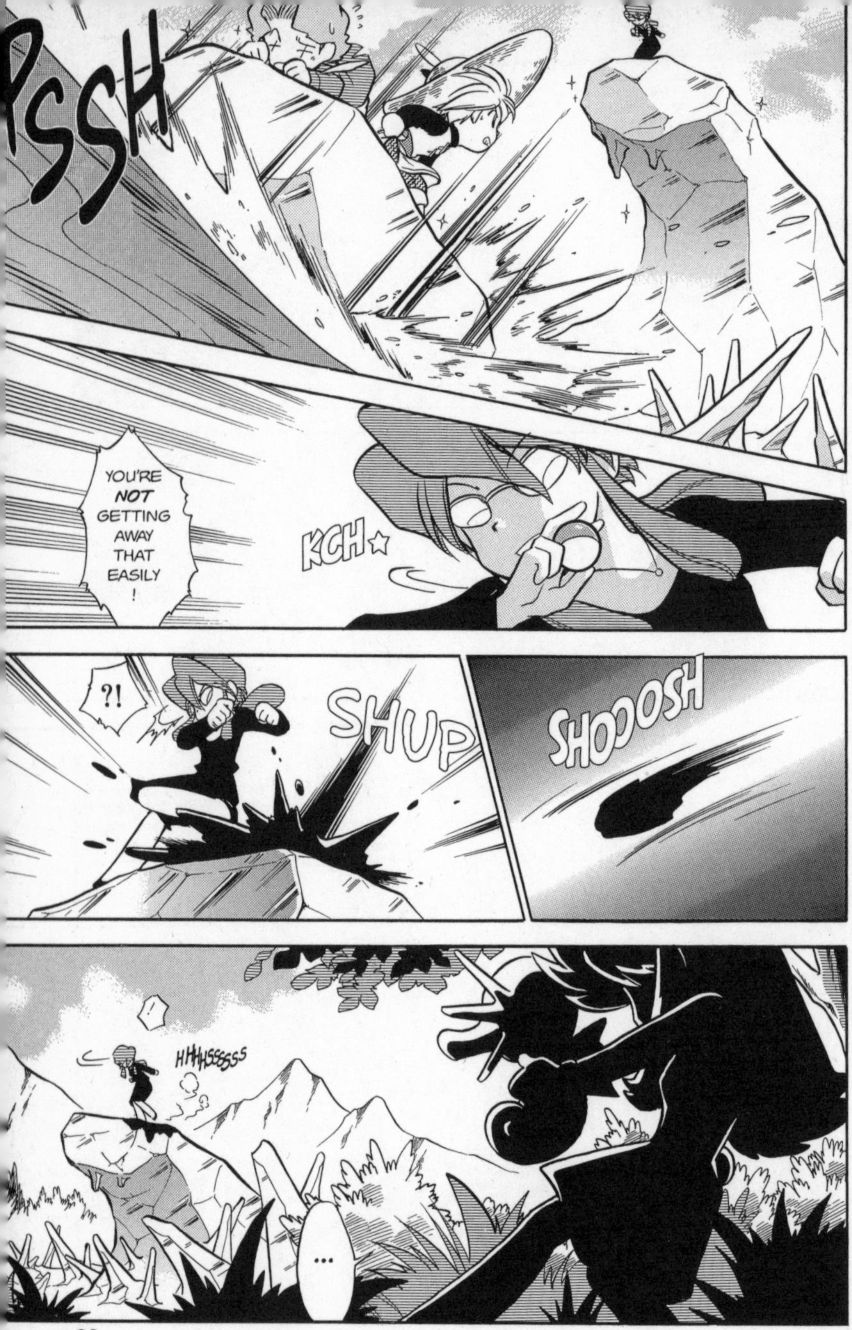

PSSH
YOU'RE *NOT* GETTING AWAY THAT EASILY !
KCH
SHOOOSH
?!
SHUP
!
HHHHSSSSS
...

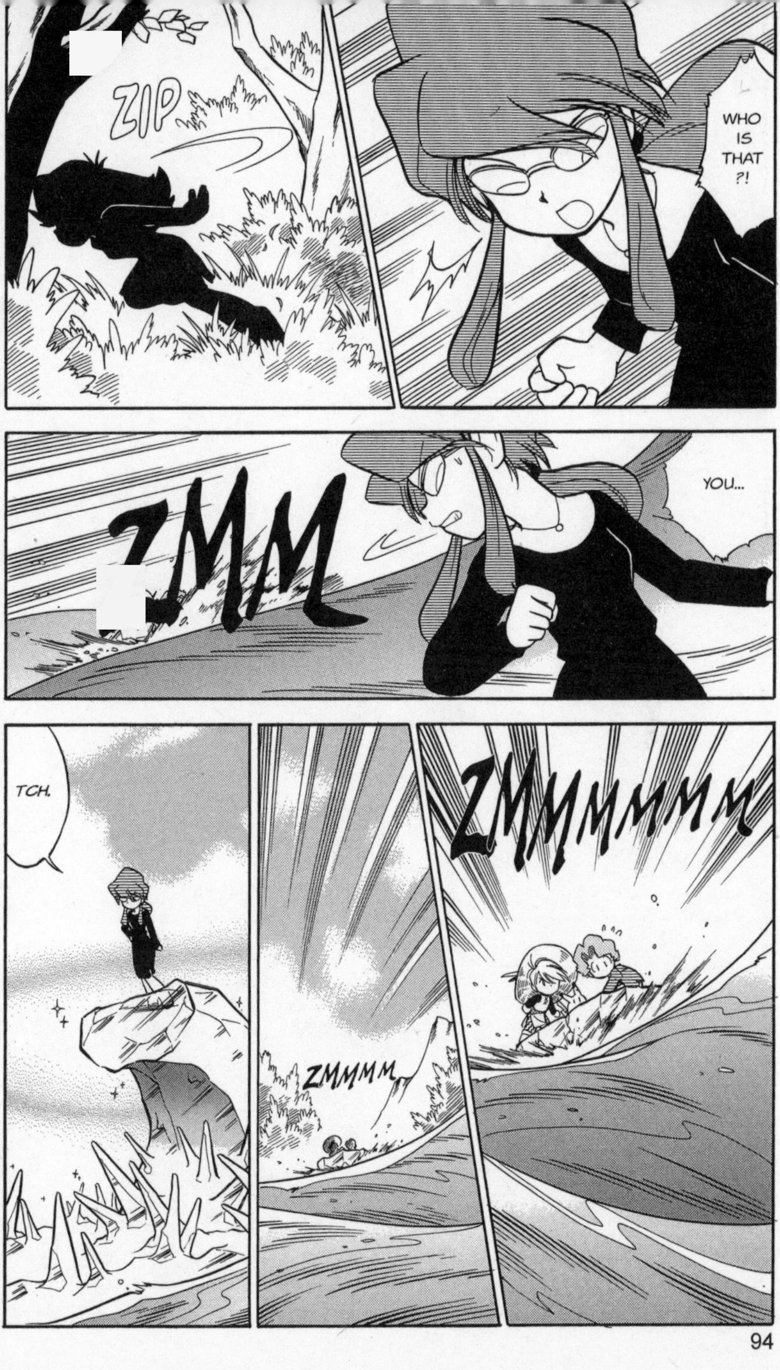
WHO IS THAT ?!
ZIP
YOU...
ZMM
ZMMMMMMM
ZMMMM
TCH.

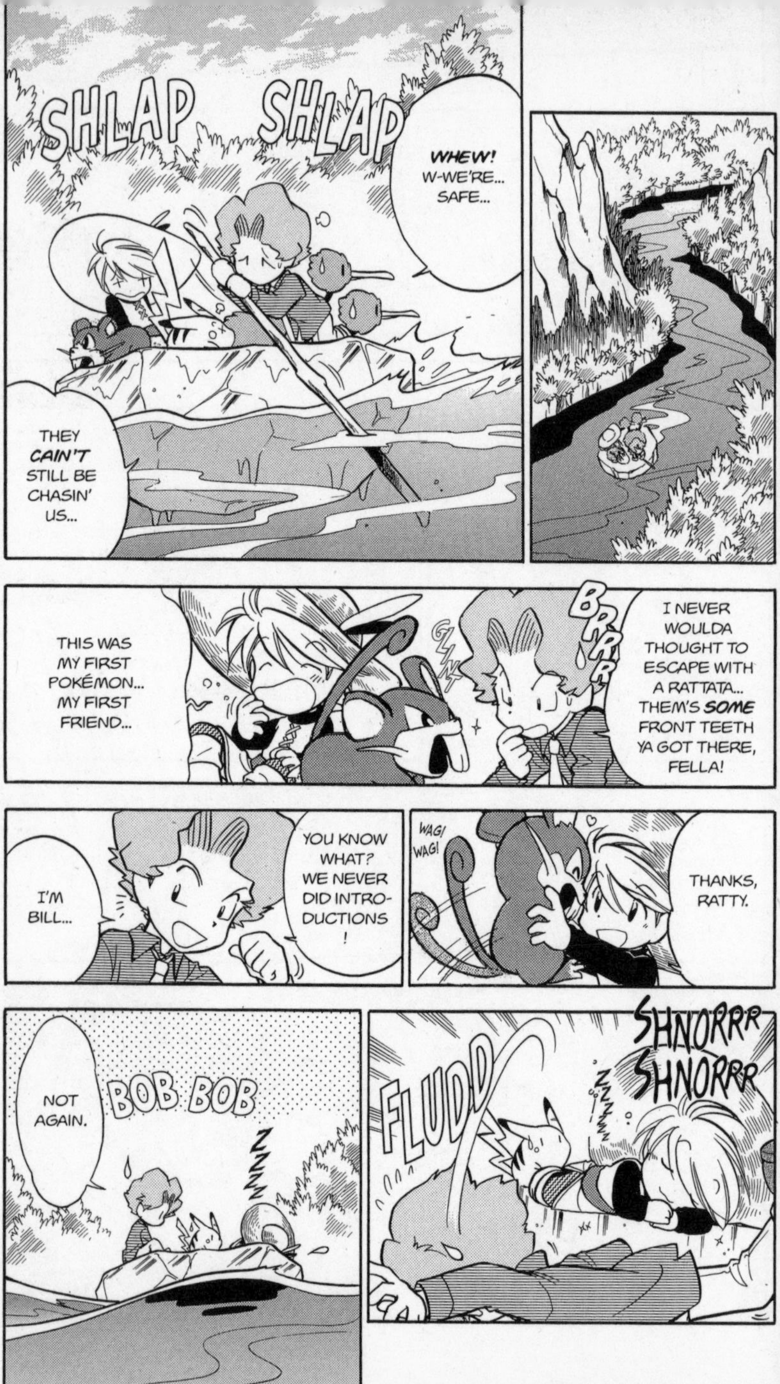

WHEW! W-WE'RE... SAFE...
SHLAP SHLAP
THEY CAIN'T STILL BE CHASIN' US...
BRRR
I NEVER WOULDA THOUGHT TO ESCAPE WITH A RATTATA... THEM'S SOME FRONT TEETH YA GOT THERE, FELLA!
GLINT
THIS WAS MY FIRST POKÉMON... MY FIRST FRIEND...
THANKS, RATTY.
WAG! WAG!
YOU KNOW WHAT? WE NEVER DID INTRO-DUCTIONS!
I'M BILL...
SHNORRR SHNORRR
FLUDD
BOB BOB
NOT AGAIN.

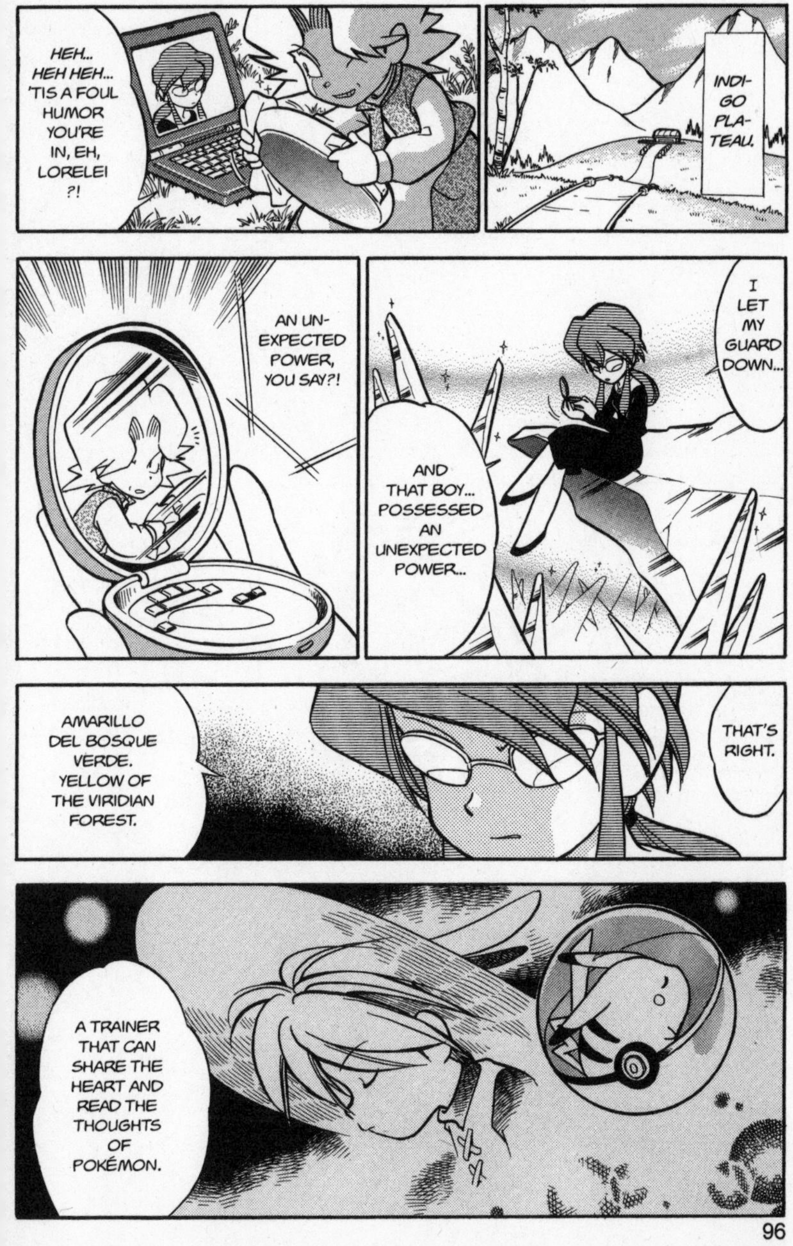
INDIGO PLATEAU.
HEH... HEH HEH... 'TIS A FOUL HUMOR YOU'RE IN, EH, LORELEI?!
I LET MY GUARD DOWN...
AND THAT BOY... POSSESSED AN UNEXPECTED POWER...
AN UNEXPECTED POWER, YOU SAY?!
THAT'S RIGHT.
AMARILLO DEL BOSQUE VERDE. YELLOW OF THE VIRIDIAN FOREST.
A TRAINER THAT CAN SHARE THE HEART AND READ THE THOUGHTS OF POKÉMON.

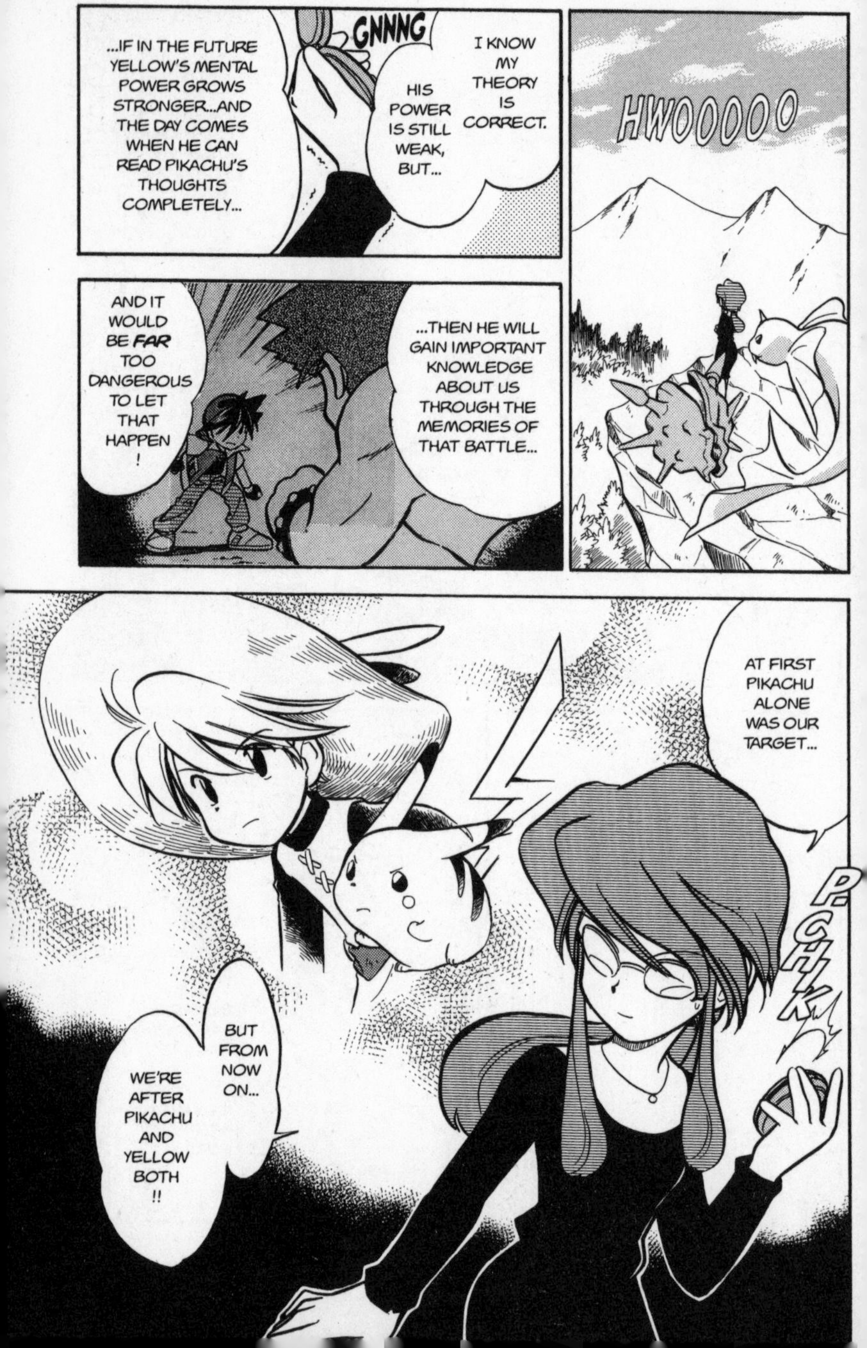
HWOOOOO
I KNOW MY THEORY IS CORRECT.
GNNNG
HIS POWER IS STILL WEAK, BUT...
...IF IN THE FUTURE YELLOW'S MENTAL POWER GROWS STRONGER...AND THE DAY COMES WHEN HE CAN READ PIKACHU'S THOUGHTS COMPLETELY...
...THEN HE WILL GAIN IMPORTANT KNOWLEDGE ABOUT US THROUGH THE MEMORIES OF THAT BATTLE...
AND IT WOULD BE FAR TOO DANGEROUS TO LET THAT HAPPEN!
AT FIRST PIKACHU ALONE WAS OUR TARGET...
P-CHK
BUT FROM NOW ON...
WE'RE AFTER PIKACHU AND YELLOW BOTH!!

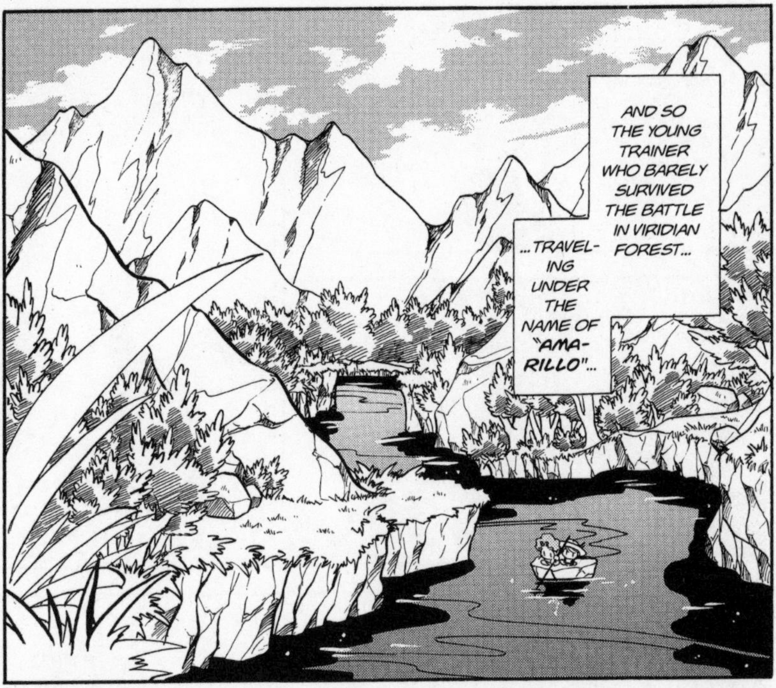
AND SO THE YOUNG TRAINER WHO BARELY SURVIVED THE BATTLE IN VIRIDIAN FOREST...
...TRAVEL-ING UNDER THE NAME OF "AMA-RILLO"...

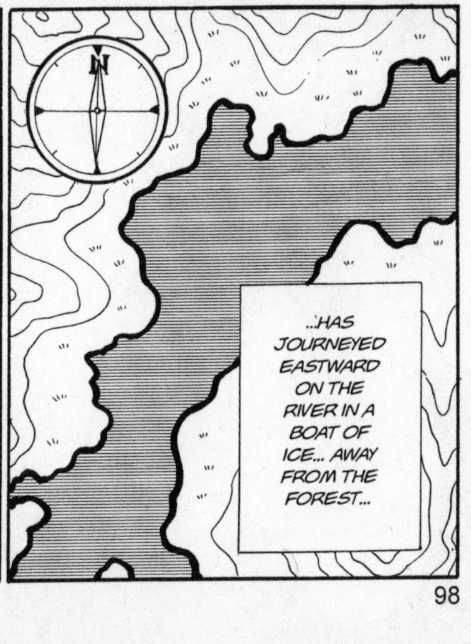
...HAS JOURNEYED EASTWARD ON THE RIVER IN A BOAT OF ICE... AWAY FROM THE FOREST...

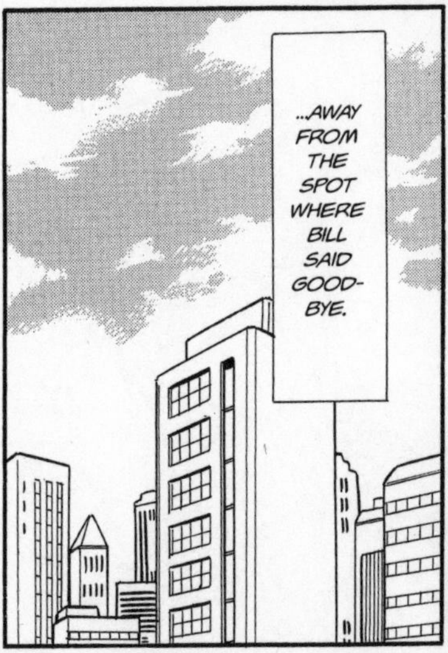
...AWAY FROM THE SPOT WHERE BILL SAID GOOD-BYE.

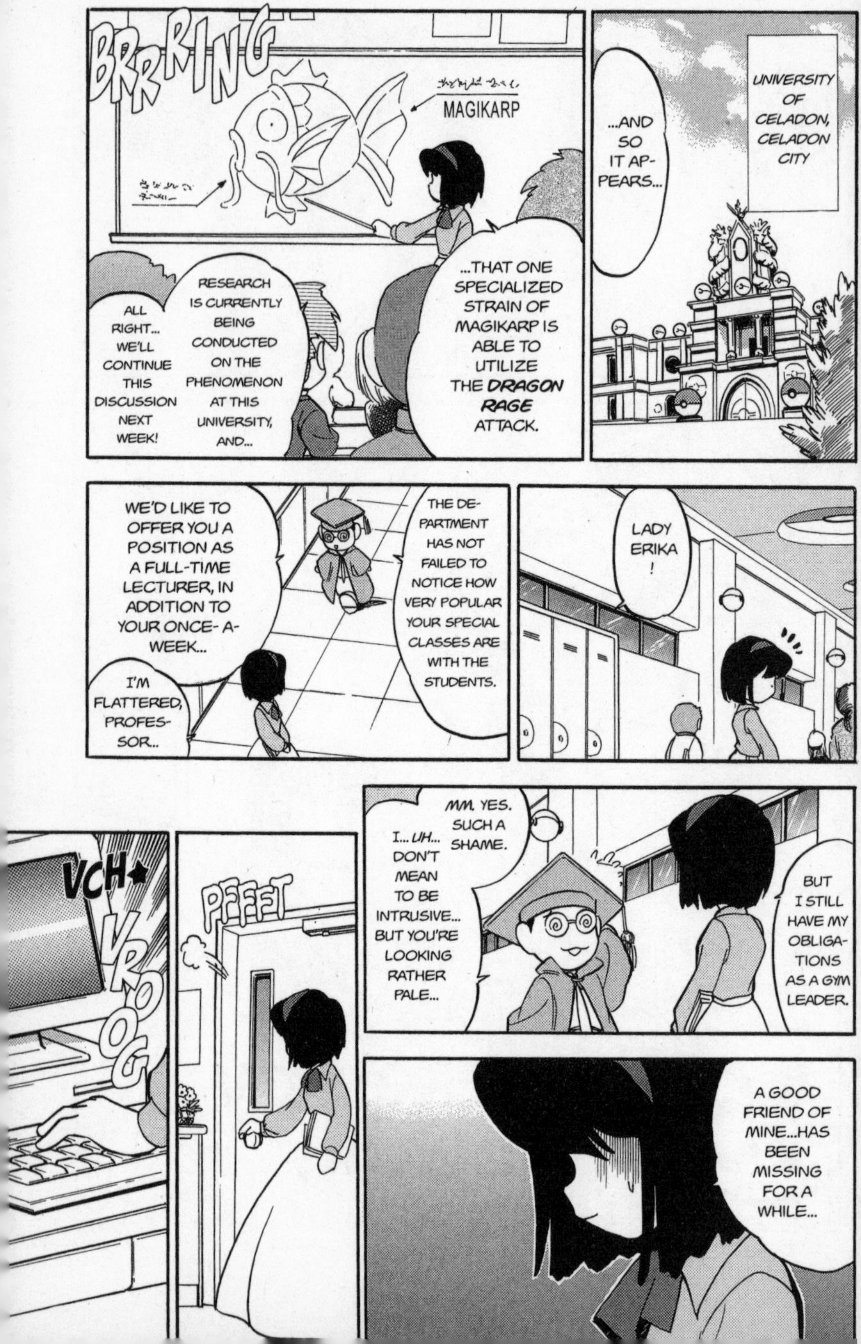

UNIVERSITY OF CELADON, CELADON CITY
...AND SO IT APPEARS...
BRRRING
MAGIKARP
...THAT ONE SPECIALIZED STRAIN OF MAGIKARP IS ABLE TO UTILIZE THE DRAGON RAGE ATTACK.
RESEARCH IS CURRENTLY BEING CONDUCTED ON THE PHENOMENON AT THIS UNIVERSITY, AND...
ALL RIGHT... WE'LL CONTINUE THIS DISCUSSION NEXT WEEK!
LADY ERIKA!
THE DEPARTMENT HAS NOT FAILED TO NOTICE HOW VERY POPULAR YOUR SPECIAL CLASSES ARE WITH THE STUDENTS.
WE'D LIKE TO OFFER YOU A POSITION AS A FULL-TIME LECTURER, IN ADDITION TO YOUR ONCE-A-WEEK...
I'M FLATTERED, PROFESSOR..
BUT I STILL HAVE MY OBLIGATIONS AS A GYM LEADER.
MM. YES. SUCH A SHAME.
I... UH... DON'T MEAN TO BE INTRUSIVE... BUT YOU'RE LOOKING RATHER PALE...
A GOOD FRIEND OF MINE...HAS BEEN MISSING FOR A WHILE...
PFFFT
VCH★
VROOOG

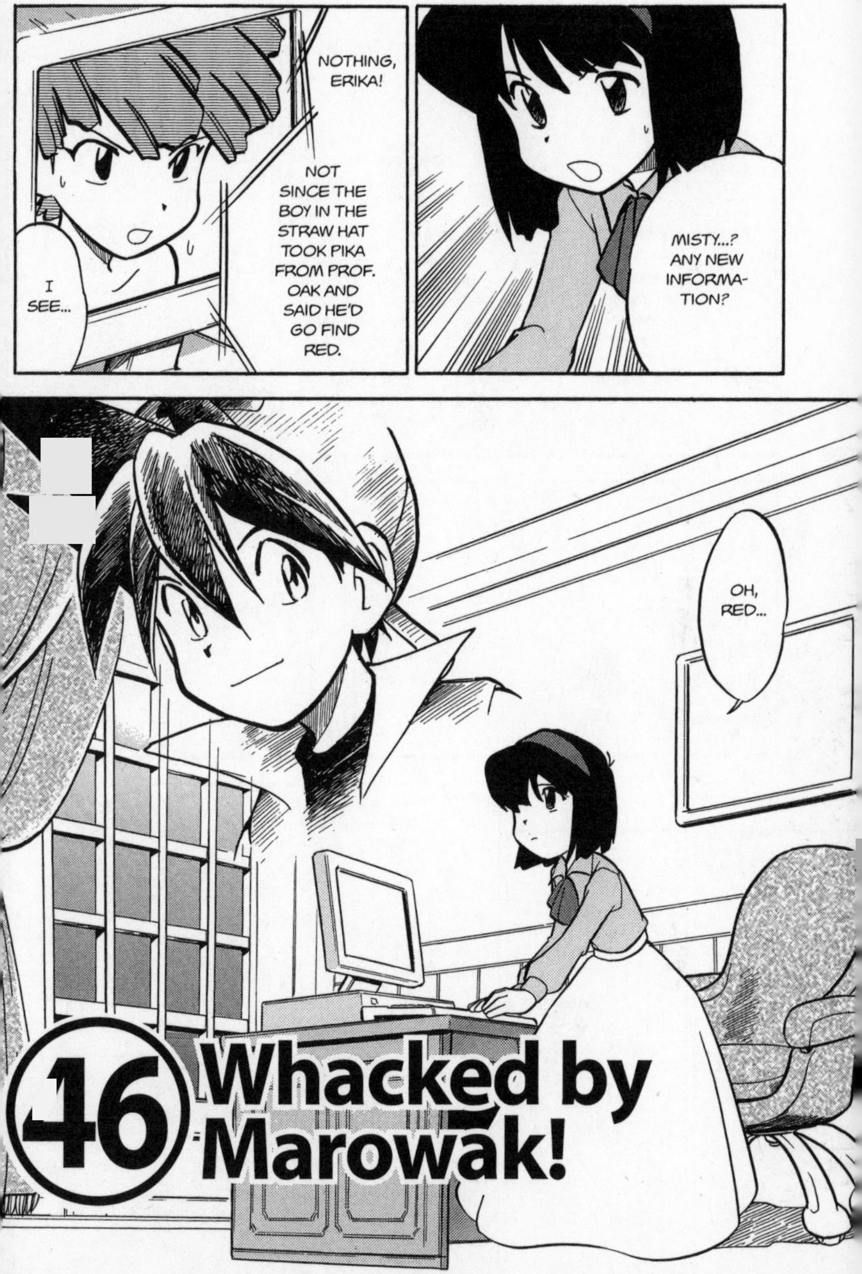
MISTY...? ANY NEW INFORMATION?
NOTHING, ERIKA!
NOT SINCE THE BOY IN THE STRAW HAT TOOK PIKA FROM PROF. OAK AND SAID HE'D GO FIND RED.
I SEE...
OH, RED...
46 Whacked by Marowak!

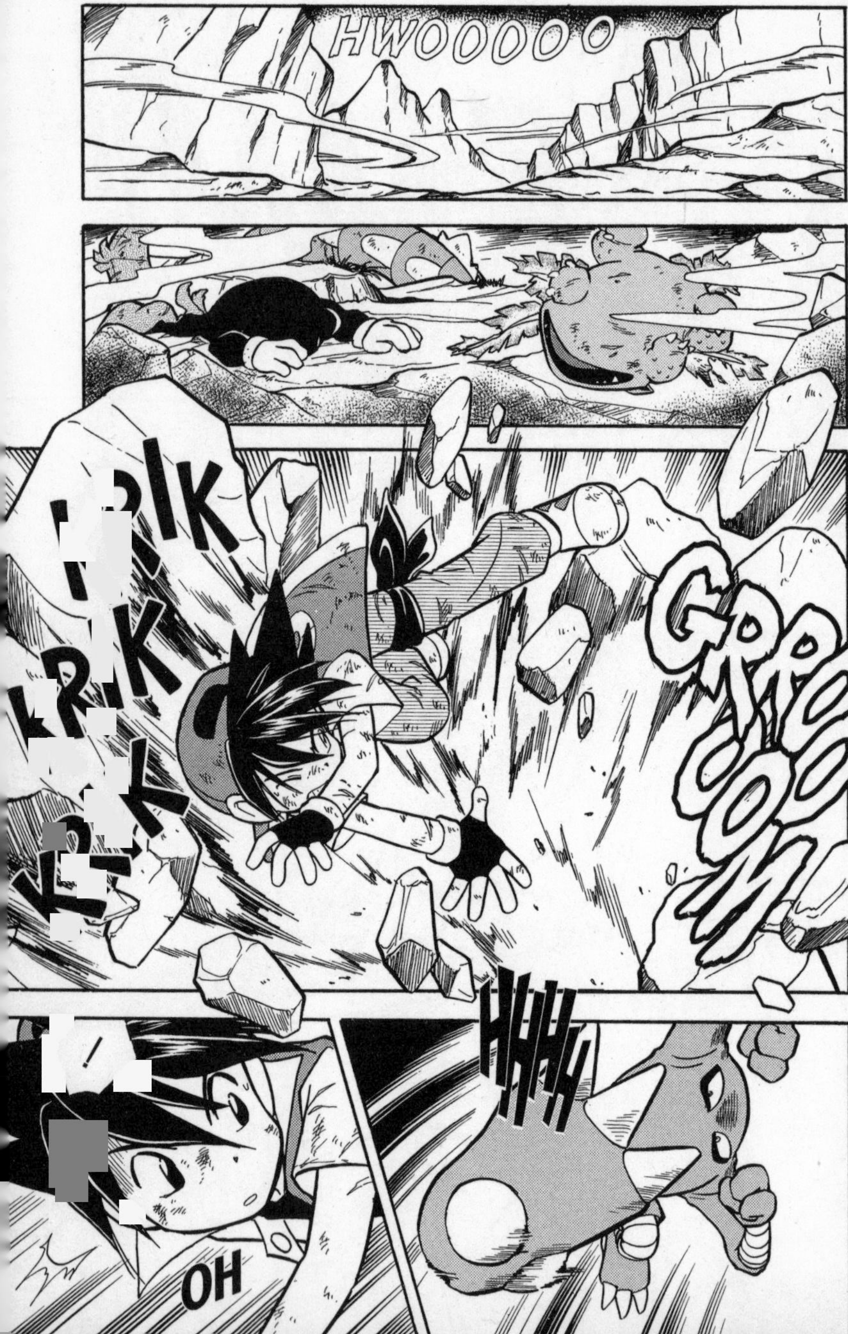
HWOOOOO
GROOOOM
KRIK
KRIK
HHHH
!
OH

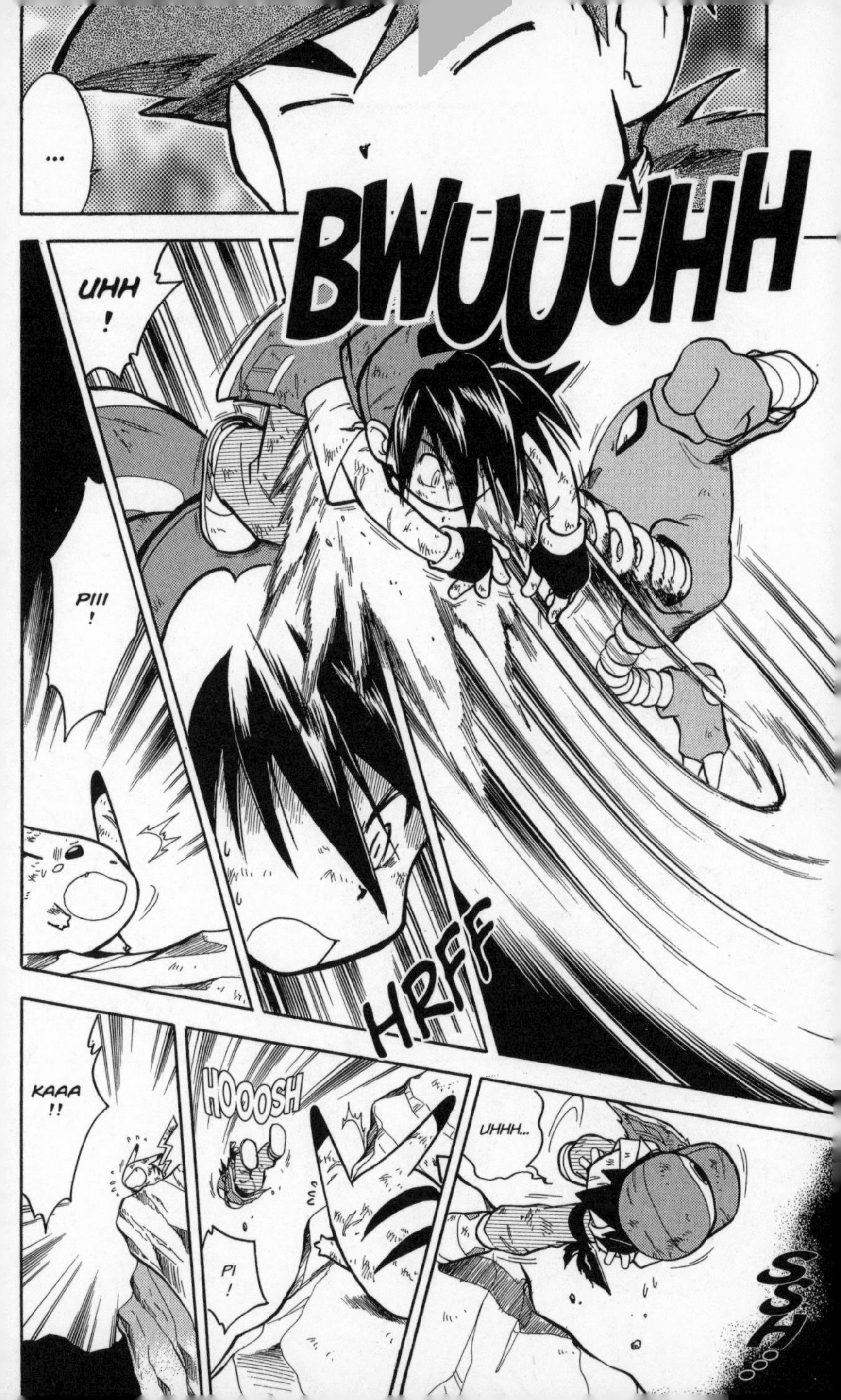
...
BWUUUUHH
HRFF
UHH !
PIII !
UHHH...
SSSH...
HOOOSH
PI !
KAAA !!

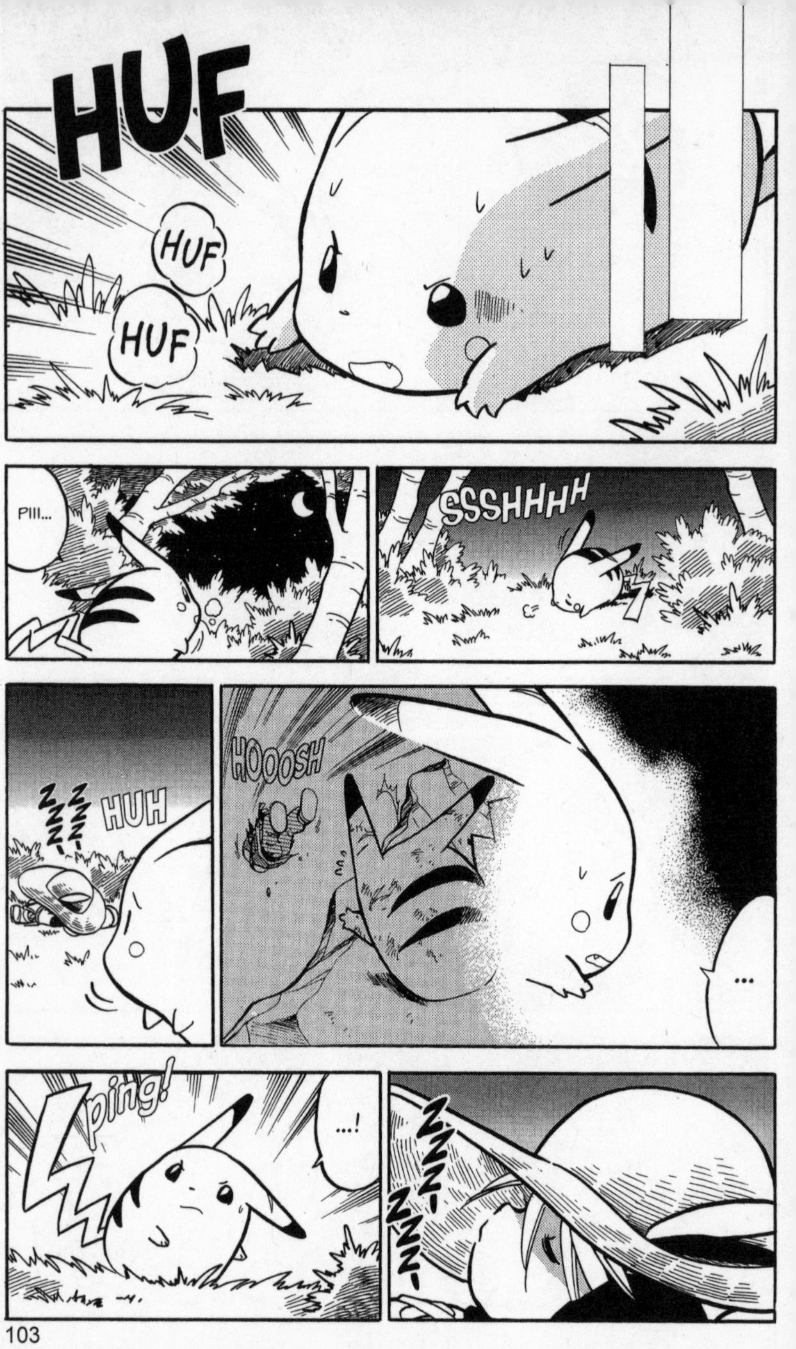

HUF
HUF
HUF
SSSHHHH
PIII...
HOOOSH
...
HUH
...!
ping!

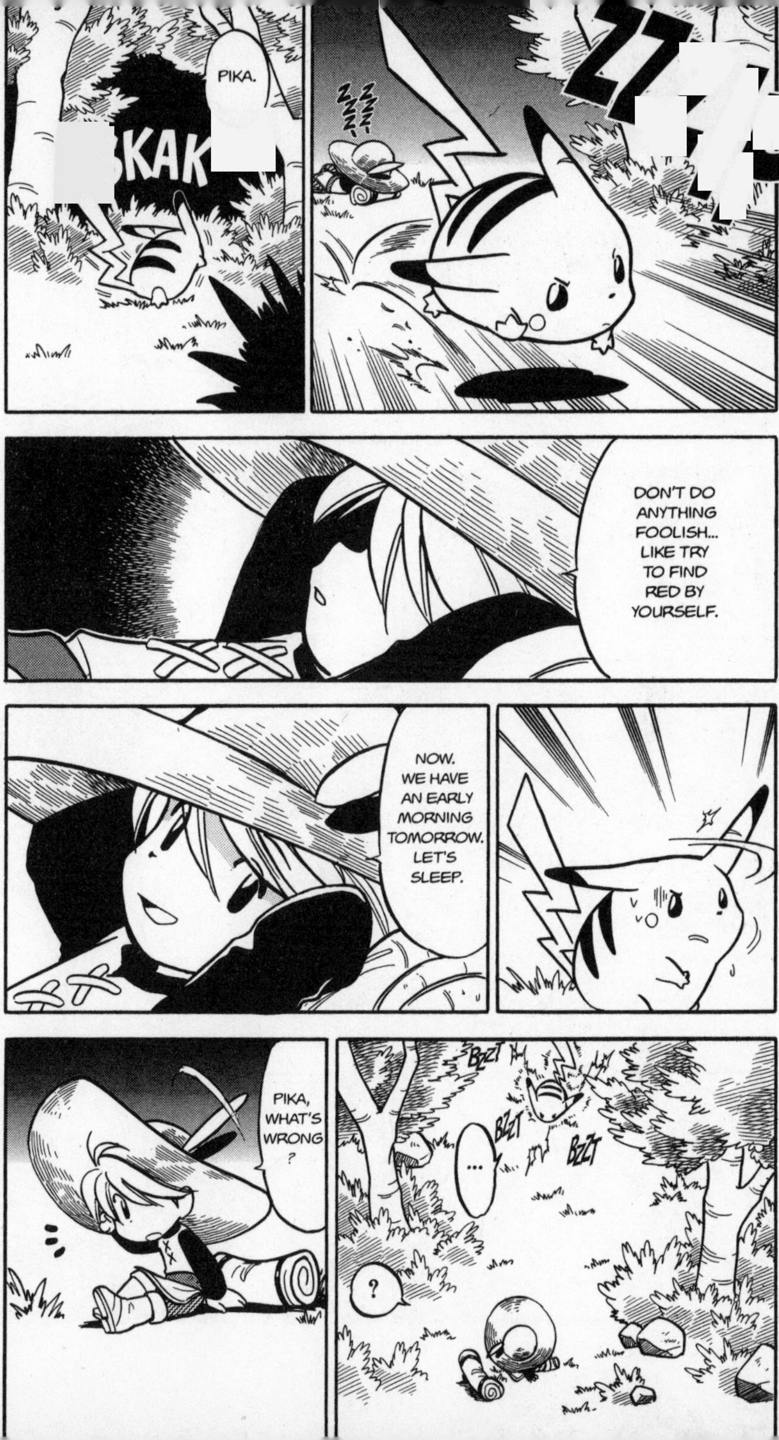
PIKA.
DON'T DO ANYTHING FOOLISH... LIKE TRY TO FIND RED BY YOURSELF.
NOW. WE HAVE AN EARLY MORNING TOMORROW. LET'S SLEEP.
BZZT
BZZT
BZZT
...
?
PIKA, WHAT'S WRONG?

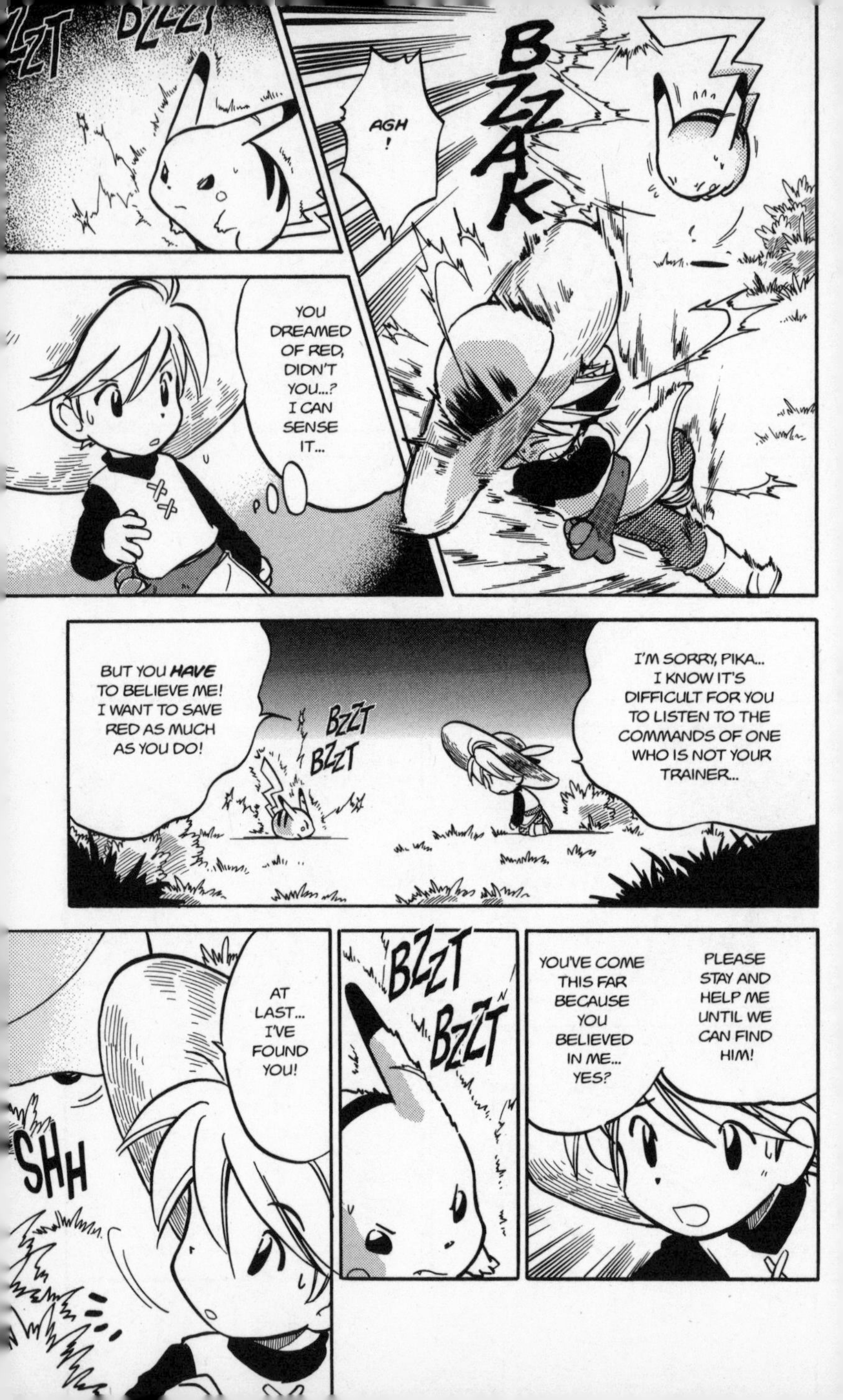
BZZAK
AGH!
ZZT
BZZZ
YOU DREAMED OF RED, DIDN'T YOU...? I CAN SENSE IT...
I'M SORRY, PIKA... I KNOW IT'S DIFFICULT FOR YOU TO LISTEN TO THE COMMANDS OF ONE WHO IS NOT YOUR TRAINER...
BZZT BZZT
BUT YOU **HAVE** TO BELIEVE ME! I WANT TO SAVE RED AS MUCH AS YOU DO!
PLEASE STAY AND HELP ME UNTIL WE CAN FIND HIM!
YOU'VE COME THIS FAR BECAUSE YOU BELIEVED IN ME... YES?
BZZT BZZT
AT LAST... I'VE FOUND YOU!
SHH

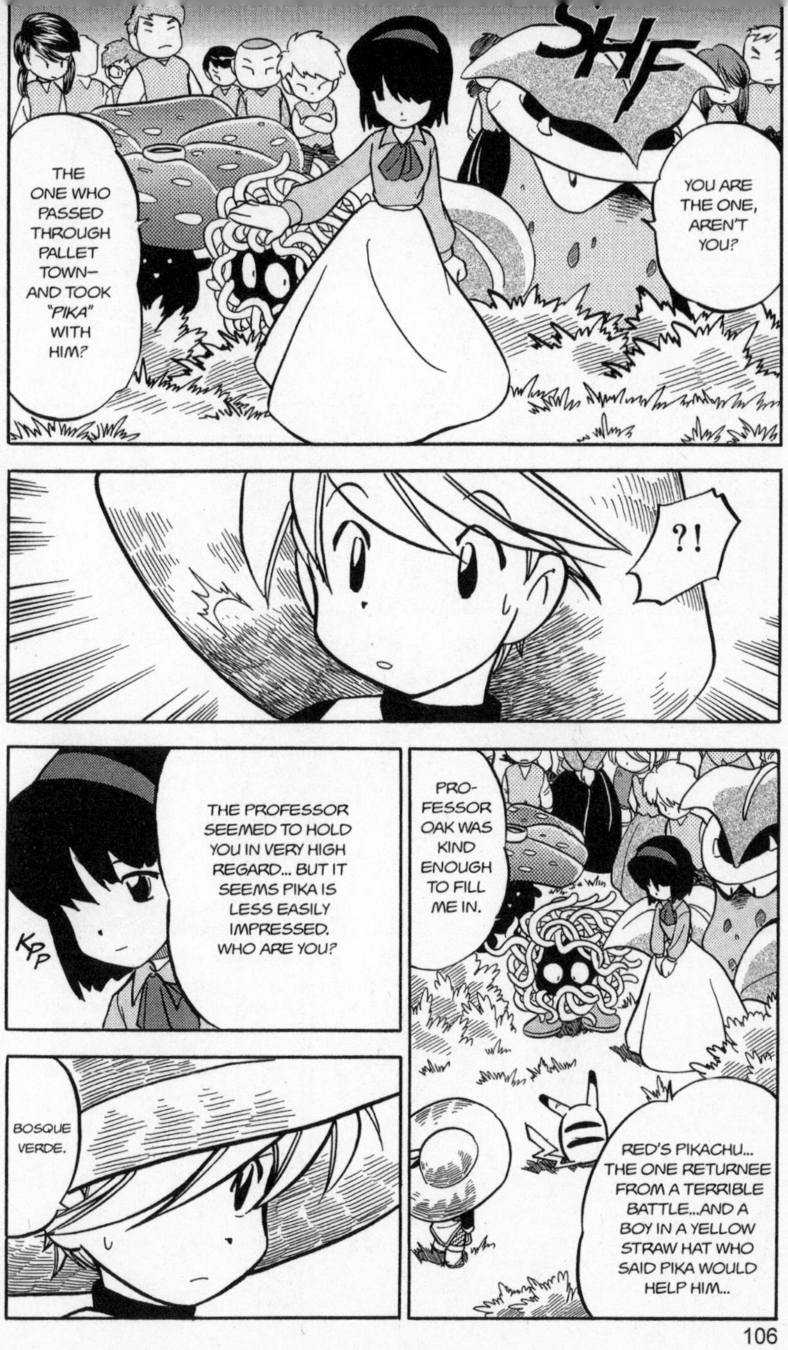
SHF
YOU ARE THE ONE, AREN'T YOU?
THE ONE WHO PASSED THROUGH PALLET TOWN— AND TOOK "PIKA" WITH HIM?
?!
PROFESSOR OAK WAS KIND ENOUGH TO FILL ME IN.
RED'S PIKACHU... THE ONE RETURNEE FROM A TERRIBLE BATTLE...AND A BOY IN A YELLOW STRAW HAT WHO SAID PIKA WOULD HELP HIM...
THE PROFESSOR SEEMED TO HOLD YOU IN VERY HIGH REGARD... BUT IT SEEMS PIKA IS LESS EASILY IMPRESSED. WHO ARE YOU?
KPP
BOSQUE VERDE.

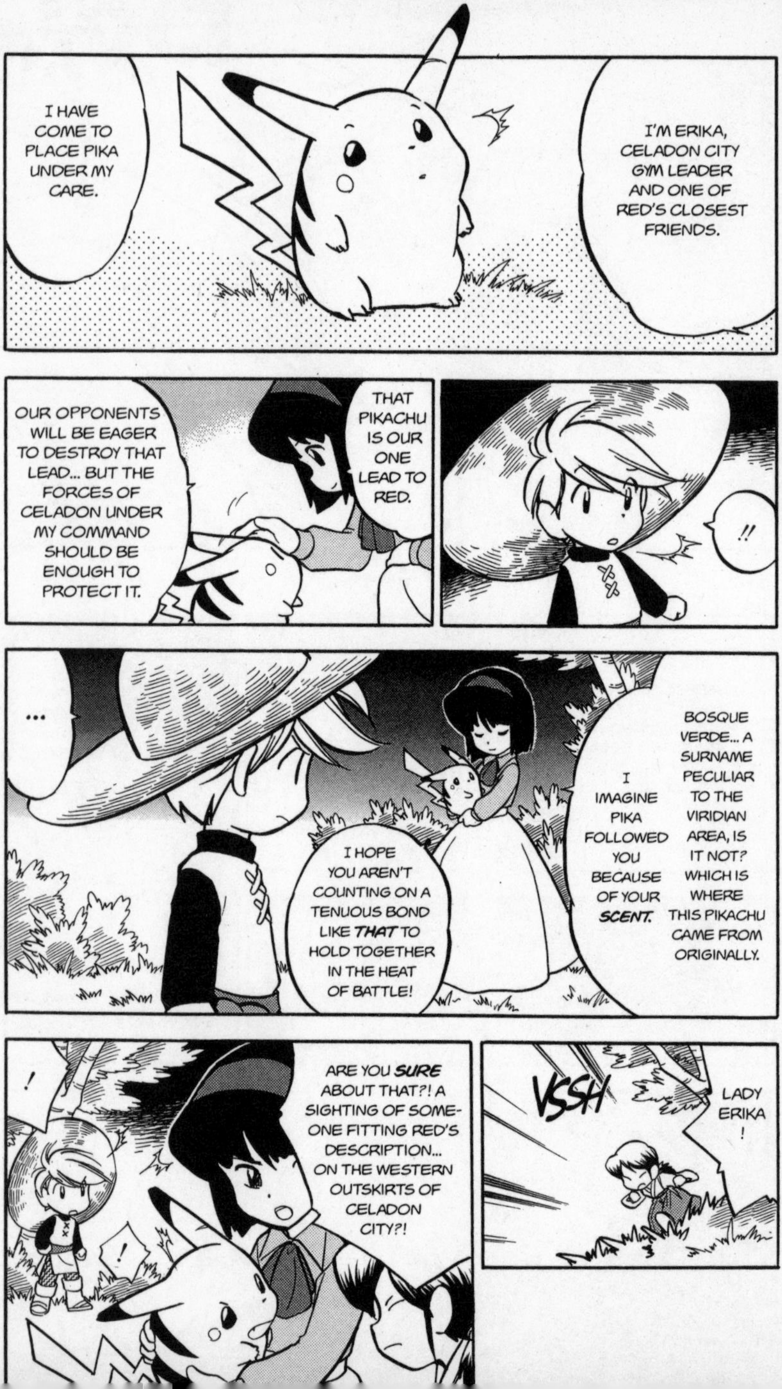
I'M ERIKA, CELADON CITY GYM LEADER AND ONE OF RED'S CLOSEST FRIENDS.
I HAVE COME TO PLACE PIKA UNDER MY CARE.
!!
THAT PIKACHU IS OUR ONE LEAD TO RED.
OUR OPPONENTS WILL BE EAGER TO DESTROY THAT LEAD... BUT THE FORCES OF CELADON UNDER MY COMMAND SHOULD BE ENOUGH TO PROTECT IT.
BOSQUE VERDE... A SURNAME PECULIAR TO THE VIRIDIAN AREA, IS IT NOT? WHICH IS WHERE THIS PIKACHU CAME FROM ORIGINALLY.
I IMAGINE PIKA FOLLOWED YOU BECAUSE OF YOUR *SCENT.*
I HOPE YOU AREN'T COUNTING ON A TENUOUS BOND LIKE *THAT* TO HOLD TOGETHER IN THE HEAT OF BATTLE!
...
VSSH
LADY ERIKA!
ARE YOU *SURE* ABOUT THAT?! A SIGHTING OF SOME-ONE FITTING RED'S DESCRIPTION... ON THE WESTERN OUTSKIRTS OF CELADON CITY?!
!
!

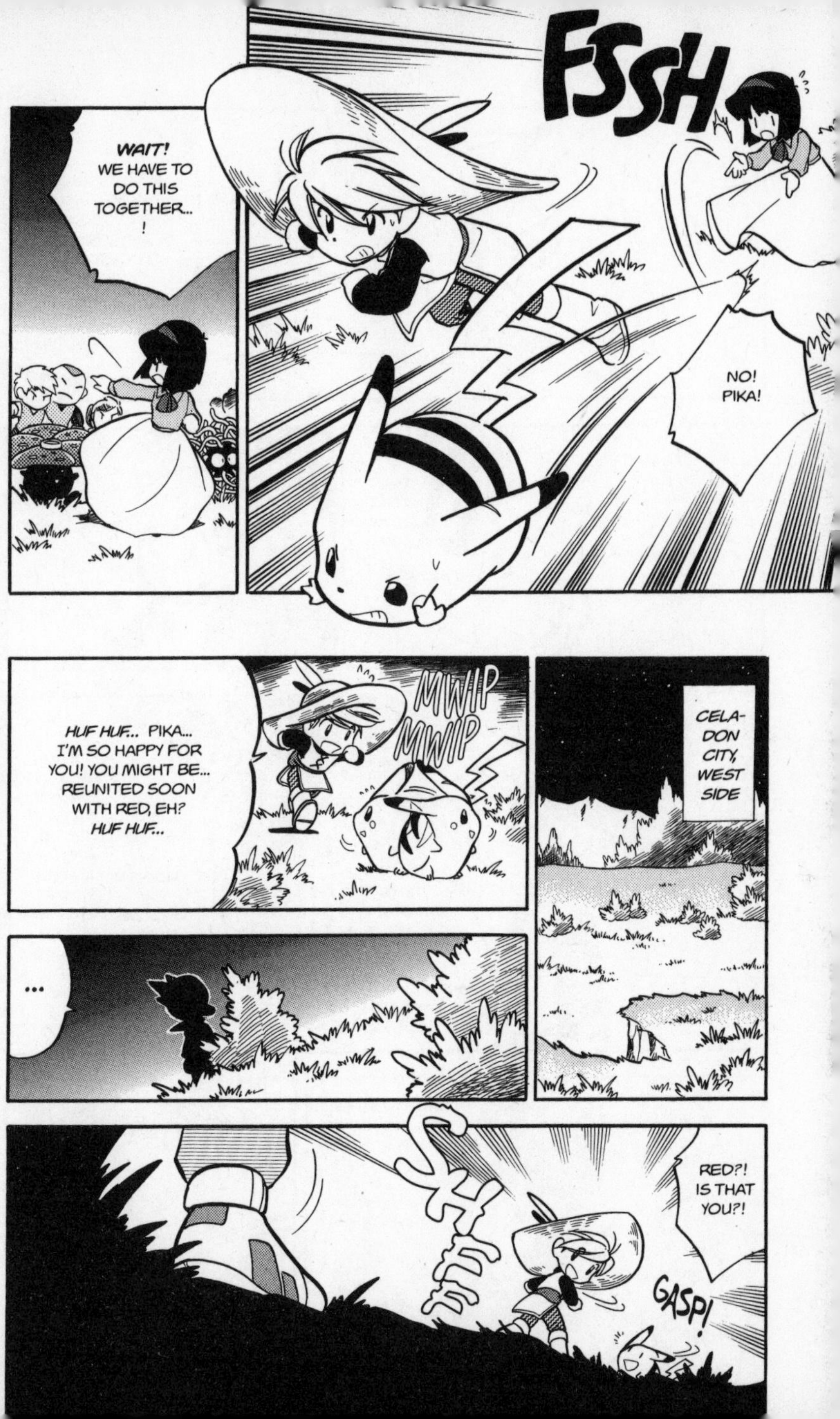
FSSH
NO! PIKA!
WAIT! WE HAVE TO DO THIS TOGETHER...!
CELADON CITY, WEST SIDE
HUF HUF... PIKA... I'M SO HAPPY FOR YOU! YOU MIGHT BE... REUNITED SOON WITH RED, EH? HUF HUF...
MWIP MWIP
...
RED?! IS THAT YOU?!
GASP!

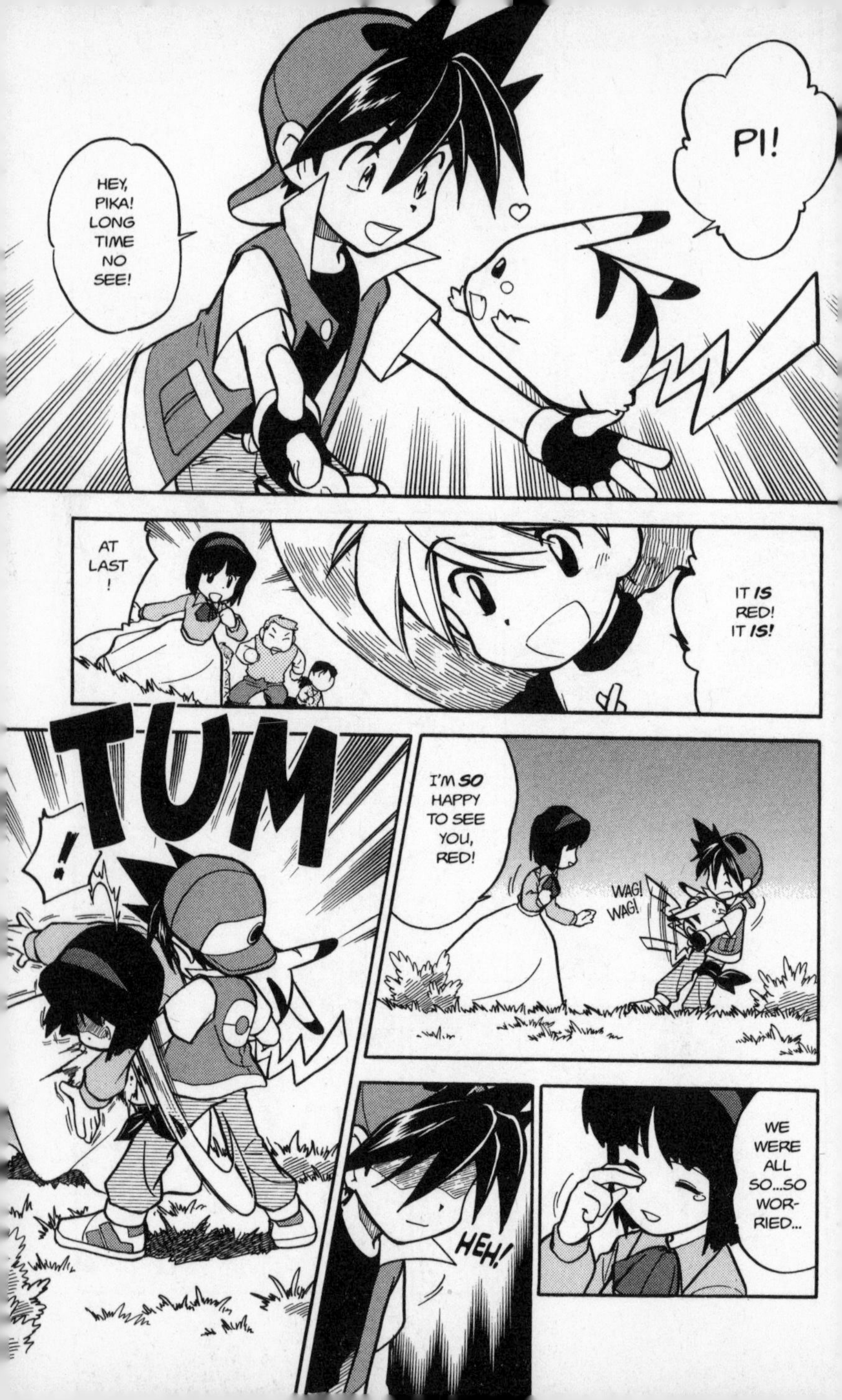
PI!
HEY, PIKA! LONG TIME NO SEE!
IT IS RED! IT IS!
AT LAST!
I'M SO HAPPY TO SEE YOU, RED!
WAG! WAG!
WE WERE ALL SO...SO WORRIED...
HEH!
TUM
!

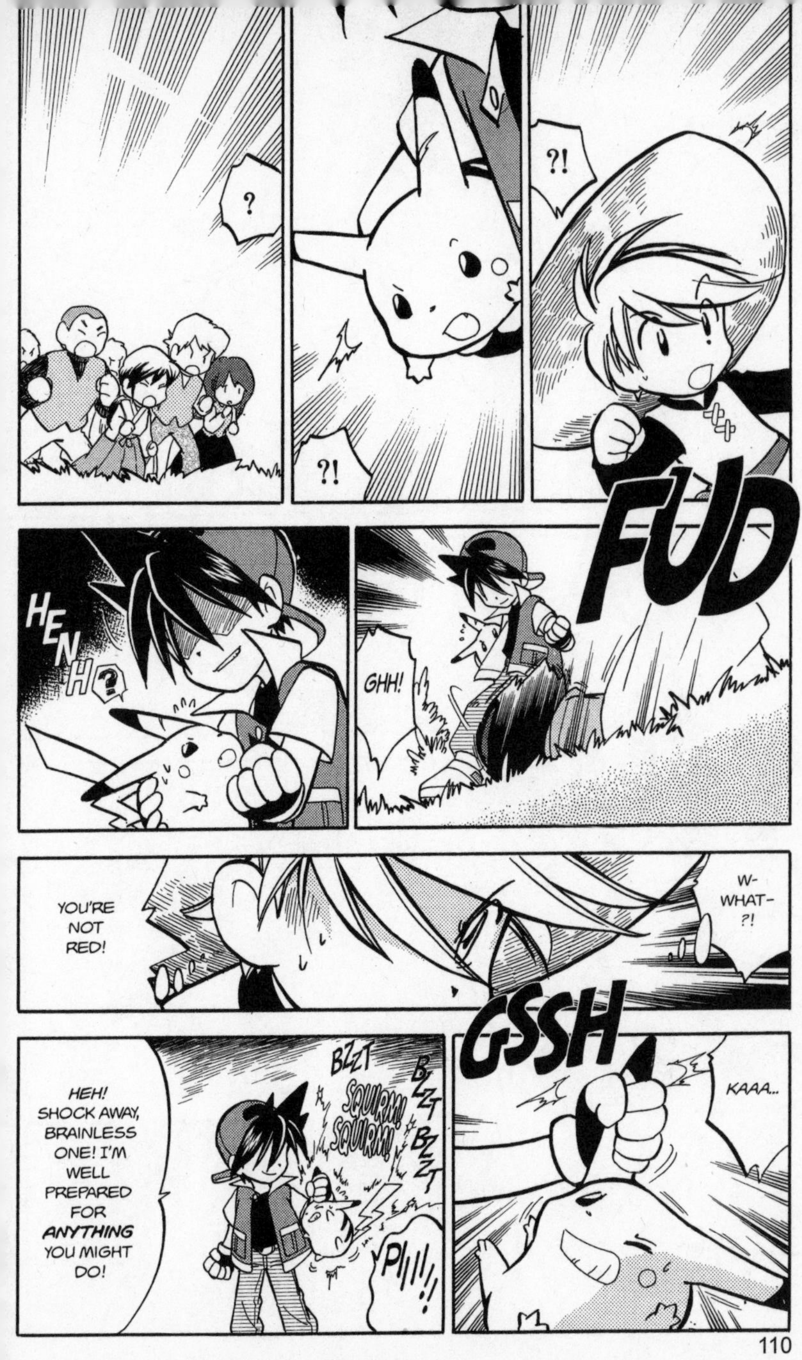
?!
?!
?
FUD
GHH!
HENH
?
W-WHAT-?!
YOU'RE NOT RED!
GSSH
KAAA...
HEH! SHOCK AWAY, BRAINLESS ONE! I'M WELL PREPARED FOR *ANYTHING* YOU MIGHT DO!
BZZT
BZZT
BZZT
SQUIRM! SQUIRM!
PI!!!!

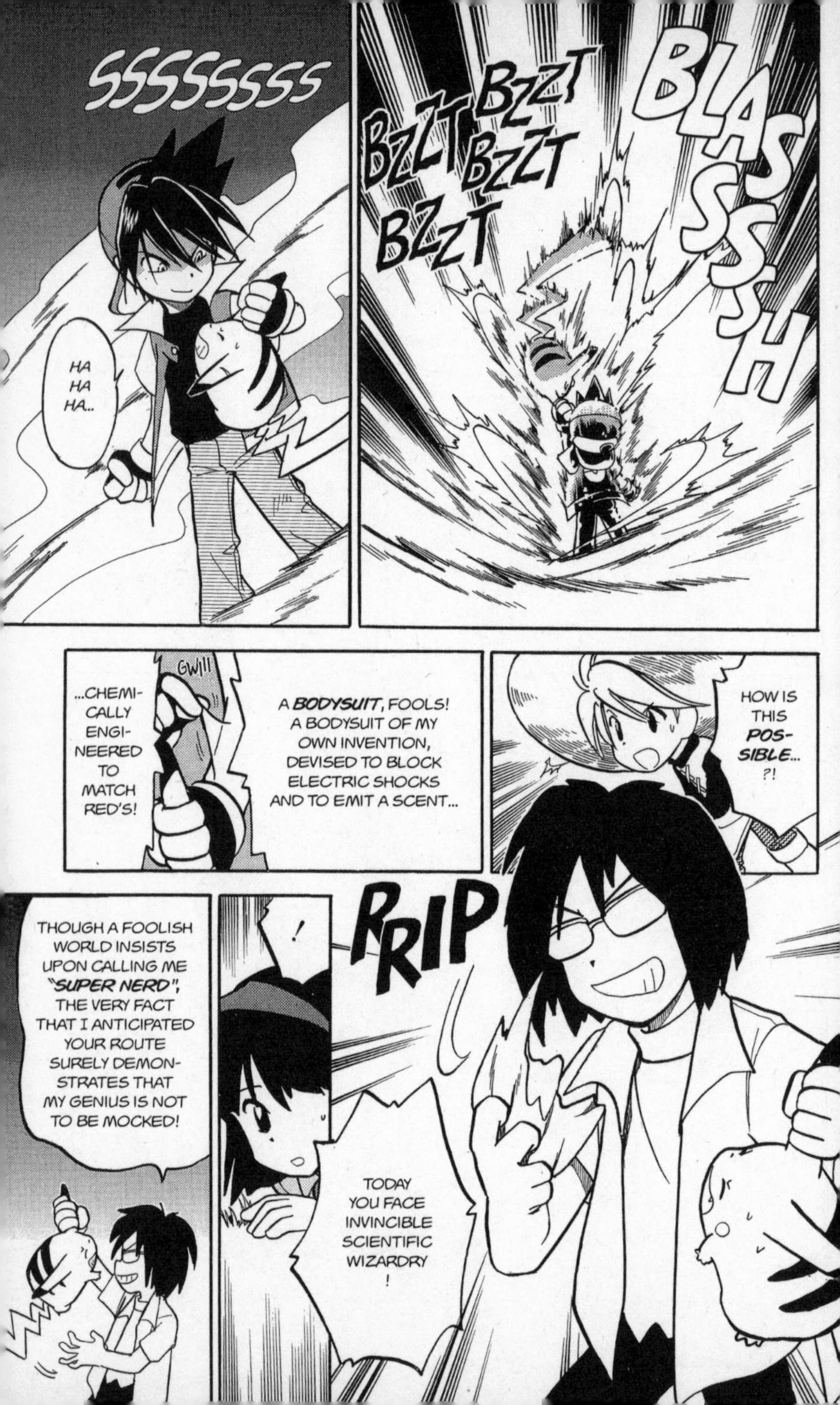
BLASSSH
BZZT BZZT BZZT BZZT
SSSSSSSS
HA HA HA...
HOW IS THIS POSSIBLE...?!
A BODYSUIT, FOOLS! A BODYSUIT OF MY OWN INVENTION, DEVISED TO BLOCK ELECTRIC SHOCKS AND TO EMIT A SCENT...
GWIII
...CHEMICALLY ENGINEERED TO MATCH RED'S!
RRIP
TODAY YOU FACE INVINCIBLE SCIENTIFIC WIZARDRY!
!
THOUGH A FOOLISH WORLD INSISTS UPON CALLING ME "SUPER NERD", THE VERY FACT THAT I ANTICIPATED YOUR ROUTE SURELY DEMONSTRATES THAT MY GENIUS IS NOT TO BE MOCKED!

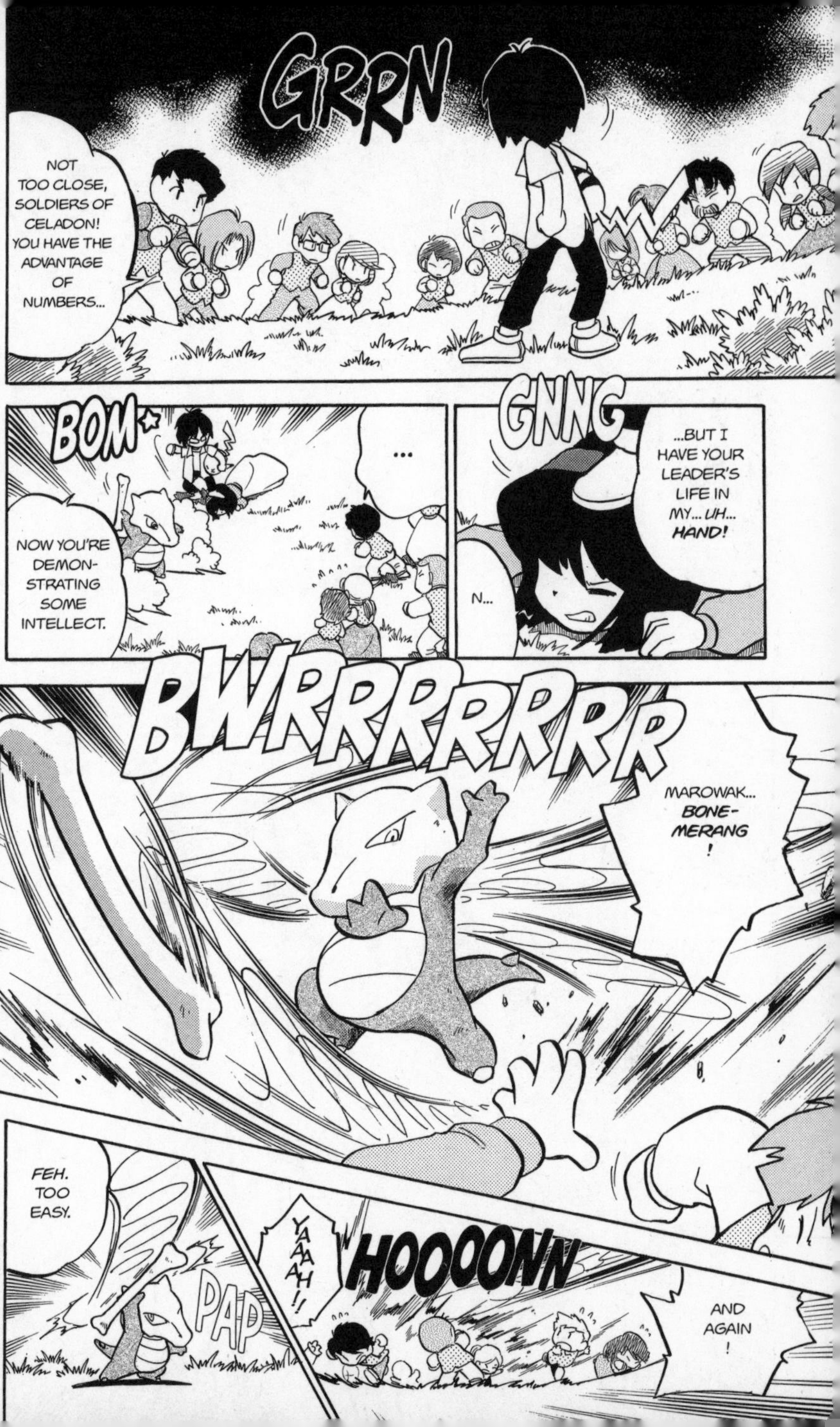
GRRN
NOT TOO CLOSE, SOLDIERS OF CELADON! YOU HAVE THE ADVANTAGE OF NUMBERS...
GNNG
...BUT I HAVE YOUR LEADER'S LIFE IN MY... UH... HAND!
N...
...
BOM
NOW YOU'RE DEMON-STRATING SOME INTELLECT.
BWRRRRRRRR
MAROWAK... BONE-MERANG!
AND AGAIN!
HOOOONN
YAAAAH!!
FEH. TOO EASY.
PAP

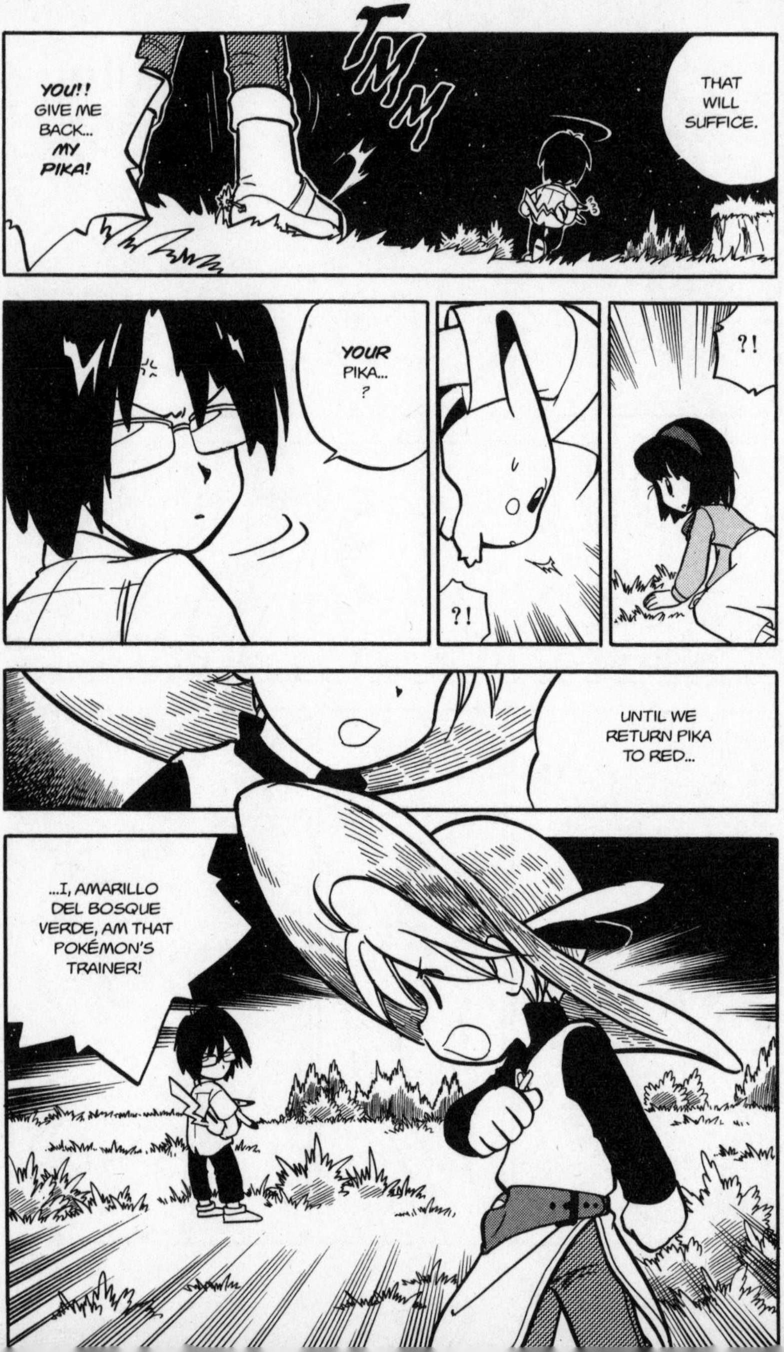
THAT WILL SUFFICE.
TMM
YOU!! GIVE ME BACK... MY PIKA!
?!
?!
YOUR PIKA...?
UNTIL WE RETURN PIKA TO RED...
...I, AMARILLO DEL BOSQUE VERDE, AM THAT POKÉMON'S TRAINER!

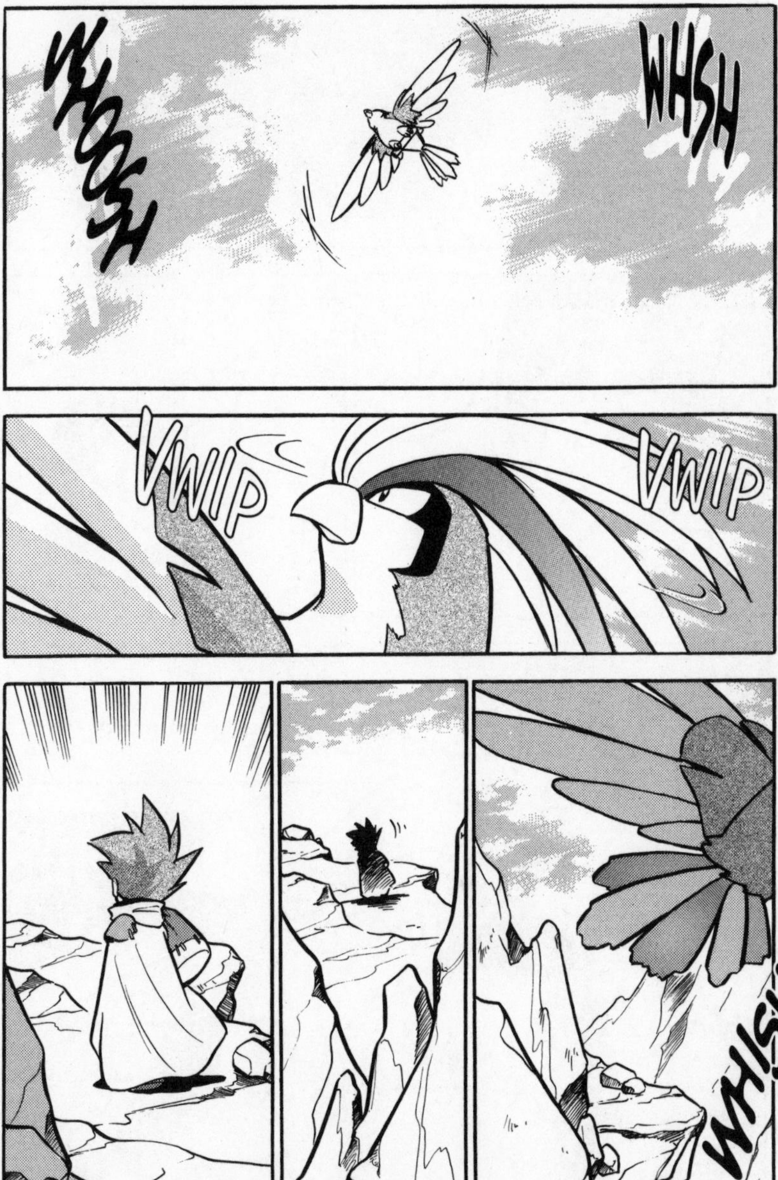
WHSH
WHOOSH
VWIP
VWIP
WHISH

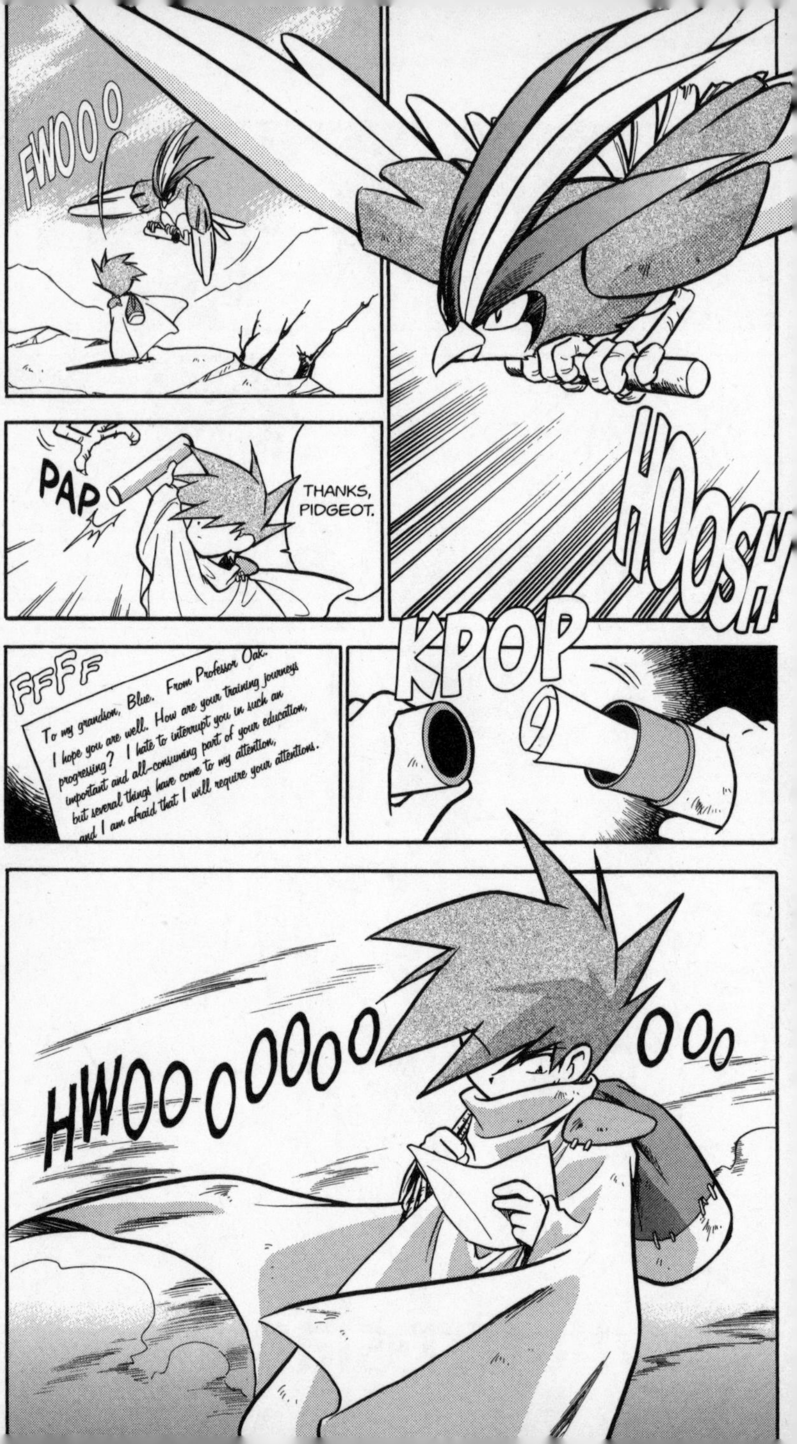
HOOSH
FWOOO
PAP
THANKS, PIDGEOT.
KPOP
FFFF
To my grandson, Blue. From Professor Oak.
I hope you are well. How are your training journeys
progressing? I hate to interrupt you in such an
important and all-consuming part of your education,
but several things have come to my attention,
and I am afraid that I will require your attentions.
HWOOOOOOOOOO

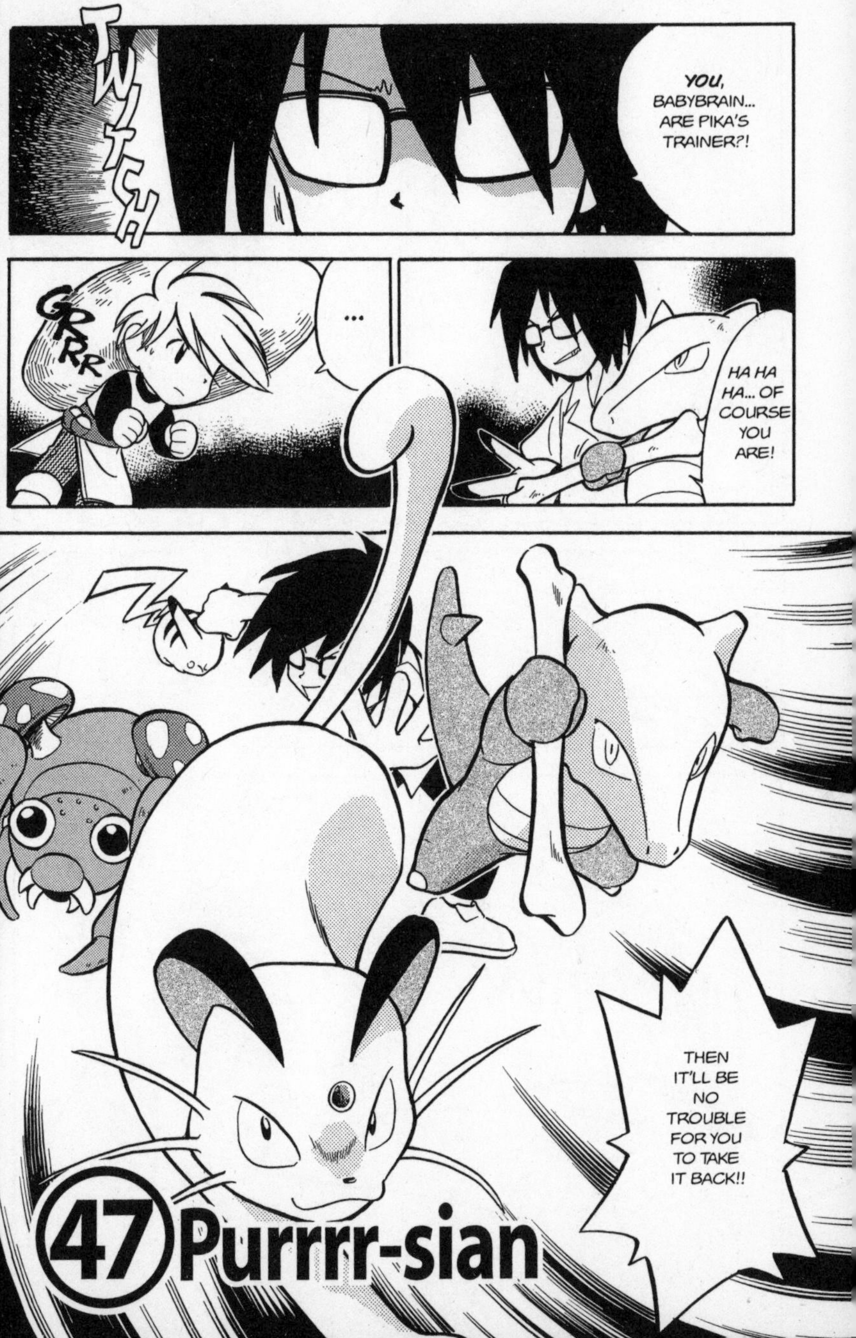
YOU, BABYBRAIN... ARE PIKA'S TRAINER?!
TWITCH
HA HA HA... OF COURSE YOU ARE!
...
GRRR
THEN IT'LL BE NO TROUBLE FOR YOU TO TAKE IT BACK!!
47 Purrrr-sian

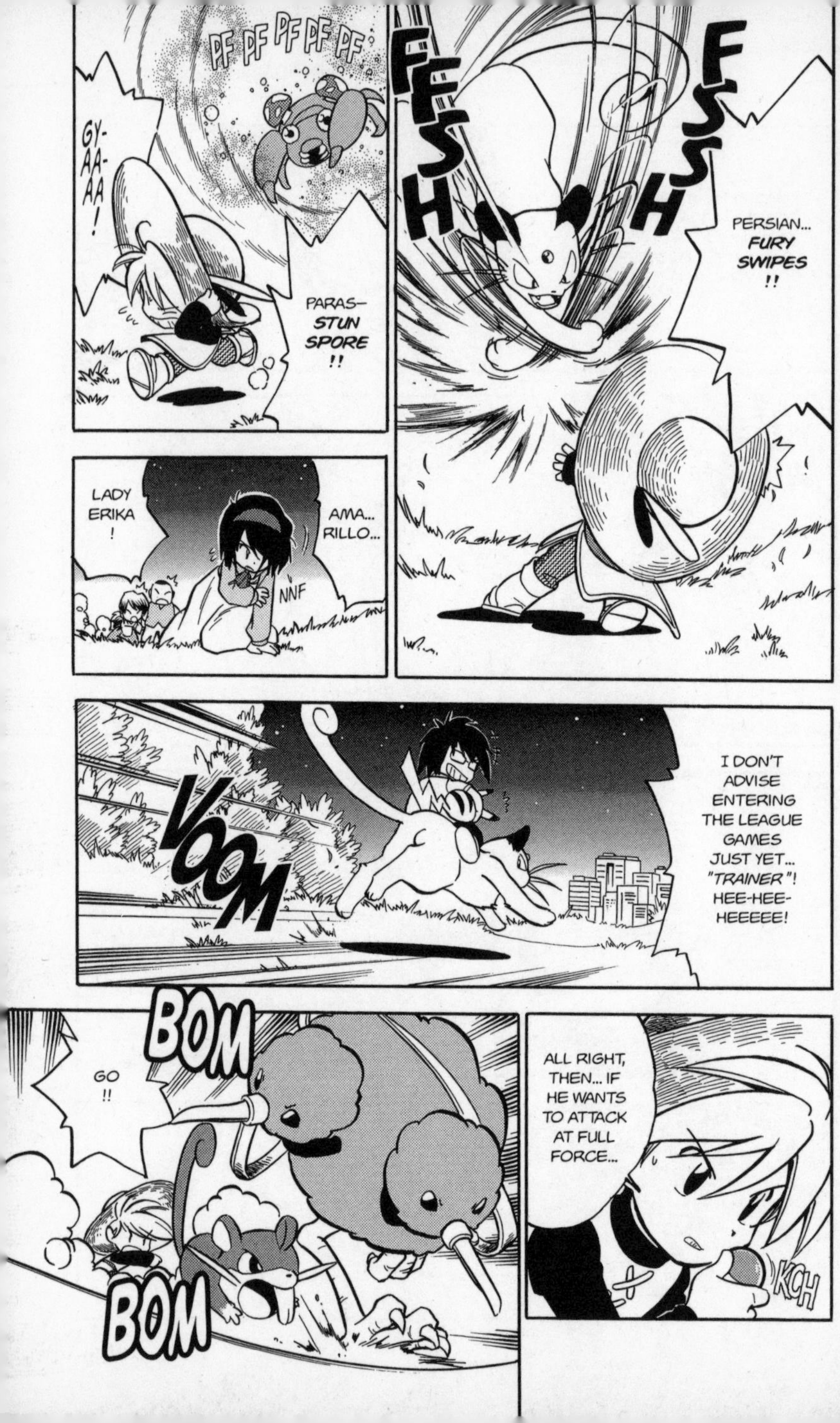
FSSH
FESH
PERSIAN... FURY SWIPES !!
PF PF PF PF PF
GY-AA-AA!
PARAS-STUN SPORE !!
AMA... RILLO...
LADY ERIKA !
NNF
I DON'T ADVISE ENTERING THE LEAGUE GAMES JUST YET... "TRAINER"! HEE-HEE-HEEEEE!
VOOM
ALL RIGHT, THEN... IF HE WANTS TO ATTACK AT FULL FORCE...
KCH
BOM
GO !!
BOM

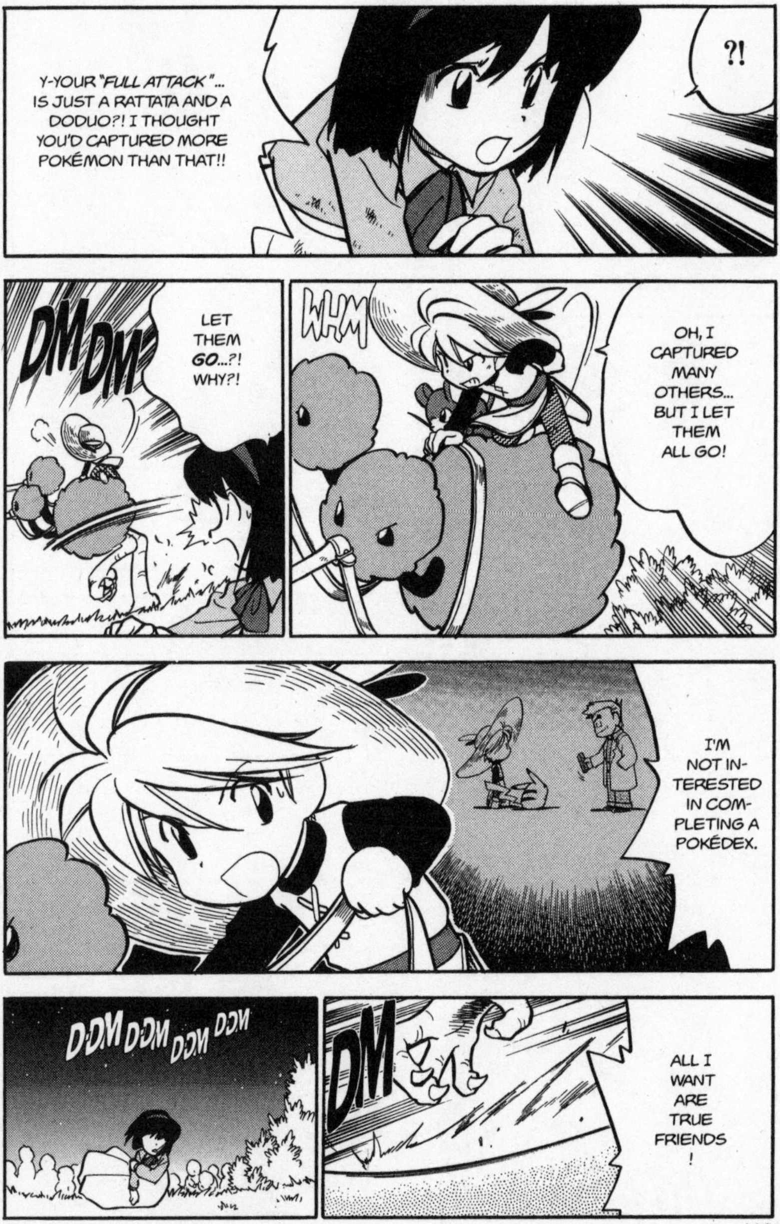
?!
Y-YOUR "FULL ATTACK"... IS JUST A RATTATA AND A DODUO?! I THOUGHT YOU'D CAPTURED MORE POKÉMON THAN THAT!!
WHM
OH, I CAPTURED MANY OTHERS... BUT I LET THEM ALL GO!
DM DM
LET THEM GO...?! WHY?!
I'M NOT INTERESTED IN COMPLETING A POKÉDEX.
DM
ALL I WANT ARE TRUE FRIENDS!
D-DM D-DM D-DM D-DM

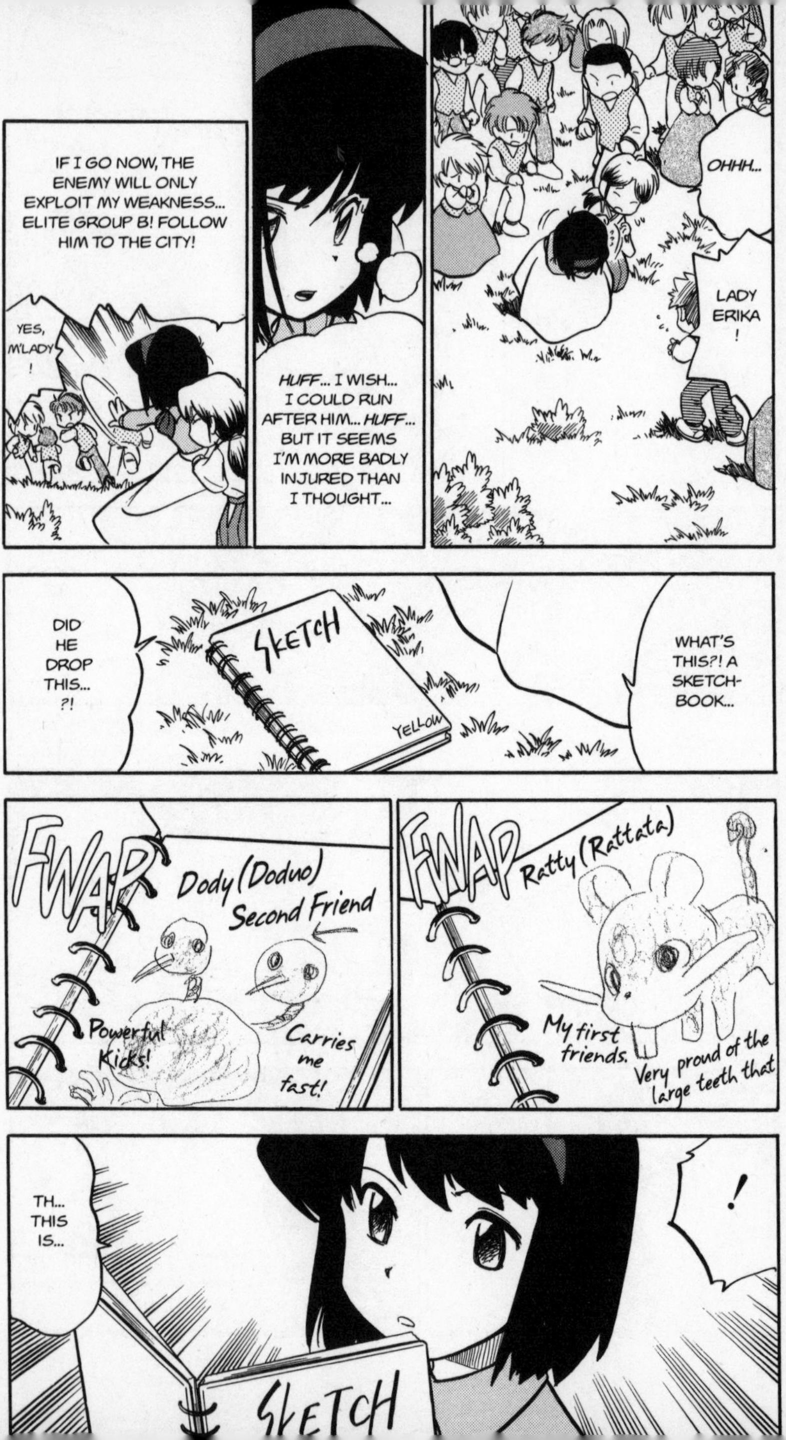
OHHH...
LADY ERIKA!
HUFF... I WISH... I COULD RUN AFTER HIM... HUFF... BUT IT SEEMS I'M MORE BADLY INJURED THAN I THOUGHT...
IF I GO NOW, THE ENEMY WILL ONLY EXPLOIT MY WEAKNESS... ELITE GROUP B! FOLLOW HIM TO THE CITY!
YES, M'LADY!
WHAT'S THIS?! A SKETCH-BOOK...
SKETCH
YELLOW
DID HE DROP THIS...?!
FWAP
Ratty (Rattata)
My first friends.
Very proud of the large teeth that
FWAP
Dody (Doduo)
Second Friend
Powerful Kicks!
Carries me fast!
!
TH... THIS IS...
SKETCH

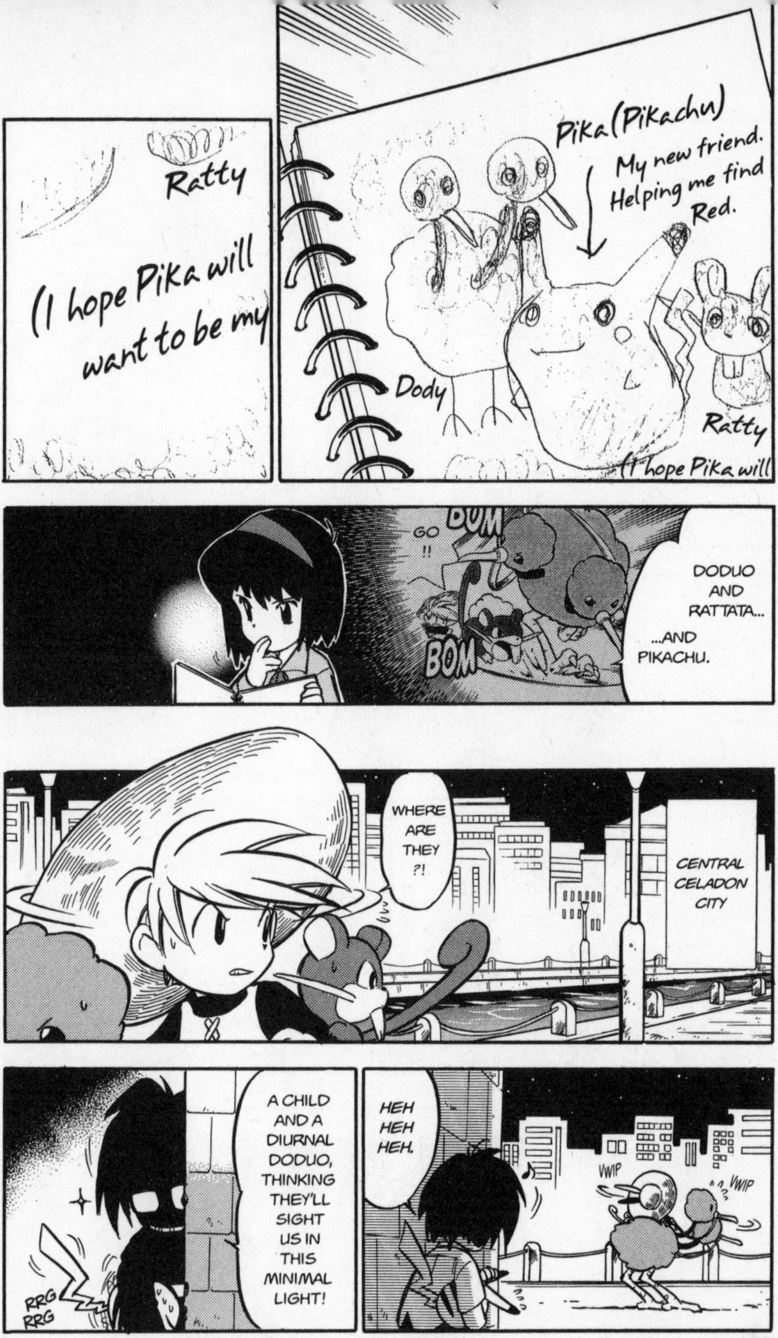
Pika (Pikachu)
My new friend. Helping me find Red.
Dody
Ratty
(I hope Pika will
Ratty
(I hope Pika will want to be my
DODUO AND RATTATA...
...AND PIKACHU.
BOM
GO !!
BOM
CENTRAL CELADON CITY
WHERE ARE THEY ?!
HEH HEH HEH.
VWIP
VWIP
A CHILD AND A DIURNAL DODUO, THINKING THEY'LL SIGHT US IN THIS MINIMAL LIGHT!
RRG RRG

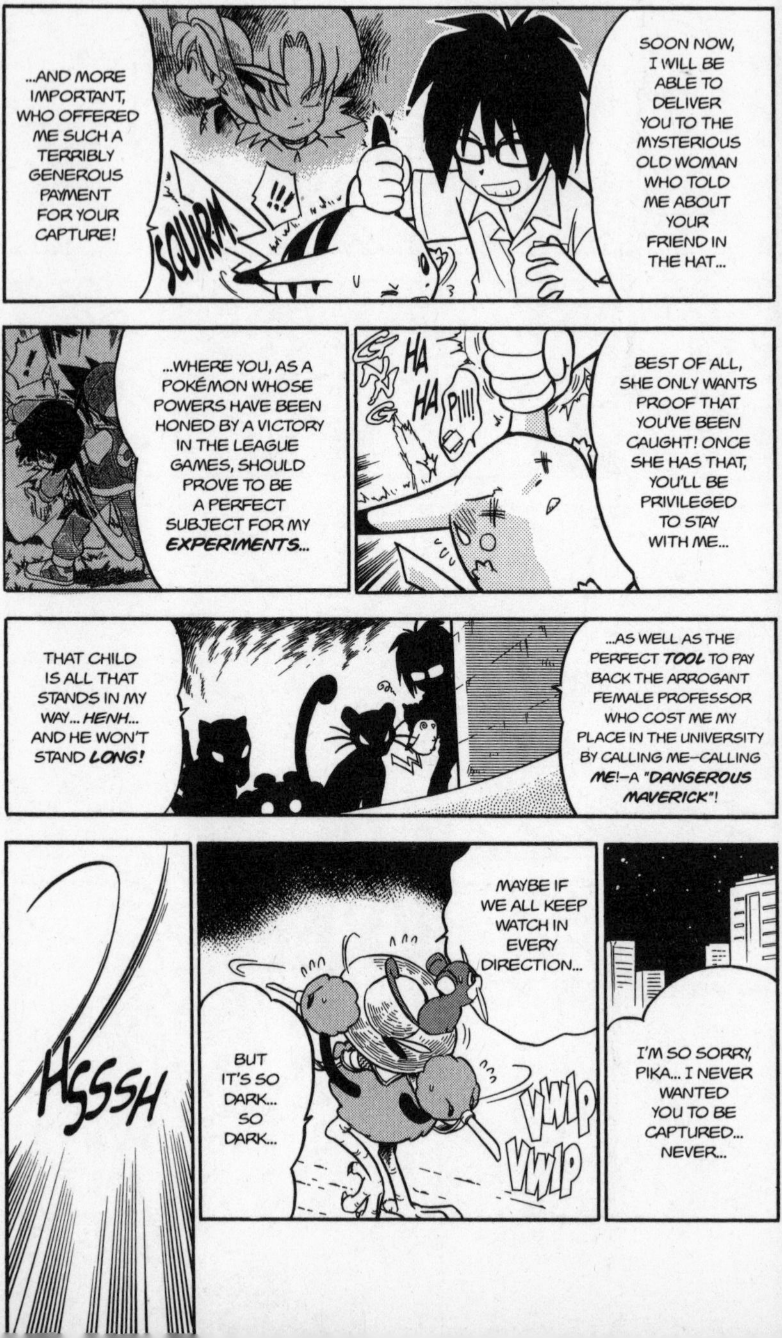
SOON NOW, I WILL BE ABLE TO DELIVER YOU TO THE MYSTERIOUS OLD WOMAN WHO TOLD ME ABOUT YOUR FRIEND IN THE HAT...
!!!
SQUIRM
...AND MORE IMPORTANT, WHO OFFERED ME SUCH A TERRIBLY GENEROUS PAYMENT FOR YOUR CAPTURE!
BEST OF ALL, SHE ONLY WANTS PROOF THAT YOU'VE BEEN CAUGHT! ONCE SHE HAS THAT, YOU'LL BE PRIVILEGED TO STAY WITH ME...
HA HA
PI!!!
...WHERE YOU, AS A POKÉMON WHOSE POWERS HAVE BEEN HONED BY A VICTORY IN THE LEAGUE GAMES, SHOULD PROVE TO BE A PERFECT SUBJECT FOR MY ***EXPERIMENTS***...
...AS WELL AS THE PERFECT ***TOOL*** TO PAY BACK THE ARROGANT FEMALE PROFESSOR WHO COST ME MY PLACE IN THE UNIVERSITY BY CALLING ME—CALLING ***ME***!—A "***DANGEROUS MAVERICK***"!
THAT CHILD IS ALL THAT STANDS IN MY WAY... ***HENH***... AND HE WON'T STAND ***LONG***!
I'M SO SORRY, PIKA... I NEVER WANTED YOU TO BE CAPTURED... NEVER...
MAYBE IF WE ALL KEEP WATCH IN EVERY DIRECTION...
BUT IT'S SO DARK... SO DARK...
VWIP VWIP
HSSSH

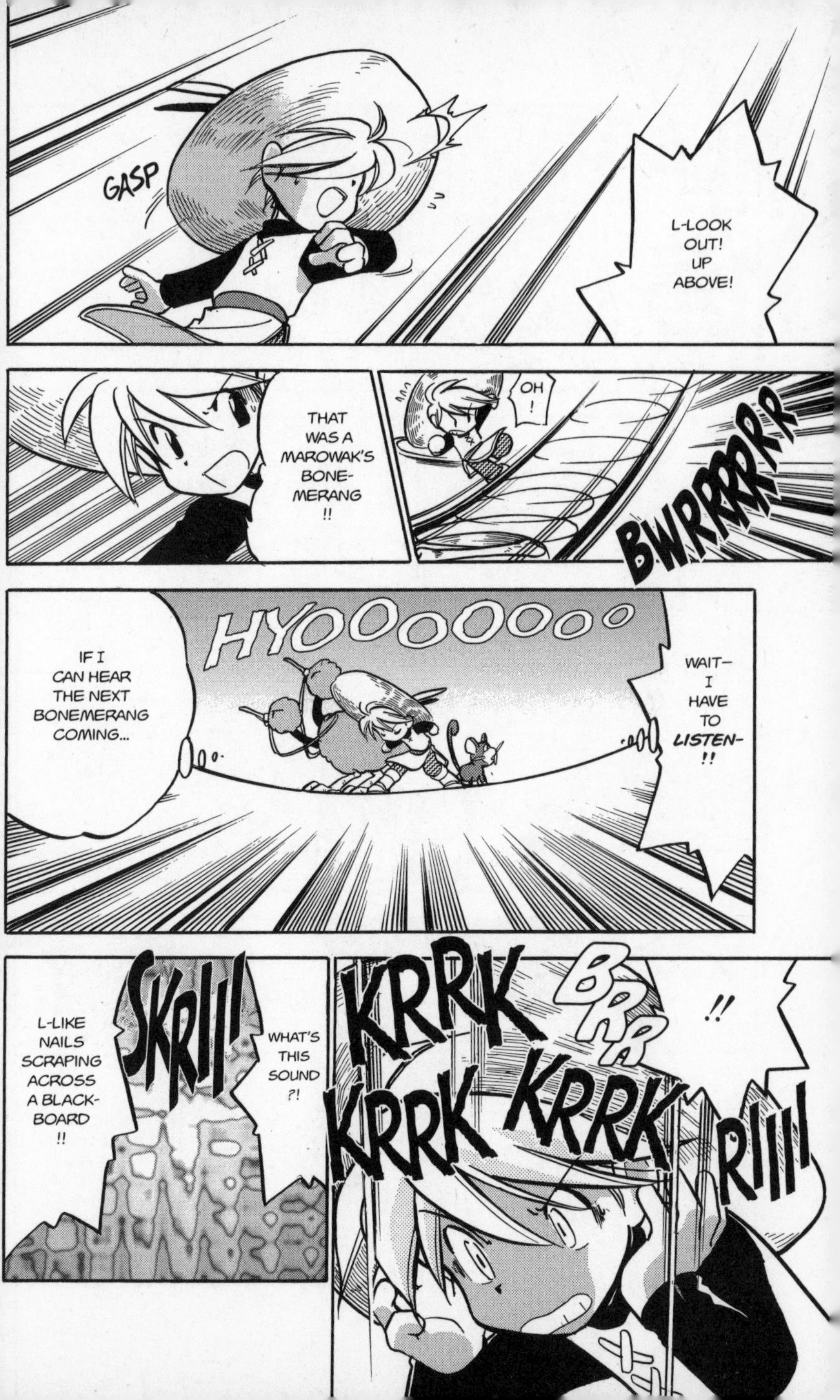
L-LOOK OUT! UP ABOVE!
GASP
OH!
BWRRRRRR
THAT WAS A MAROWAK'S BONE-MERANG!!
HYOOOOOOO
WAIT— I HAVE TO LISTEN—!!
IF I CAN HEAR THE NEXT BONEMERANG COMING...
!!
BRRA
KRRK KRRK KRRK KRRK
RIII
WHAT'S THIS SOUND?!
SKRIII
L-LIKE NAILS SCRAPING ACROSS A BLACK-BOARD!!

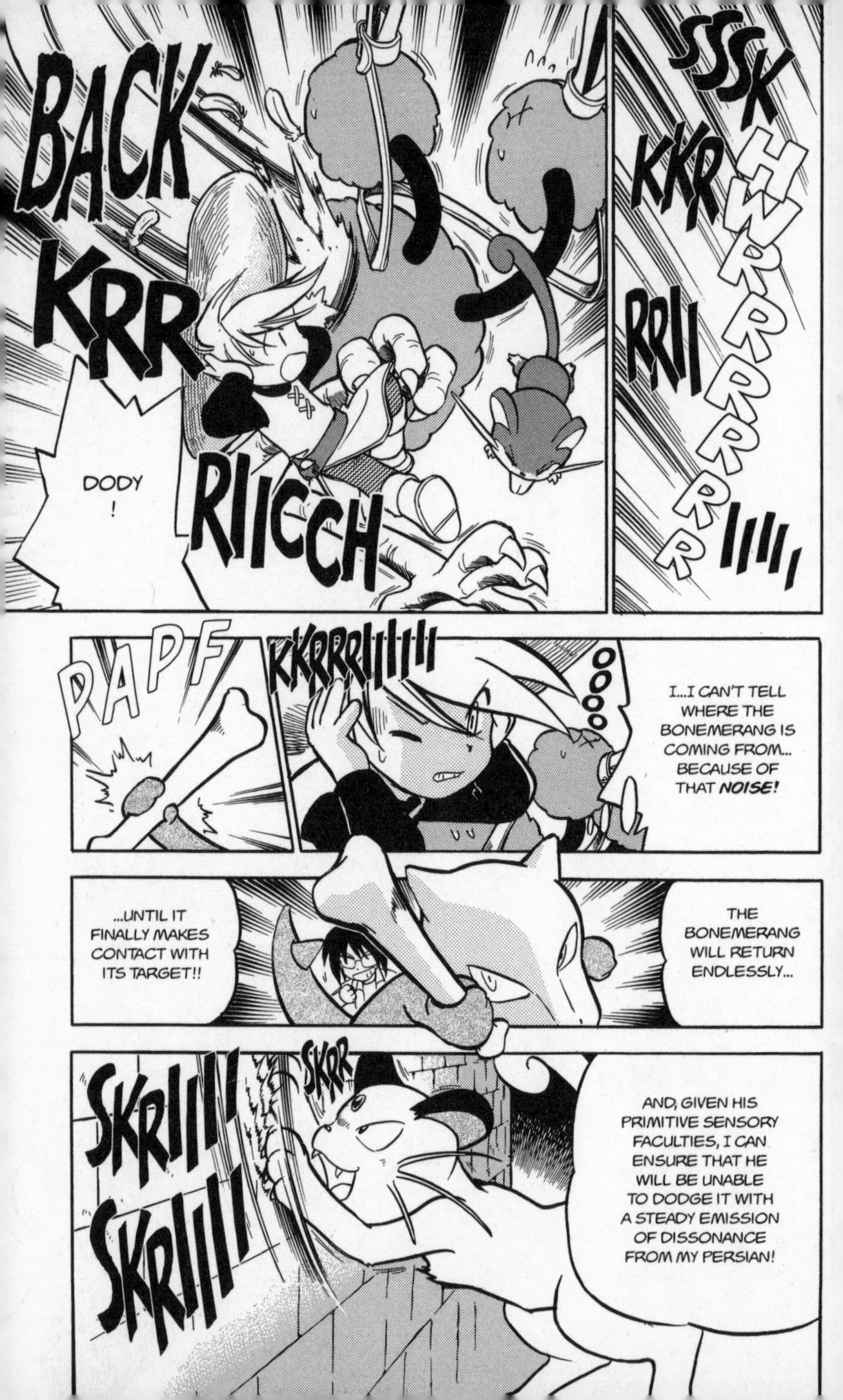

SSSK
KKR
RRII
HWRRRRRRRIIII
BACK
KRR
DODY!
RIICCH
OOOO
I...I CAN'T TELL WHERE THE BONEMERANG IS COMING FROM... BECAUSE OF THAT ***NOISE!***
KKRRRIIIIII
PAPF
THE BONEMERANG WILL RETURN ENDLESSLY...
...UNTIL IT FINALLY MAKES CONTACT WITH ITS TARGET!!
AND, GIVEN HIS PRIMITIVE SENSORY FACULTIES, I CAN ENSURE THAT HE WILL BE UNABLE TO DODGE IT WITH A STEADY EMISSION OF DISSONANCE FROM MY PERSIAN!
SKRR
SKRIIII
SKRIIII

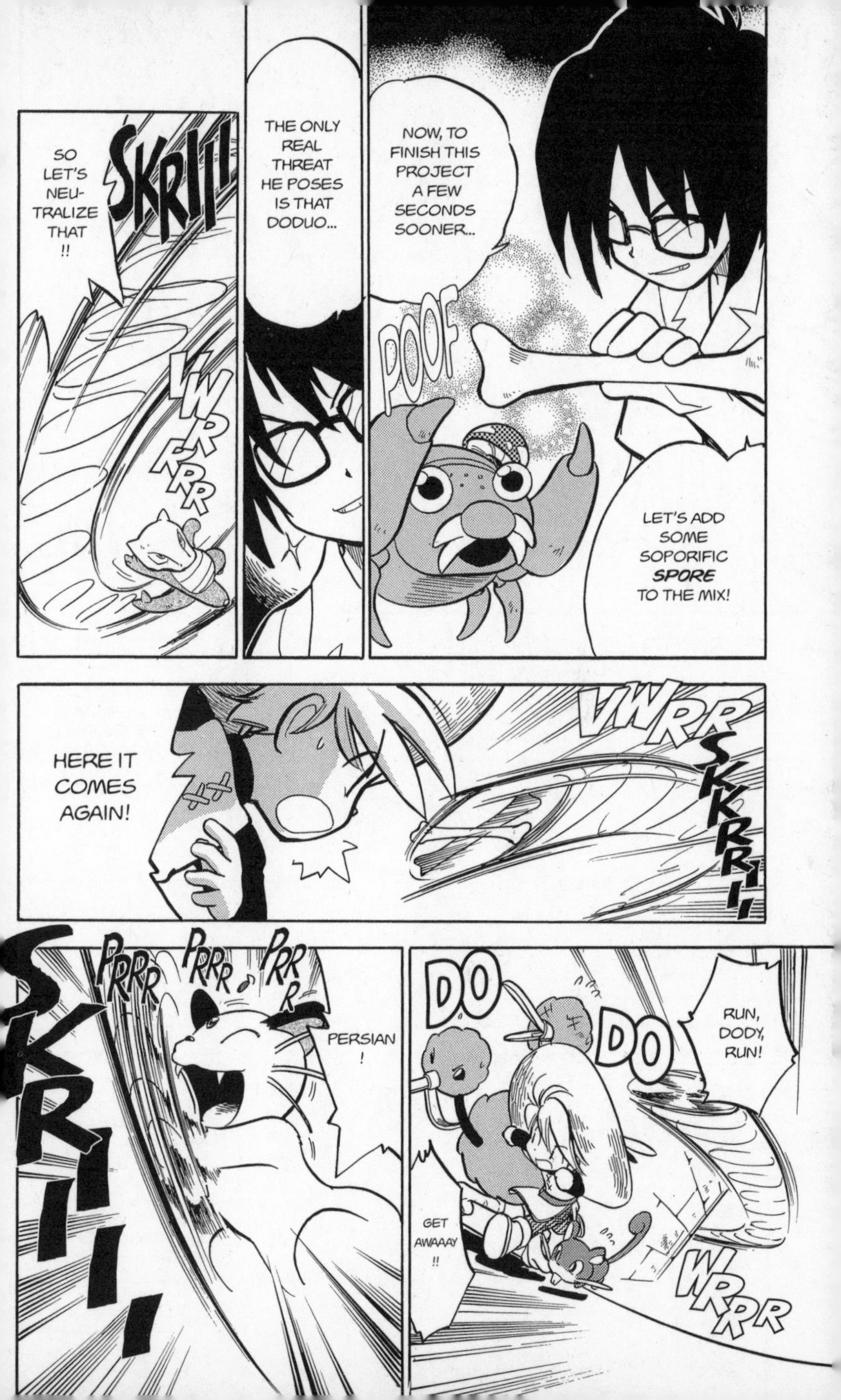
NOW, TO FINISH THIS PROJECT A FEW SECONDS SOONER...
POOF
LET'S ADD SOME SOPORIFIC **SPORE** TO THE MIX!
THE ONLY REAL THREAT HE POSES IS THAT DODUO...
SKRIII
SO LET'S NEU-TRALIZE THAT !!
VWRRRR
VWRR
SKKRRII
HERE IT COMES AGAIN!
RUN, DODY, RUN!
DO
DO
GET AWAAAY !!
WRRR
PRRR
PRRR
PRRR
PERSIAN !
SKRII

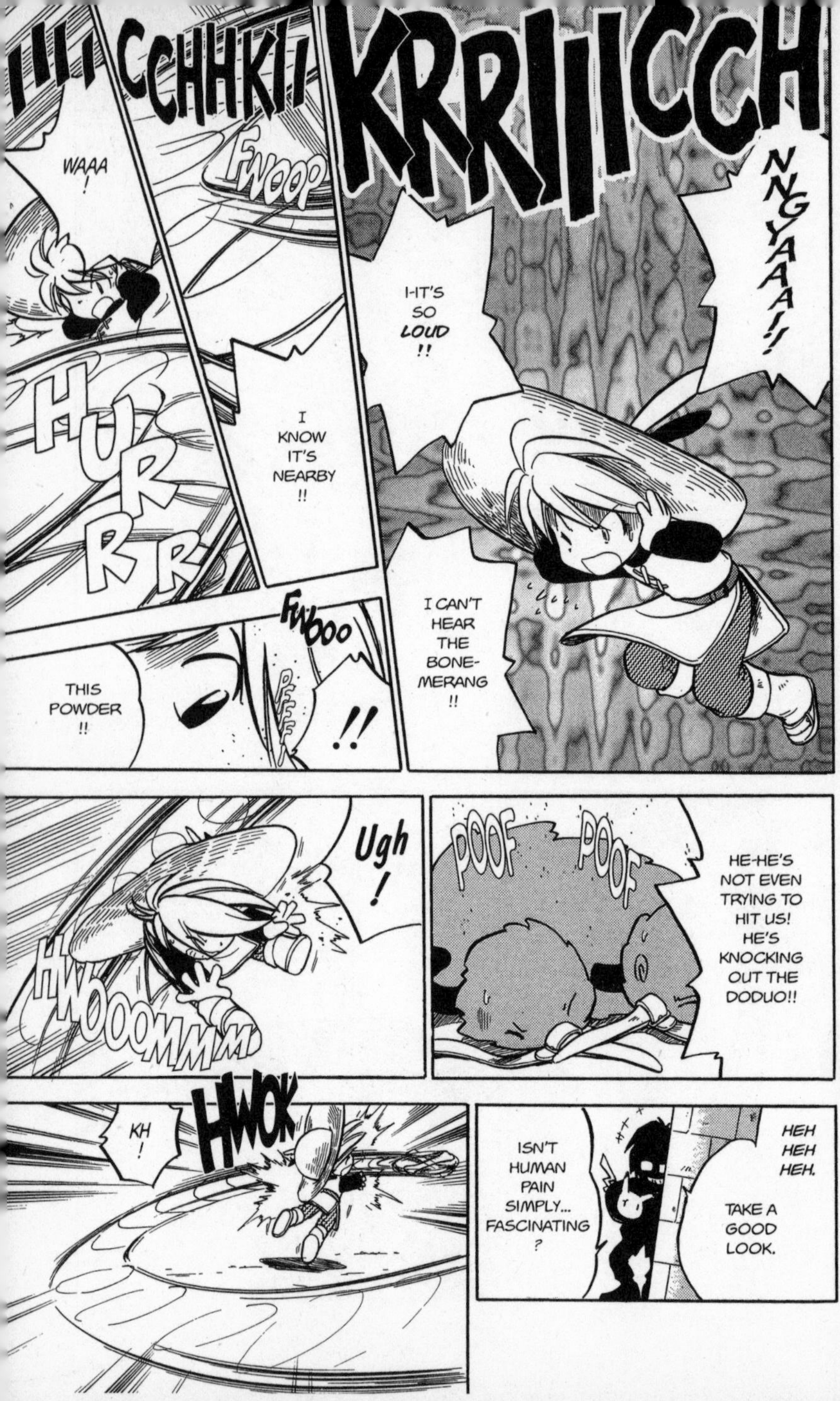

KRRIIICCH
NNGYAAAA!!
I-IT'S SO LOUD!!
I CAN'T HEAR THE BONE-MERANG!!
CCHHKII
FWOOP
I KNOW IT'S NEARBY!!
WAAA!
HURRR
FWOOO
PFFF
!!
THIS POWDER!!
POOF POOF
HE-HE'S NOT EVEN TRYING TO HIT US! HE'S KNOCKING OUT THE DODUO!!
Ugh!
HWOOOMMM
HEH HEH HEH.
TAKE A GOOD LOOK.
ISN'T HUMAN PAIN SIMPLY... FASCINATING?
HWOK
KH!

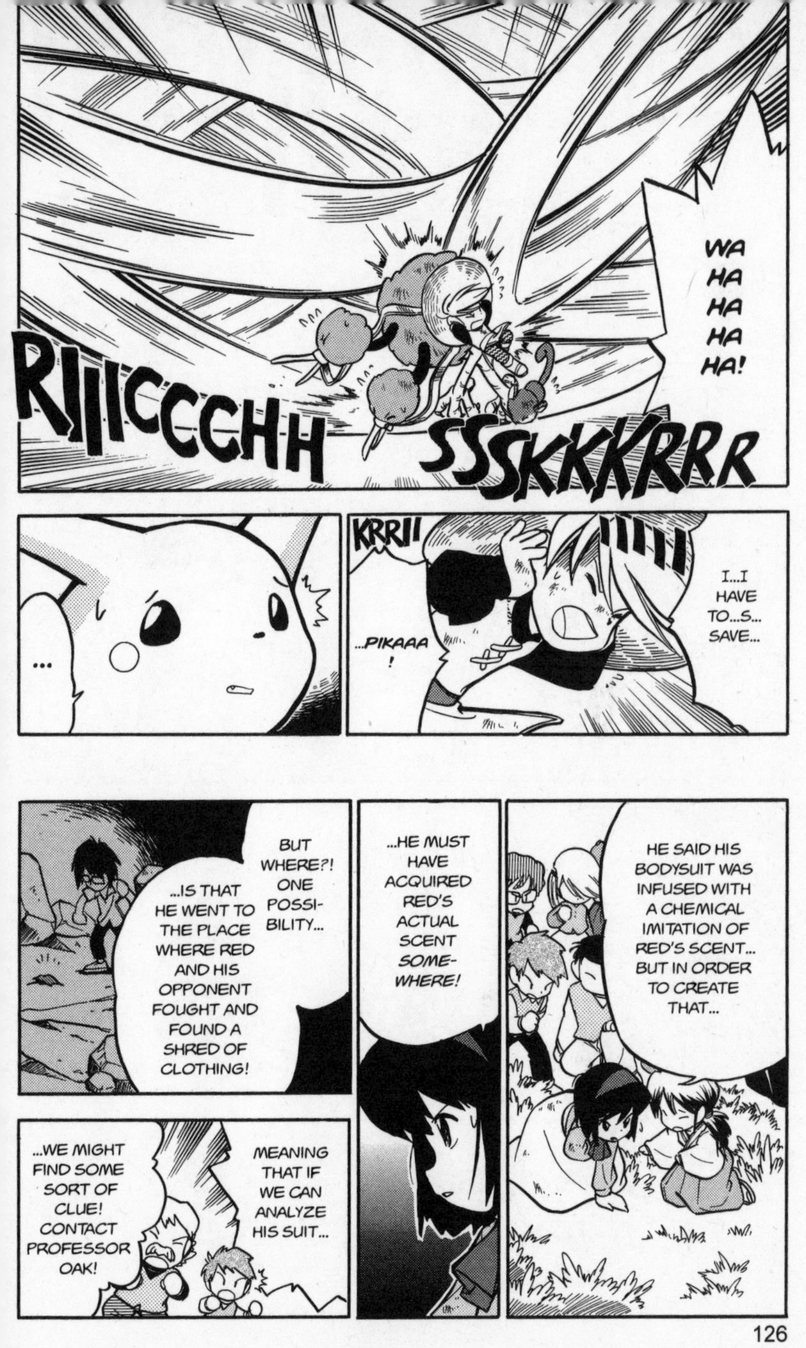
WA HA HA HA HA!
RIIICCCHH
SSSKKKRRR
KRRII
I...I HAVE TO...S... SAVE...
...PIKAAA!
...
HE SAID HIS BODYSUIT WAS INFUSED WITH A CHEMICAL IMITATION OF RED'S SCENT... BUT IN ORDER TO CREATE THAT...
...HE MUST HAVE ACQUIRED RED'S ACTUAL SCENT SOME-WHERE!
BUT WHERE?! ONE POSSI-BILITY...
...IS THAT HE WENT TO THE PLACE WHERE RED AND HIS OPPONENT FOUGHT AND FOUND A SHRED OF CLOTHING!
MEANING THAT IF WE CAN ANALYZE HIS SUIT...
...WE MIGHT FIND SOME SORT OF CLUE! CONTACT PROFESSOR OAK!

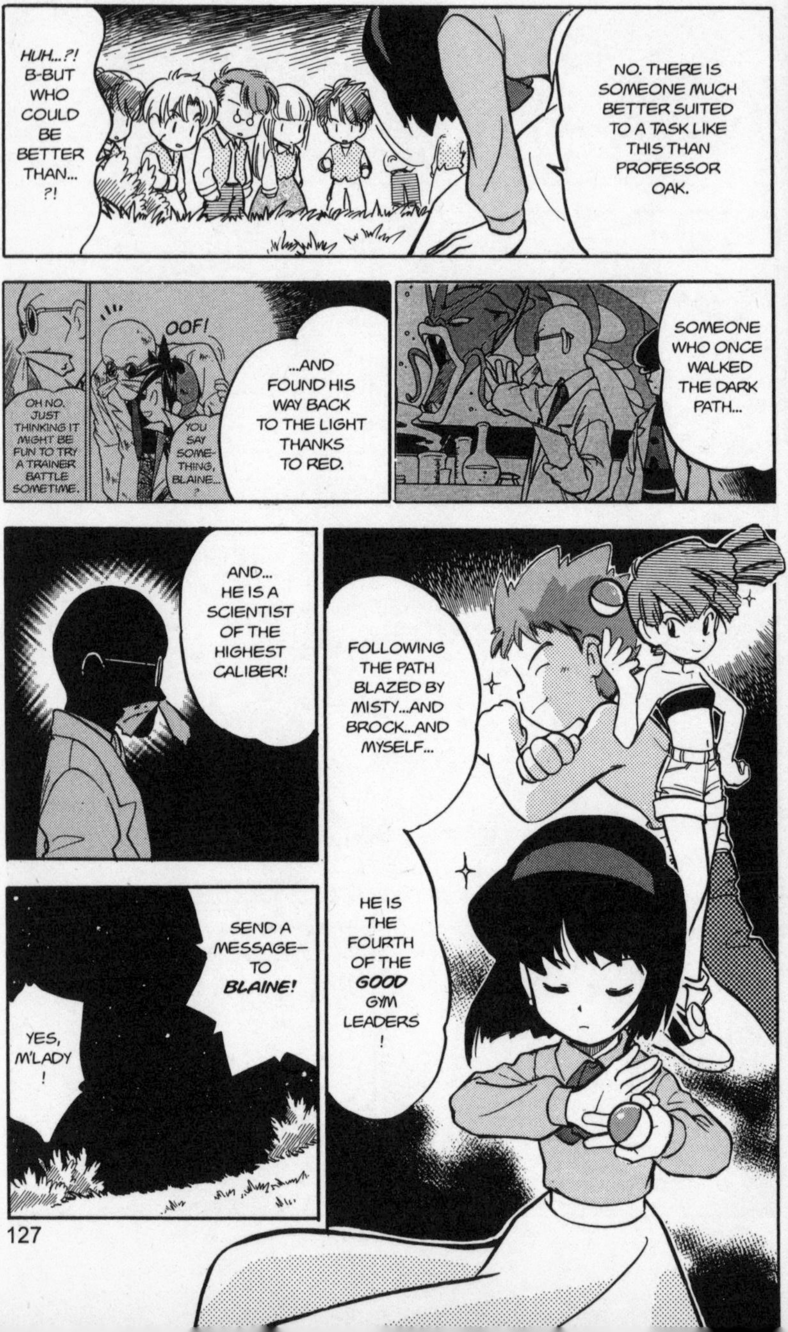
NO. THERE IS SOMEONE MUCH BETTER SUITED TO A TASK LIKE THIS THAN PROFESSOR OAK.
HUH...?! B-BUT WHO COULD BE BETTER THAN... ?!
SOMEONE WHO ONCE WALKED THE DARK PATH...
...AND FOUND HIS WAY BACK TO THE LIGHT THANKS TO RED.
OOF!
YOU SAY SOME-THING, BLAINE...
OH NO. JUST THINKING IT MIGHT BE FUN TO TRY A TRAINER BATTLE SOMETIME.
FOLLOWING THE PATH BLAZED BY MISTY...AND BROCK...AND MYSELF...
HE IS THE FOURTH OF THE GOOD GYM LEADERS!
AND... HE IS A SCIENTIST OF THE HIGHEST CALIBER!
SEND A MESSAGE— TO BLAINE!
YES, M'LADY!

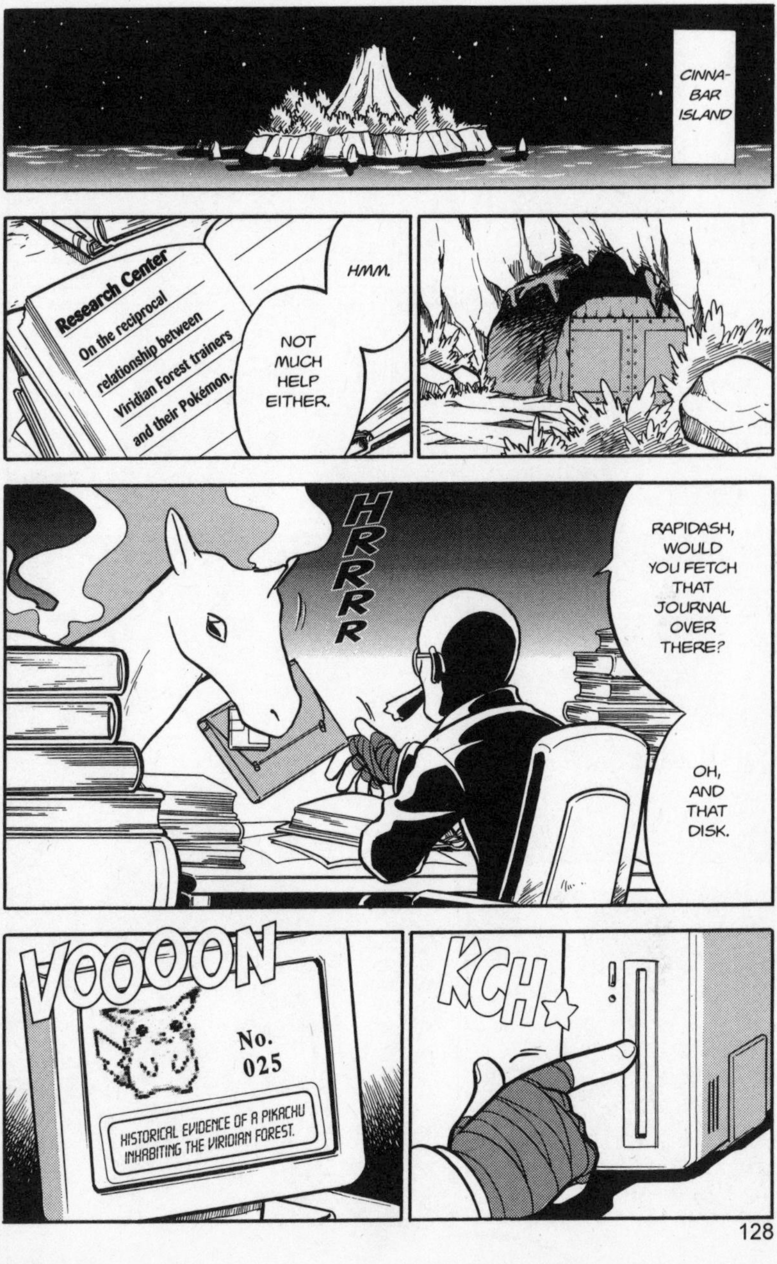
CINNA-BAR ISLAND
HMM.
NOT MUCH HELP EITHER.
Research Center
On the reciprocal relationship between Viridian Forest trainers and their Pokémon.
RAPIDASH, WOULD YOU FETCH THAT JOURNAL OVER THERE?
HRRRR
OH, AND THAT DISK.
KCH
VOOOON
No. 025
HISTORICAL EVIDENCE OF A PIKACHU INHABITING THE VIRIDIAN FOREST.

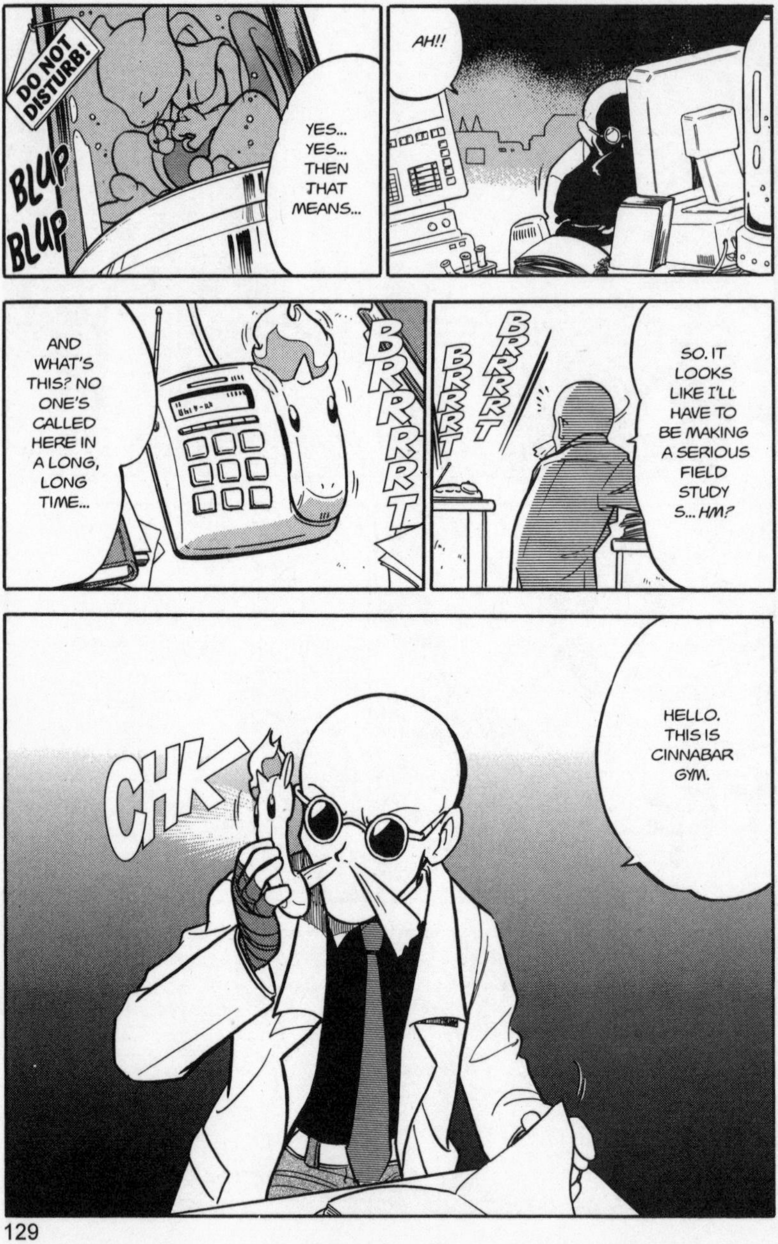
AH!!
YES... YES... THEN THAT MEANS...
DO NOT DISTURB!
BLUP BLUP
SO. IT LOOKS LIKE I'LL HAVE TO BE MAKING A SERIOUS FIELD STUDY S... HM?
BRRRRT
BRRRRT
BRRRRRT
AND WHAT'S THIS? NO ONE'S CALLED HERE IN A LONG, LONG TIME...
HELLO. THIS IS CINNABAR GYM.
CHK

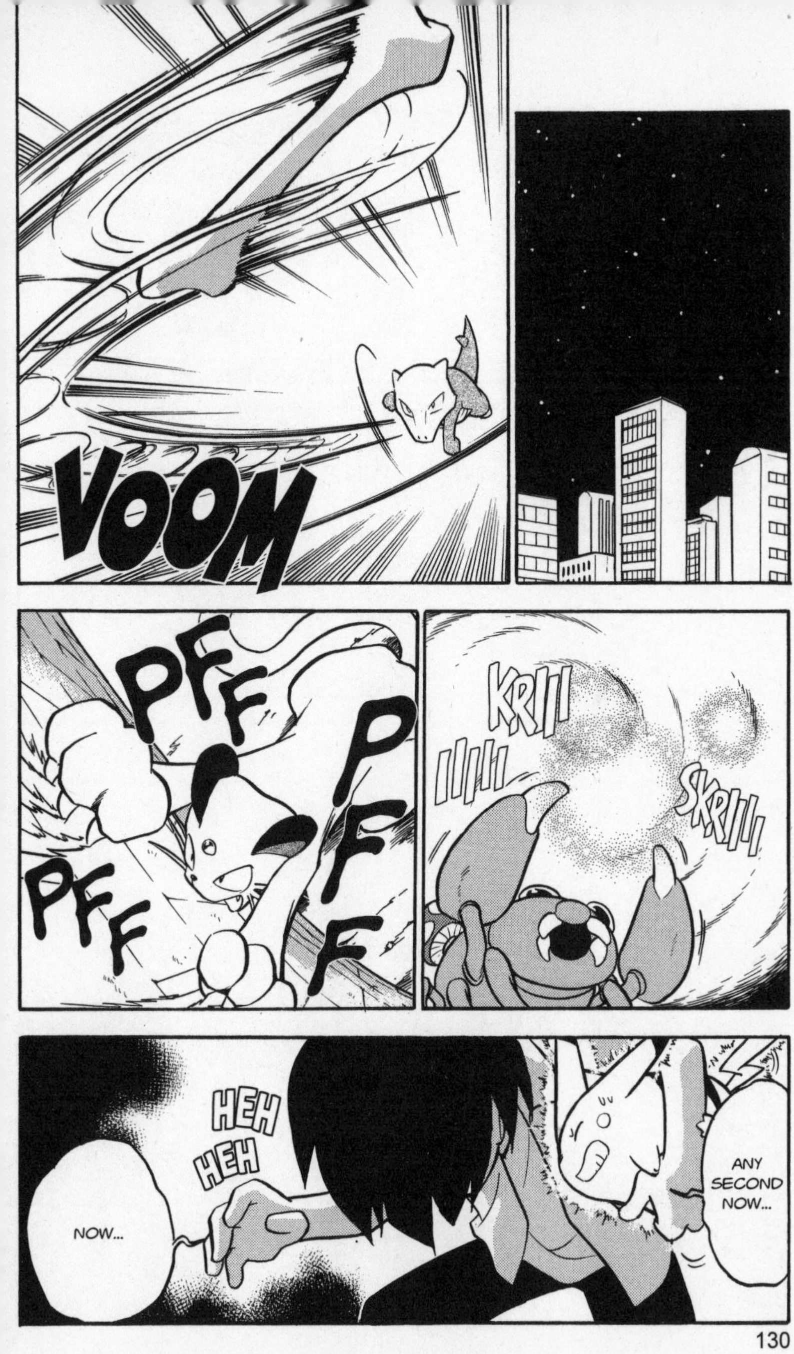

VOOM
KRIII
IIIII
SKRIIII
PFFF
PFFF
PFFF
ANY SECOND NOW...
HEH HEH
NOW...

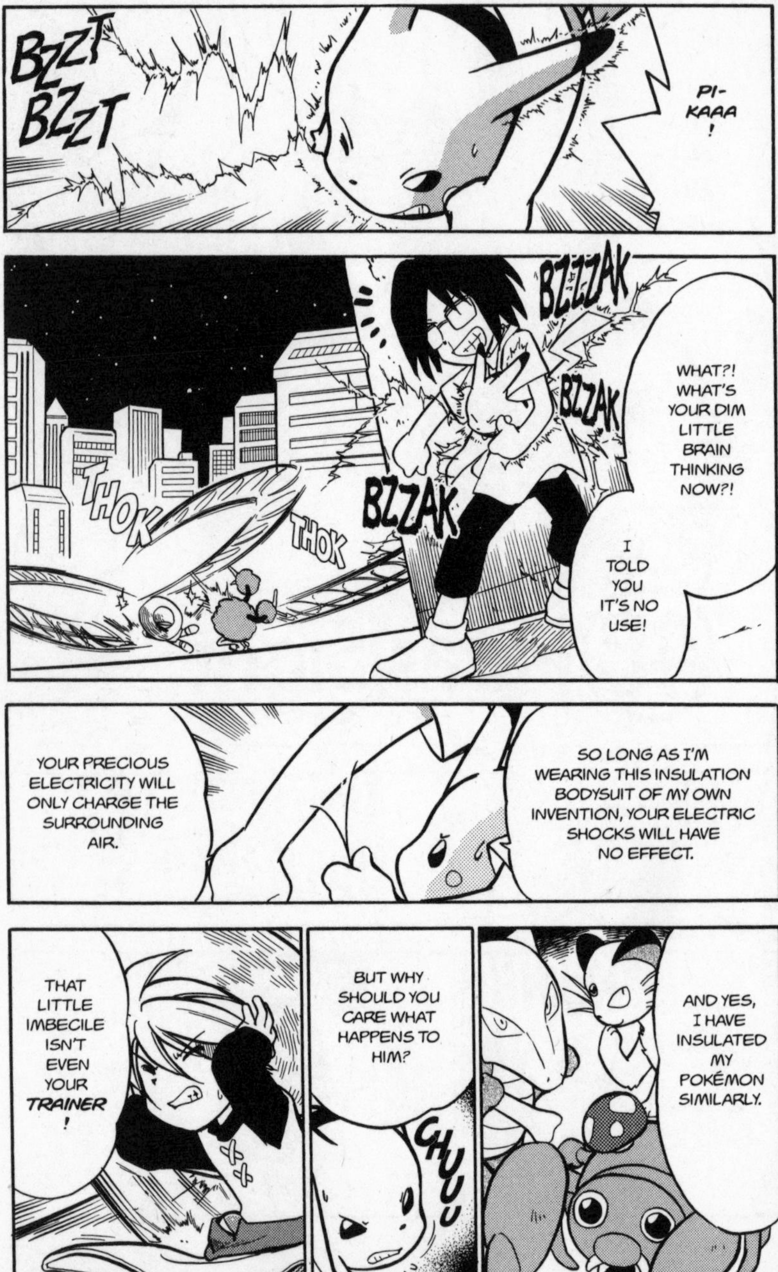
BZZZT BZZZT
PI-KAAA!
BZZZAK
WHAT?! WHAT'S YOUR DIM LITTLE BRAIN THINKING NOW?!
BZZAK
I TOLD YOU IT'S NO USE!
BZZAK
THOK
THOK
SO LONG AS I'M WEARING THIS INSULATION BODYSUIT OF MY OWN INVENTION, YOUR ELECTRIC SHOCKS WILL HAVE NO EFFECT.
YOUR PRECIOUS ELECTRICITY WILL ONLY CHARGE THE SURROUNDING AIR.
AND YES, I HAVE INSULATED MY POKÉMON SIMILARLY.
BUT WHY SHOULD YOU CARE WHAT HAPPENS TO HIM?
CHUUU
THAT LITTLE IMBECILE ISN'T EVEN YOUR *TRAINER*!

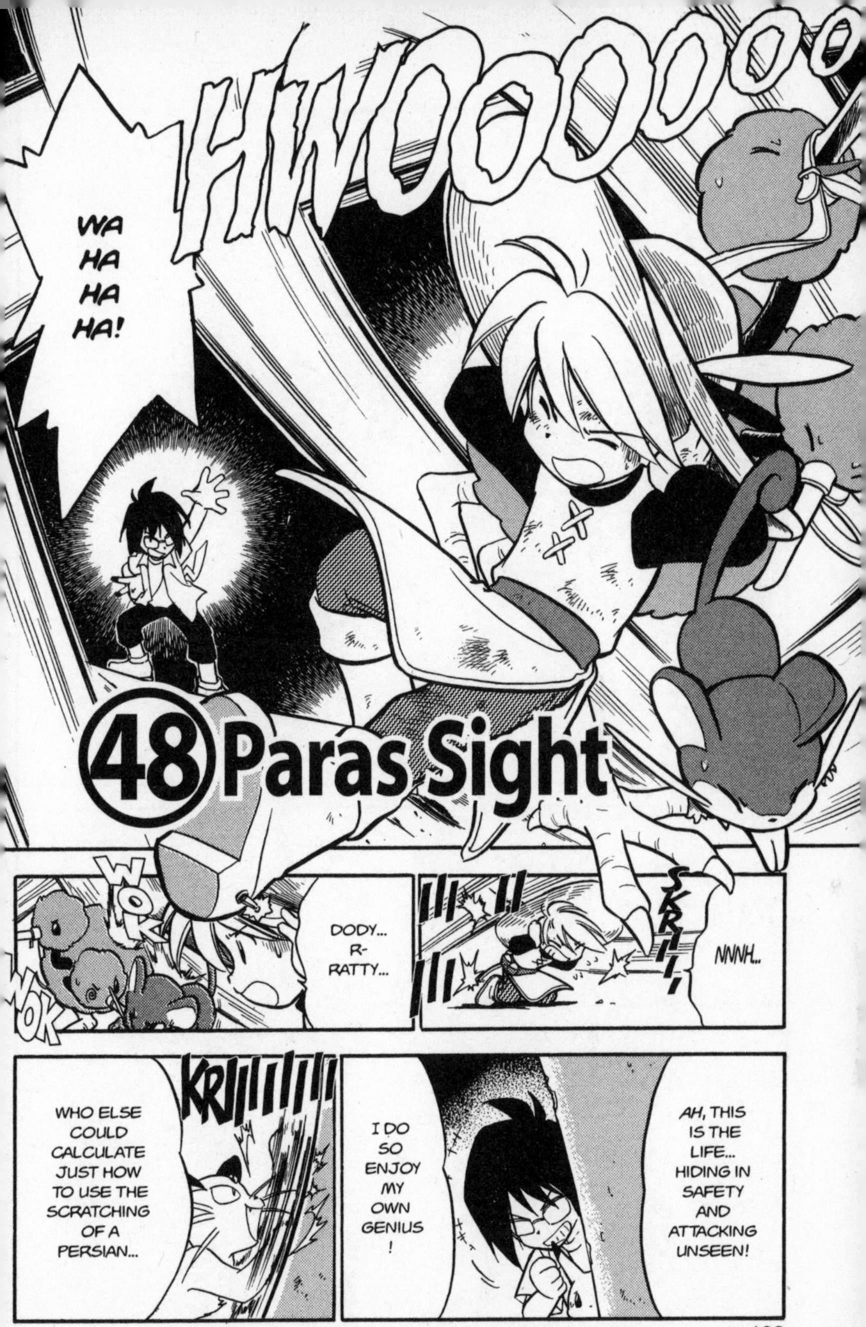
HWOOOOOOO
WA HA HA HA!
48 Paras Sight
SKRIIII
NNNH...
WOK
DODY... R-RATTY...
WOK
AH, THIS IS THE LIFE... HIDING IN SAFETY AND ATTACKING UNSEEN!
I DO SO ENJOY MY OWN GENIUS!
KRIIIIIII
WHO ELSE COULD CALCULATE JUST HOW TO USE THE SCRATCHING OF A PERSIAN...

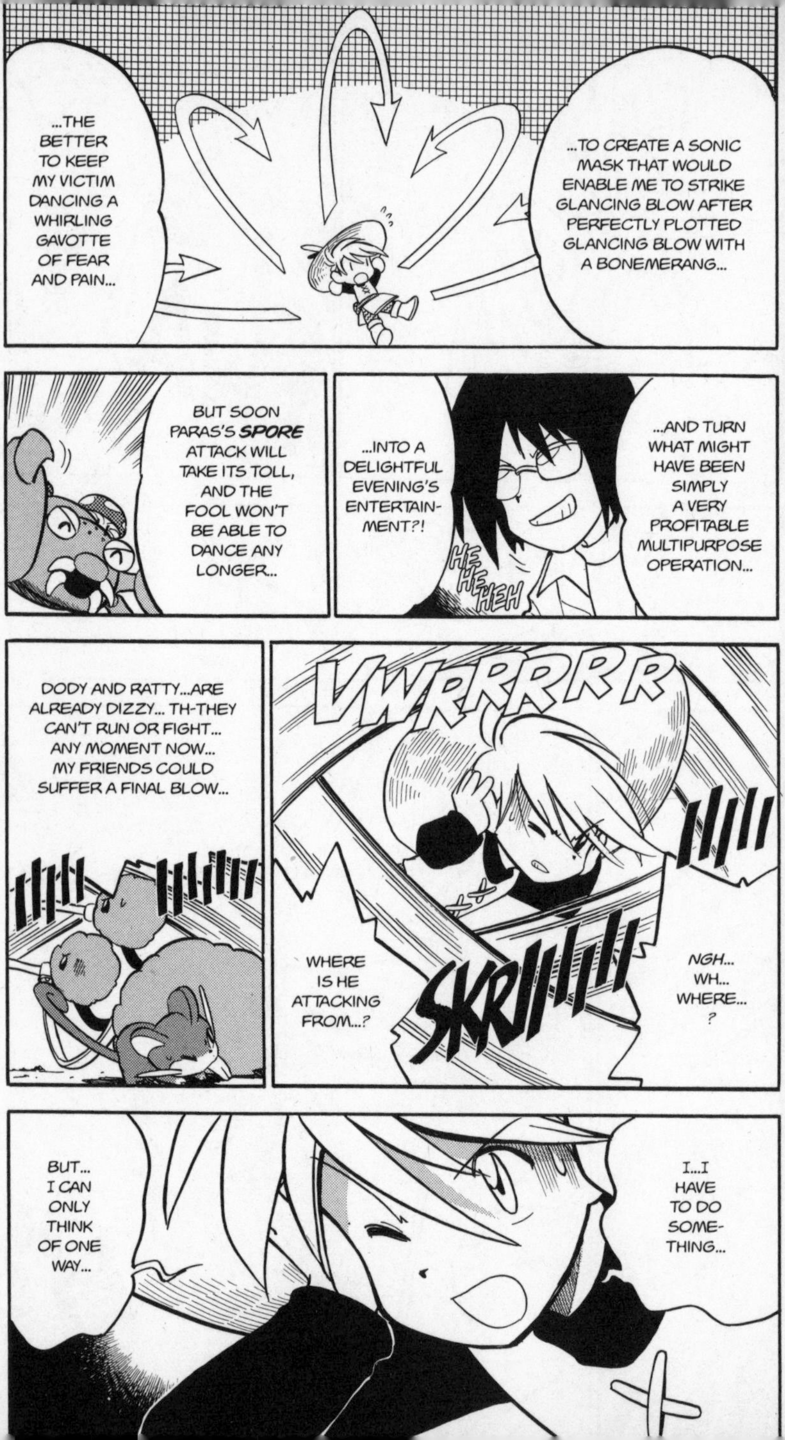
...TO CREATE A SONIC MASK THAT WOULD ENABLE ME TO STRIKE GLANCING BLOW AFTER PERFECTLY PLOTTED GLANCING BLOW WITH A BONEMERANG...
...THE BETTER TO KEEP MY VICTIM DANCING A WHIRLING GAVOTTE OF FEAR AND PAIN...
...AND TURN WHAT MIGHT HAVE BEEN SIMPLY A VERY PROFITABLE MULTIPURPOSE OPERATION...
...INTO A DELIGHTFUL EVENING'S ENTERTAIN-MENT?!
HE HE HEH
BUT SOON PARAS'S **SPORE** ATTACK WILL TAKE ITS TOLL, AND THE FOOL WON'T BE ABLE TO DANCE ANY LONGER...
VWRRRRR
NGH... WH... WHERE...?
WHERE IS HE ATTACKING FROM...?
SKRIIIII
DODY AND RATTY...ARE ALREADY DIZZY... TH-THEY CAN'T RUN OR FIGHT... ANY MOMENT NOW... MY FRIENDS COULD SUFFER A FINAL BLOW...
I...I HAVE TO DO SOME-THING...
BUT... I CAN ONLY THINK OF ONE WAY...

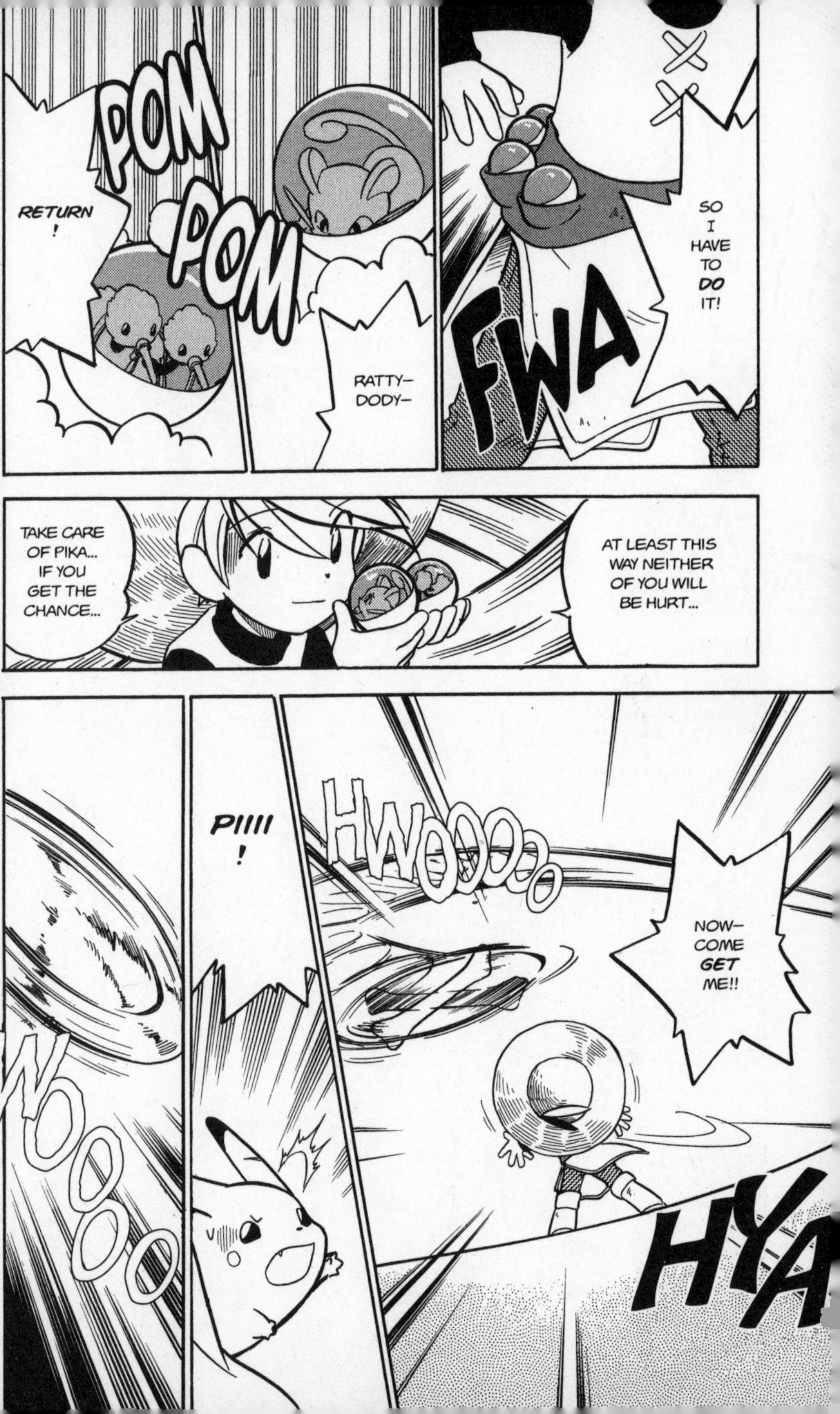
SO I HAVE TO DO IT!
FWA
RATTY—DODY—
POM POM
RETURN!
AT LEAST THIS WAY NEITHER OF YOU WILL BE HURT...
TAKE CARE OF PIKA... IF YOU GET THE CHANCE...
HWOOOOO
NOW— COME GET ME!!
HYA
PIIII!
WOOOOOO

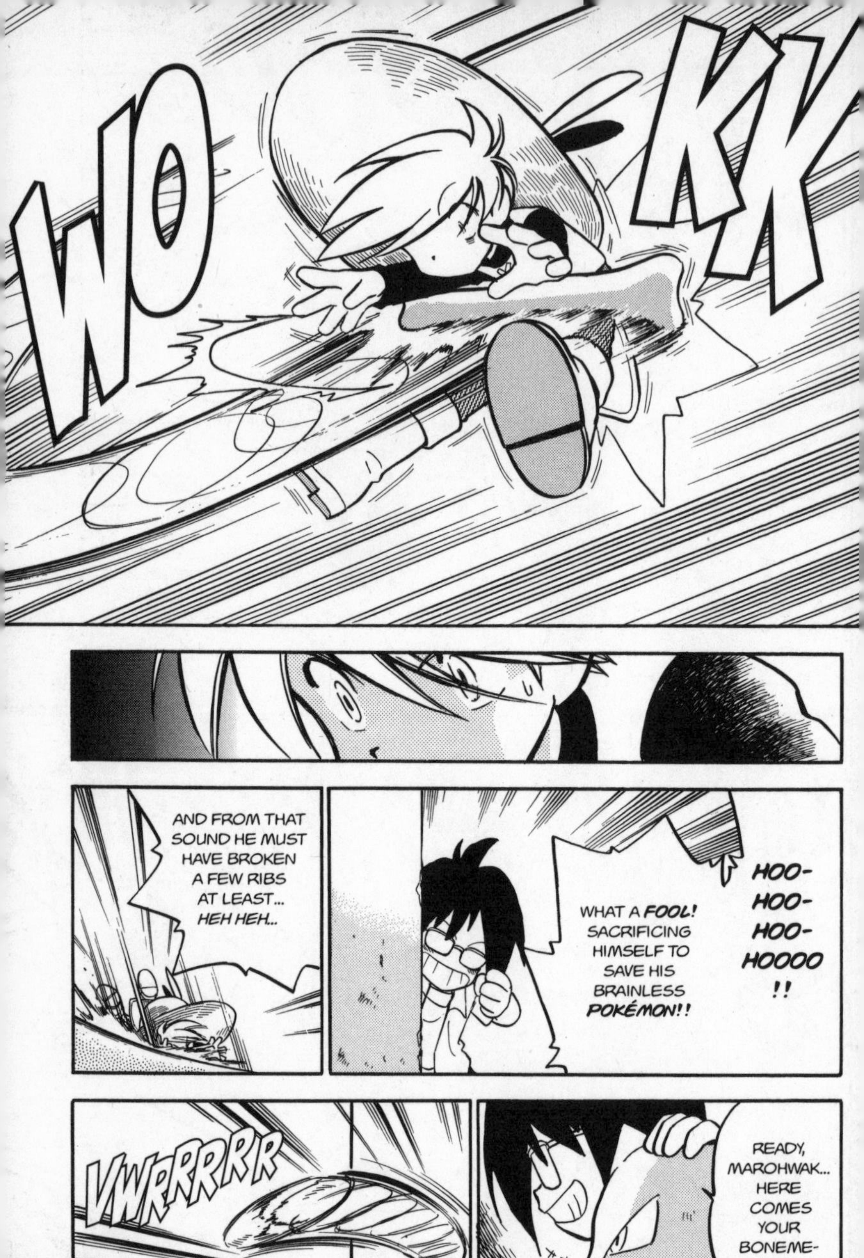
WOKK
HOO-HOO-HOO-HOOOO!!
WHAT A **FOOL**! SACRIFICING HIMSELF TO SAVE HIS BRAINLESS **POKÉMON**!!
AND FROM THAT SOUND HE MUST HAVE BROKEN A FEW RIBS AT LEAST... **HEH HEH...**
READY, MAROHWAK... HERE COMES YOUR BONEME-RANG!
VWRRRRR

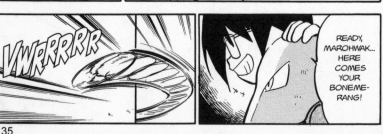

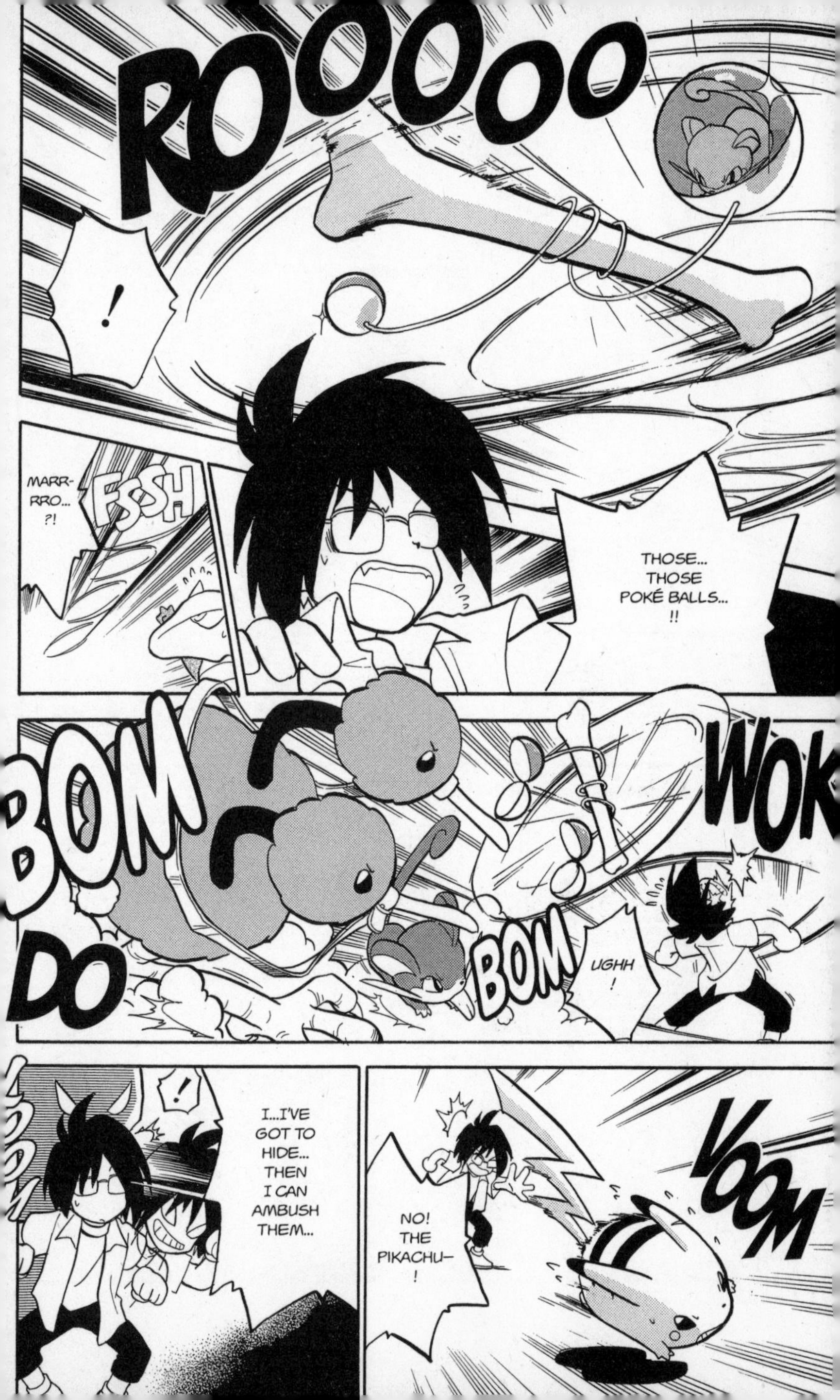
ROOOOO
!
THOSE... THOSE POKÉ BALLS... !!
FSSH
MARR-RRO... ?!
WOK
UGHH !
BOM
BOM
DO
VOOM
NO! THE PIKACHU— !
I...I'VE GOT TO HIDE... THEN I CAN AMBUSH THEM...
!

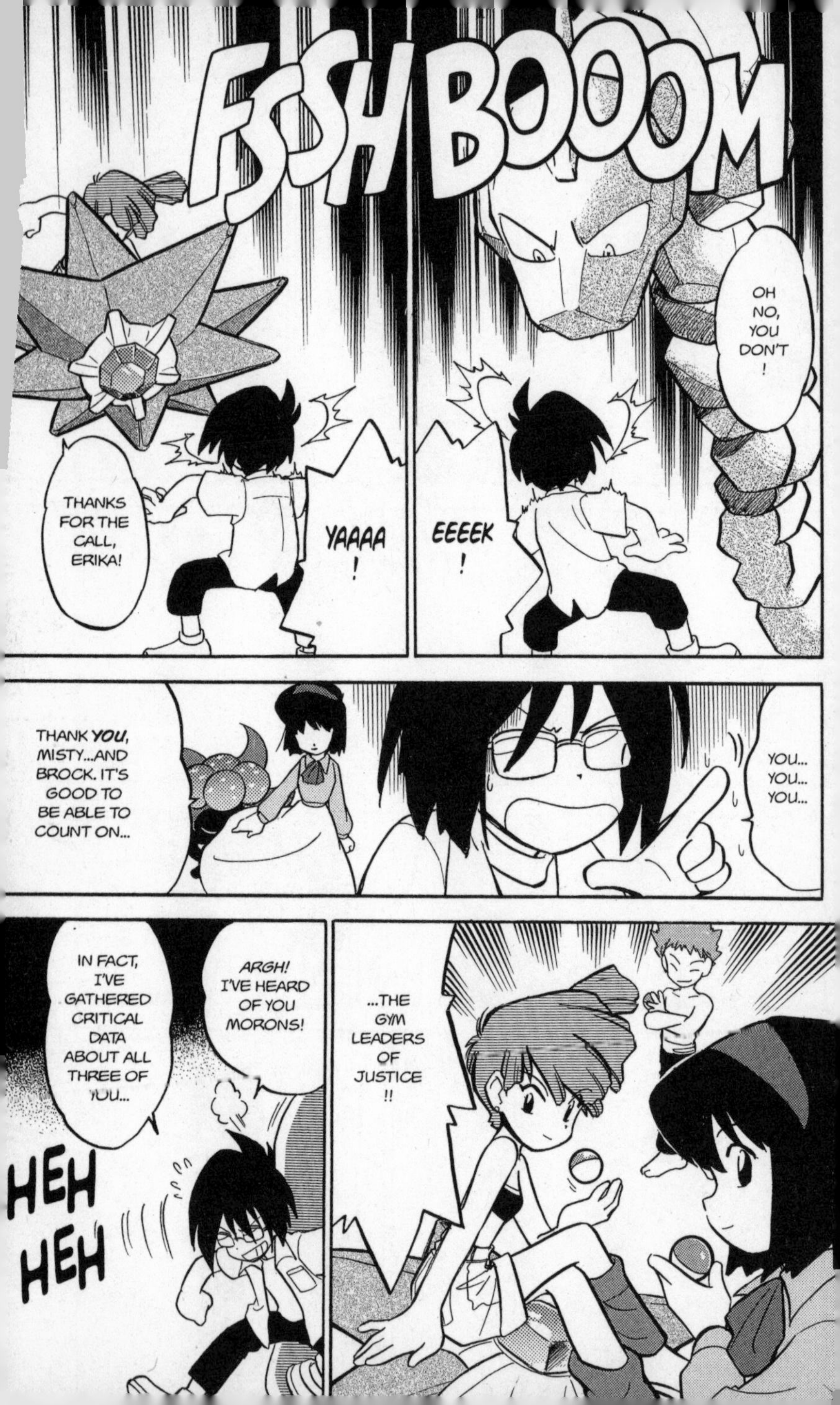
FSH BOOOOM
OH NO, YOU DON'T!
EEEEK!
THANKS FOR THE CALL, ERIKA!
YAAAA!
YOU... YOU... YOU...
THANK *YOU*, MISTY...AND BROCK. IT'S GOOD TO BE ABLE TO COUNT ON...
...THE GYM LEADERS OF JUSTICE!!
ARGH! I'VE HEARD OF YOU MORONS!
IN FACT, I'VE GATHERED CRITICAL DATA ABOUT ALL THREE OF YOU...
HEH HEH

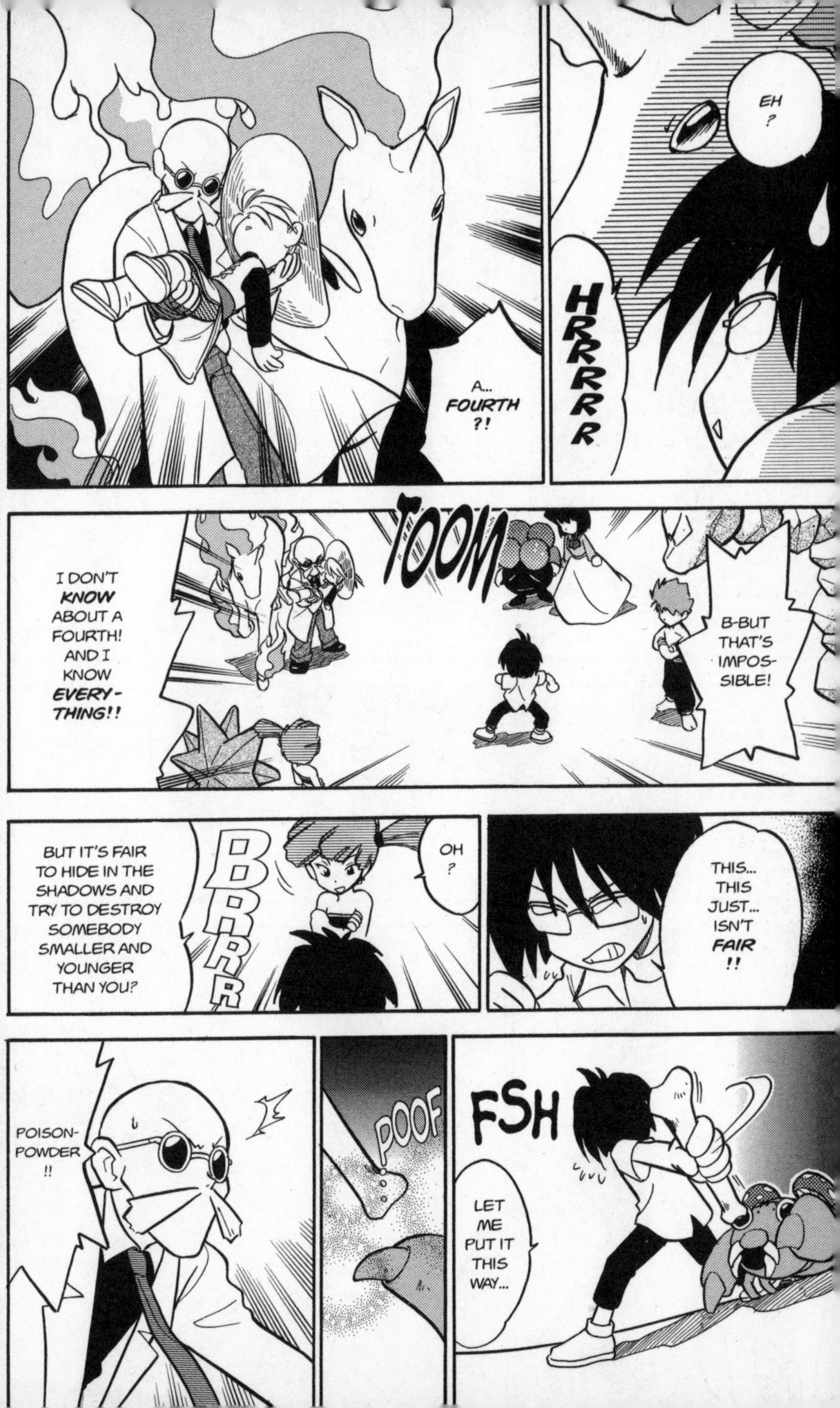
EH ?
HRRRRR
A... FOURTH ?!
B-BUT THAT'S IMPOS-SIBLE!
TOOM
I DON'T KNOW ABOUT A FOURTH! AND I KNOW EVERY-THING!!
THIS... THIS JUST... ISN'T FAIR !!
OH ?
BRRRR
BUT IT'S FAIR TO HIDE IN THE SHADOWS AND TRY TO DESTROY SOMEBODY SMALLER AND YOUNGER THAN YOU?
FSH
LET ME PUT IT THIS WAY...
POOF
POISON-POWDER !!

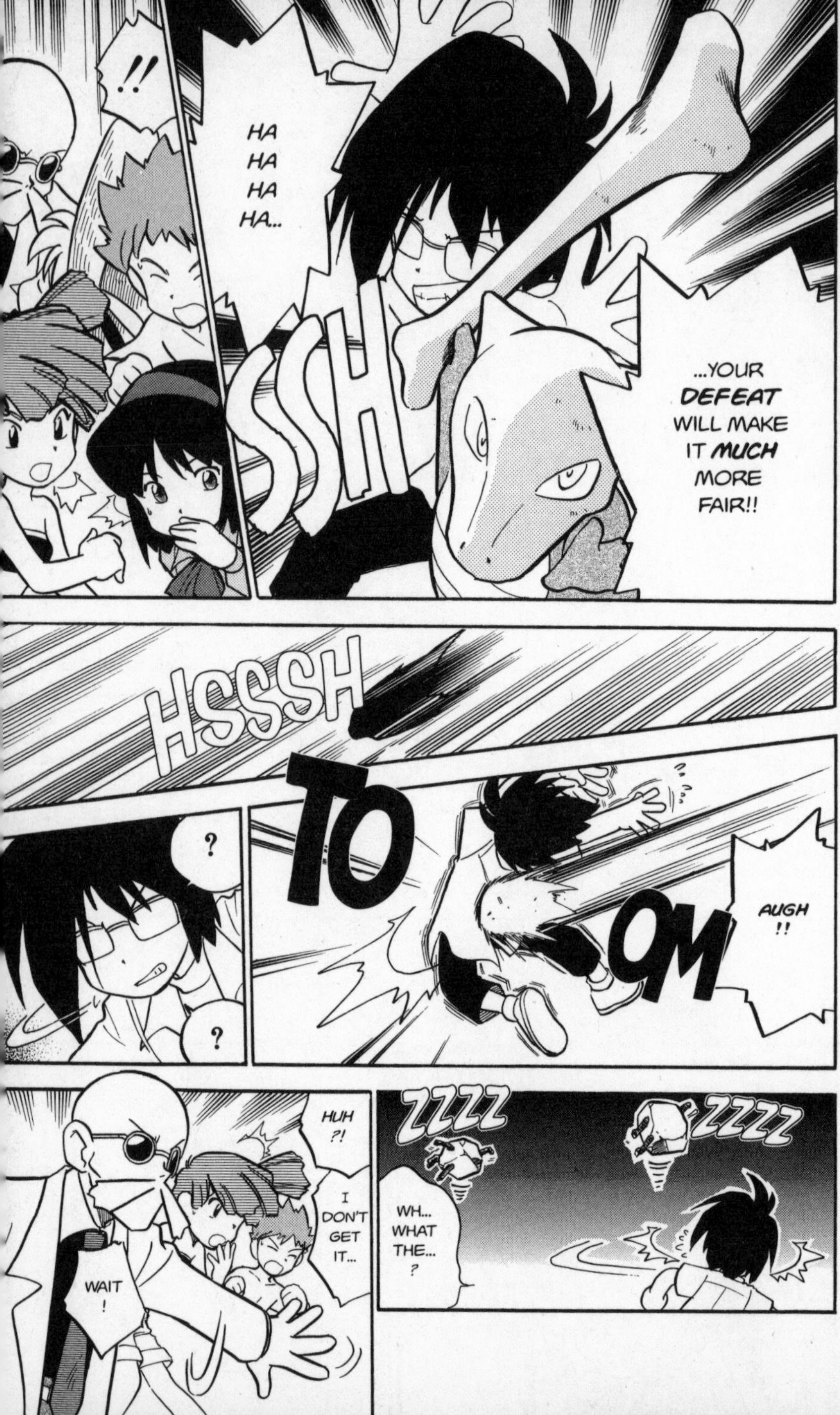
...YOUR DEFEAT WILL MAKE IT MUCH MORE FAIR!!
SSH
HA HA HA HA...
!!
HSSSH
TO
OM
AUGH !!
?
?
ZZZZ
ZZZZ
WH... WHAT THE... ?
HUH ?!
I DON'T GET IT...
WAIT !

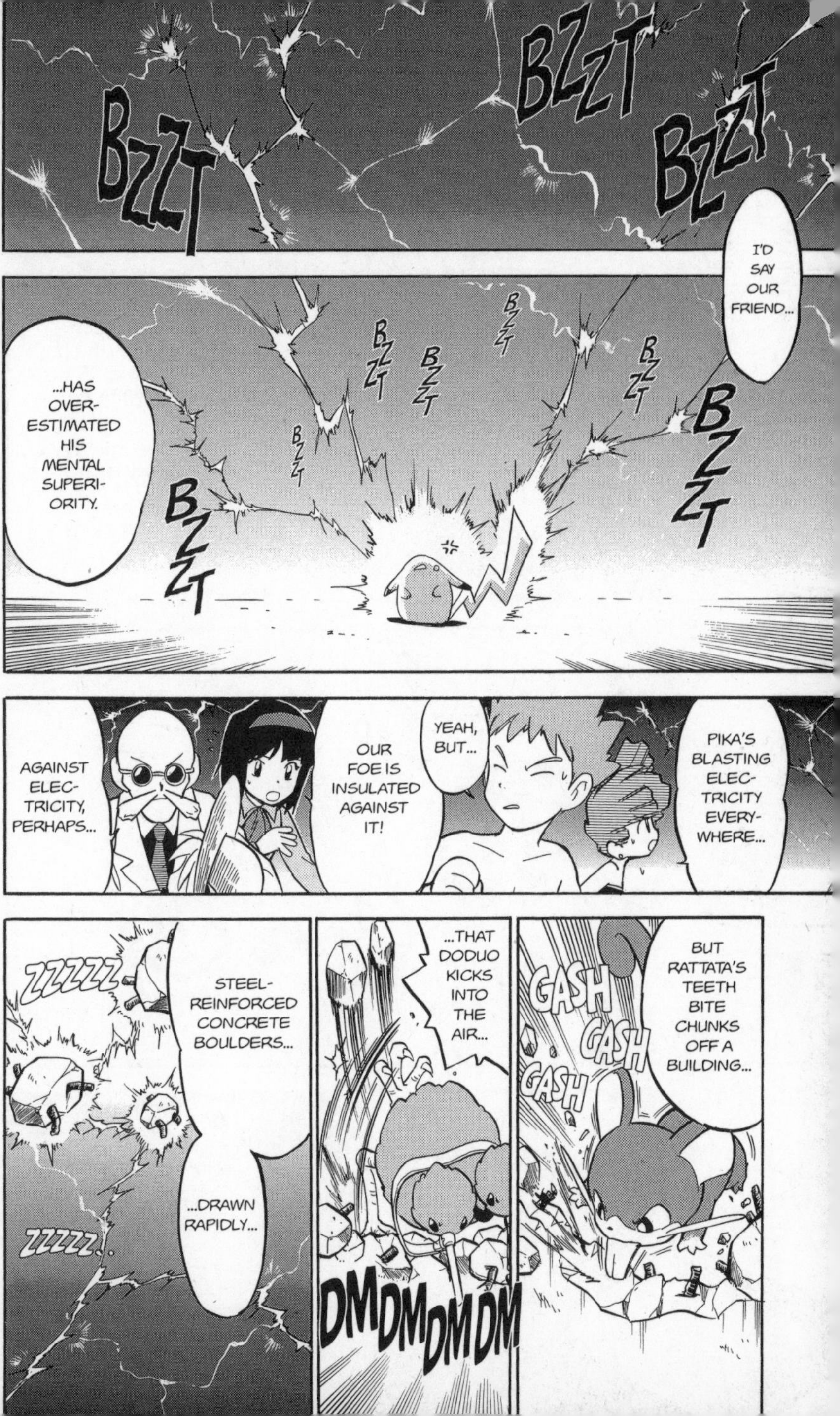
BZZT
BZZT
BZZT
I'D SAY OUR FRIEND...
BZZZT
BZZT
BZZT
BZZT
BZZT
BZZT
...HAS OVER-ESTIMATED HIS MENTAL SUPERIORITY.
BZZZT
PIKA'S BLASTING ELECTRICITY EVERYWHERE...
YEAH, BUT...
OUR FOE IS INSULATED AGAINST IT!
AGAINST ELECTRICITY, PERHAPS...
BUT RATTATA'S TEETH BITE CHUNKS OFF A BUILDING...
GASH
GASH
GASH
...THAT DODUO KICKS INTO THE AIR...
DMDMDMDM
STEEL-REINFORCED CONCRETE BOULDERS...
ZZZZZ
...DRAWN RAPIDLY...
ZZZZZ

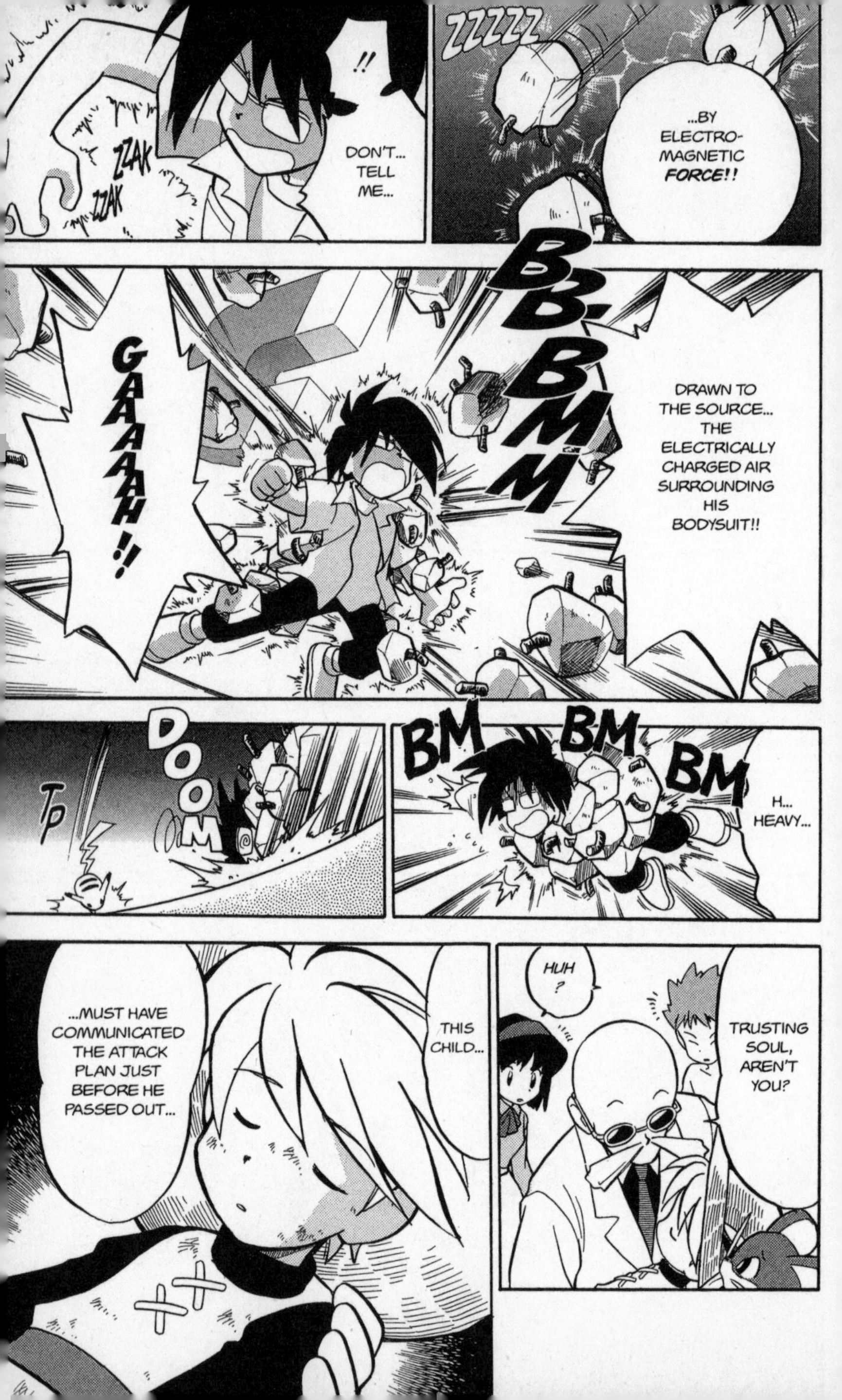
ZZZZZ
...BY ELECTRO-MAGNETIC FORCE!!
!!
DON'T... TELL ME...
ZZAK
ZZAK
BB-BMMM
DRAWN TO THE SOURCE... THE ELECTRICALLY CHARGED AIR SURROUNDING HIS BODYSUIT!!
GAAAAAH!!
BM
BM
BM
H... HEAVY...
DOOOM
TP
TRUSTING SOUL, AREN'T YOU?
HUH?
THIS CHILD...
...MUST HAVE COMMUNICATED THE ATTACK PLAN JUST BEFORE HE PASSED OUT...

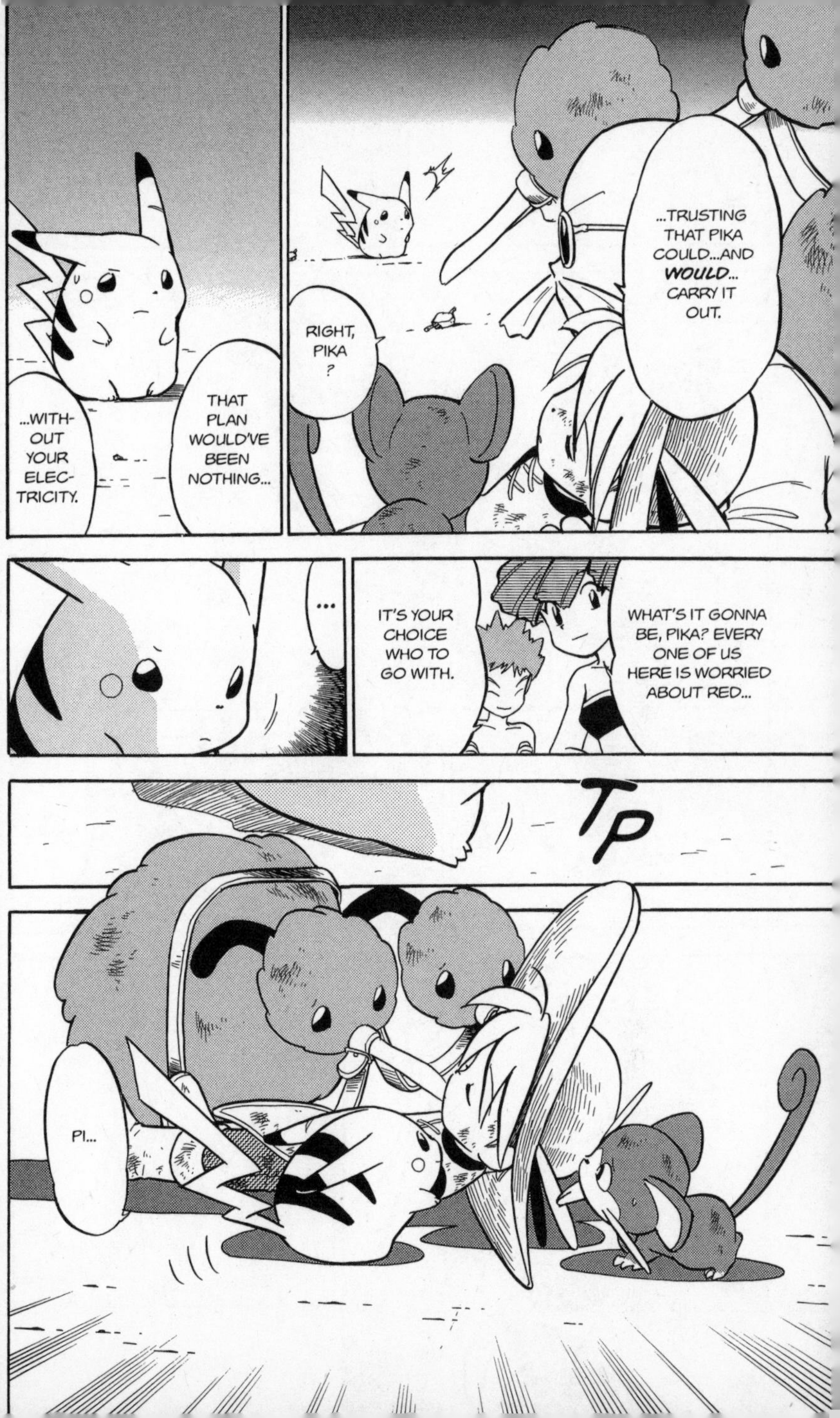

...TRUSTING THAT PIKA COULD...AND ***WOULD***... CARRY IT OUT.
RIGHT, PIKA?
THAT PLAN WOULD'VE BEEN NOTHING...
...WITH-OUT YOUR ELEC-TRICITY.
WHAT'S IT GONNA BE, PIKA? EVERY ONE OF US HERE IS WORRIED ABOUT RED...
IT'S YOUR CHOICE WHO TO GO WITH.
...
TP
PI...

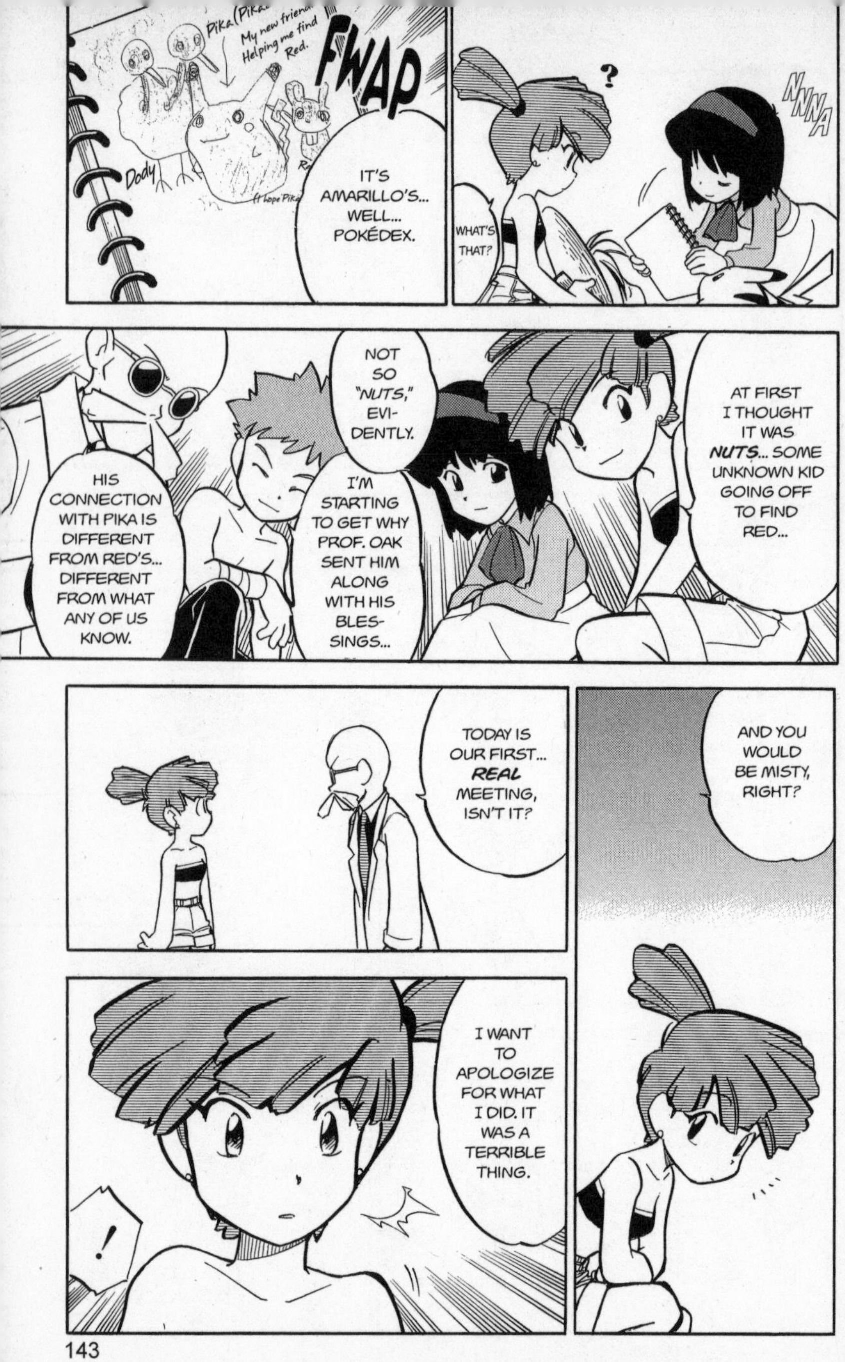

NNNA
?
WHAT'S THAT?
FWAP
IT'S AMARILLO'S... WELL... POKÉDEX.
Pika
My new friend
Helping me find Red.
Dody
AT FIRST I THOUGHT IT WAS ***NUTS***... SOME UNKNOWN KID GOING OFF TO FIND RED...
NOT SO *"NUTS,"* EVI-DENTLY.
I'M STARTING TO GET WHY PROF. OAK SENT HIM ALONG WITH HIS BLES-SINGS...
HIS CONNECTION WITH PIKA IS DIFFERENT FROM RED'S... DIFFERENT FROM WHAT ANY OF US KNOW.
AND YOU WOULD BE MISTY, RIGHT?
...
TODAY IS OUR FIRST... ***REAL*** MEETING, ISN'T IT?
I WANT TO APOLOGIZE FOR WHAT I DID. IT WAS A TERRIBLE THING.
!

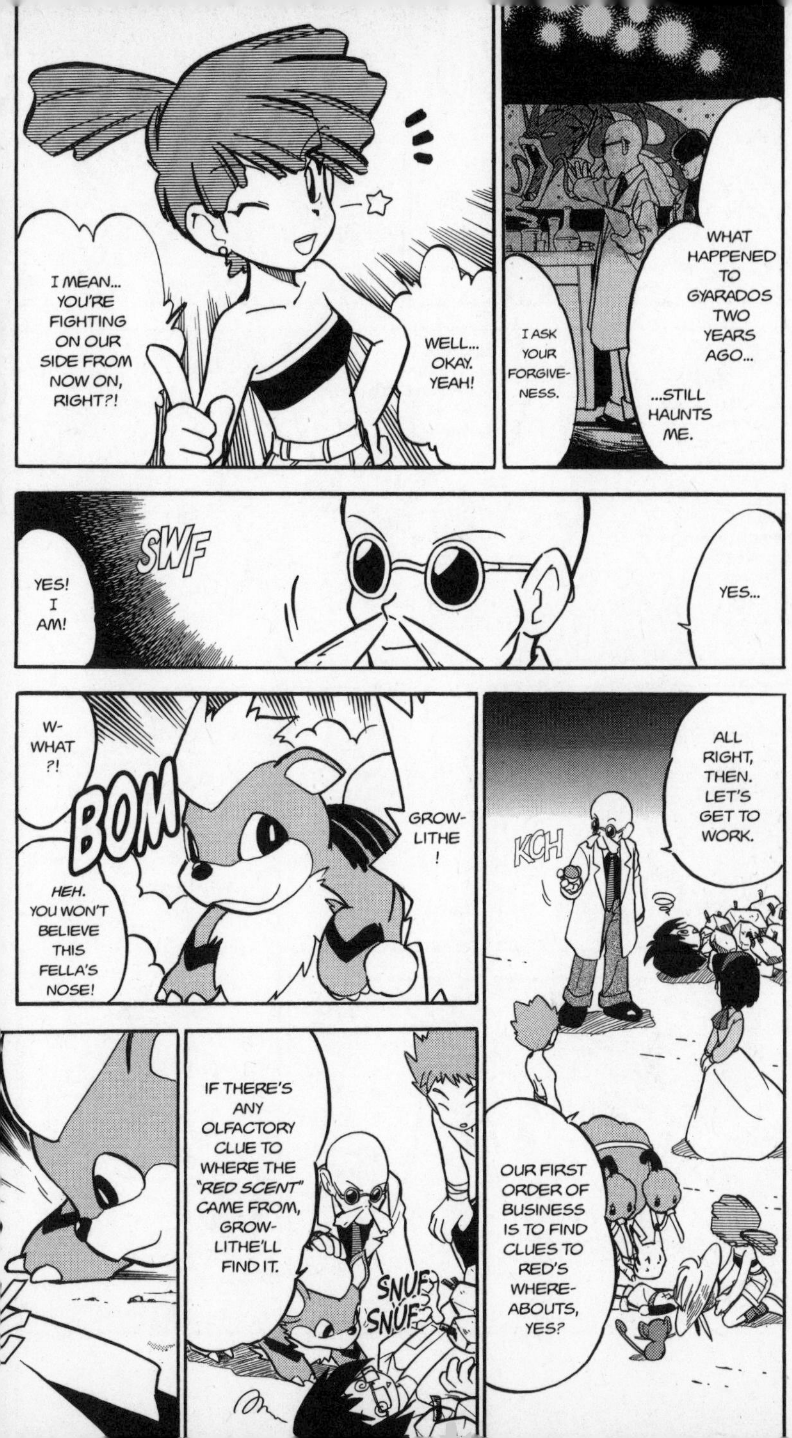
WHAT HAPPENED TO GYARADOS TWO YEARS AGO...
...STILL HAUNTS ME.
I ASK YOUR FORGIVE-NESS.
WELL... OKAY. YEAH!
I MEAN... YOU'RE FIGHTING ON OUR SIDE FROM NOW ON, RIGHT?!
YES...
SWF
YES! I AM!
ALL RIGHT, THEN. LET'S GET TO WORK.
KCH
OUR FIRST ORDER OF BUSINESS IS TO FIND CLUES TO RED'S WHERE-ABOUTS, YES?
W-WHAT?!
GROW-LITHE!
BOM
HEH. YOU WON'T BELIEVE THIS FELLA'S NOSE!
IF THERE'S ANY OLFACTORY CLUE TO WHERE THE "RED SCENT" CAME FROM, GROW-LITHE'LL FIND IT.
SNUF SNUF

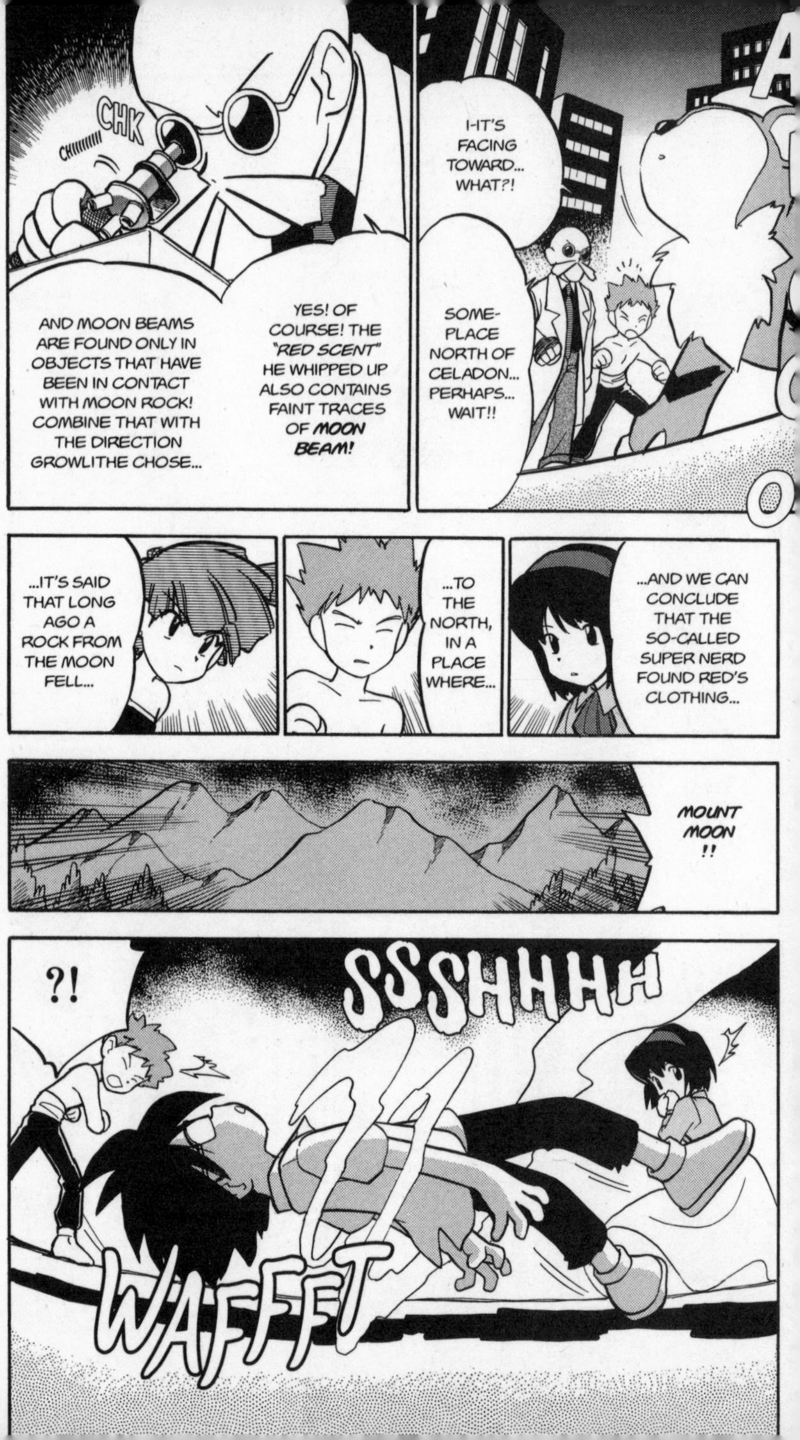
I-IT'S FACING TOWARD... WHAT?!
SOME-PLACE NORTH OF CELADON... PERHAPS... WAIT!!
CHK
CHIIIIIII
YES! OF COURSE! THE "RED SCENT" HE WHIPPED UP ALSO CONTAINS FAINT TRACES OF MOON BEAM!
AND MOON BEAMS ARE FOUND ONLY IN OBJECTS THAT HAVE BEEN IN CONTACT WITH MOON ROCK! COMBINE THAT WITH THE DIRECTION GROWLITHE CHOSE...
...AND WE CAN CONCLUDE THAT THE SO-CALLED SUPER NERD FOUND RED'S CLOTHING...
...TO THE NORTH, IN A PLACE WHERE...
...IT'S SAID THAT LONG AGO A ROCK FROM THE MOON FELL...
MOUNT MOON !!
SSSHHHH
?!
WAFFFT

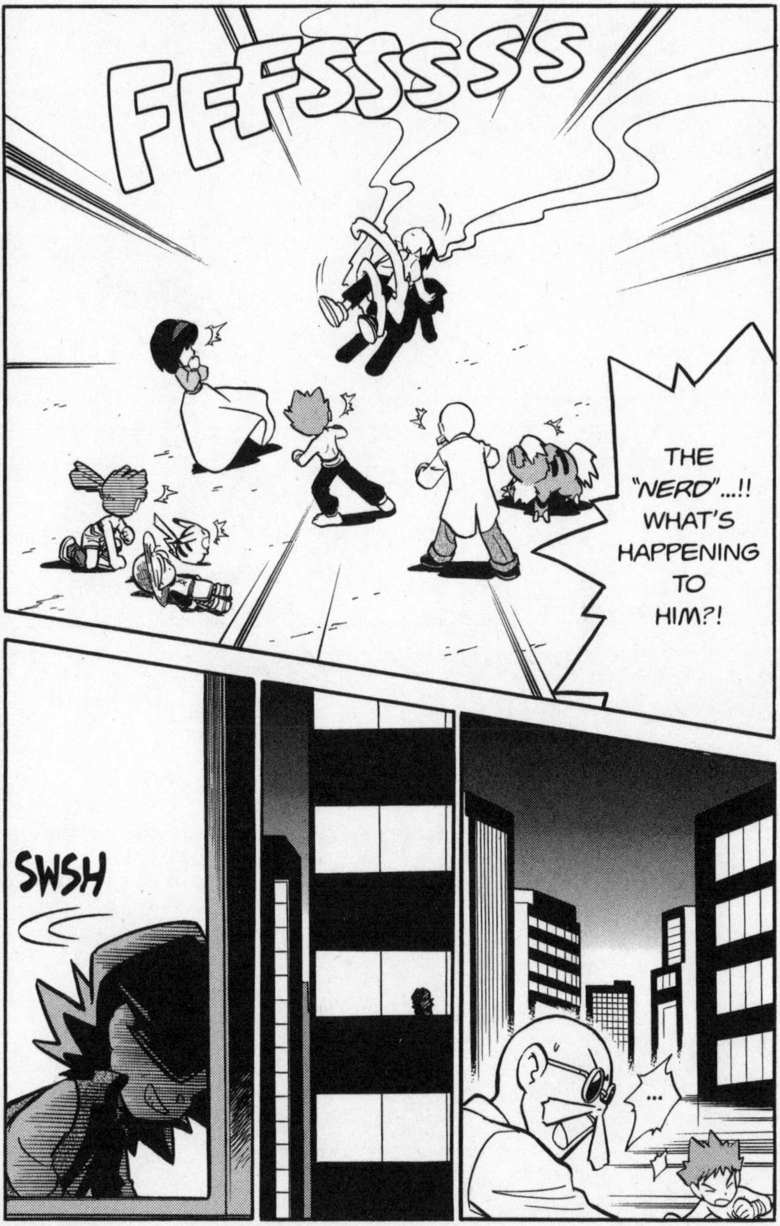
FFFSSSSS
THE "NERD"...!! WHAT'S HAPPENING TO HIM?!
...
SWSH

49 As Gastly As Before

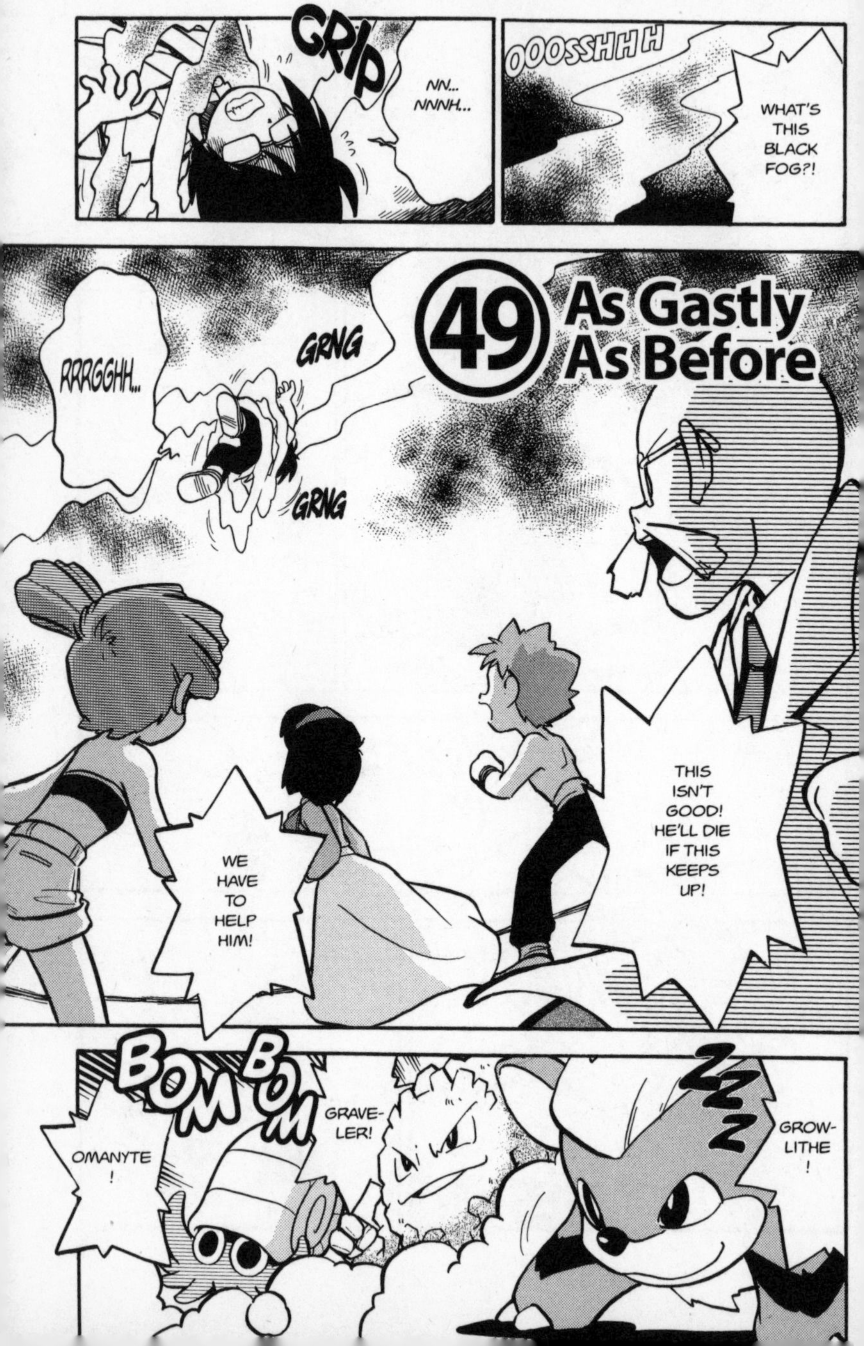
OOOSSHHH
WHAT'S THIS BLACK FOG?!
GRIP
NN... NNNH...
GRNG
RRRGGHH...
GRNG
THIS ISN'T GOOD! HE'LL DIE IF THIS KEEPS UP!
WE HAVE TO HELP HIM!
GROWLITHE!
ZZZ
GRAVELER!
BOM BOM
OMANYTE!

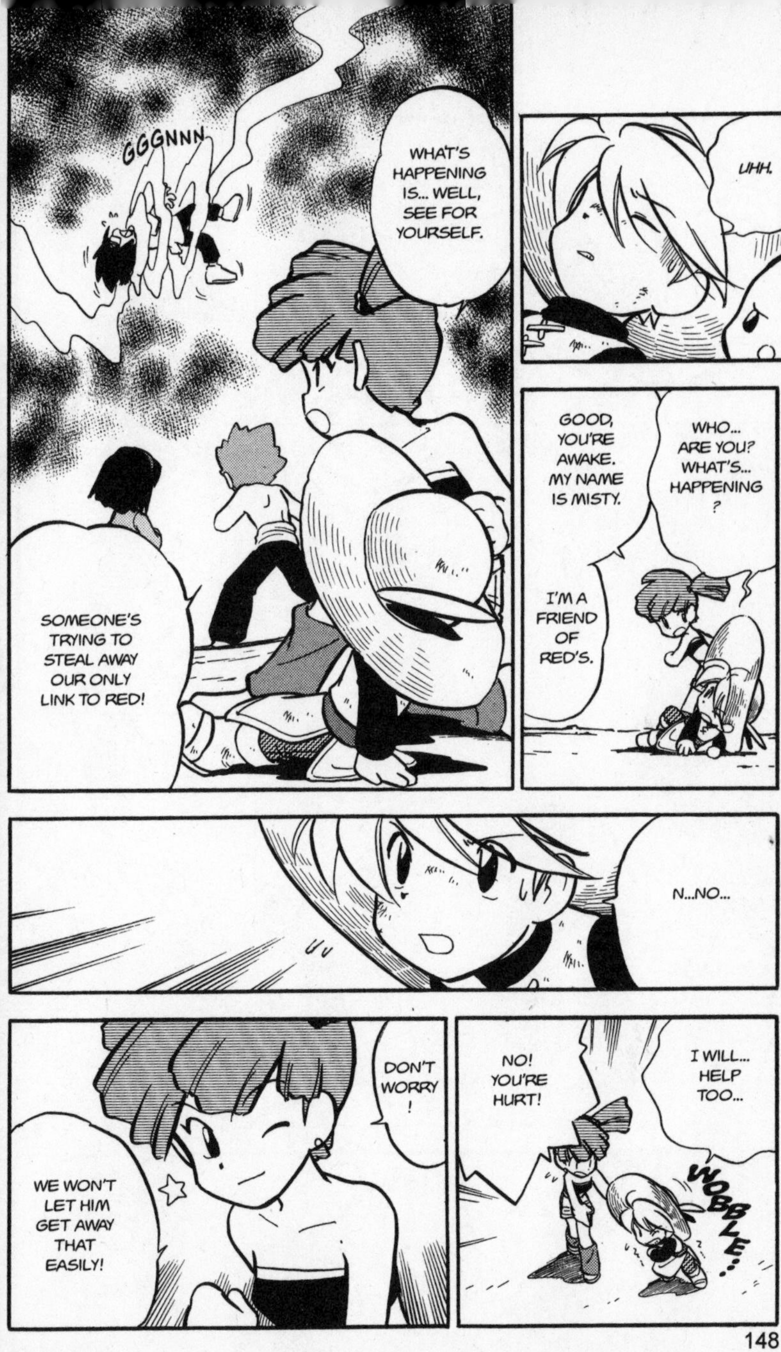
UHH.
WHO... ARE YOU? WHAT'S... HAPPENING ?
GOOD, YOU'RE AWAKE. MY NAME IS MISTY.
I'M A FRIEND OF RED'S.
WHAT'S HAPPENING IS... WELL, SEE FOR YOURSELF.
GGGNNN
SOMEONE'S TRYING TO STEAL AWAY OUR ONLY LINK TO RED!
N...NO...
I WILL... HELP TOO...
WOBBLE...
NO! YOU'RE HURT!
DON'T WORRY !
WE WON'T LET HIM GET AWAY THAT EASILY!

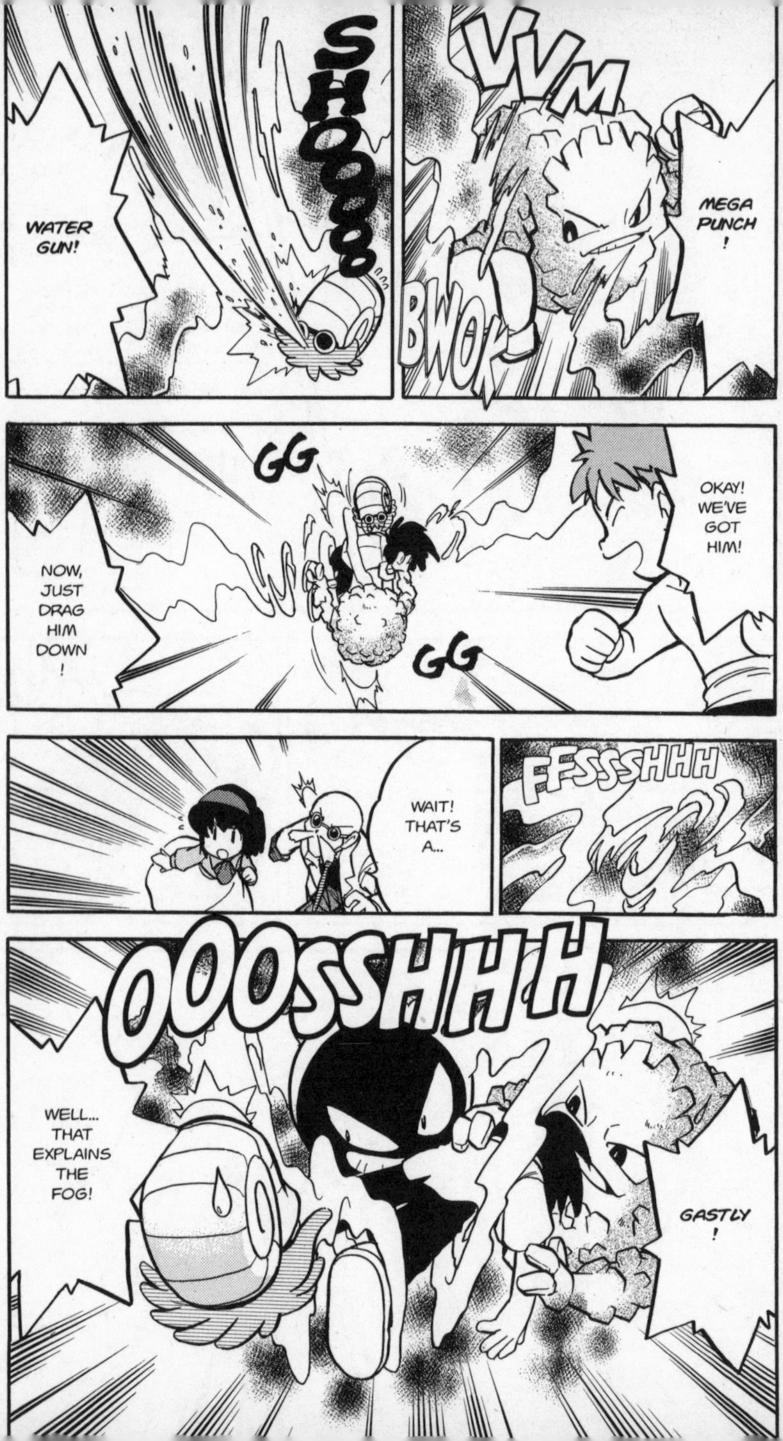
VVM
MEGA PUNCH!
BWOK
SHOOOOO
WATER GUN!
OKAY! WE'VE GOT HIM!
GG
NOW, JUST DRAG HIM DOWN!
GG
FFSSSHHH
WAIT! THAT'S A...
OOOSSHHHH
GASTLY!
WELL... THAT EXPLAINS THE FOG!

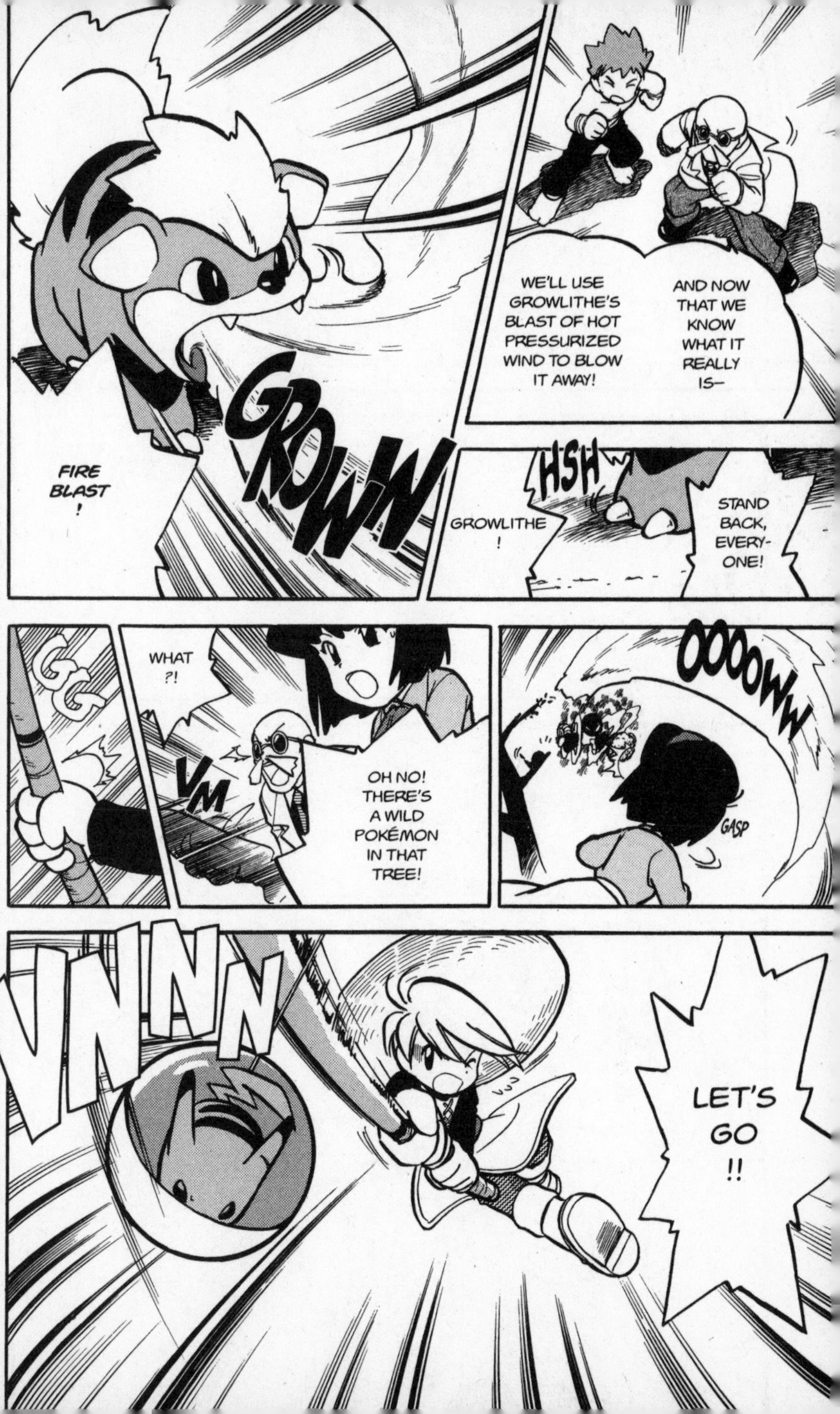
AND NOW THAT WE KNOW WHAT IT REALLY IS—
WE'LL USE GROWLITHE'S BLAST OF HOT PRESSURIZED WIND TO BLOW IT AWAY!
STAND BACK, EVERY-ONE!
HSH
GROWLITHE!
GROWW
FIRE BLAST!
OOOOWW
GASP
WHAT?!
OH NO! THERE'S A WILD POKÉMON IN THAT TREE!
VM
GG
LET'S GO!!
VNNN

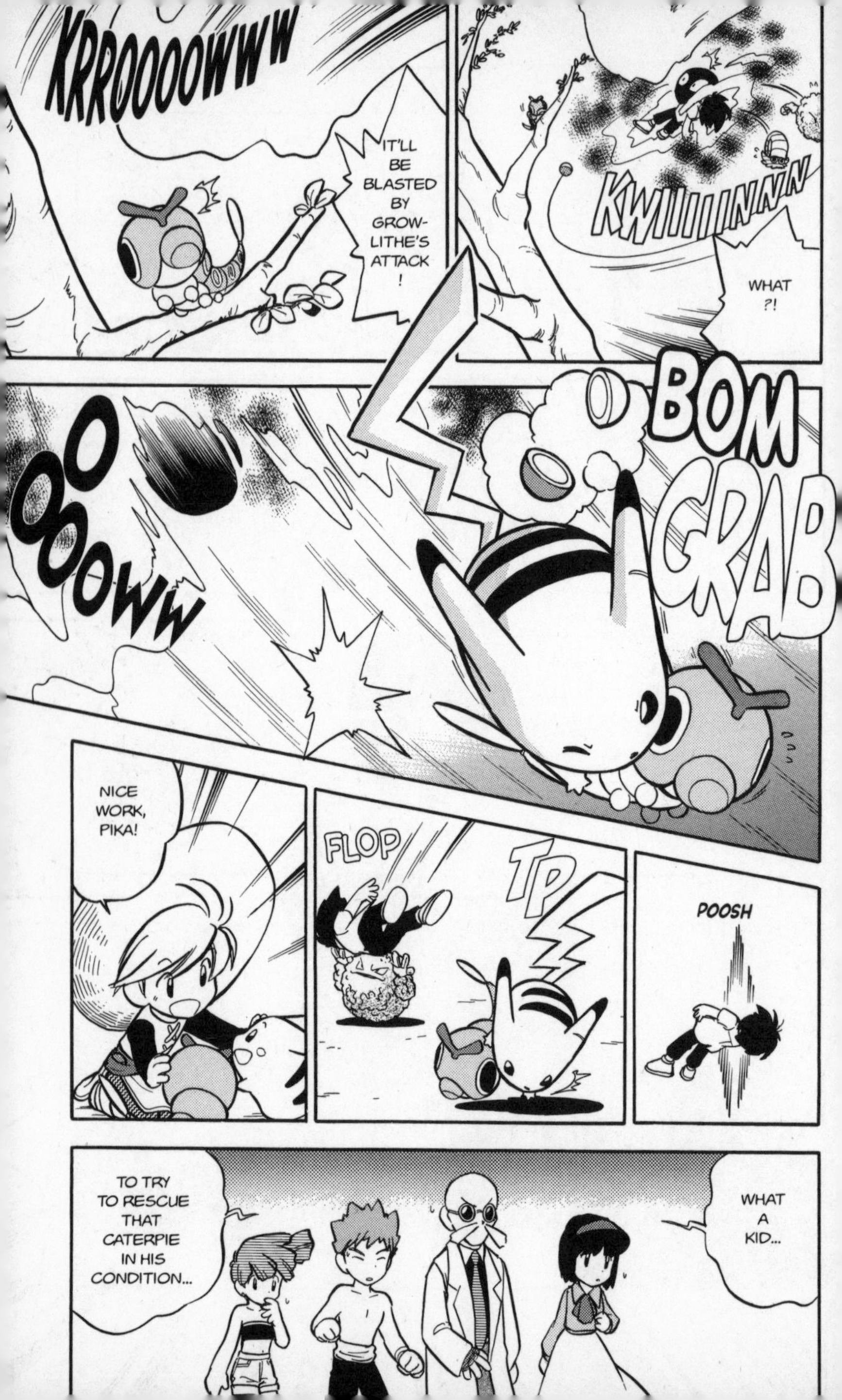
KWIIIIINNN
WHAT ?!
KRROOOOWWW
IT'LL BE BLASTED BY GROWLITHE'S ATTACK !
BOM
GRAB
OOOOOWW
POOSH
TP
FLOP
NICE WORK, PIKA!
WHAT A KID...
TO TRY TO RESCUE THAT CATERPIE IN HIS CONDITION...

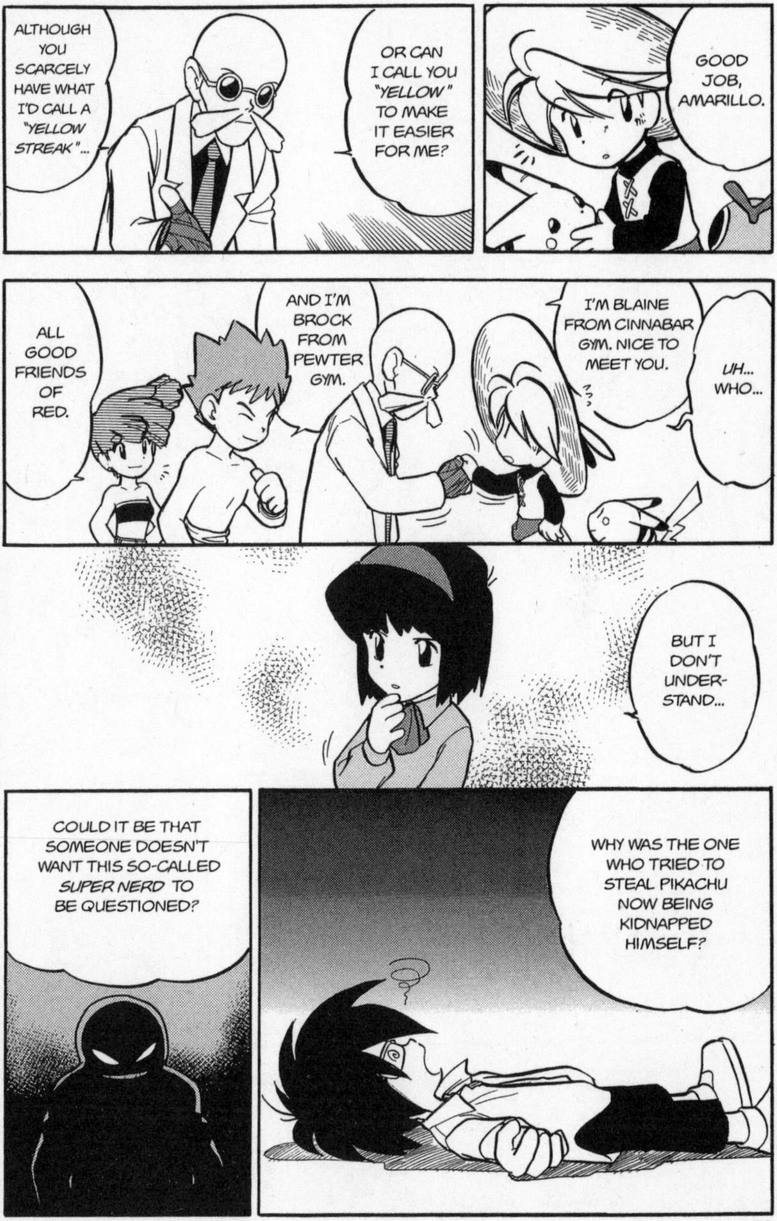
GOOD JOB, AMARILLO.
ALTHOUGH YOU SCARCELY HAVE WHAT I'D CALL A "YELLOW STREAK"...
OR CAN I CALL YOU "YELLOW" TO MAKE IT EASIER FOR ME?
UH... WHO...
I'M BLAINE FROM CINNABAR GYM. NICE TO MEET YOU.
AND I'M BROCK FROM PEWTER GYM.
ALL GOOD FRIENDS OF RED.
BUT I DON'T UNDERSTAND...
WHY WAS THE ONE WHO TRIED TO STEAL PIKACHU NOW BEING KIDNAPPED HIMSELF?
COULD IT BE THAT SOMEONE DOESN'T WANT THIS SO-CALLED SUPER NERD TO BE QUESTIONED?

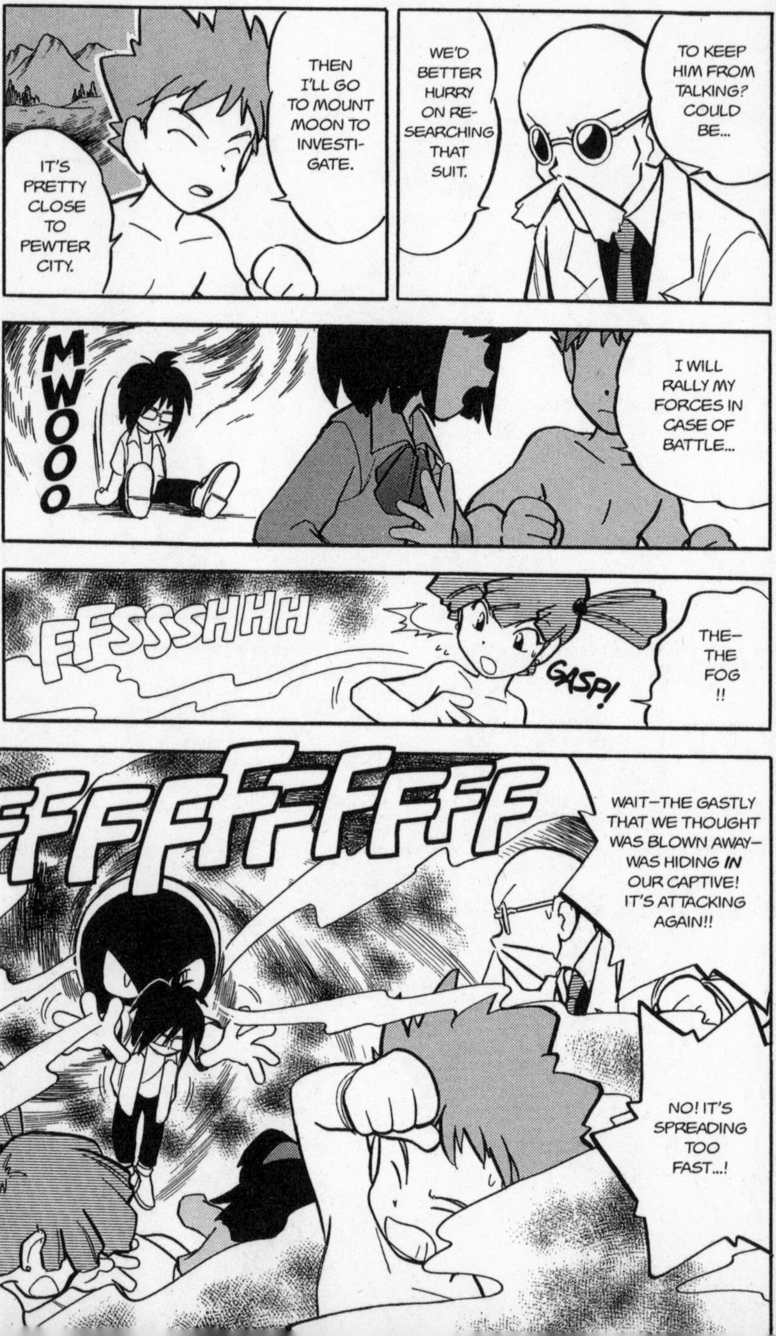
TO KEEP HIM FROM TALKING? COULD BE...
WE'D BETTER HURRY ON RE-SEARCHING THAT SUIT.
THEN I'LL GO TO MOUNT MOON TO INVESTI-GATE.
IT'S PRETTY CLOSE TO PEWTER CITY.
I WILL RALLY MY FORCES IN CASE OF BATTLE...
MWOOOO
THE— THE FOG !!
GASP!
FFSSSHHH
WAIT—THE GASTLY THAT WE THOUGHT WAS BLOWN AWAY— WAS HIDING *IN* OUR CAPTIVE! IT'S ATTACKING AGAIN!!
FFFFFFFFFF
NO! IT'S SPREADING TOO FAST...!

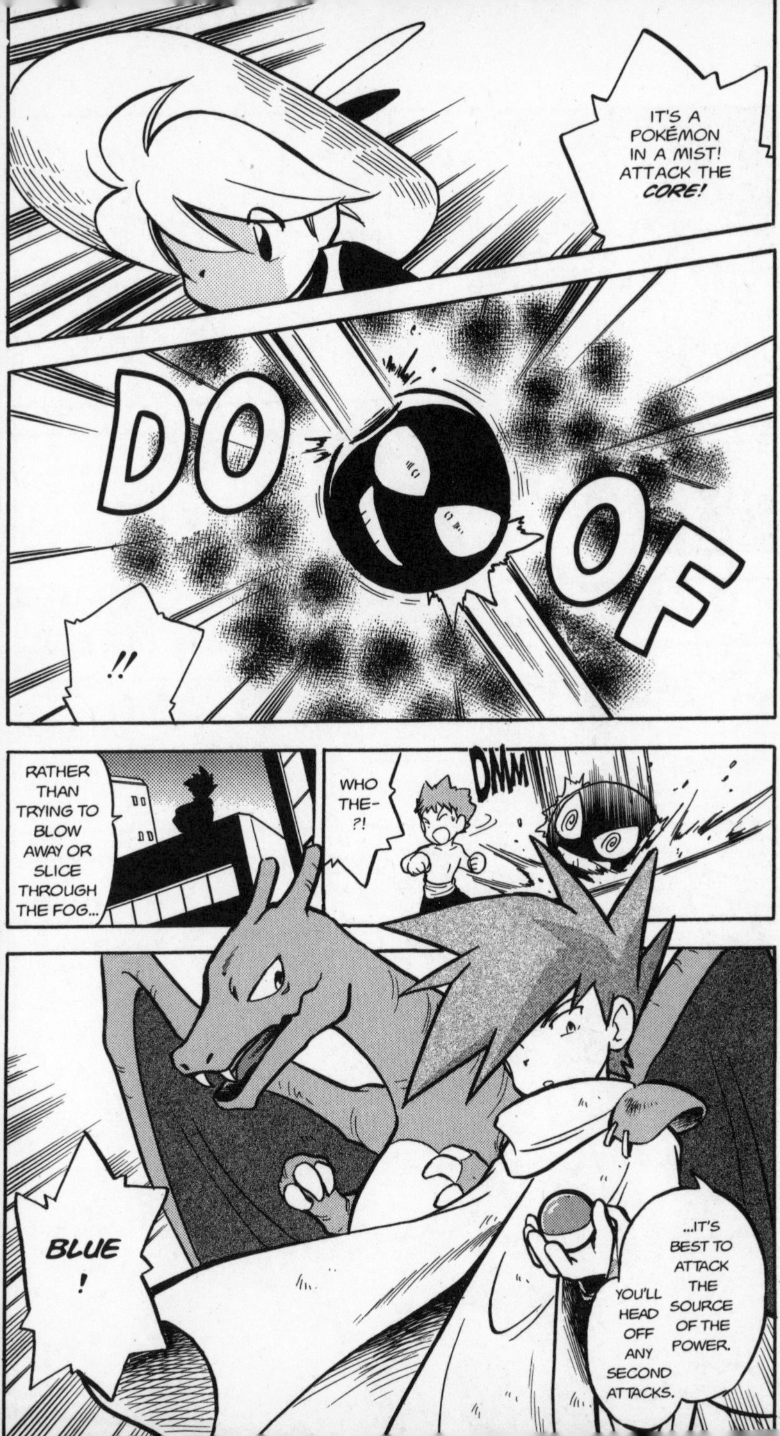
IT'S A POKÉMON IN A MIST! ATTACK THE CORE!
DOOF
!!
DMM
WHO THE-?!
RATHER THAN TRYING TO BLOW AWAY OR SLICE THROUGH THE FOG...
...IT'S BEST TO ATTACK THE SOURCE OF THE POWER.
YOU'LL HEAD OFF ANY SECOND ATTACKS.
BLUE!

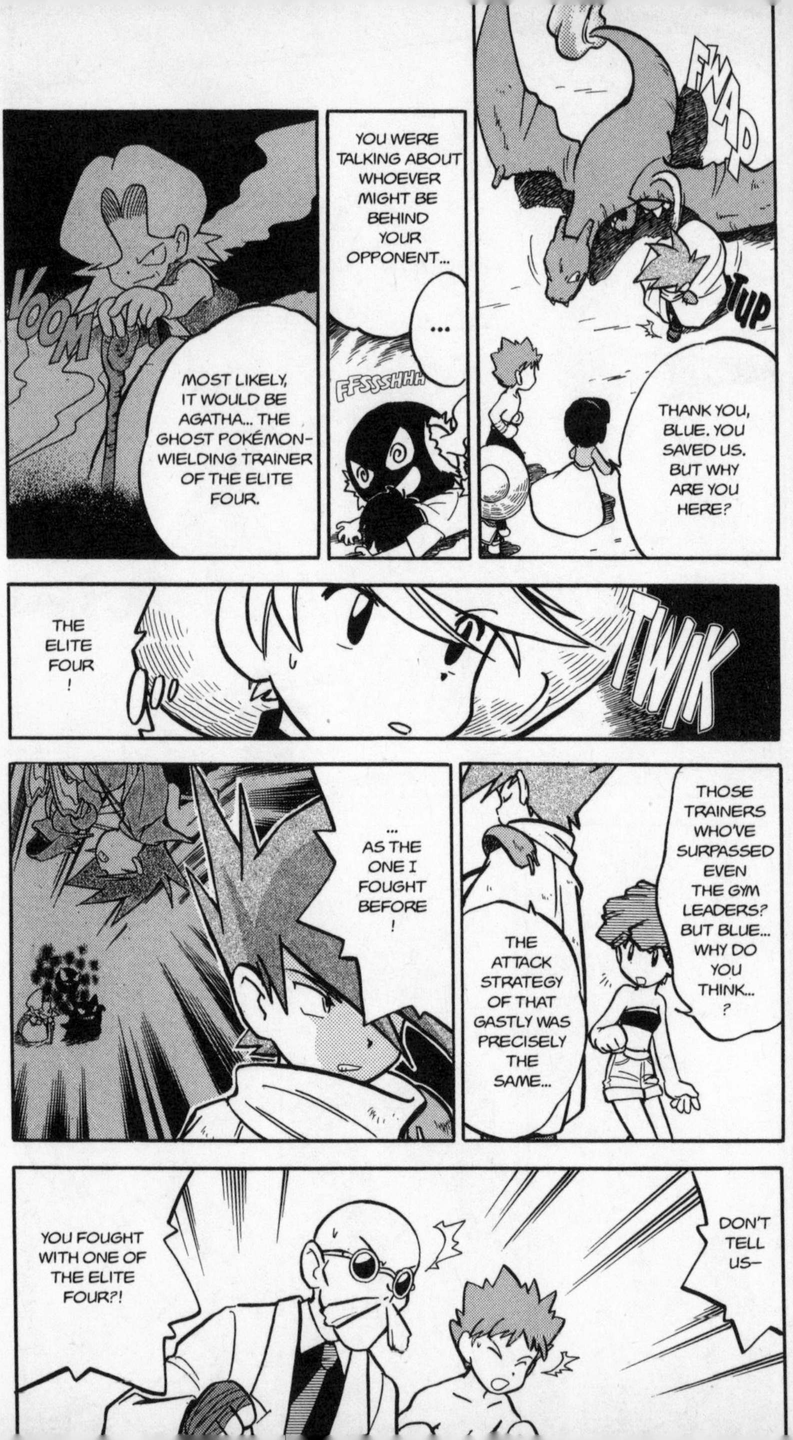
FWAP
TUP
THANK YOU, BLUE. YOU SAVED US. BUT WHY ARE YOU HERE?
YOU WERE TALKING ABOUT WHOEVER MIGHT BE BEHIND YOUR OPPONENT...
...
FFSSSHHH
VOOM
MOST LIKELY, IT WOULD BE AGATHA... THE GHOST POKÉMON-WIELDING TRAINER OF THE ELITE FOUR.
TWIK
THE ELITE FOUR!
THOSE TRAINERS WHO'VE SURPASSED EVEN THE GYM LEADERS? BUT BLUE... WHY DO YOU THINK...?
THE ATTACK STRATEGY OF THAT GASTLY WAS PRECISELY THE SAME...
...AS THE ONE I FOUGHT BEFORE!
DON'T TELL US—
YOU FOUGHT WITH ONE OF THE ELITE FOUR?!

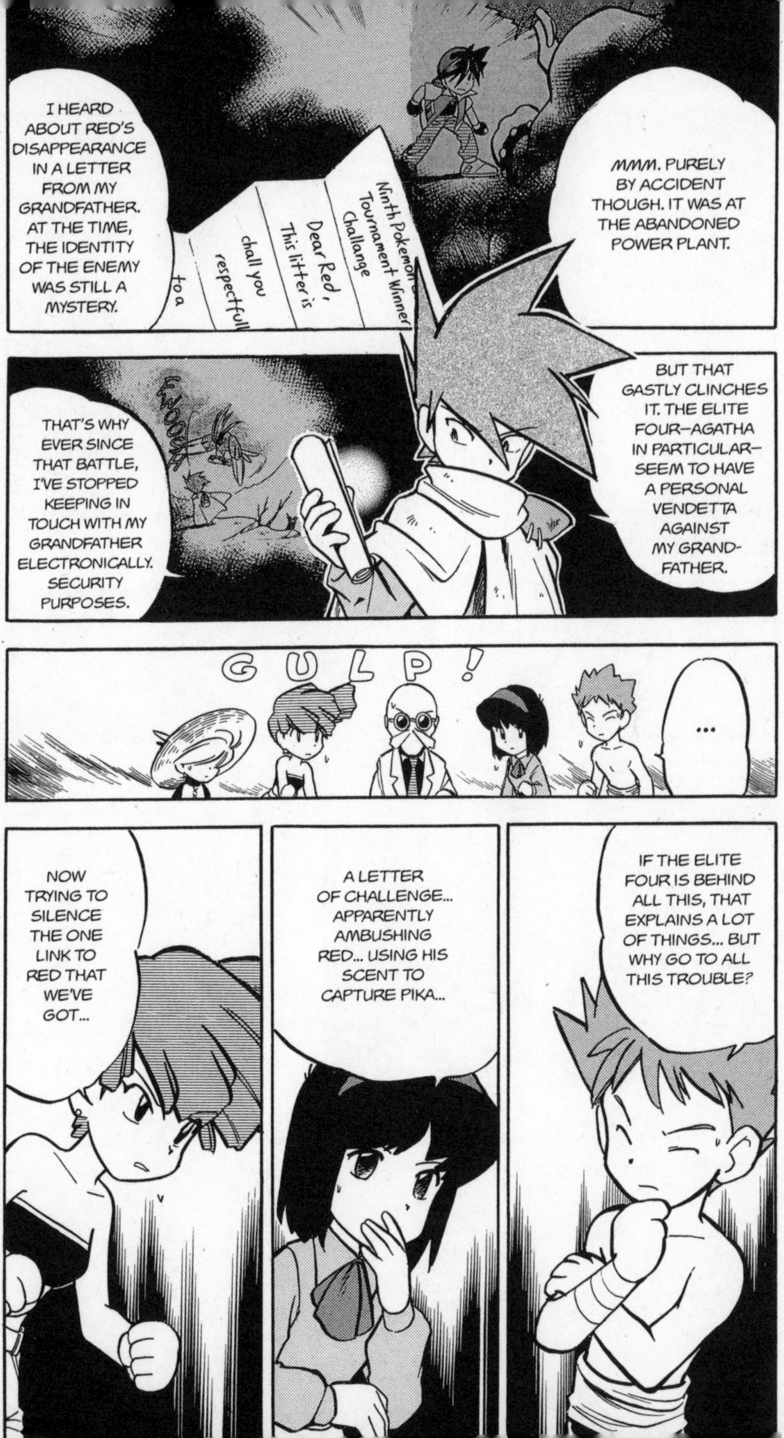
MMM. PURELY BY ACCIDENT THOUGH. IT WAS AT THE ABANDONED POWER PLANT.
Ninth Pokemon Tournament Winner Challange
Dear Red, This litter is
chall you respectfull
to a
I HEARD ABOUT RED'S DISAPPEARANCE IN A LETTER FROM MY GRANDFATHER. AT THE TIME, THE IDENTITY OF THE ENEMY WAS STILL A MYSTERY.
BUT THAT GASTLY CLINCHES IT. THE ELITE FOUR—AGATHA IN PARTICULAR—SEEM TO HAVE A PERSONAL VENDETTA AGAINST MY GRAND-FATHER.
THAT'S WHY EVER SINCE THAT BATTLE, I'VE STOPPED KEEPING IN TOUCH WITH MY GRANDFATHER ELECTRONICALLY. SECURITY PURPOSES.
...
GULP!
IF THE ELITE FOUR IS BEHIND ALL THIS, THAT EXPLAINS A LOT OF THINGS... BUT WHY GO TO ALL THIS TROUBLE?
A LETTER OF CHALLENGE... APPARENTLY AMBUSHING RED... USING HIS SCENT TO CAPTURE PIKA...
NOW TRYING TO SILENCE THE ONE LINK TO RED THAT WE'VE GOT...

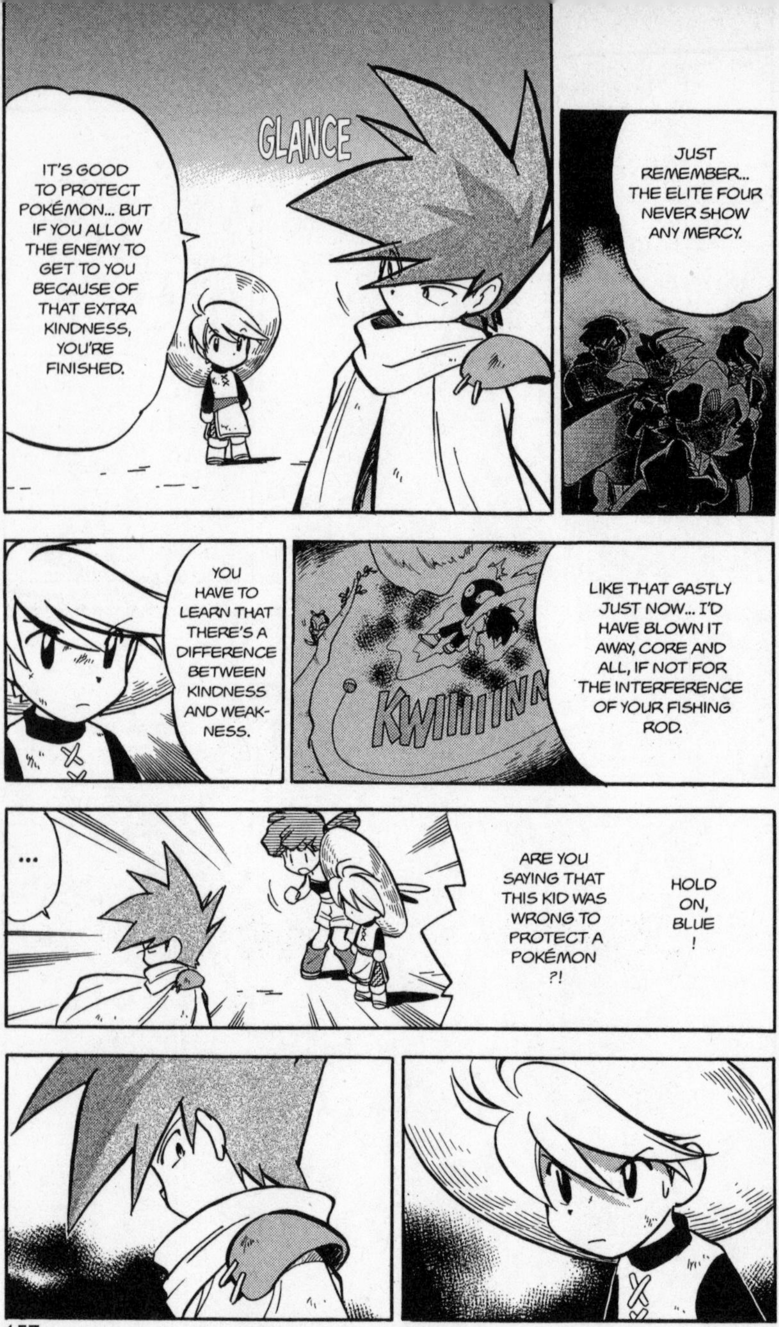
JUST REMEMBER... THE ELITE FOUR NEVER SHOW ANY MERCY.
GLANCE
IT'S GOOD TO PROTECT POKéMON... BUT IF YOU ALLOW THE ENEMY TO GET TO YOU BECAUSE OF THAT EXTRA KINDNESS, YOU'RE FINISHED.
LIKE THAT GASTLY JUST NOW... I'D HAVE BLOWN IT AWAY, CORE AND ALL, IF NOT FOR THE INTERFERENCE OF YOUR FISHING ROD.
KWIIIIIN
YOU HAVE TO LEARN THAT THERE'S A DIFFERENCE BETWEEN KINDNESS AND WEAK-NESS.
HOLD ON, BLUE!
ARE YOU SAYING THAT THIS KID WAS WRONG TO PROTECT A POKéMON?!
...

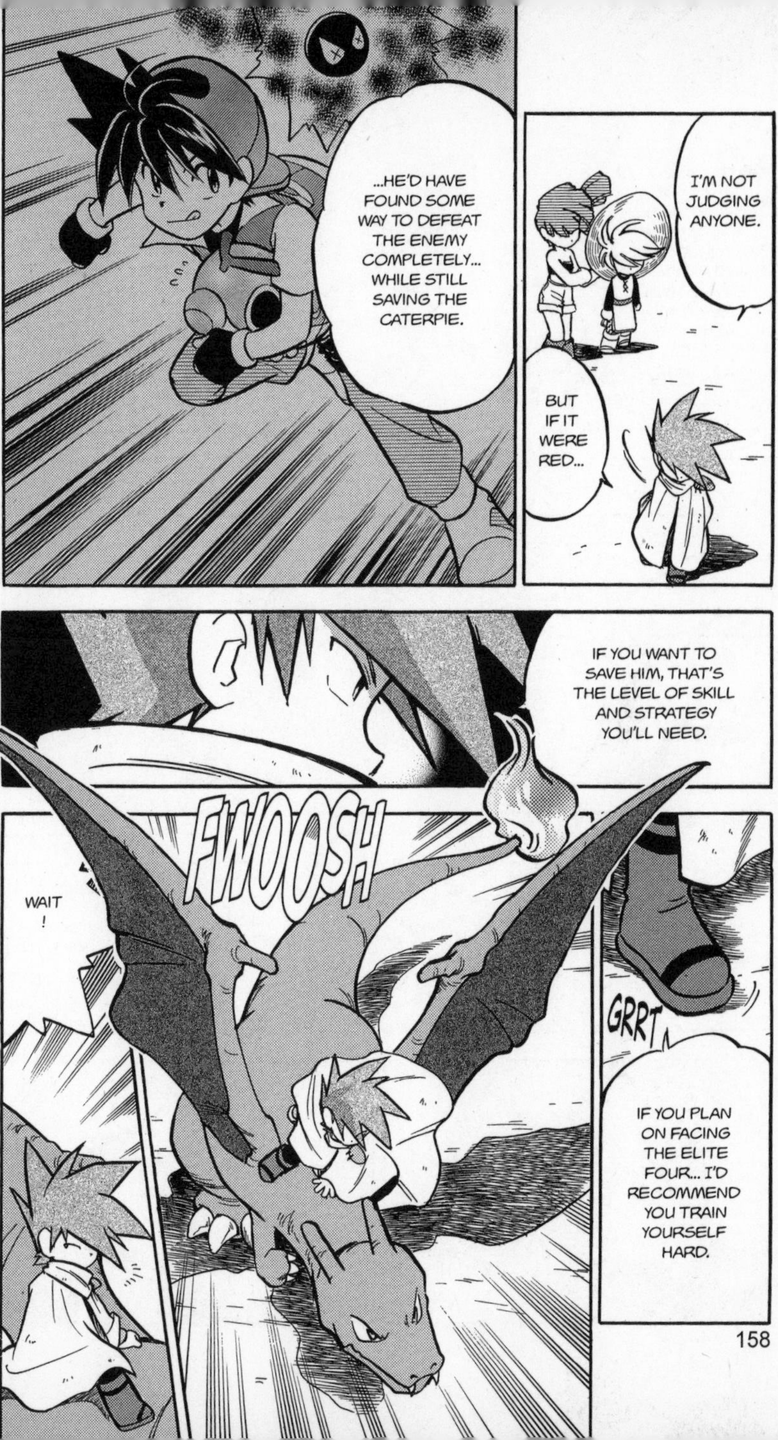
I'M NOT JUDGING ANYONE.
BUT IF IT WERE RED...
...HE'D HAVE FOUND SOME WAY TO DEFEAT THE ENEMY COMPLETELY... WHILE STILL SAVING THE CATERPIE.
IF YOU WANT TO SAVE HIM, THAT'S THE LEVEL OF SKILL AND STRATEGY YOU'LL NEED.
GRRT
IF YOU PLAN ON FACING THE ELITE FOUR... I'D RECOMMEND YOU TRAIN YOURSELF HARD.
FWOOSH
WAIT!

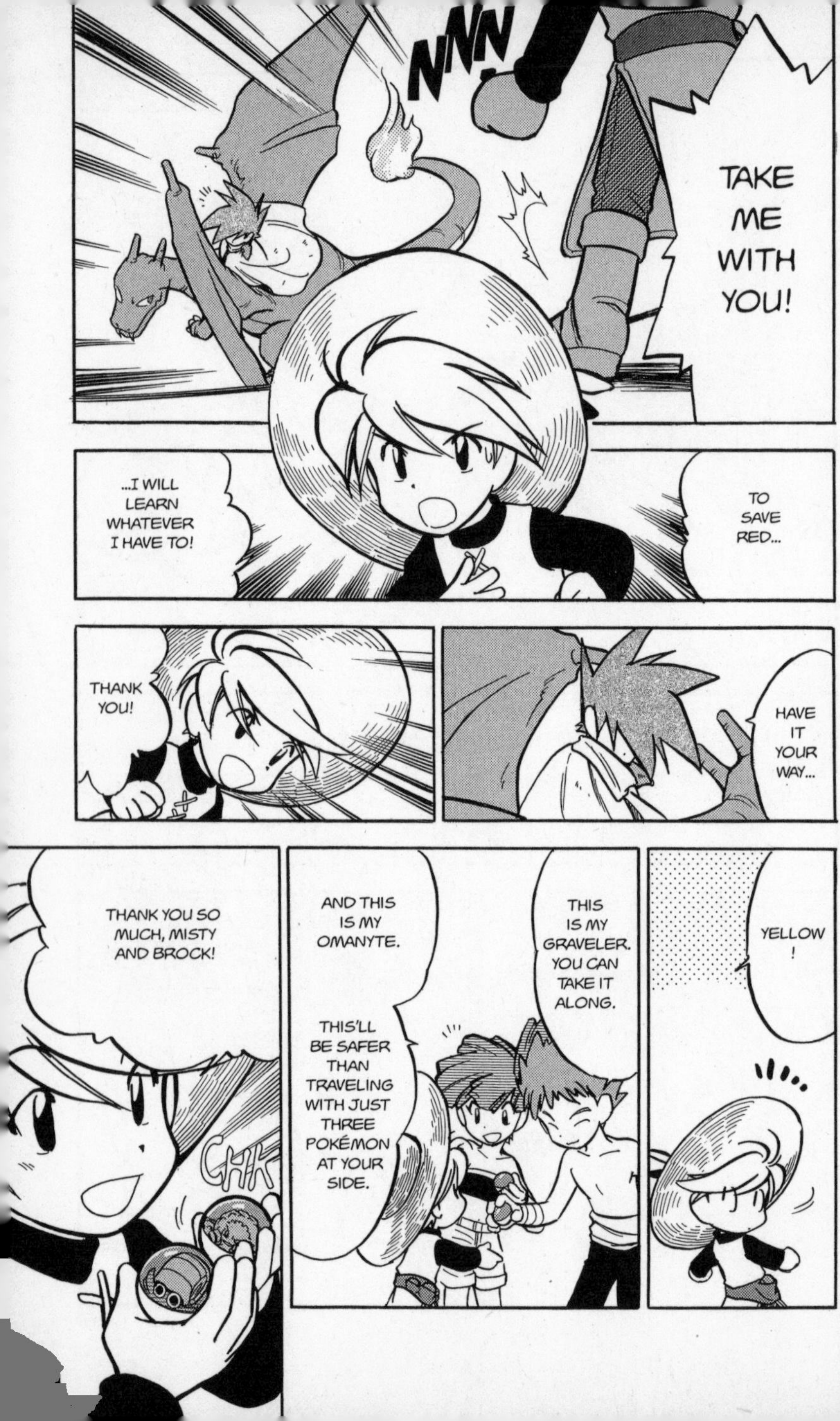
NNN
TAKE ME WITH YOU!
TO SAVE RED...
...I WILL LEARN WHATEVER I HAVE TO!
HAVE IT YOUR WAY...
THANK YOU!
YELLOW!
THIS IS MY GRAVELER. YOU CAN TAKE IT ALONG.
AND THIS IS MY OMANYTE.
THIS'LL BE SAFER THAN TRAVELING WITH JUST THREE POKÉMON AT YOUR SIDE.
THANK YOU SO MUCH, MISTY AND BROCK!
CHK

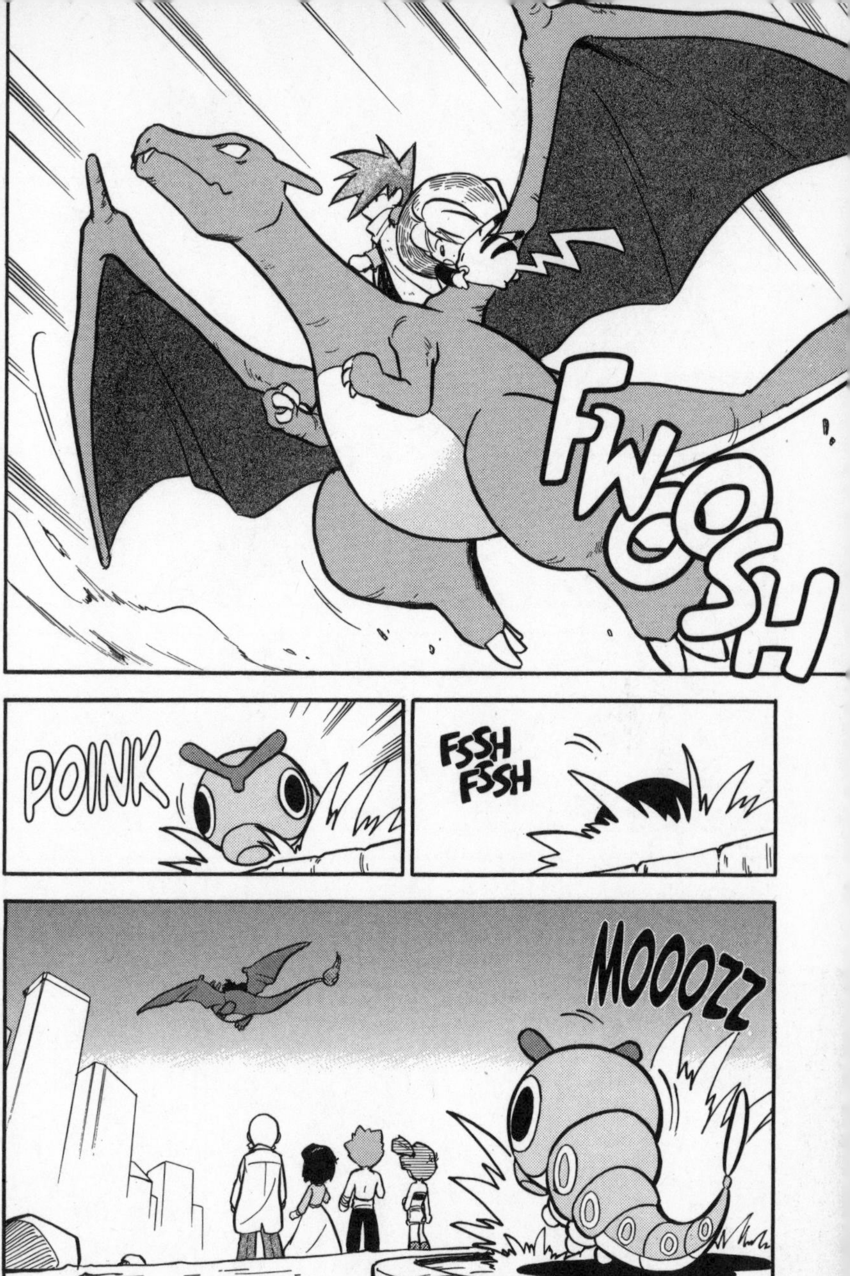
FWOOSH
FSSH FSSH
POINK
MOOOZZ

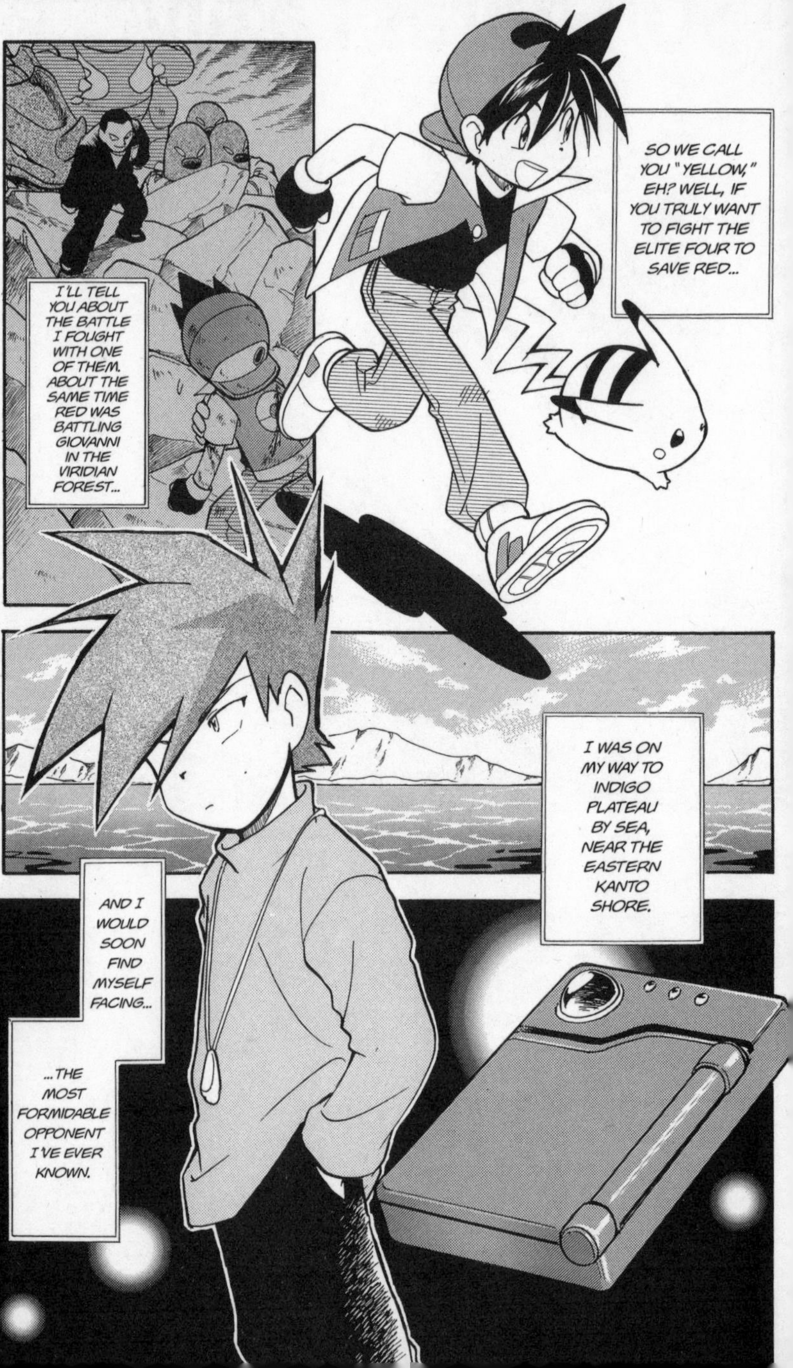
SO WE CALL YOU "YELLOW," EH? WELL, IF YOU TRULY WANT TO FIGHT THE ELITE FOUR TO SAVE RED...
I'LL TELL YOU ABOUT THE BATTLE I FOUGHT WITH ONE OF THEM. ABOUT THE SAME TIME RED WAS BATTLING GIOVANNI IN THE VIRIDIAN FOREST...
I WAS ON MY WAY TO INDIGO PLATEAU BY SEA, NEAR THE EASTERN KANTO SHORE.
AND I WOULD SOON FIND MYSELF FACING...
...THE MOST FORMIDABLE OPPONENT I'VE EVER KNOWN.

50 Lapras Lazily

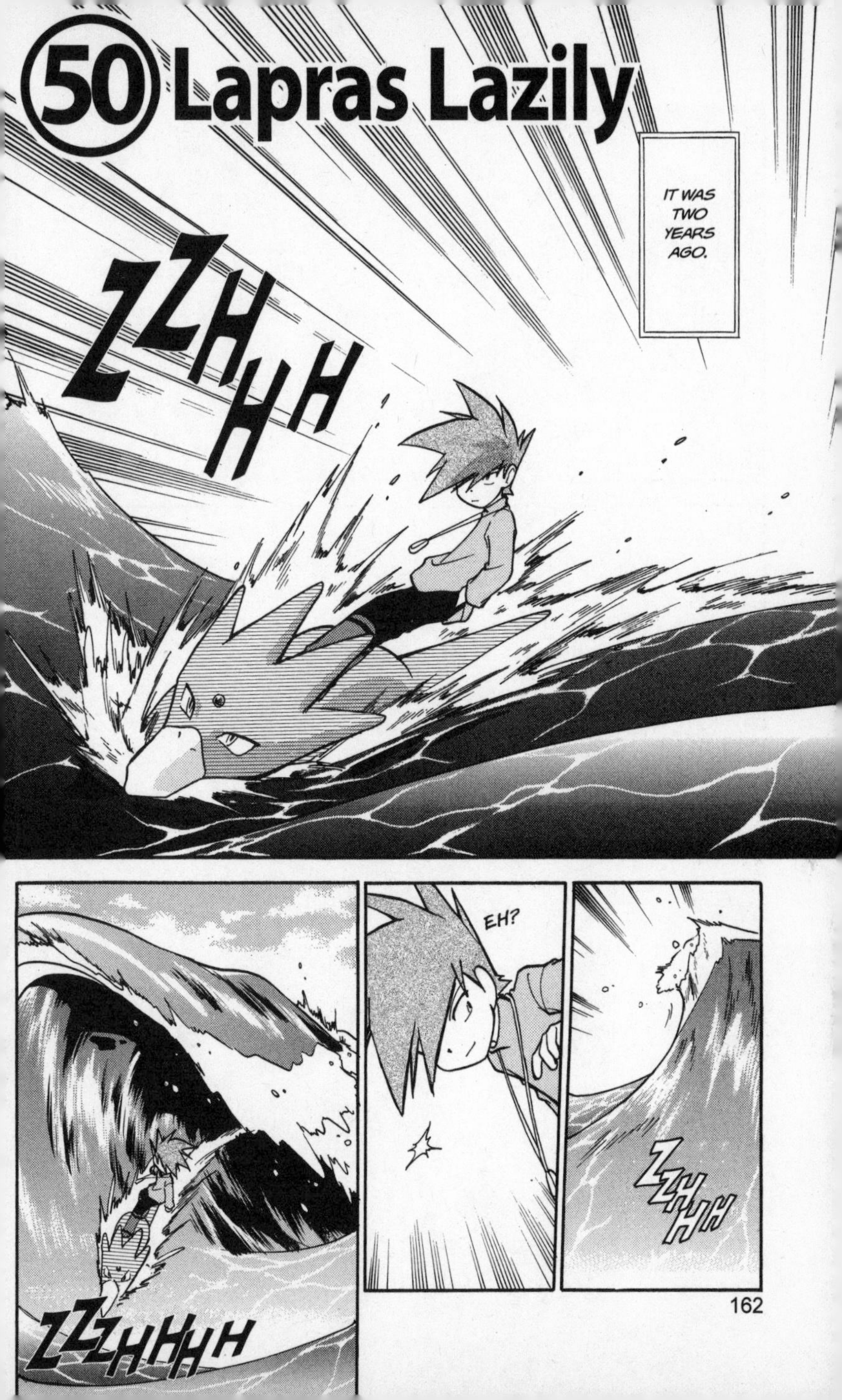

IT WAS TWO YEARS AGO.
ZZHHHH
ZZHHH
EH?
ZZZHHHHH

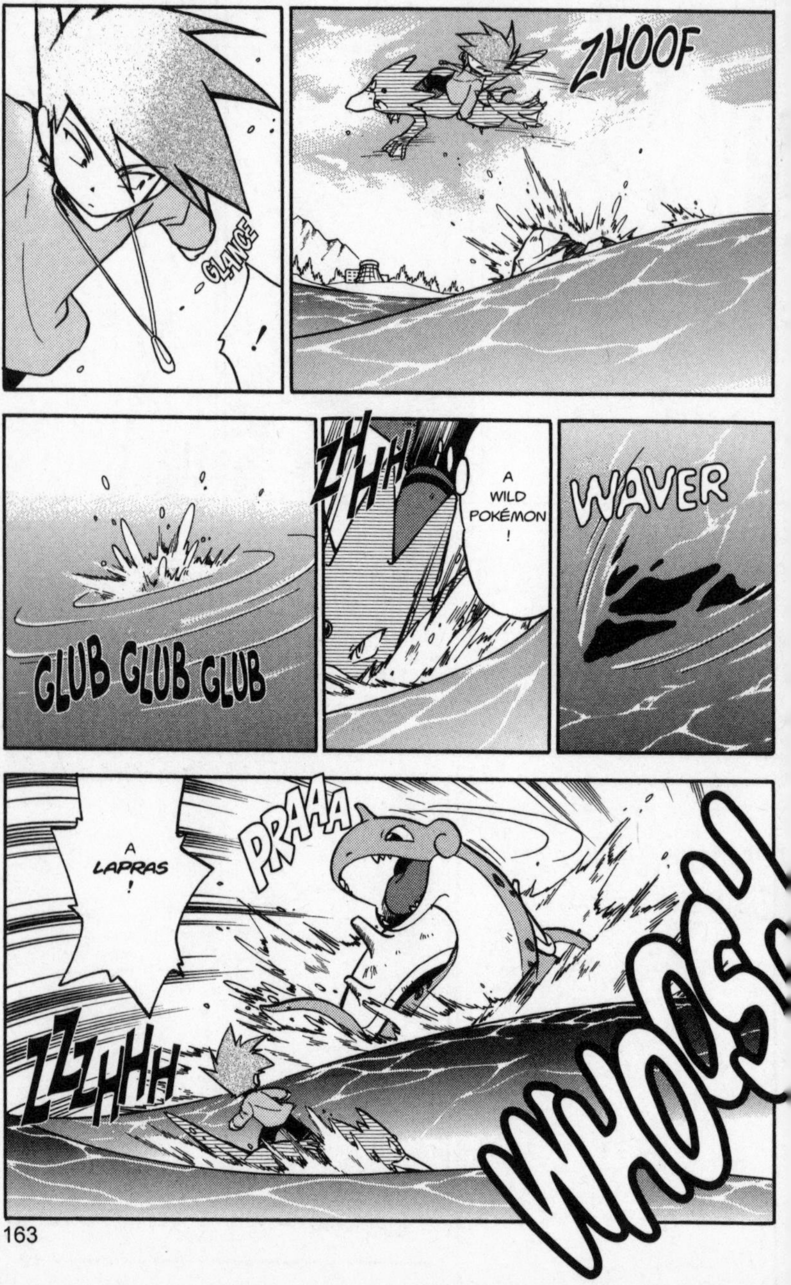
ZHOOF
GLANCE
!
WAVER
ZHHH
A WILD POKÉMON !
GLUB GLUB GLUB
WHOOS
PRAAA
A LAPRAS !
ZZZHHH

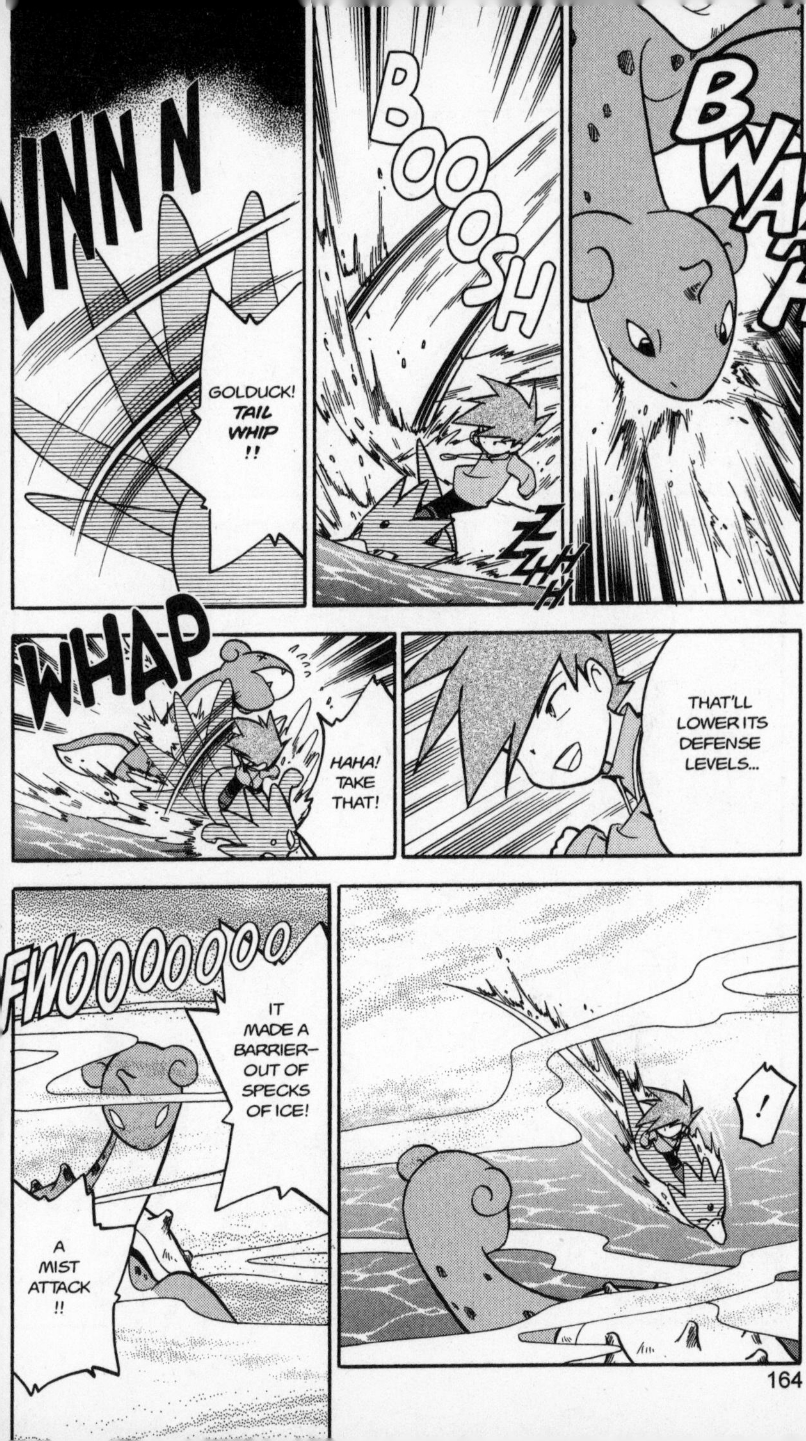
BWAAAH
BOOOSH
ZZHHH
VNNN N
GOLDUCK! TAIL WHIP!!
THAT'LL LOWER ITS DEFENSE LEVELS...
WHAP
HAHA! TAKE THAT!
!
FWOOOOOOO
IT MADE A BARRIER— OUT OF SPECKS OF ICE!
A MIST ATTACK!!

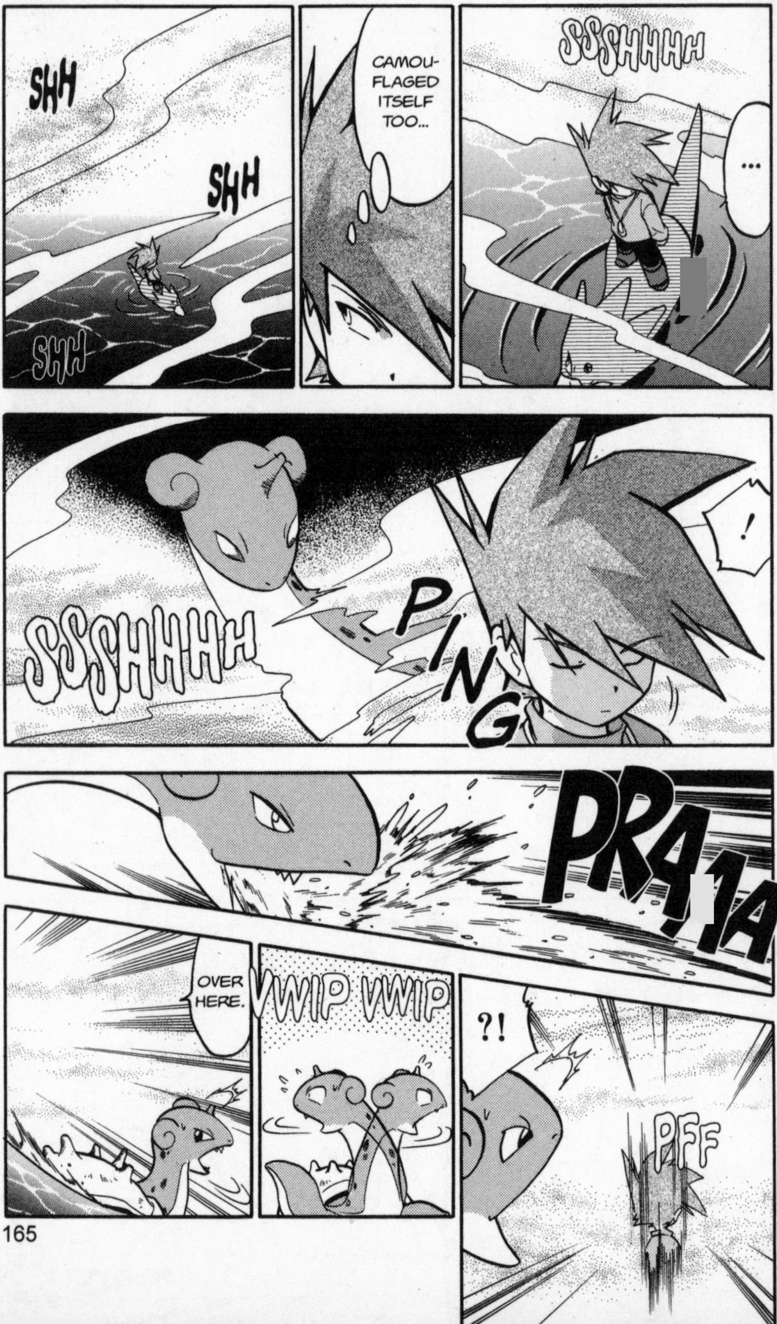
SSSHHHH
...
CAMOUFLAGED ITSELF TOO...
SHH
SHH
SHH
!
PING
SSSHHHH
PRA
?!
PFF
VWIP VWIP
OVER HERE.

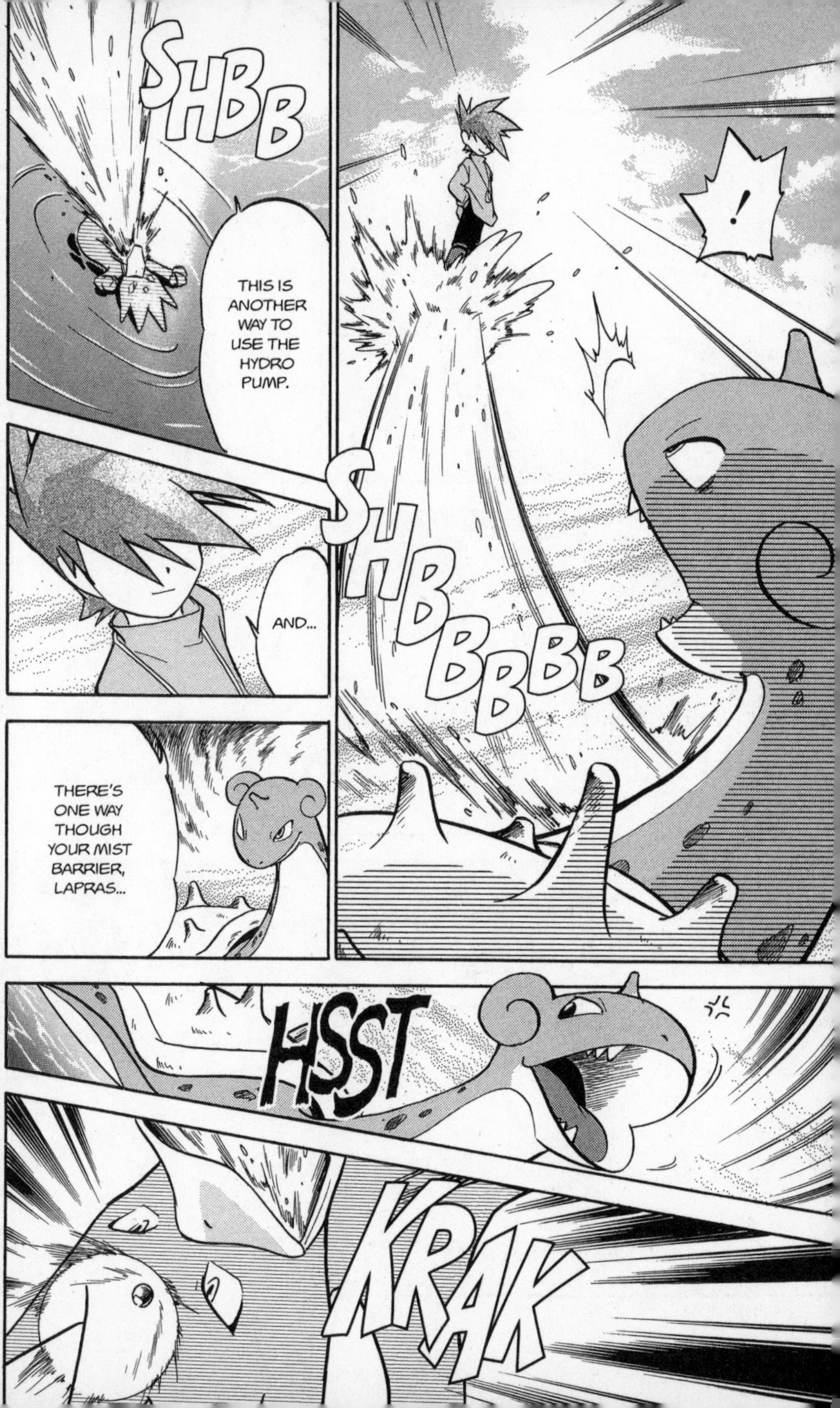
!
SHBBBBBB
SHBB
THIS IS ANOTHER WAY TO USE THE HYDRO PUMP.
AND...
THERE'S ONE WAY THOUGH YOUR MIST BARRIER, LAPRAS...
HSST
KRAK

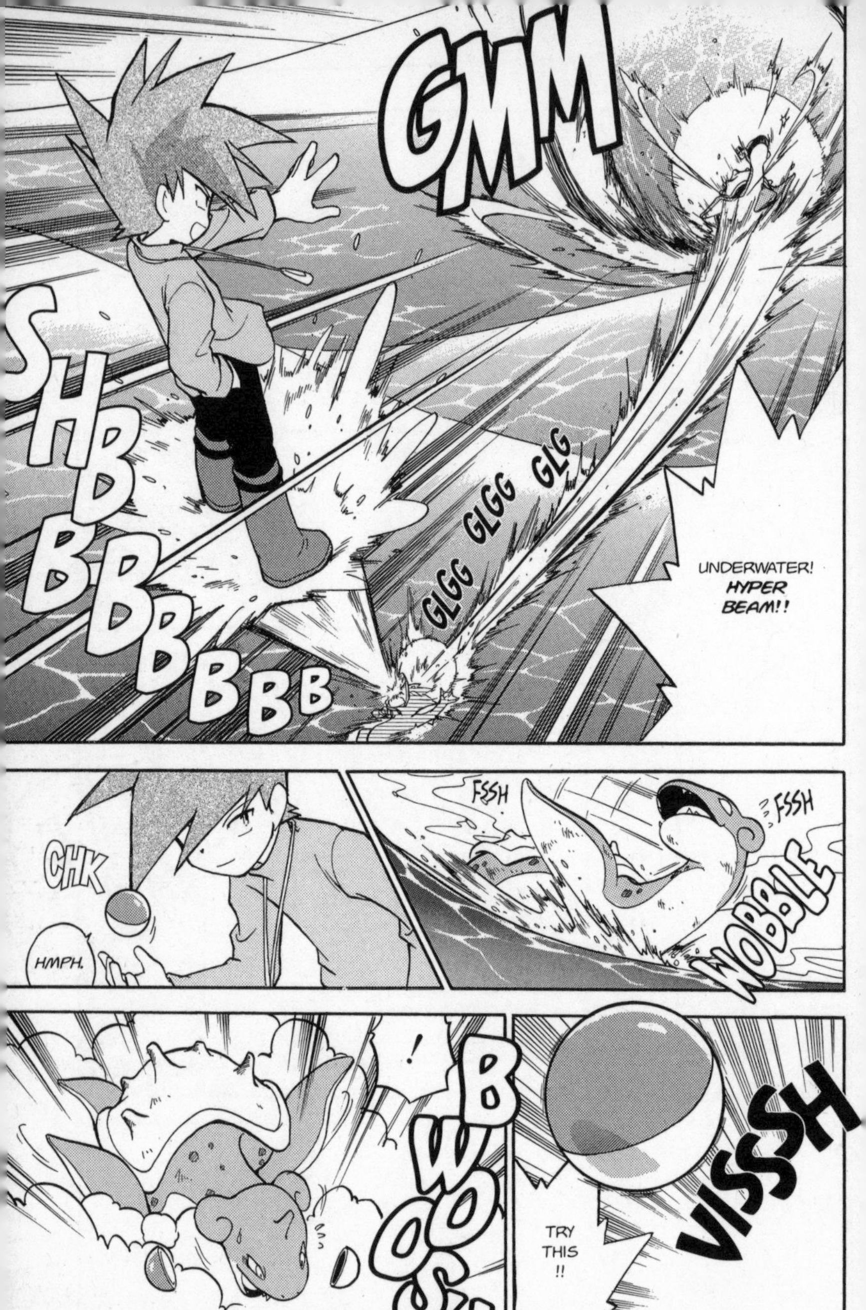
GMM
UNDERWATER! HYPER BEAM!!
GLG GLGG GLGG
SHBBBBBBB
FSSH
FSSH
WOBBLE
CHK
HMPH.
VISSSH
TRY THIS !!
!
BWOOOSH

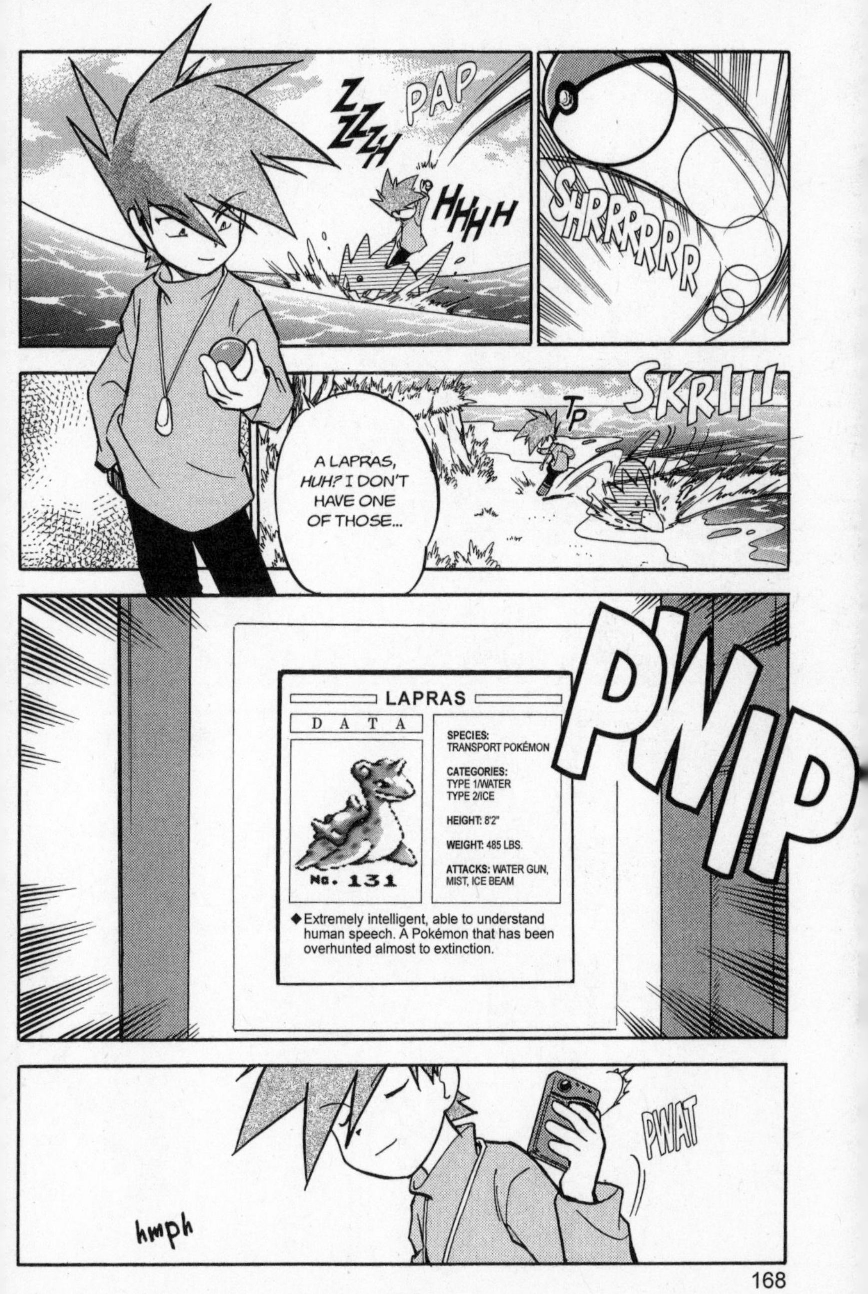
SHRRRRRRRR
ZZZZH
PAP
HHHH
SKRIII'
TP
A LAPRAS, HUH? I DON'T HAVE ONE OF THOSE...
PWIP
LAPRAS
DATA
No. 131
SPECIES: TRANSPORT POKÉMON
CATEGORIES: TYPE 1/WATER TYPE 2/ICE
HEIGHT: 8'2"
WEIGHT: 485 LBS.
ATTACKS: WATER GUN, MIST, ICE BEAM
◆Extremely intelligent, able to understand human speech. A Pokémon that has been overhunted almost to extinction.
PWAT
hmph

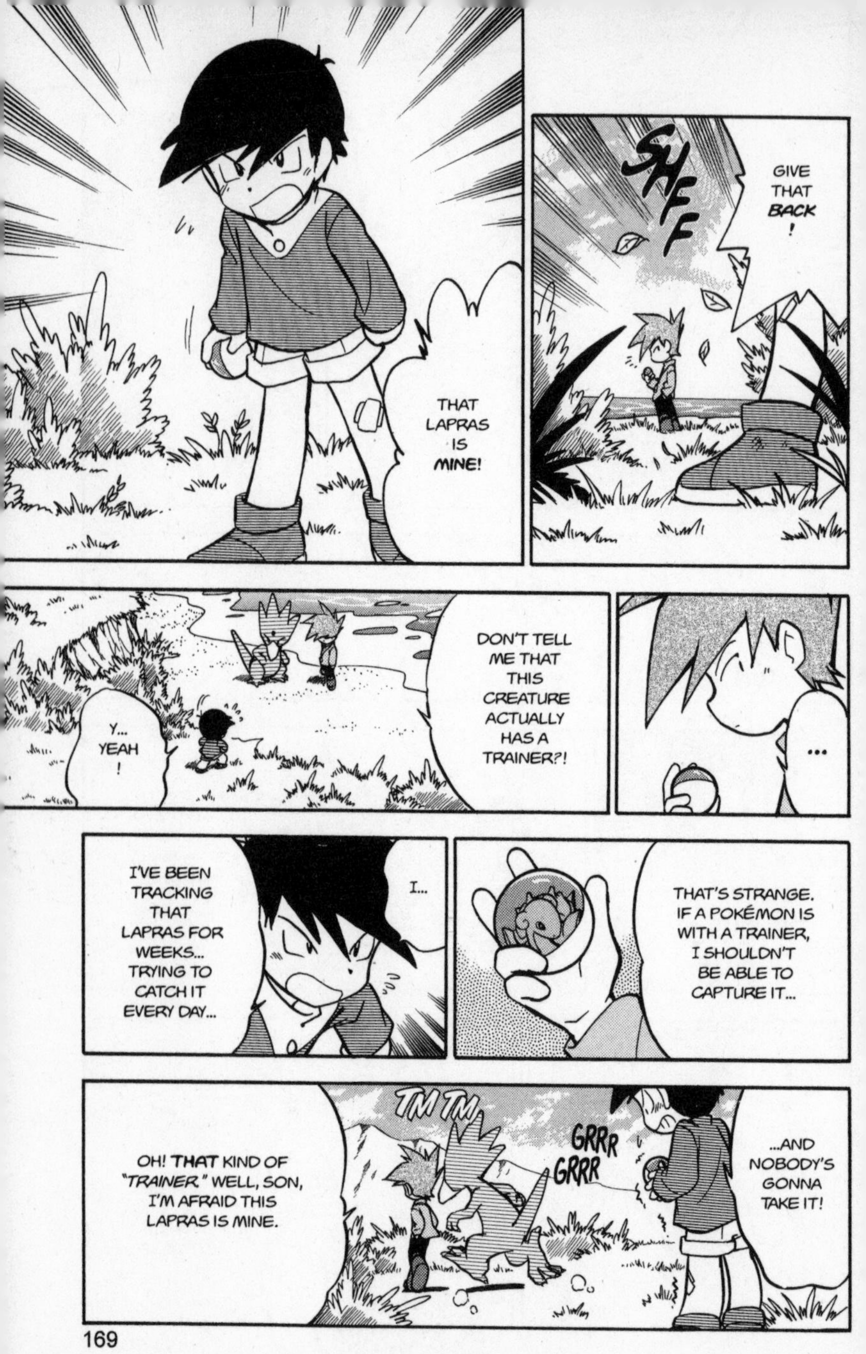
GIVE THAT BACK!
SHFF
THAT LAPRAS IS MINE!
...
DON'T TELL ME THAT THIS CREATURE ACTUALLY HAS A TRAINER?!
Y... YEAH!
THAT'S STRANGE. IF A POKÉMON IS WITH A TRAINER, I SHOULDN'T BE ABLE TO CAPTURE IT...
I...
I'VE BEEN TRACKING THAT LAPRAS FOR WEEKS... TRYING TO CATCH IT EVERY DAY...
...AND NOBODY'S GONNA TAKE IT!
GRRR GRRR
TM TM
OH! THAT KIND OF "TRAINER." WELL, SON, I'M AFRAID THIS LAPRAS IS MINE.

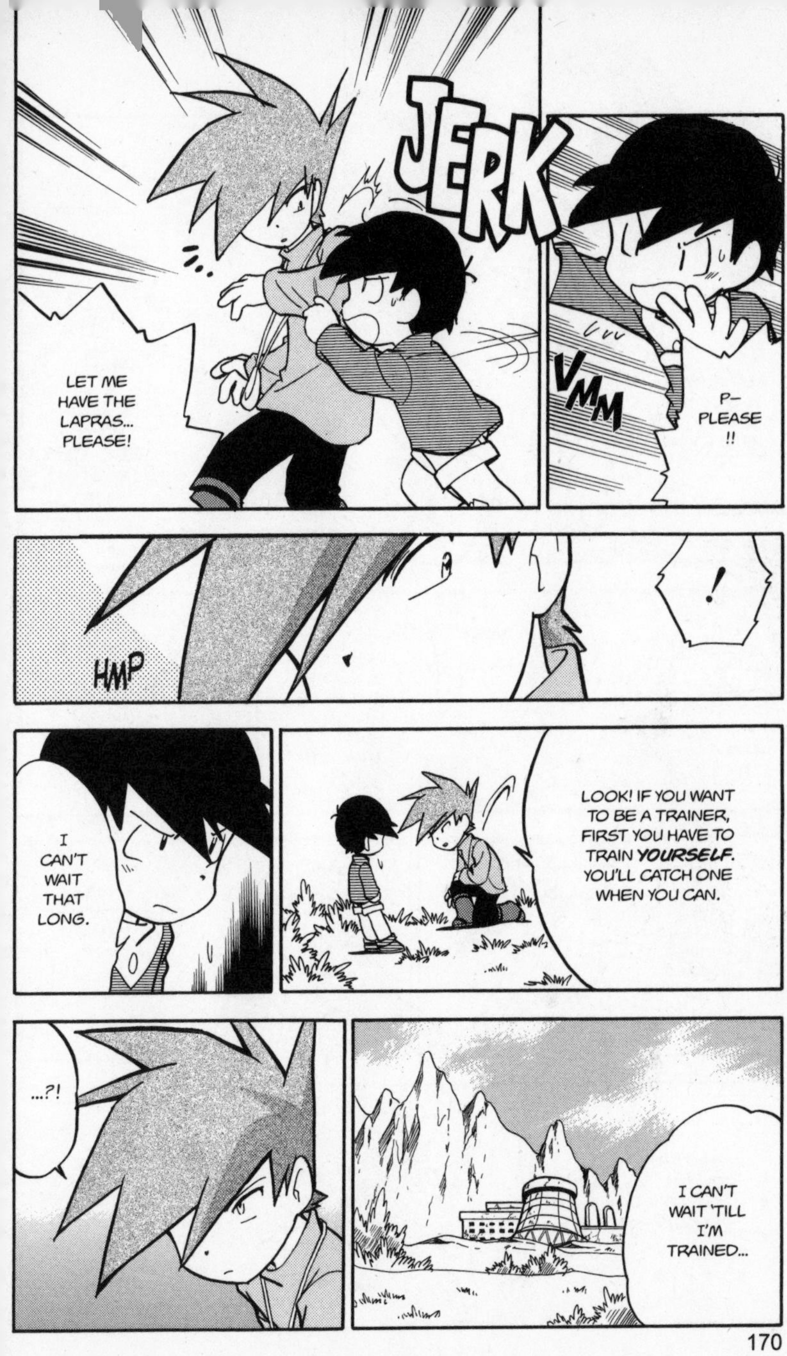

VMM
P— PLEASE !!
JERK
LET ME HAVE THE LAPRAS... PLEASE!
!
HMP
LOOK! IF YOU WANT TO BE A TRAINER, FIRST YOU HAVE TO TRAIN ***YOURSELF***. YOU'LL CATCH ONE WHEN YOU CAN.
I CAN'T WAIT THAT LONG.
I CAN'T WAIT 'TILL I'M TRAINED...
...?!

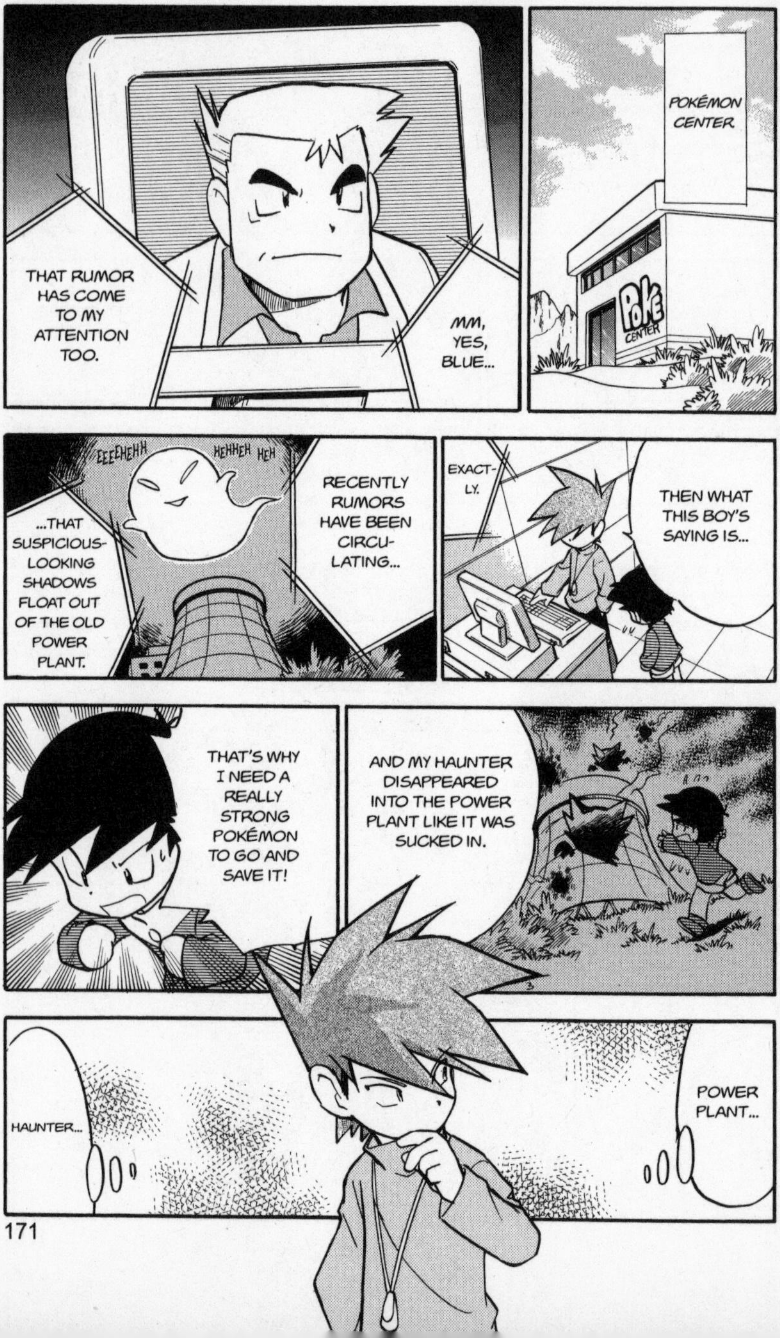
POKÉMON CENTER
POKé CENTER
MM, YES, BLUE...
THAT RUMOR HAS COME TO MY ATTENTION TOO.
THEN WHAT THIS BOY'S SAYING IS...
EXACT-LY.
RECENTLY RUMORS HAVE BEEN CIRCU-LATING...
HEHHEH HEH
EEEEHEHH
...THAT SUSPICIOUS-LOOKING SHADOWS FLOAT OUT OF THE OLD POWER PLANT.
AND MY HAUNTER DISAPPEARED INTO THE POWER PLANT LIKE IT WAS SUCKED IN.
THAT'S WHY I NEED A REALLY STRONG POKÉMON TO GO AND SAVE IT!
POWER PLANT...
HAUNTER...

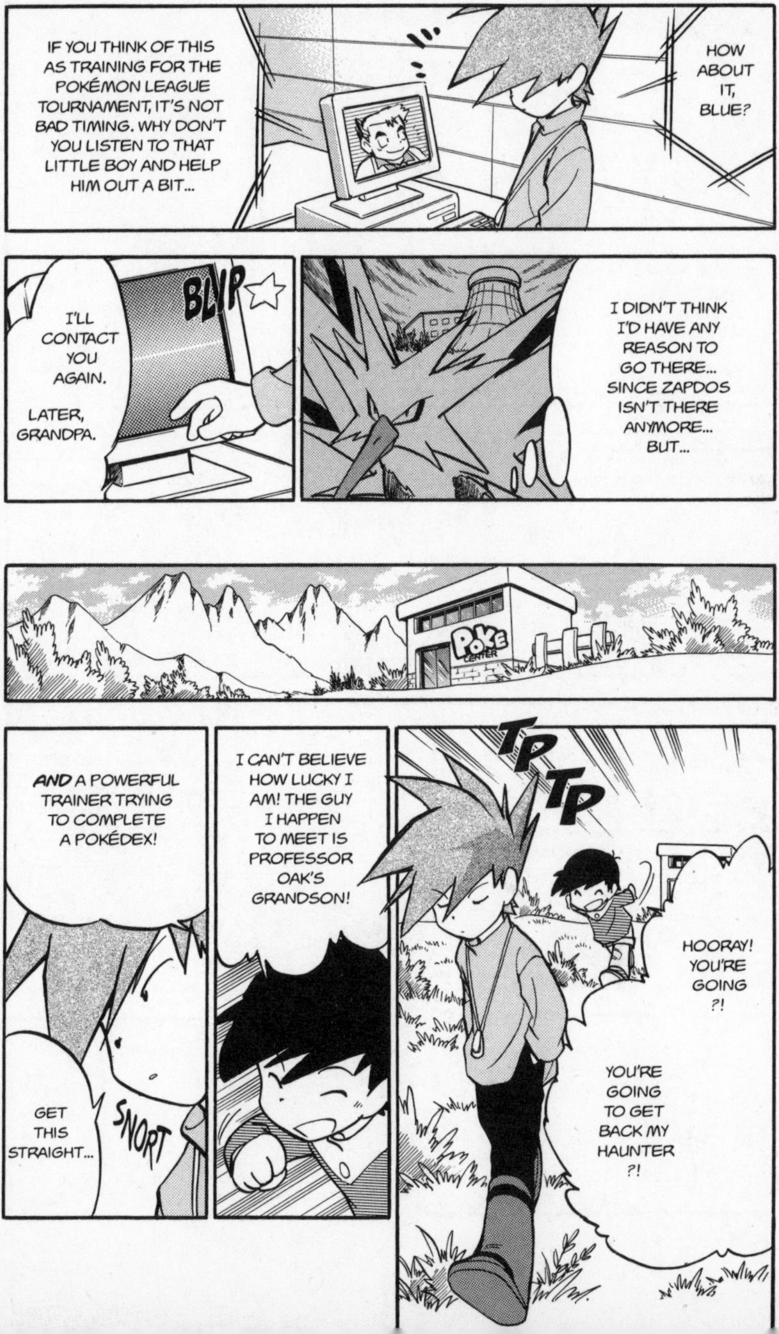
HOW ABOUT IT, BLUE?
IF YOU THINK OF THIS AS TRAINING FOR THE POKÉMON LEAGUE TOURNAMENT, IT'S NOT BAD TIMING. WHY DON'T YOU LISTEN TO THAT LITTLE BOY AND HELP HIM OUT A BIT...
I DIDN'T THINK I'D HAVE ANY REASON TO GO THERE... SINCE ZAPDOS ISN'T THERE ANYMORE... BUT...
BLIP
I'LL CONTACT YOU AGAIN.
LATER, GRANDPA.
POKE CENTER
TPTP
HOORAY! YOU'RE GOING?!
YOU'RE GOING TO GET BACK MY HAUNTER?!
I CAN'T BELIEVE HOW LUCKY I AM! THE GUY I HAPPEN TO MEET IS PROFESSOR OAK'S GRANDSON!
AND A POWERFUL TRAINER TRYING TO COMPLETE A POKÉDEX!
GET THIS STRAIGHT...
SNORT

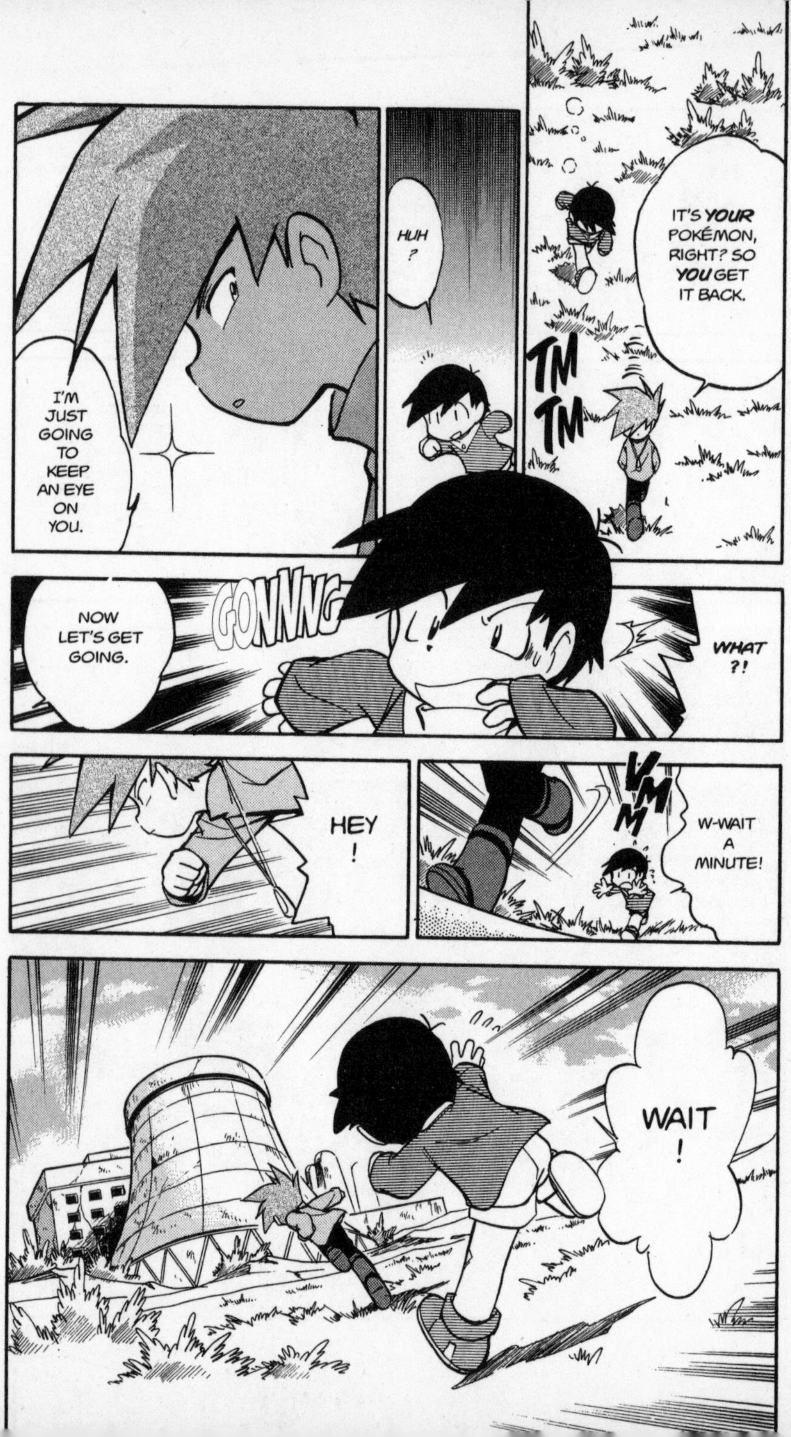
IT'S **YOUR** POKÉMON, RIGHT? SO **YOU** GET IT BACK.
TM TM
HUH ?
I'M JUST GOING TO KEEP AN EYE ON YOU.
WHAT ?!
GONNNG
NOW LET'S GET GOING.
VMMM
W-WAIT A MINUTE!
HEY !
WAIT !

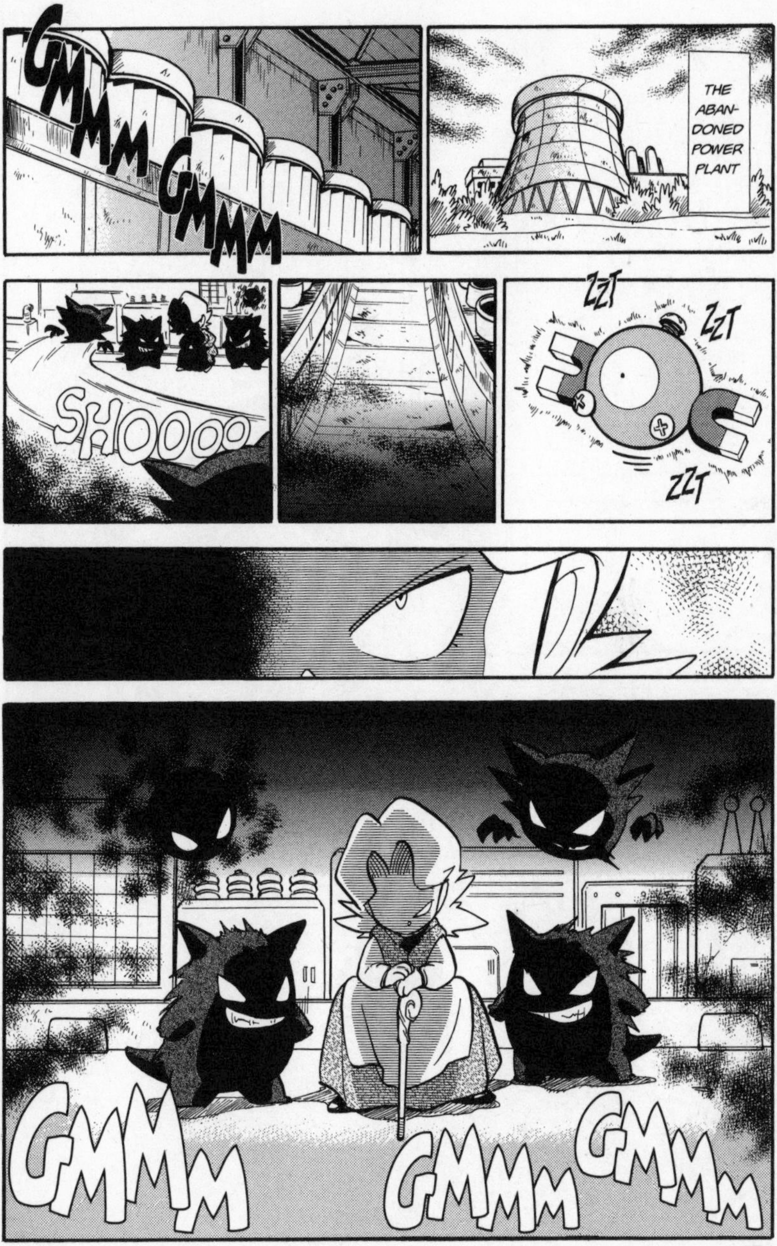

THE ABAN-
DONED
POWER
PLANT
GMMM GMMMM
ZZT
ZZT
ZZT
SHOOOO
GMMMM
GMMMM
GMMMM

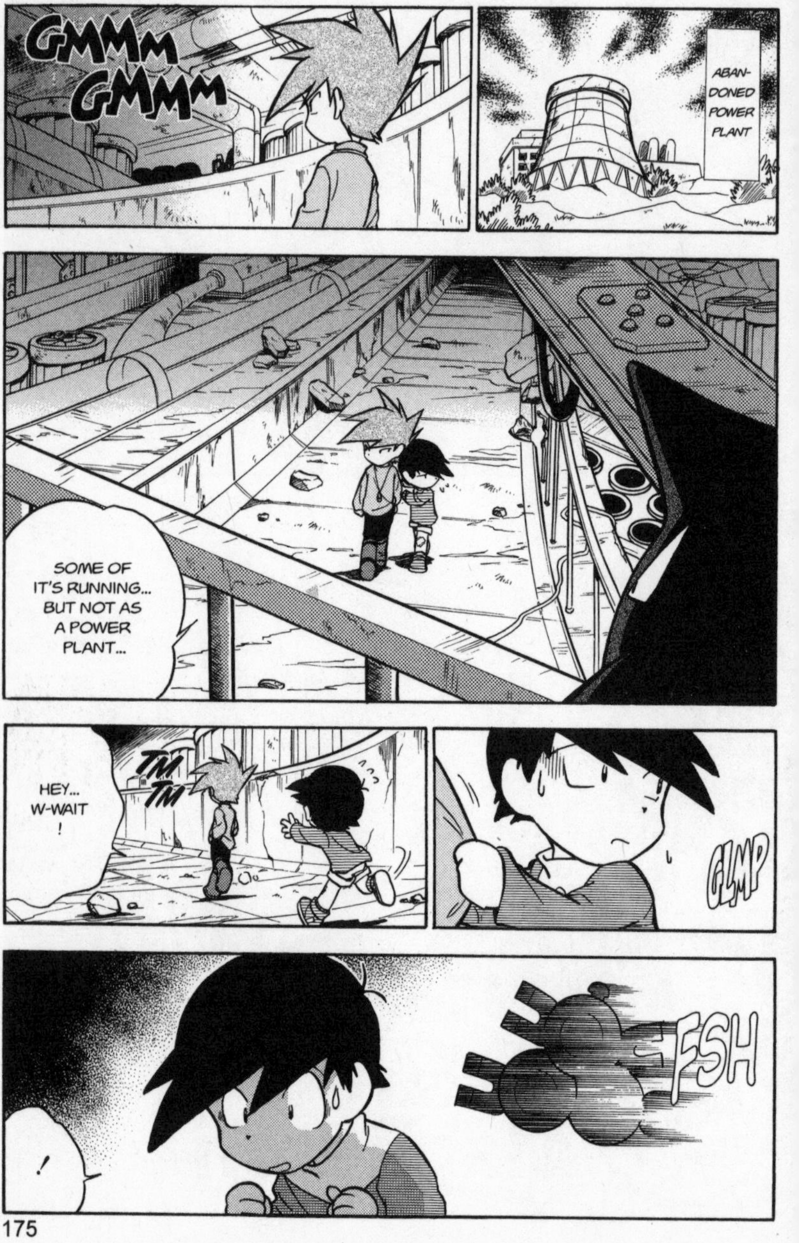
ABAN-
DONED
POWER
PLANT
GMMM GMMM
SOME OF IT'S RUNNING... BUT NOT AS A POWER PLANT...
GLMP
TM TM
HEY... W-WAIT !
FSH
!

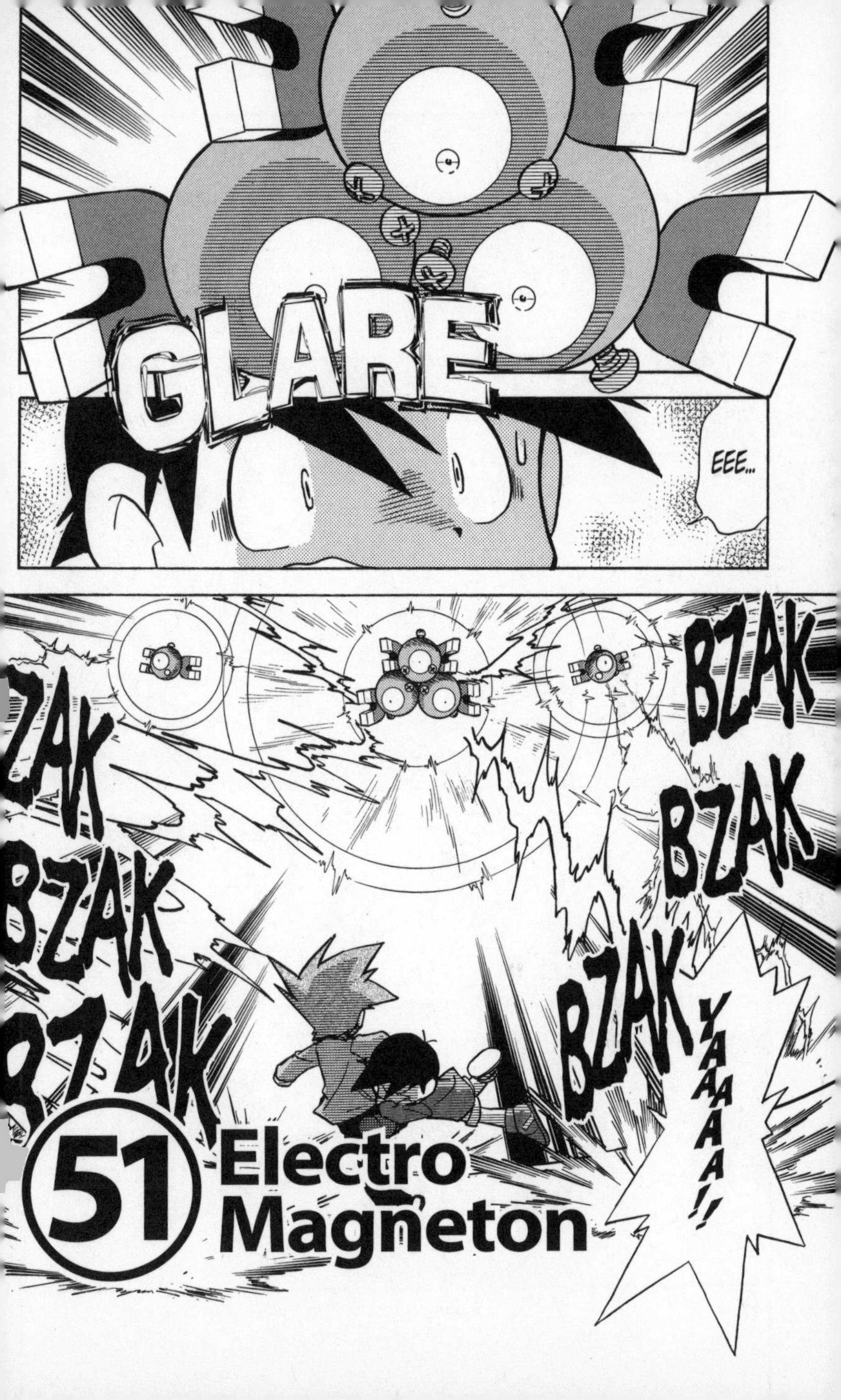
GLARE
EEE...
BZAK
BZAK
BZAK
BZAK
YAAAAA!!
ZAK
BZAK
BZAK

51 Electro Magneton

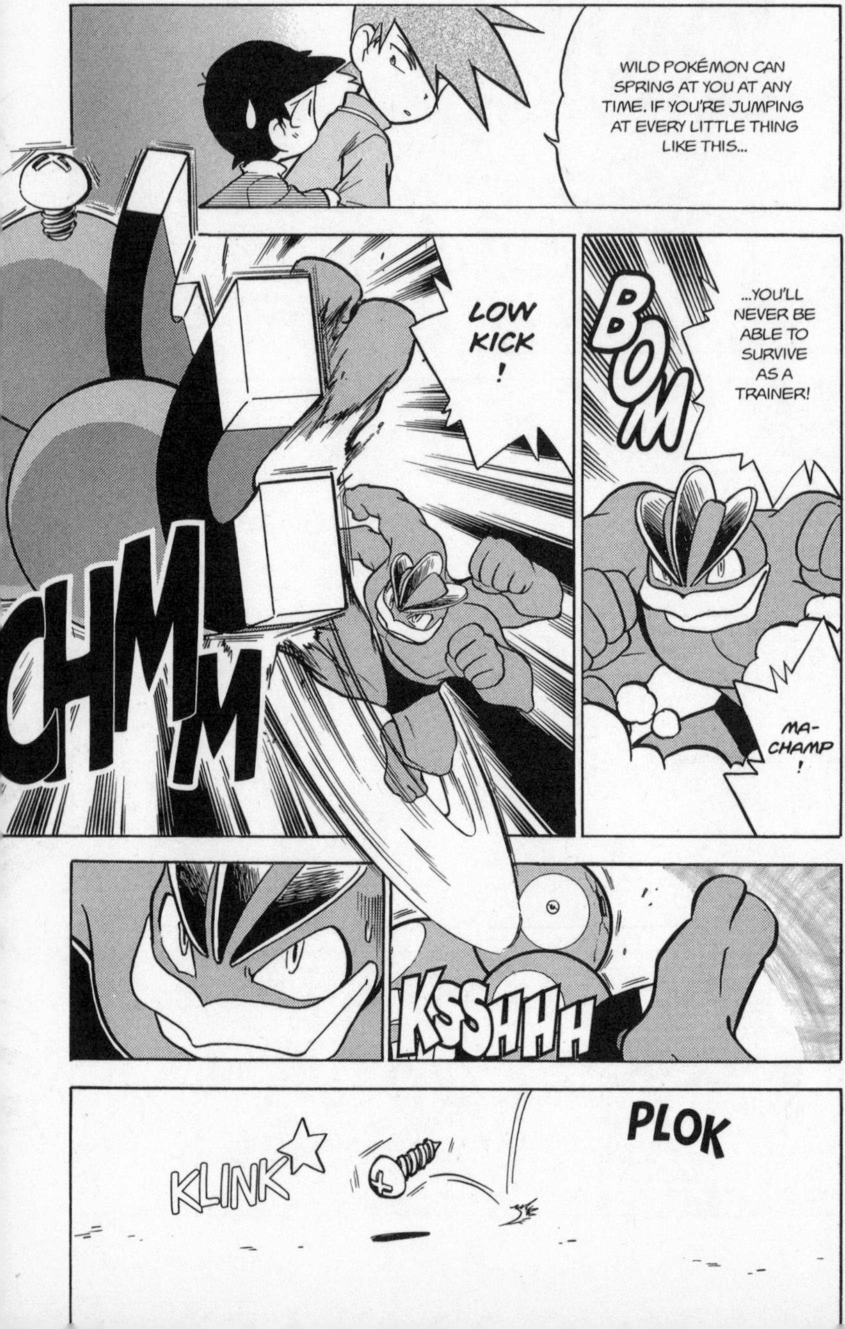
WILD POKÉMON CAN SPRING AT YOU AT ANY TIME. IF YOU'RE JUMPING AT EVERY LITTLE THING LIKE THIS...
BOM
...YOU'LL NEVER BE ABLE TO SURVIVE AS A TRAINER!
MA-CHAMP!
LOW KICK!
CHMMM
KSSHHH
PLOK
KLINK

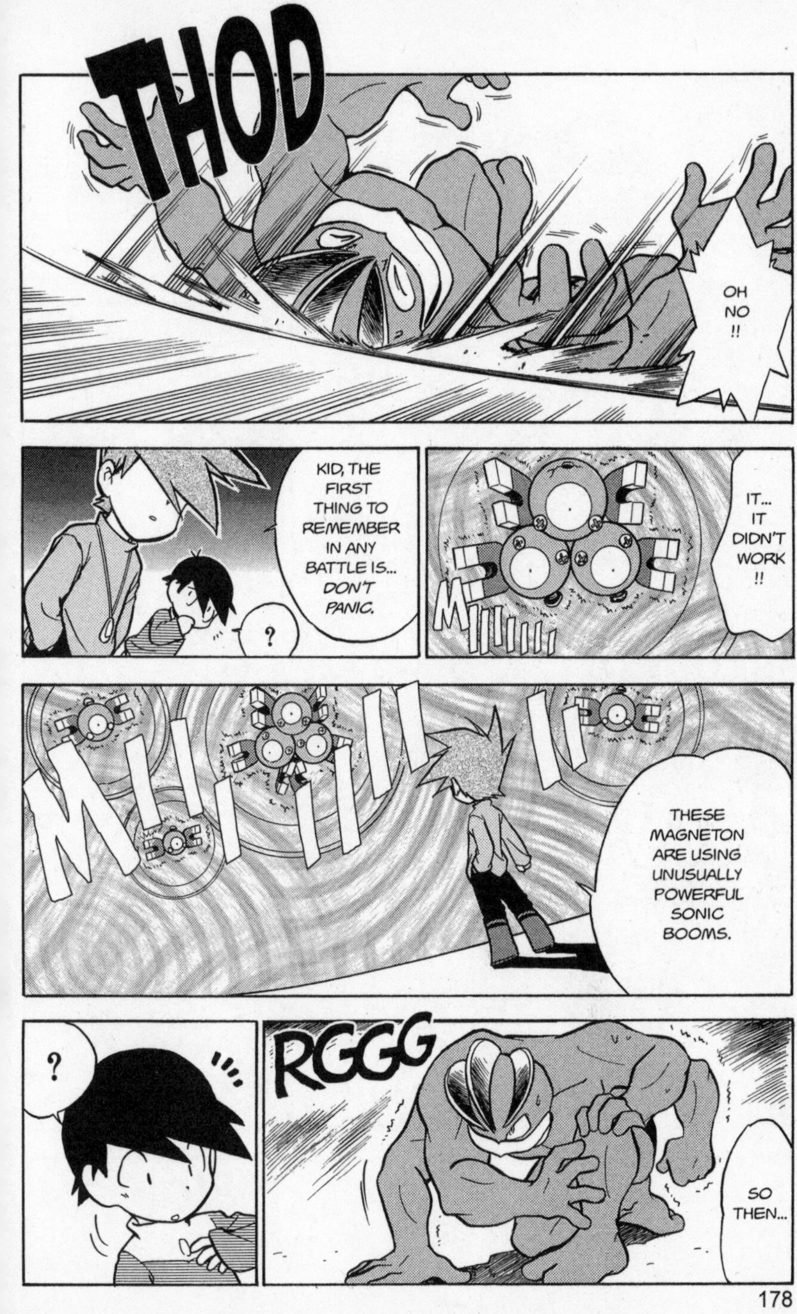
THOD
OH NO !!
IT... IT DIDN'T WORK !!
MIIIIIII
KID, THE FIRST THING TO REMEMBER IN ANY BATTLE IS... DON'T PANIC.
?
MIIIIIII
THESE MAGNETON ARE USING UNUSUALLY POWERFUL SONIC BOOMS.
RGGG
SO THEN...
?

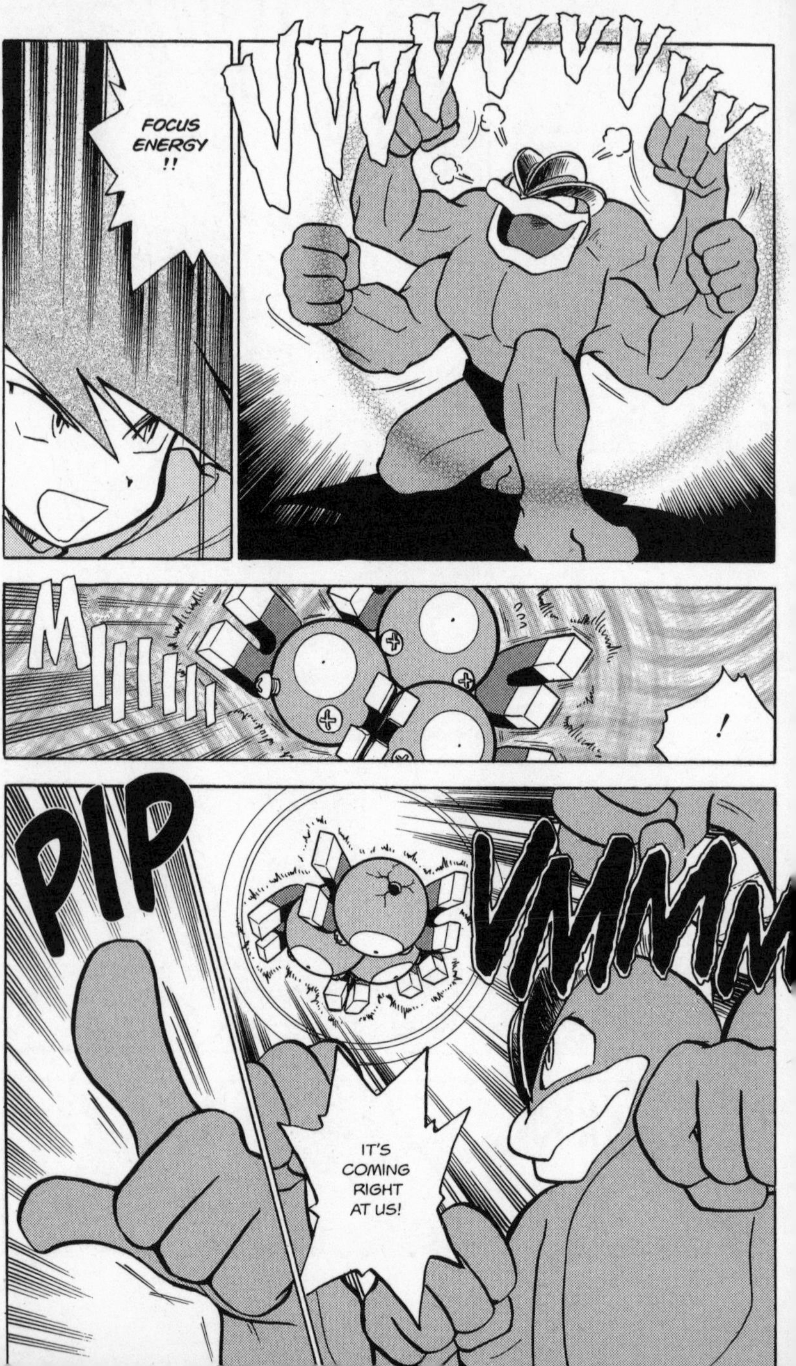
FOCUS ENERGY !!
M
!
PIP
IT'S COMING RIGHT AT US!

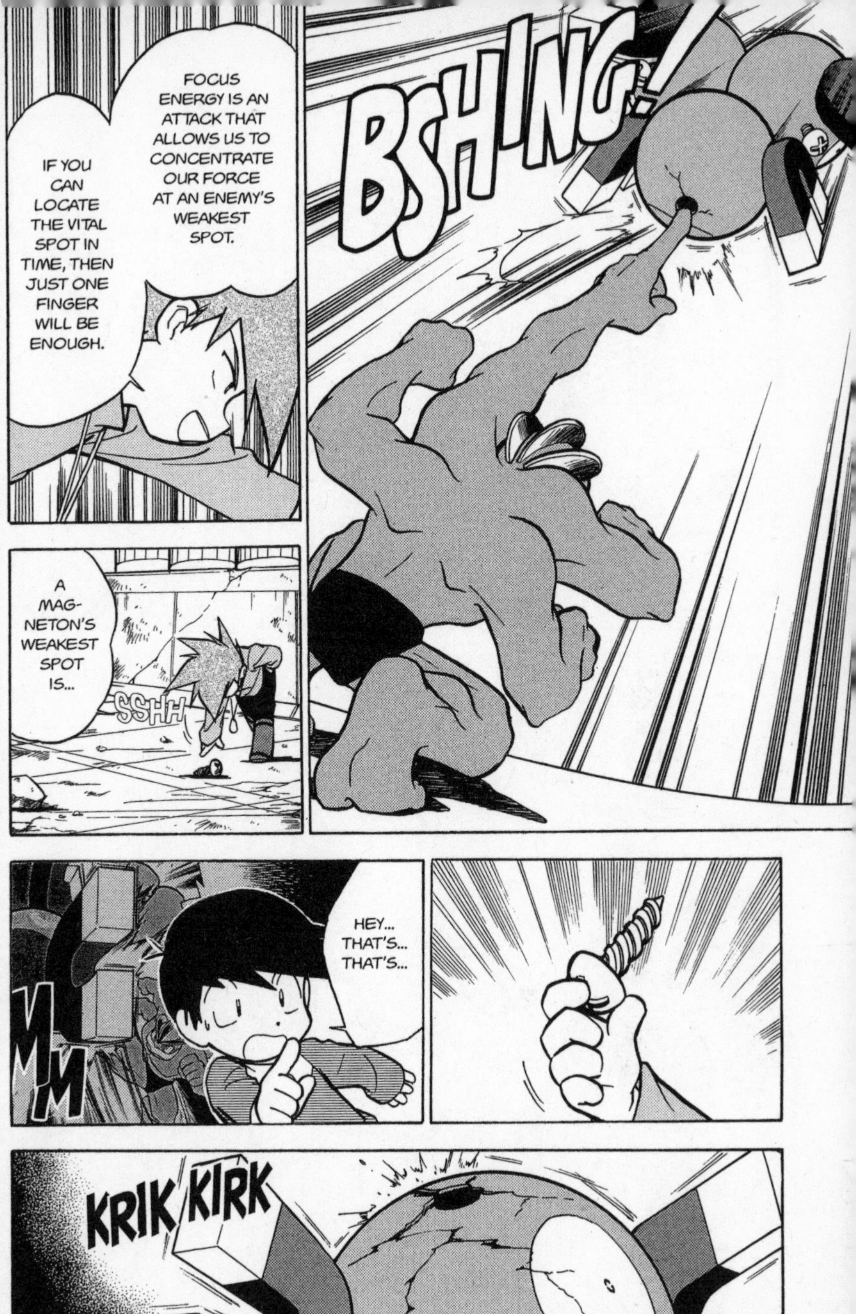
BSHING!
FOCUS ENERGY IS AN ATTACK THAT ALLOWS US TO CONCENTRATE OUR FORCE AT AN ENEMY'S WEAKEST SPOT.
IF YOU CAN LOCATE THE VITAL SPOT IN TIME, THEN JUST ONE FINGER WILL BE ENOUGH.
A MAG-NETON'S WEAKEST SPOT IS...
SSHH
HEY... THAT'S... THAT'S...
MMM
KRIK KIRK

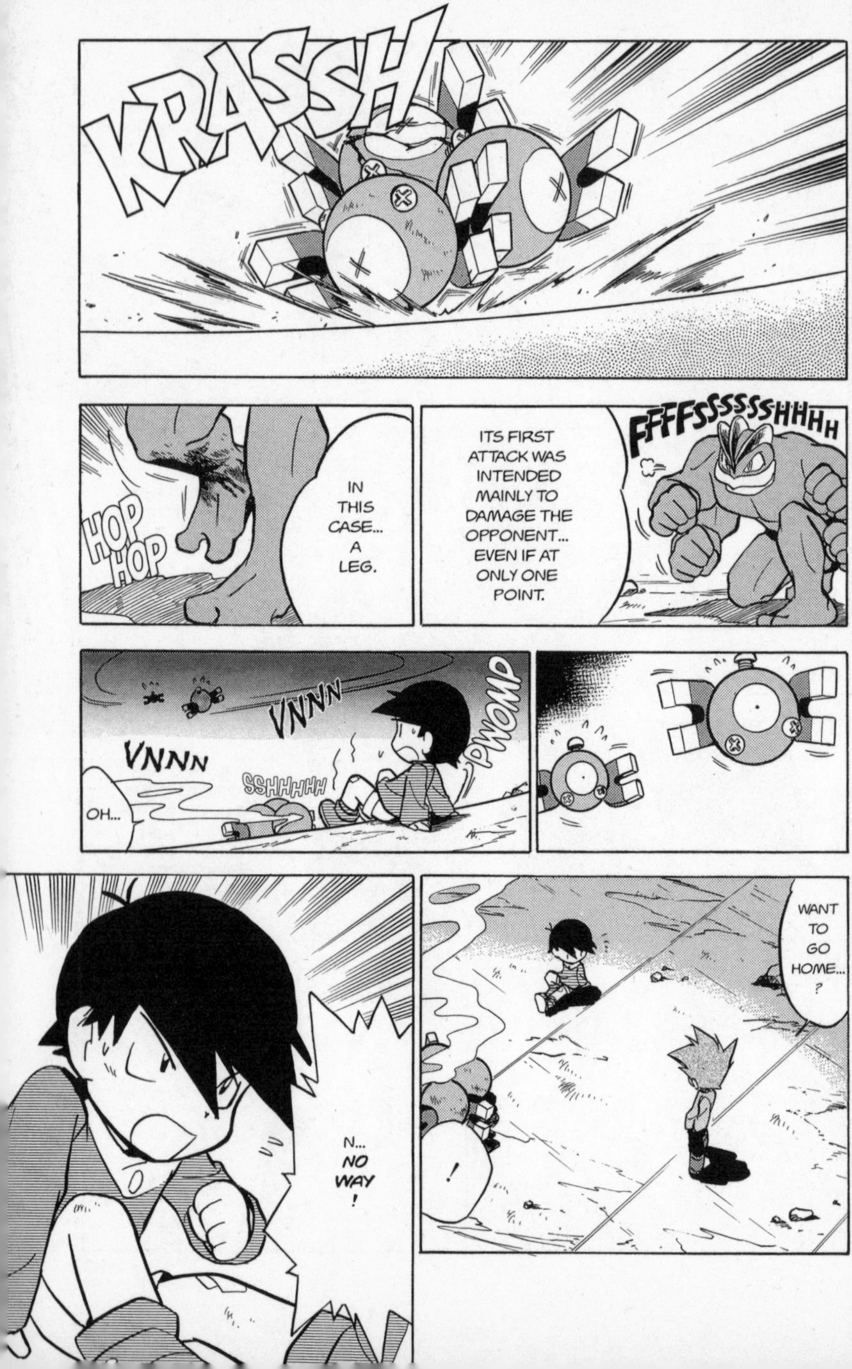
KRASSH!
FFFSSSSSSHHHH
ITS FIRST ATTACK WAS INTENDED MAINLY TO DAMAGE THE OPPONENT... EVEN IF AT ONLY ONE POINT.
HOP HOP
IN THIS CASE... A LEG.
PWOMP
VNNN
VNNN
SSHHHHH
OH...
WANT TO GO HOME...?
!
N... NO WAY!

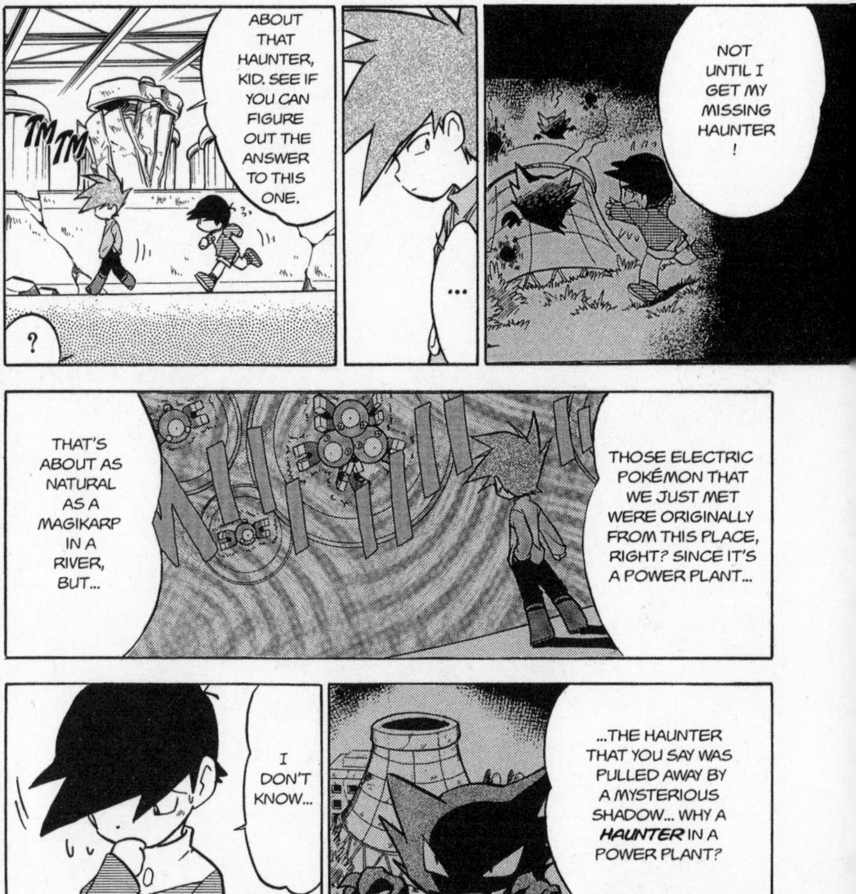
NOT UNTIL I GET MY MISSING HAUNTER!
...
ABOUT THAT HAUNTER, KID. SEE IF YOU CAN FIGURE OUT THE ANSWER TO THIS ONE.
TM TM
?
THOSE ELECTRIC POKÉMON THAT WE JUST MET WERE ORIGINALLY FROM THIS PLACE, RIGHT? SINCE IT'S A POWER PLANT...
THAT'S ABOUT AS NATURAL AS A MAGIKARP IN A RIVER, BUT...
...THE HAUNTER THAT YOU SAY WAS PULLED AWAY BY A MYSTERIOUS SHADOW... WHY A **HAUNTER** IN A POWER PLANT?
I DON'T KNOW...
TM TM TM
BUT I **SAW** IT! I'M NOT MAKING IT UP!
I REALLY DON'T CARE WHETHER YOU GET YOUR POKÉMON BACK OR NOT. I JUST WANT TO KNOW THE REASON BEHIND THIS WEIRDNESS.

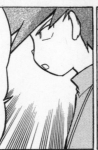

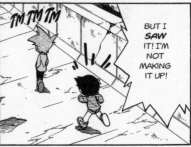

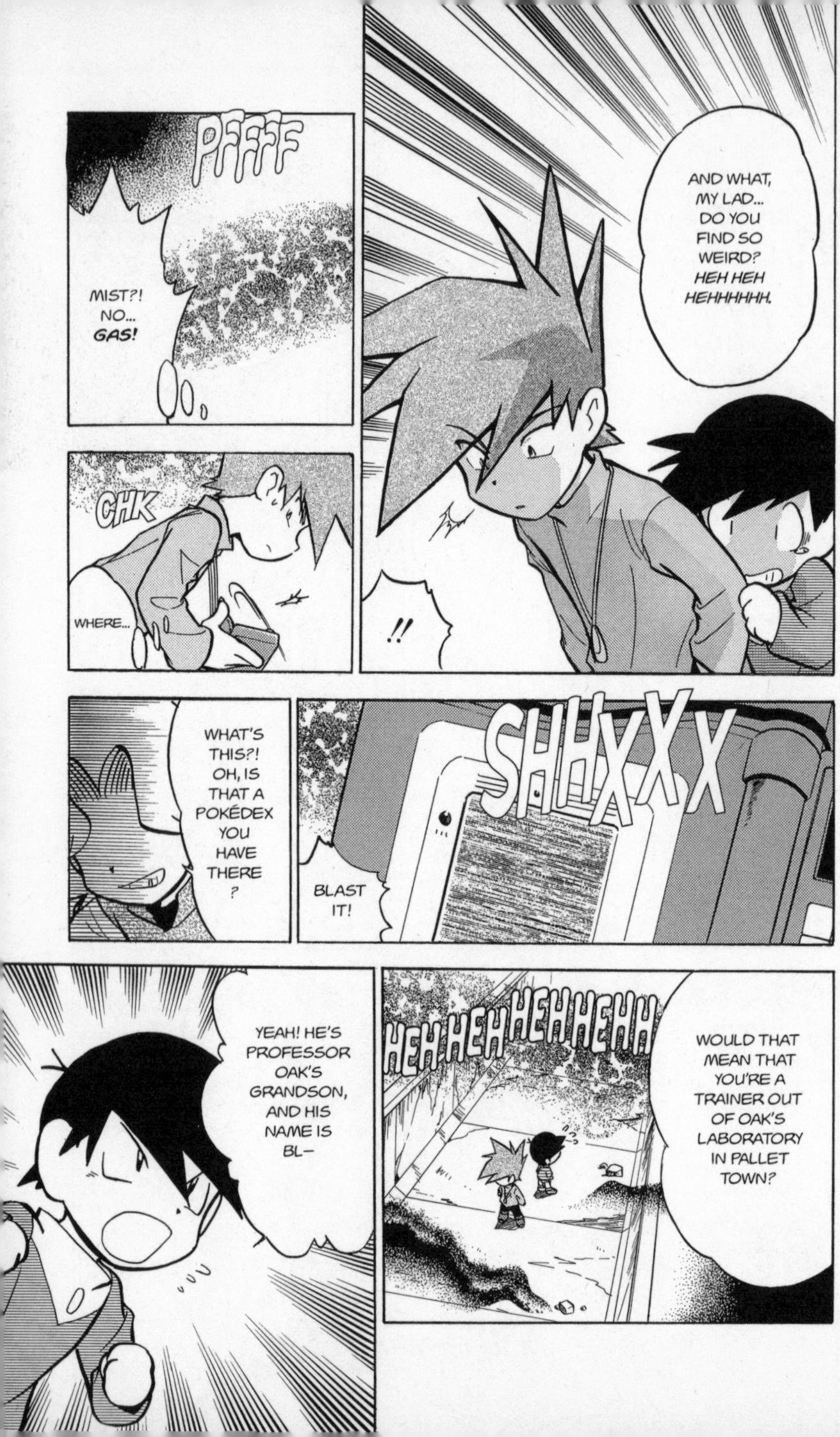
AND WHAT, MY LAD... DO YOU FIND SO WEIRD? HEH HEH HEHHHHHH.
!!
PFFFF
MIST?! NO... GAS!
CHK
WHERE...
SHHXXX
BLAST IT!
WHAT'S THIS?! OH, IS THAT A POKÉDEX YOU HAVE THERE?
HEH HEH HEH HEH HEH
WOULD THAT MEAN THAT YOU'RE A TRAINER OUT OF OAK'S LABORATORY IN PALLET TOWN?
YEAH! HE'S PROFESSOR OAK'S GRANDSON, AND HIS NAME IS BL–

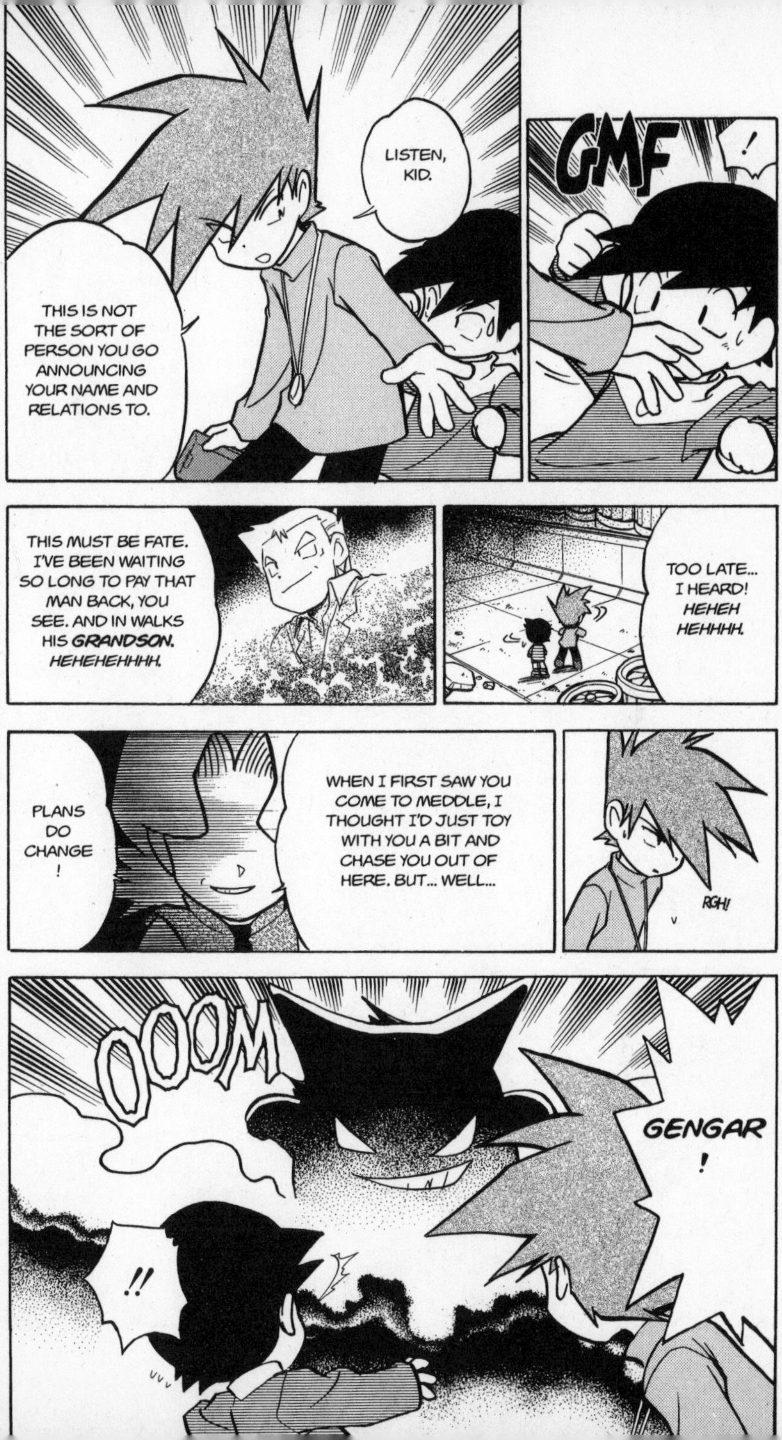
GMF
!
LISTEN, KID.
THIS IS NOT THE SORT OF PERSON YOU GO ANNOUNCING YOUR NAME AND RELATIONS TO.
TOO LATE... I HEARD! *HEHEH HEHHHH.*
THIS MUST BE FATE. I'VE BEEN WAITING SO LONG TO PAY THAT MAN BACK, YOU SEE. AND IN WALKS HIS ***GRANDSON. HEHEHEHHHH.***
RGH!
WHEN I FIRST SAW YOU COME TO MEDDLE, I THOUGHT I'D JUST TOY WITH YOU A BIT AND CHASE YOU OUT OF HERE. BUT... WELL...
PLANS DO CHANGE!
GENGAR!
OOOM
!!

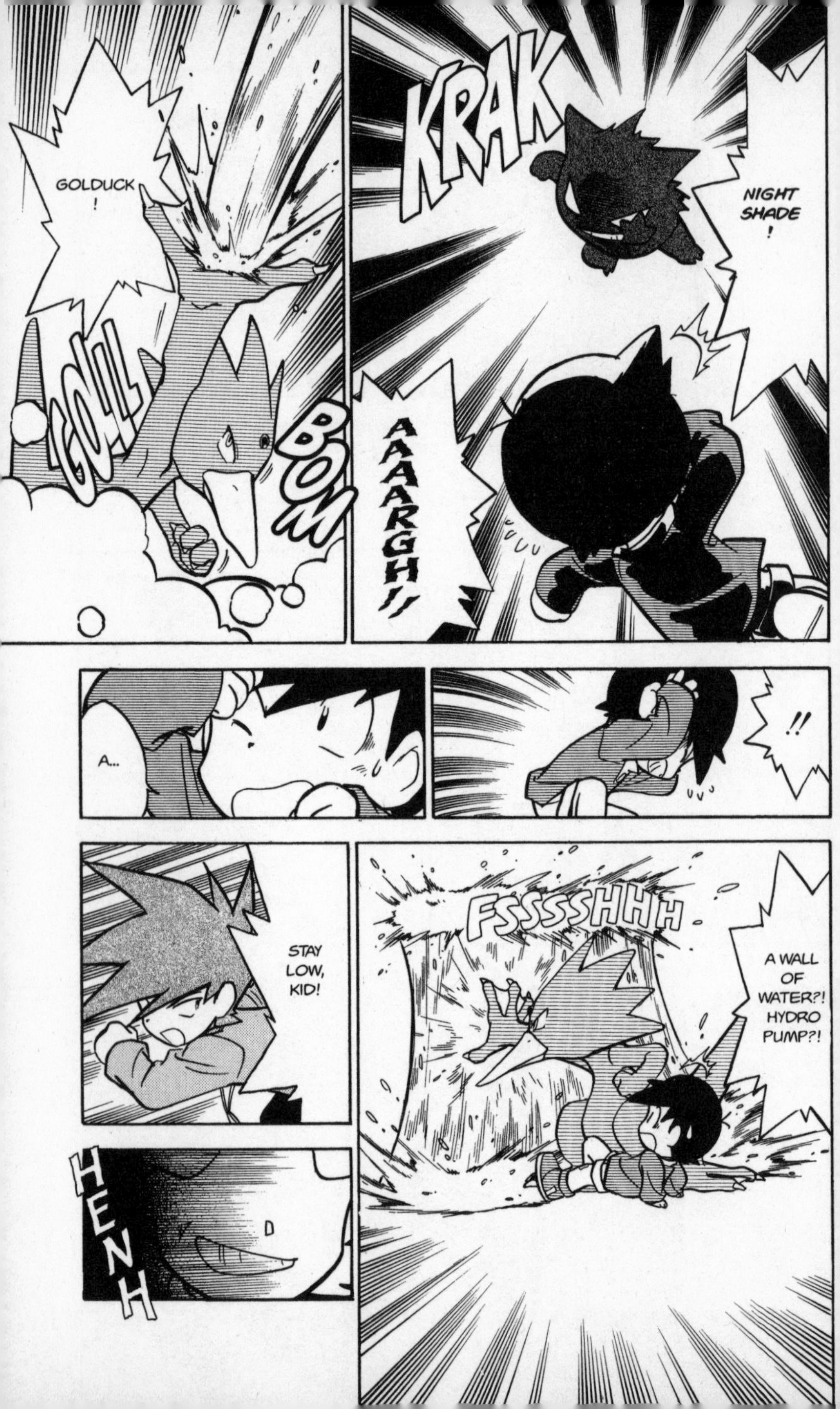
KRAK
NIGHT SHADE!
AAAARGH!!
GOLDUCK!
GOLL
BOM
!!
A...
FSSSSHHH
A WALL OF WATER?! HYDRO PUMP?!
STAY LOW, KID!
HENH

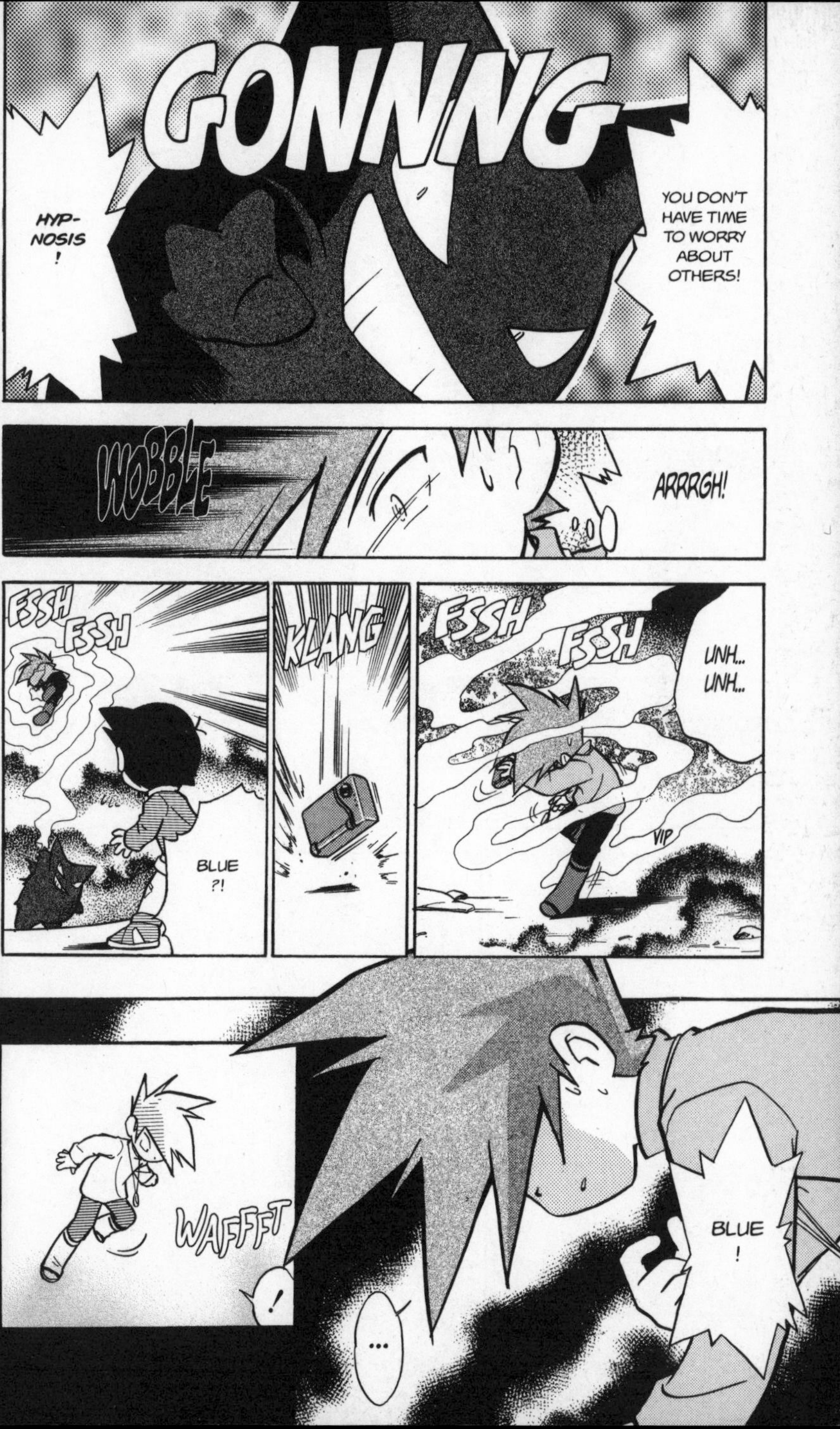
GONNNG
YOU DON'T HAVE TIME TO WORRY ABOUT OTHERS!
HYP-NOSIS!
ARRRGH!
WOBBLE
FSSH
FSSH
UNH... UNH...
VIP
KLANG
FSSH
FSSH
BLUE?!
BLUE!
...
WAFFFT
!

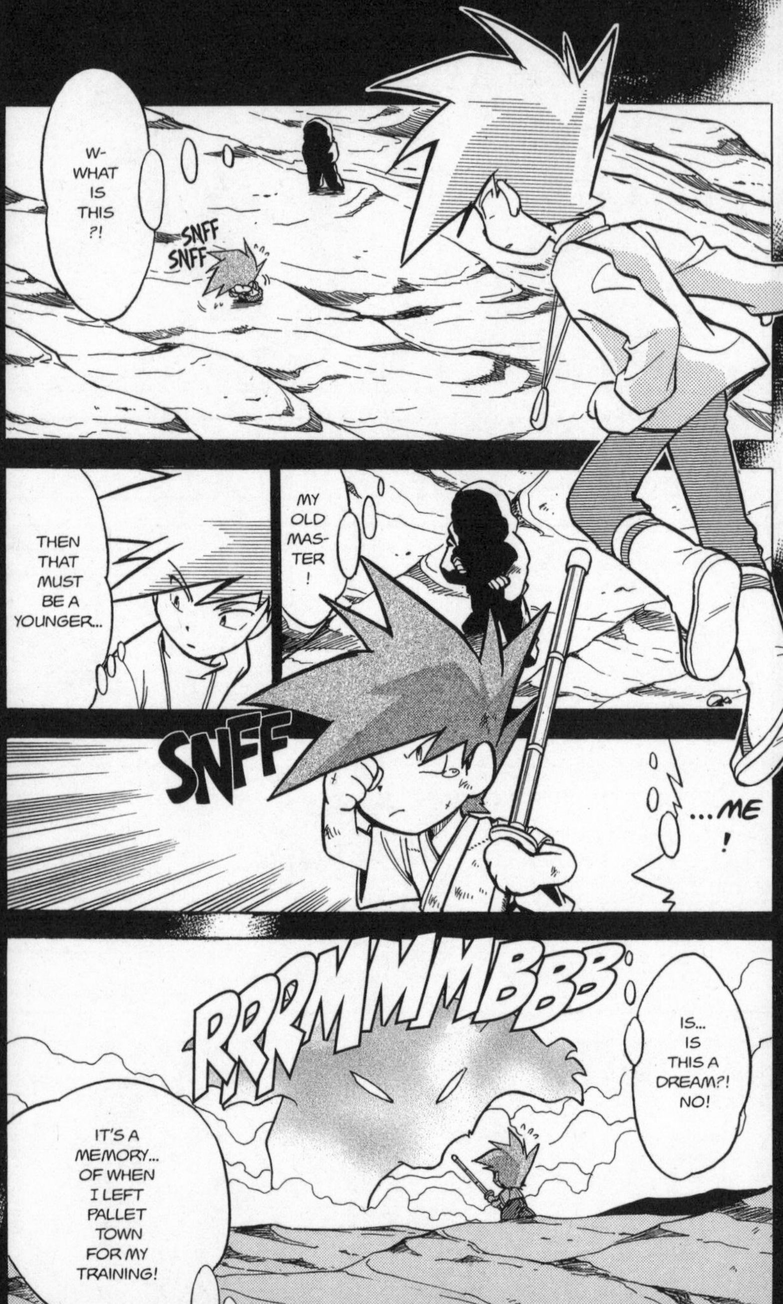
W-WHAT IS THIS?!
SNFF SNFF
MY OLD MASTER!
THEN THAT MUST BE A YOUNGER...
...ME!
SNFF
IS... IS THIS A DREAM?! NO!
RRRMMMMBBB
IT'S A MEMORY... OF WHEN I LEFT PALLET TOWN FOR MY TRAINING!

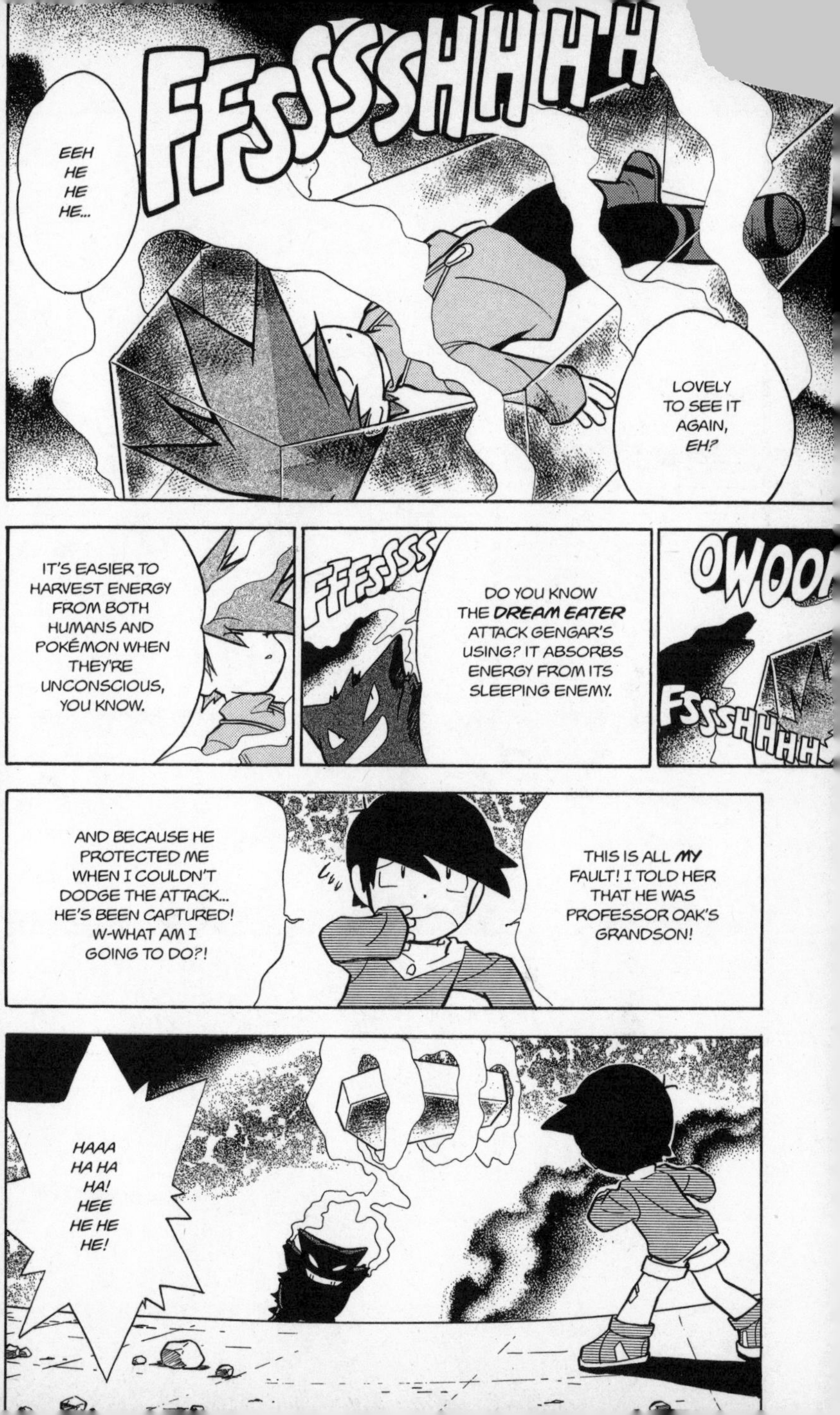
FFSSSSHHHHH
EEH HE HE HE...
LOVELY TO SEE IT AGAIN, EH?
OWOO
FSSSHHHHS
FFFSSSS
DO YOU KNOW THE DREAM EATER ATTACK GENGAR'S USING? IT ABSORBS ENERGY FROM ITS SLEEPING ENEMY.
IT'S EASIER TO HARVEST ENERGY FROM BOTH HUMANS AND POKÉMON WHEN THEY'RE UNCONSCIOUS, YOU KNOW.
THIS IS ALL MY FAULT! I TOLD HER THAT HE WAS PROFESSOR OAK'S GRANDSON!
AND BECAUSE HE PROTECTED ME WHEN I COULDN'T DODGE THE ATTACK... HE'S BEEN CAPTURED! W-WHAT AM I GOING TO DO?!
HAAA HA HA HA! HEE HE HE HE!

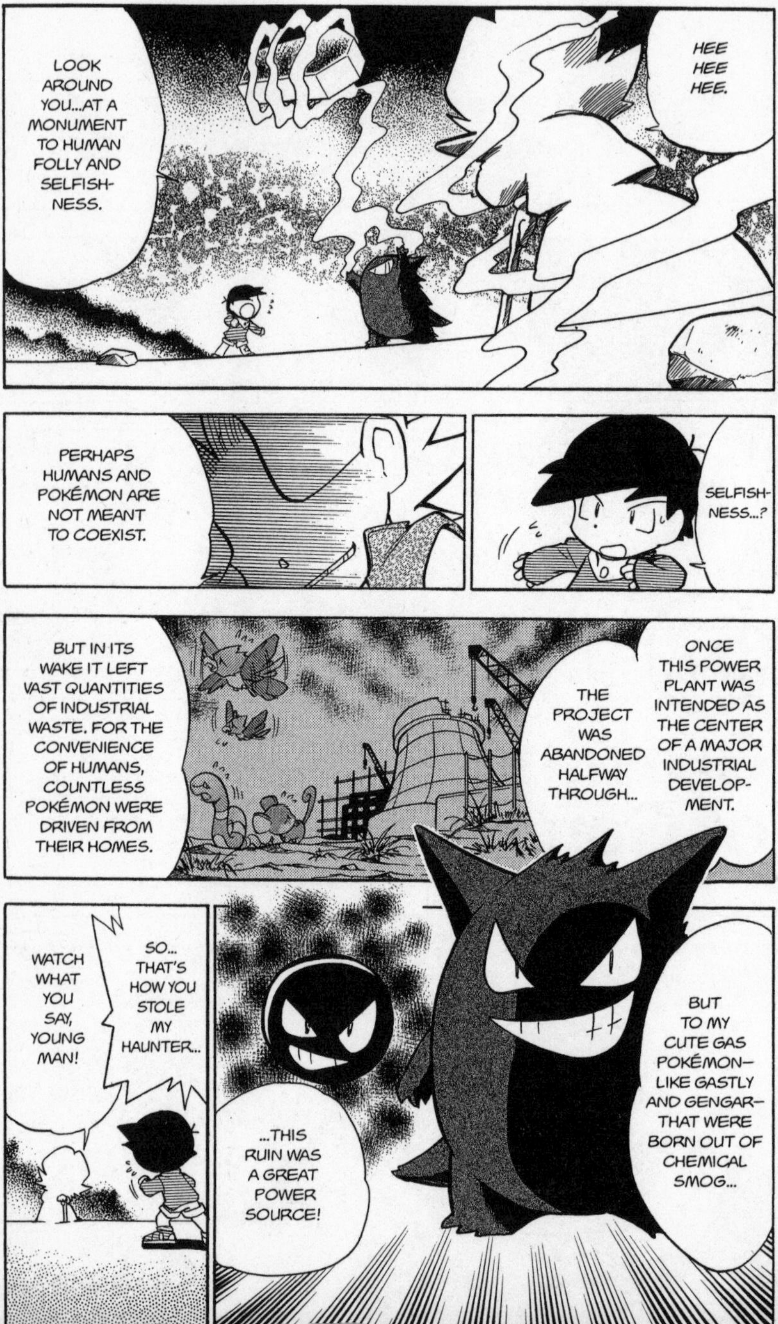
HEE HEE HEE.
LOOK AROUND YOU...AT A MONUMENT TO HUMAN FOLLY AND SELFISH-NESS.
SELFISH-NESS...?
PERHAPS HUMANS AND POKÉMON ARE NOT MEANT TO COEXIST.
ONCE THIS POWER PLANT WAS INTENDED AS THE CENTER OF A MAJOR INDUSTRIAL DEVELOP-MENT.
THE PROJECT WAS ABANDONED HALFWAY THROUGH...
BUT IN ITS WAKE IT LEFT VAST QUANTITIES OF INDUSTRIAL WASTE. FOR THE CONVENIENCE OF HUMANS, COUNTLESS POKÉMON WERE DRIVEN FROM THEIR HOMES.
BUT TO MY CUTE GAS POKÉMON— LIKE GASTLY AND GENGAR— THAT WERE BORN OUT OF CHEMICAL SMOG...
...THIS RUIN WAS A GREAT POWER SOURCE!
SO... THAT'S HOW YOU STOLE MY HAUNTER...
WATCH WHAT YOU SAY, YOUNG MAN!

52 Growing Out of Gengar

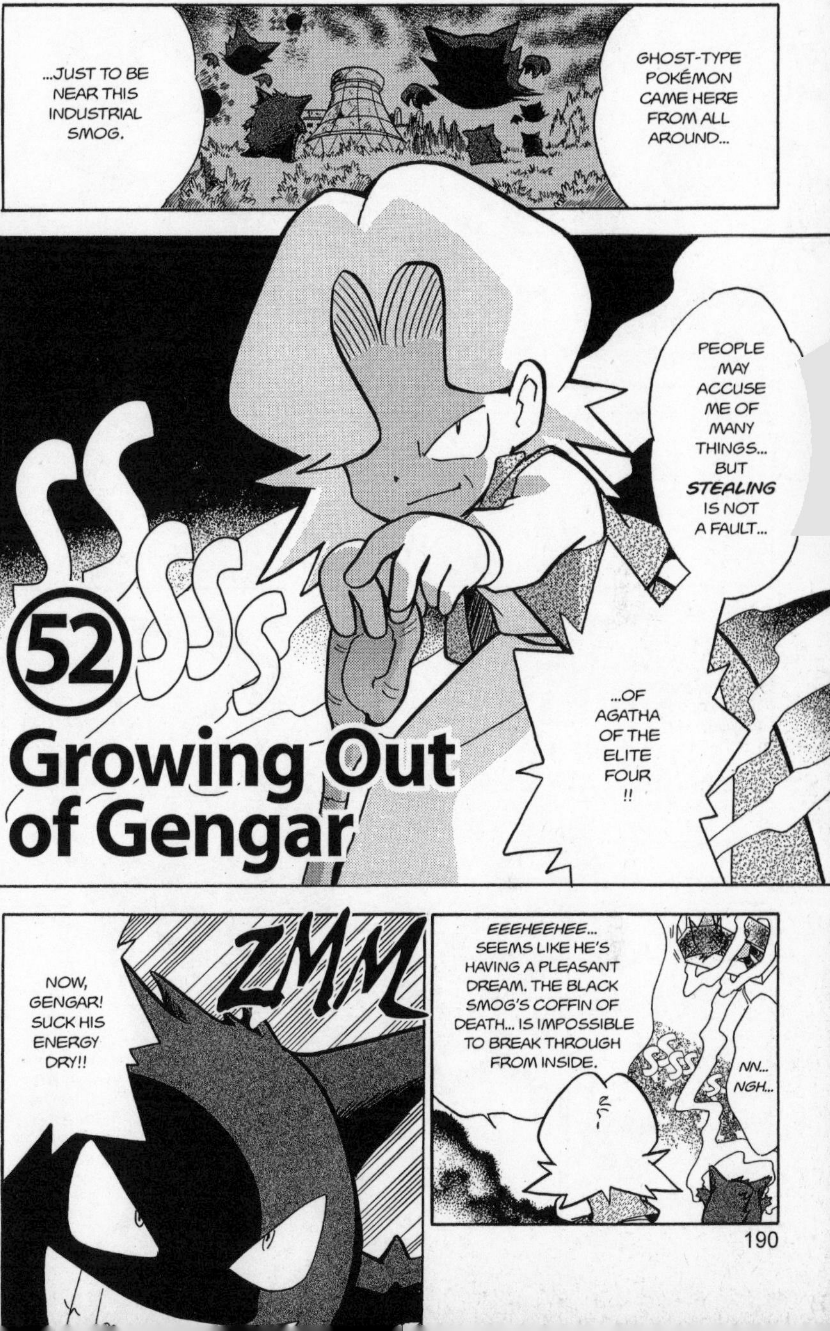
GHOST-TYPE POKÉMON CAME HERE FROM ALL AROUND...
...JUST TO BE NEAR THIS INDUSTRIAL SMOG.
PEOPLE MAY ACCUSE ME OF MANY THINGS... BUT **STEALING** IS NOT A FAULT...
...OF AGATHA OF THE ELITE FOUR !!
SSSSSSSS
EEEHEEHEE... SEEMS LIKE HE'S HAVING A PLEASANT DREAM. THE BLACK SMOG'S COFFIN OF DEATH... IS IMPOSSIBLE TO BREAK THROUGH FROM INSIDE.
SSSS
NN... NGH...
ZMM
NOW, GENGAR! SUCK HIS ENERGY DRY!!

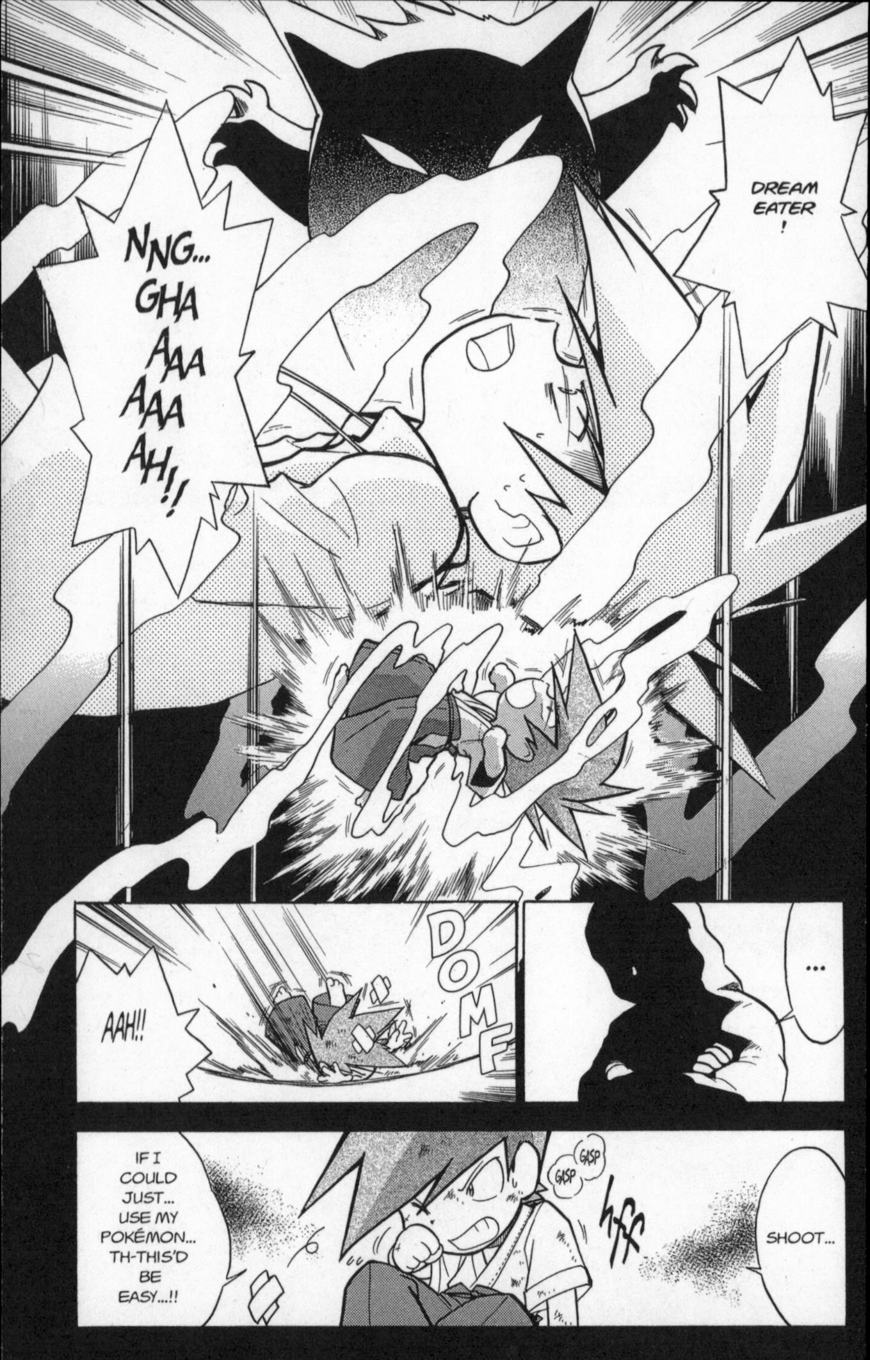
DREAM EATER!
NNG... GHAAAAAAAAAH!!
...
DOMF
AAH!!
SHOOT...
GASP GASP
hff
IF I COULD JUST... USE MY POKéMON... TH-THIS'D BE EASY...!!

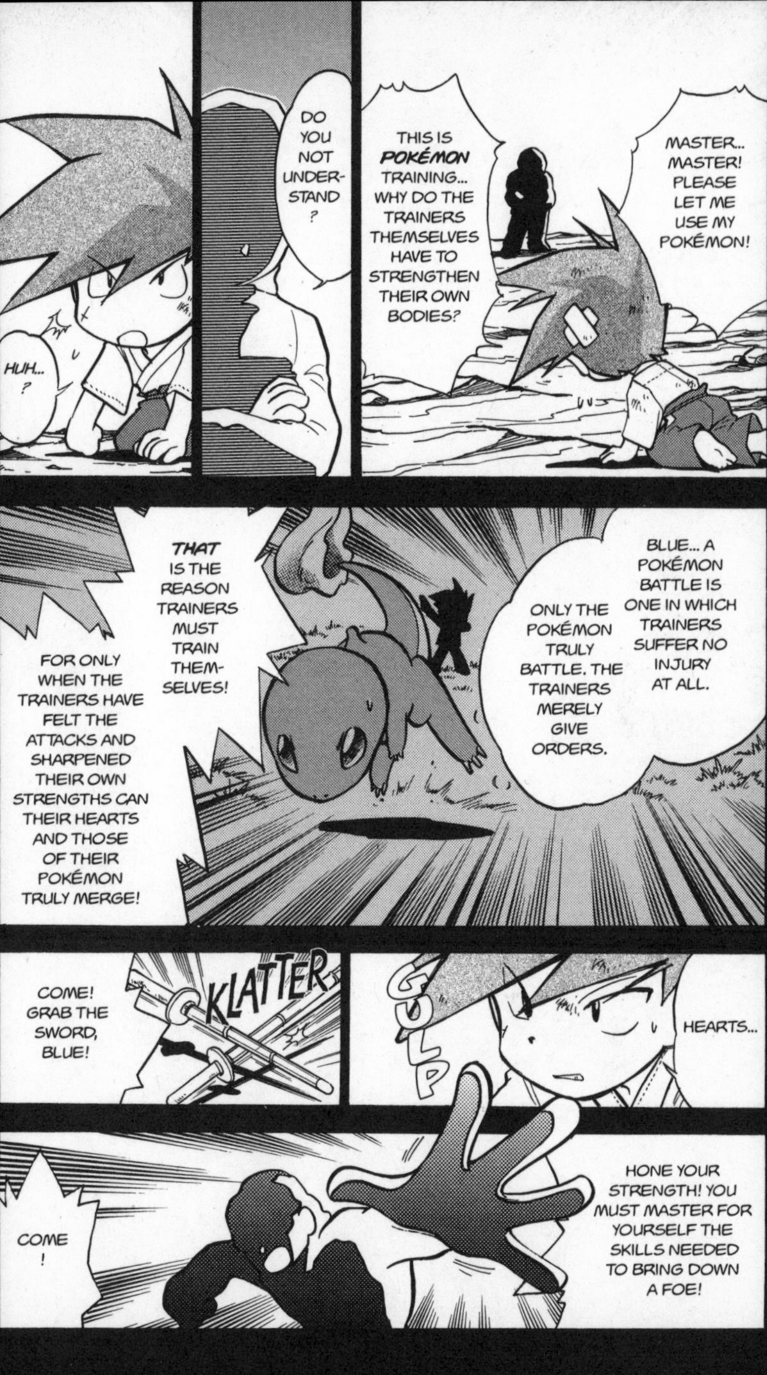
MASTER... MASTER! PLEASE LET ME USE MY POKÉMON!
THIS IS *POKÉMON* TRAINING... WHY DO THE TRAINERS THEMSELVES HAVE TO STRENGTHEN THEIR OWN BODIES?
DO YOU NOT UNDERSTAND?
HUH...?
BLUE... A POKÉMON BATTLE IS ONE IN WHICH TRAINERS SUFFER NO INJURY AT ALL.
ONLY THE POKÉMON TRULY BATTLE. THE TRAINERS MERELY GIVE ORDERS.
THAT IS THE REASON TRAINERS MUST TRAIN THEMSELVES!
FOR ONLY WHEN THE TRAINERS HAVE FELT THE ATTACKS AND SHARPENED THEIR OWN STRENGTHS CAN THEIR HEARTS AND THOSE OF THEIR POKÉMON TRULY MERGE!
GULP
HEARTS...
KLATTER
COME! GRAB THE SWORD, BLUE!
HONE YOUR STRENGTH! YOU MUST MASTER FOR YOURSELF THE SKILLS NEEDED TO BRING DOWN A FOE!
COME!

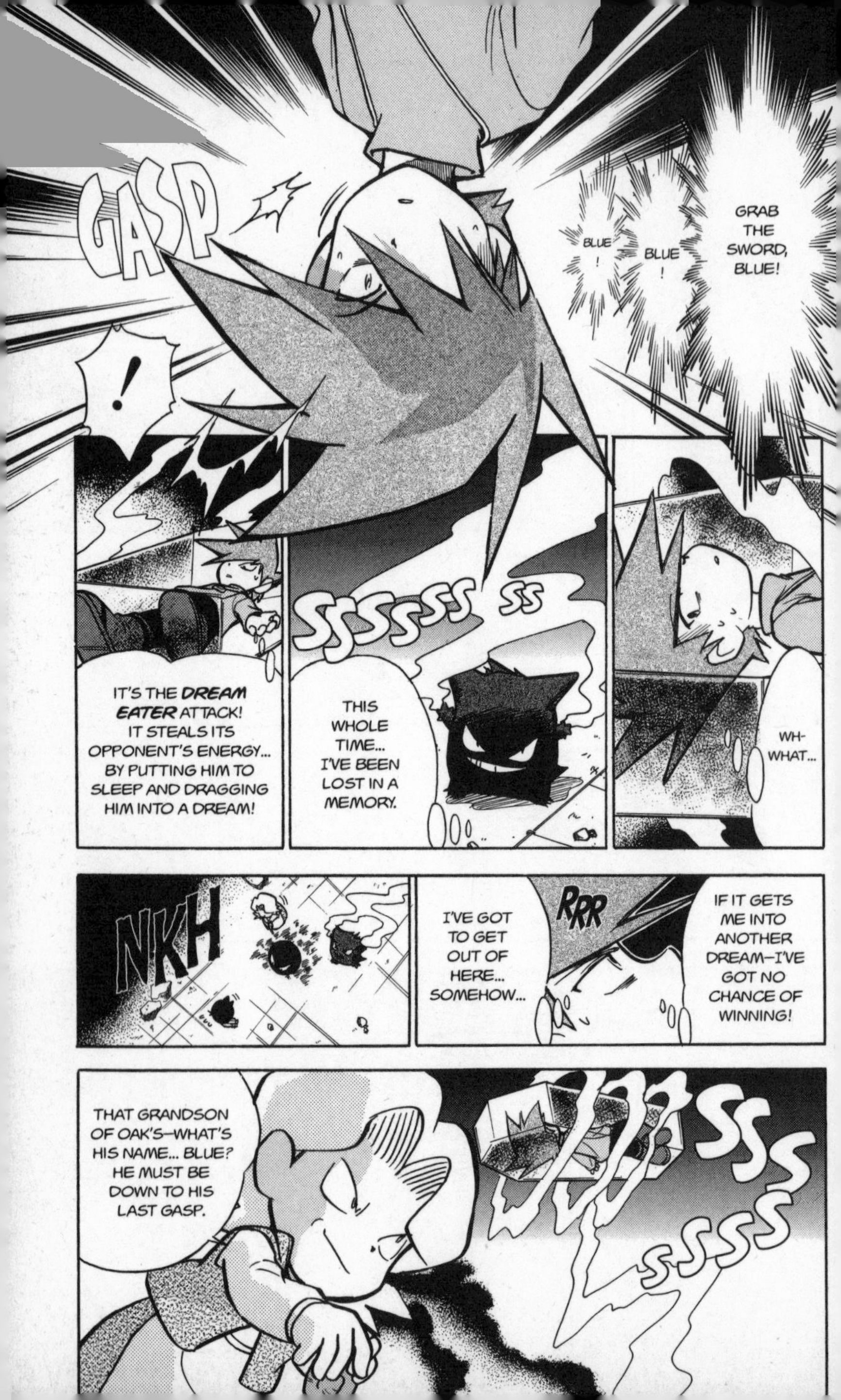
GRAB THE SWORD, BLUE!
BLUE!
BLUE!
GASP
!
WH-WHAT...
SSSSSS SS
THIS WHOLE TIME... I'VE BEEN LOST IN A MEMORY.
IT'S THE DREAM EATER ATTACK! IT STEALS ITS OPPONENT'S ENERGY... BY PUTTING HIM TO SLEEP AND DRAGGING HIM INTO A DREAM!
IF IT GETS ME INTO ANOTHER DREAM—I'VE GOT NO CHANCE OF WINNING!
RRR
I'VE GOT TO GET OUT OF HERE... SOMEHOW...
NKH
SSS
SSSS
THAT GRANDSON OF OAK'S—WHAT'S HIS NAME... BLUE? HE MUST BE DOWN TO HIS LAST GASP.

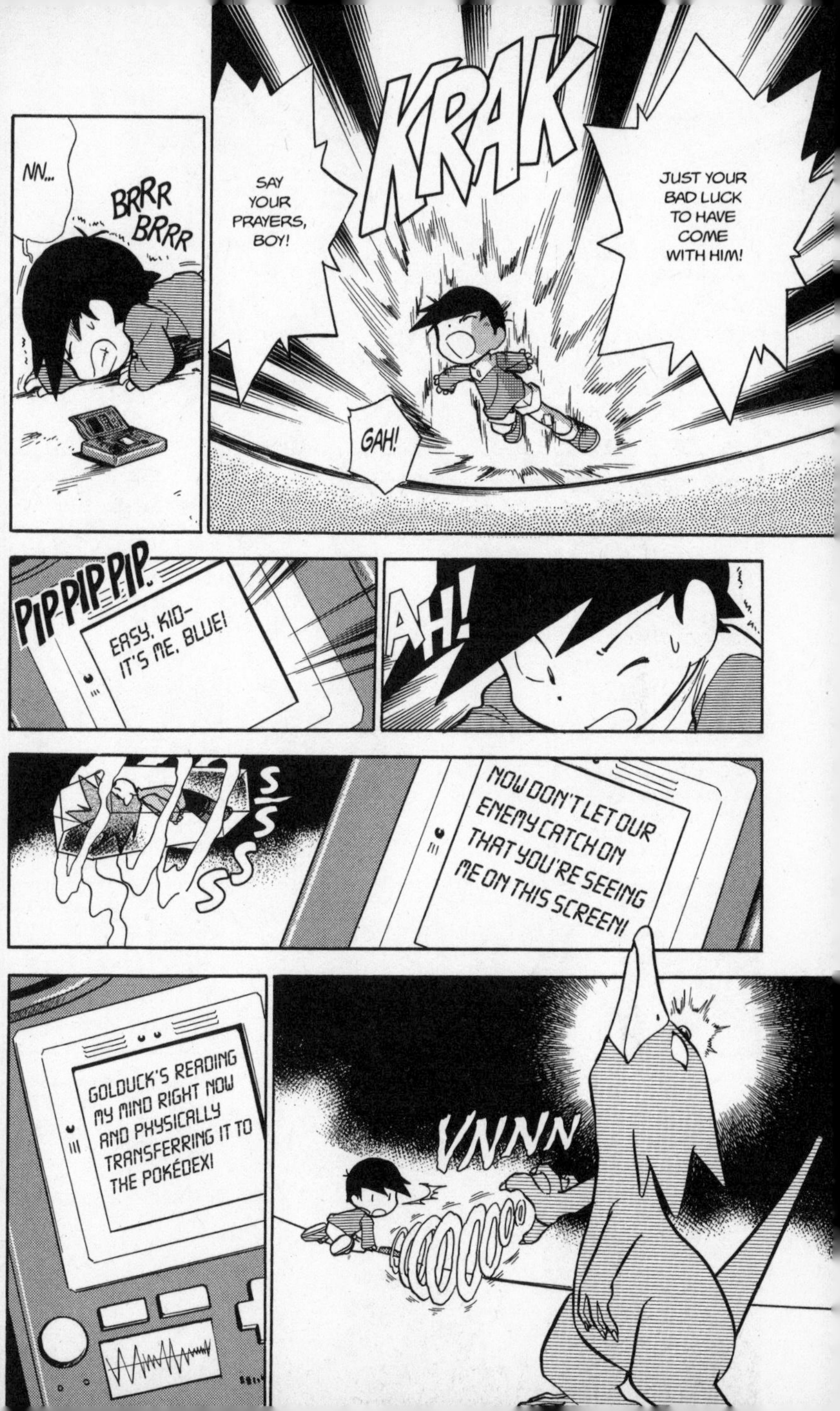
KRAK
JUST YOUR BAD LUCK TO HAVE COME WITH HIM!
SAY YOUR PRAYERS, BOY!
GAH!
NN...
BRRR BRRR
AH!
PIPPIPPIP
EASY, KID- IT'S ME, BLUE!
NOW DON'T LET OUR ENEMY CATCH ON THAT YOU'RE SEEING ME ON THIS SCREEN!
SSSS
VNNN
GOLDUCK'S READING MY MIND RIGHT NOW AND PHYSICALLY TRANSFERRING IT TO THE POKÉDEX!

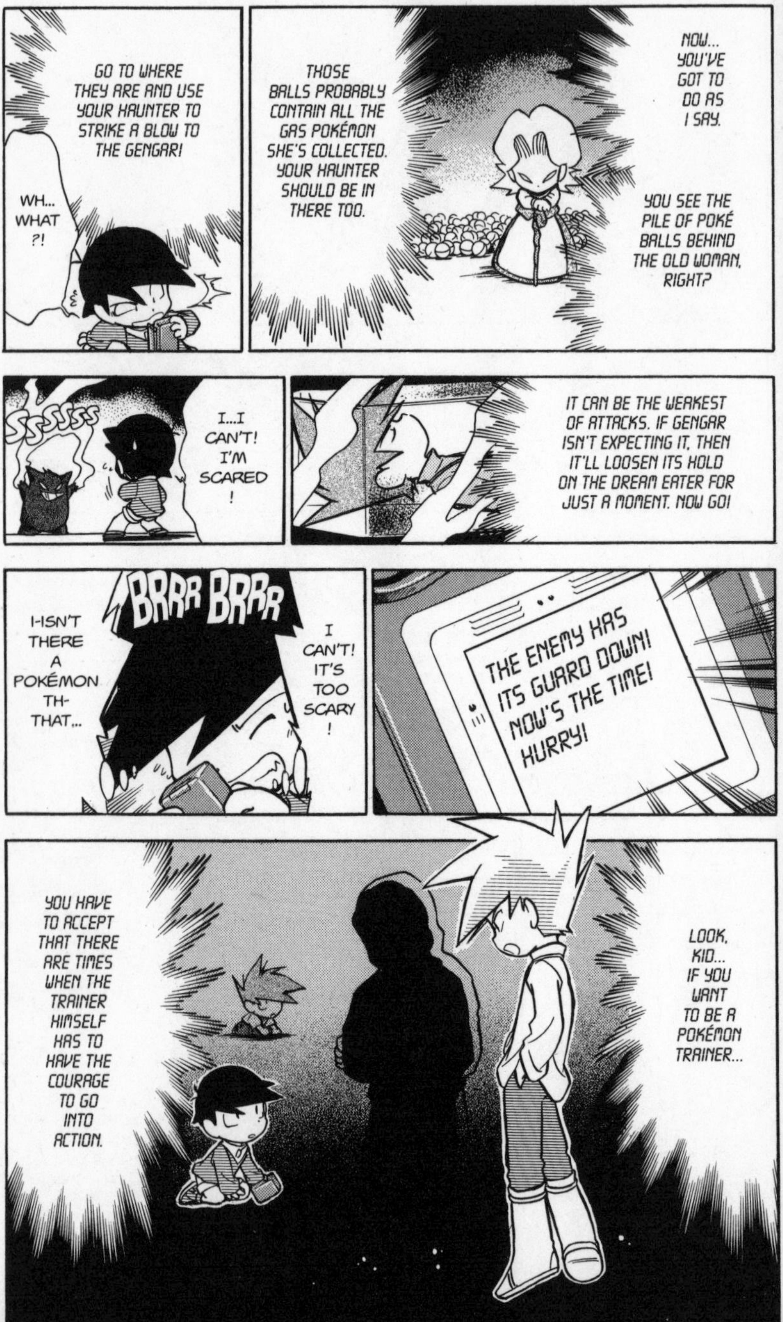
NOW... YOU'VE GOT TO DO AS I SAY.
YOU SEE THE PILE OF POKÉ BALLS BEHIND THE OLD WOMAN, RIGHT?
THOSE BALLS PROBABLY CONTAIN ALL THE GAS POKÉMON SHE'S COLLECTED. YOUR HAUNTER SHOULD BE IN THERE TOO.
GO TO WHERE THEY ARE AND USE YOUR HAUNTER TO STRIKE A BLOW TO THE GENGAR!
WH... WHAT ?!
IT CAN BE THE WEAKEST OF ATTACKS. IF GENGAR ISN'T EXPECTING IT, THEN IT'LL LOOSEN ITS HOLD ON THE DREAM EATER FOR JUST A MOMENT. NOW GO!
SSSSSS
I...I CAN'T! I'M SCARED !
THE ENEMY HAS ITS GUARD DOWN! NOW'S THE TIME! HURRY!
BRRR BRRR
I CAN'T! IT'S TOO SCARY !
I-ISN'T THERE A POKÉMON TH- THAT...
LOOK, KID... IF YOU WANT TO BE A POKÉMON TRAINER...
YOU HAVE TO ACCEPT THAT THERE ARE TIMES WHEN THE TRAINER HIMSELF HAS TO HAVE THE COURAGE TO GO INTO ACTION.

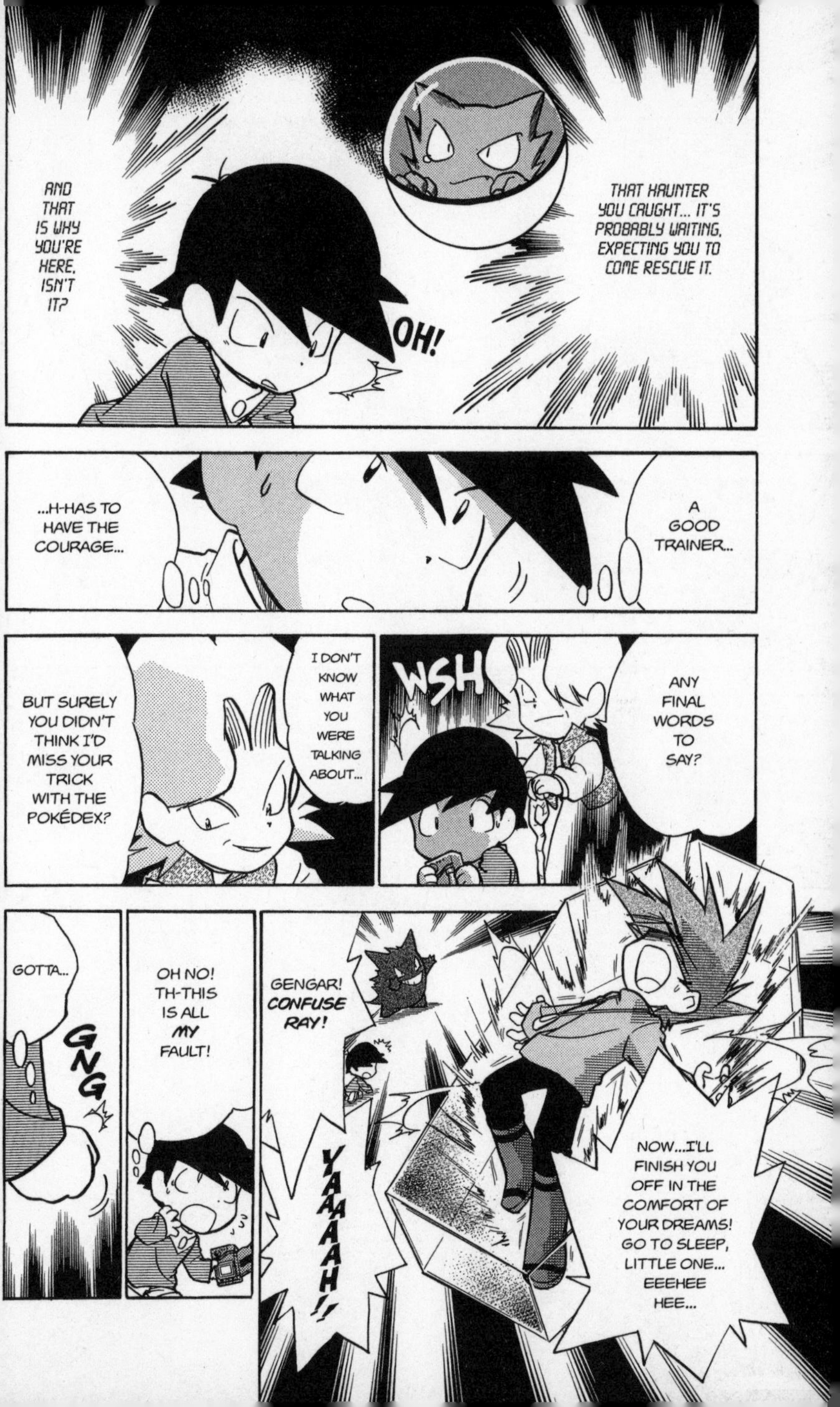

THAT HAUNTER YOU CAUGHT... IT'S PROBABLY WAITING, EXPECTING YOU TO COME RESCUE IT.
AND THAT IS WHY YOU'RE HERE, ISN'T IT?
OH!
A GOOD TRAINER...
...H-HAS TO HAVE THE COURAGE...
ANY FINAL WORDS TO SAY?
WSH
I DON'T KNOW WHAT YOU WERE TALKING ABOUT...
BUT SURELY YOU DIDN'T THINK I'D MISS YOUR TRICK WITH THE POKÉDEX?
GENGAR! CONFUSE RAY!
YAAAAAH!!
NOW...I'LL FINISH YOU OFF IN THE COMFORT OF YOUR DREAMS! GO TO SLEEP, LITTLE ONE... EEEHEE HEE...
OH NO! TH-THIS IS ALL MY FAULT!
GOTTA...
GNG

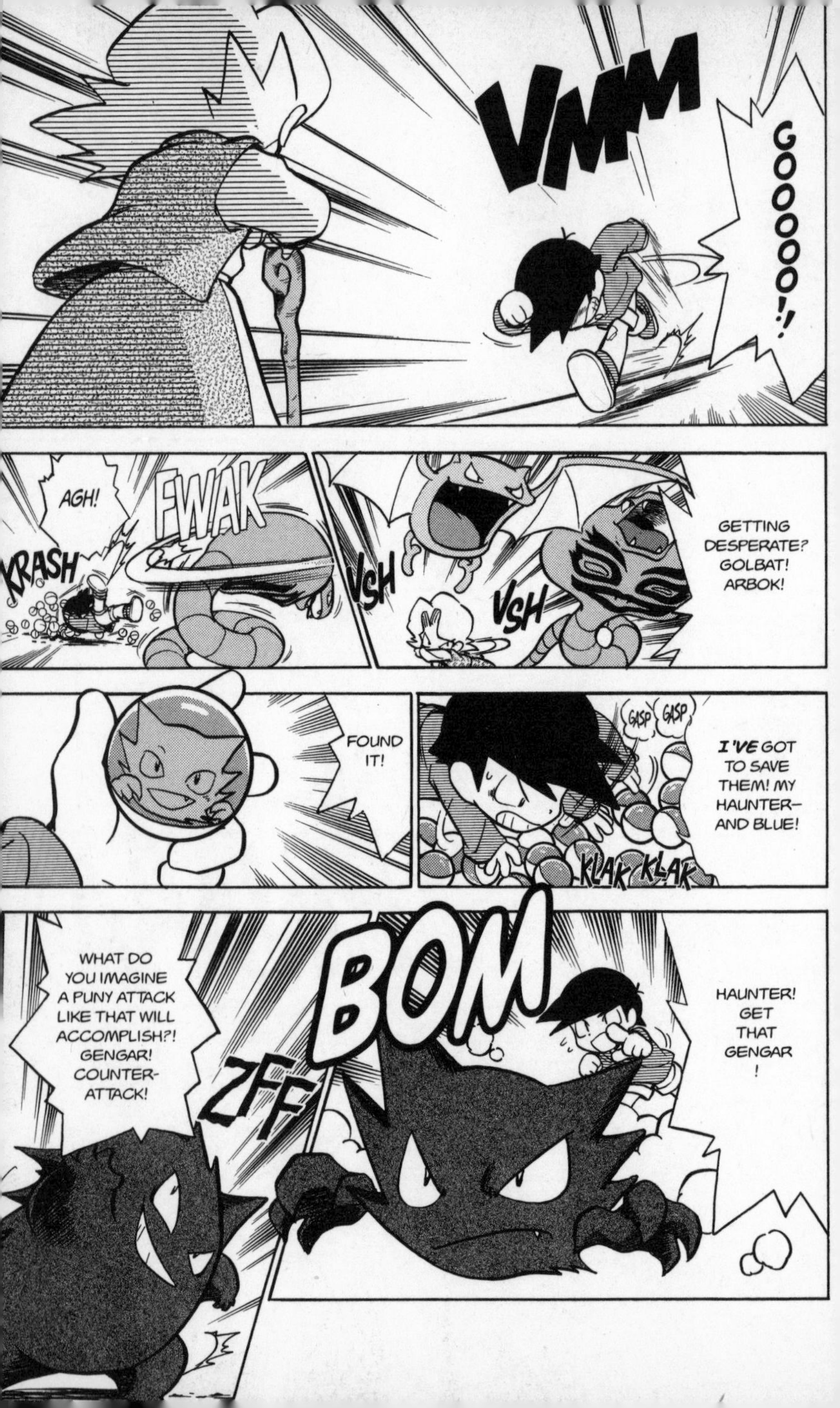
VMM
GOOOOOO!!
GETTING DESPERATE? GOLBAT! ARBOK!
VSH
VSH
AGH!
FWAK
KRASH
GASP GASP
I'VE GOT TO SAVE THEM! MY HAUNTER— AND BLUE!
KLAK KLAK
FOUND IT!
HAUNTER! GET THAT GENGAR!
BOM
ZFF
WHAT DO YOU IMAGINE A PUNY ATTACK LIKE THAT WILL ACCOMPLISH?! GENGAR! COUNTER-ATTACK!

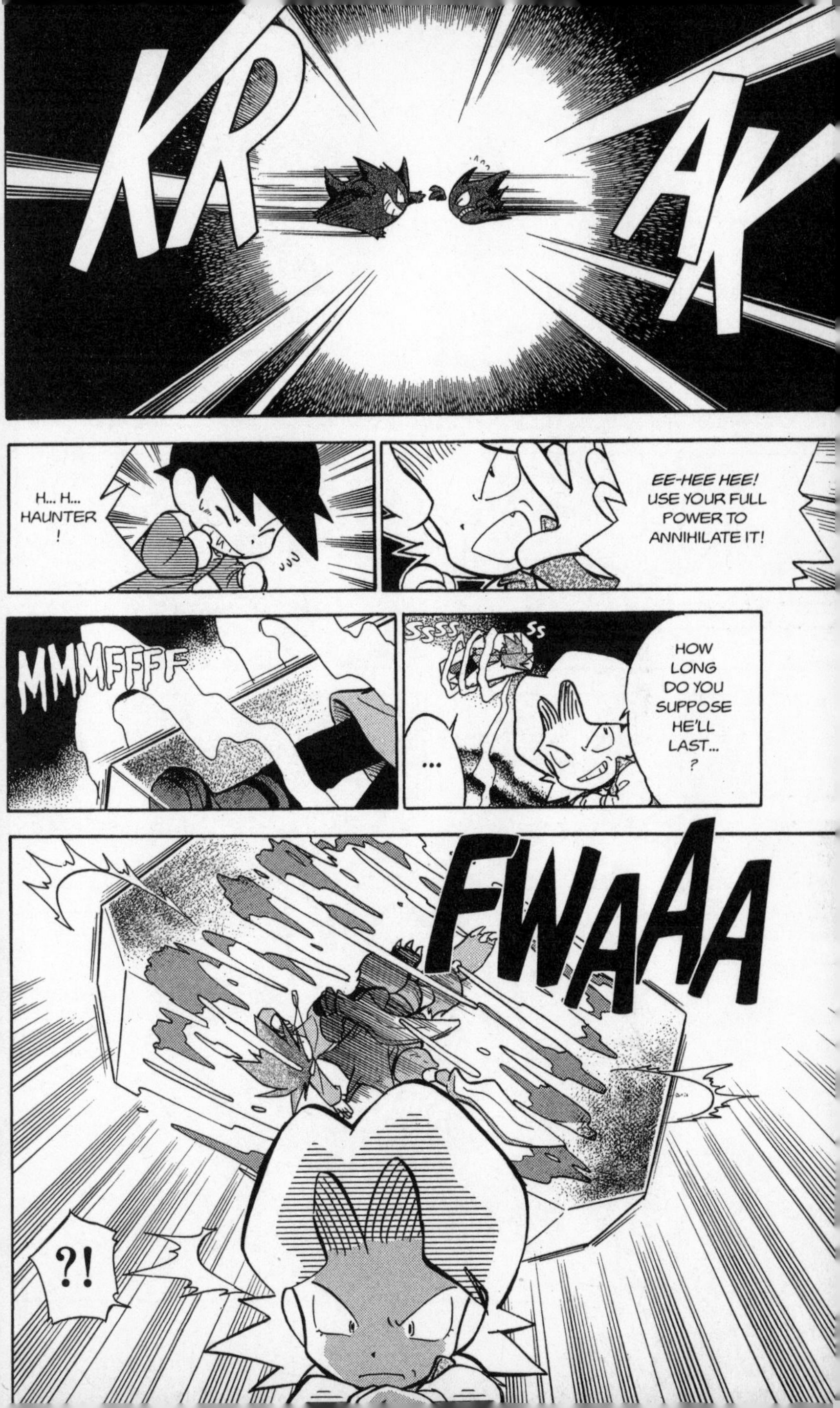
KRAK
EE-HEE HEE! USE YOUR FULL POWER TO ANNIHILATE IT!
H... H... HAUNTER !
HOW LONG DO YOU SUPPOSE HE'LL LAST... ?
...
SSSS SS
MMMFFFF
FWAAA
?!

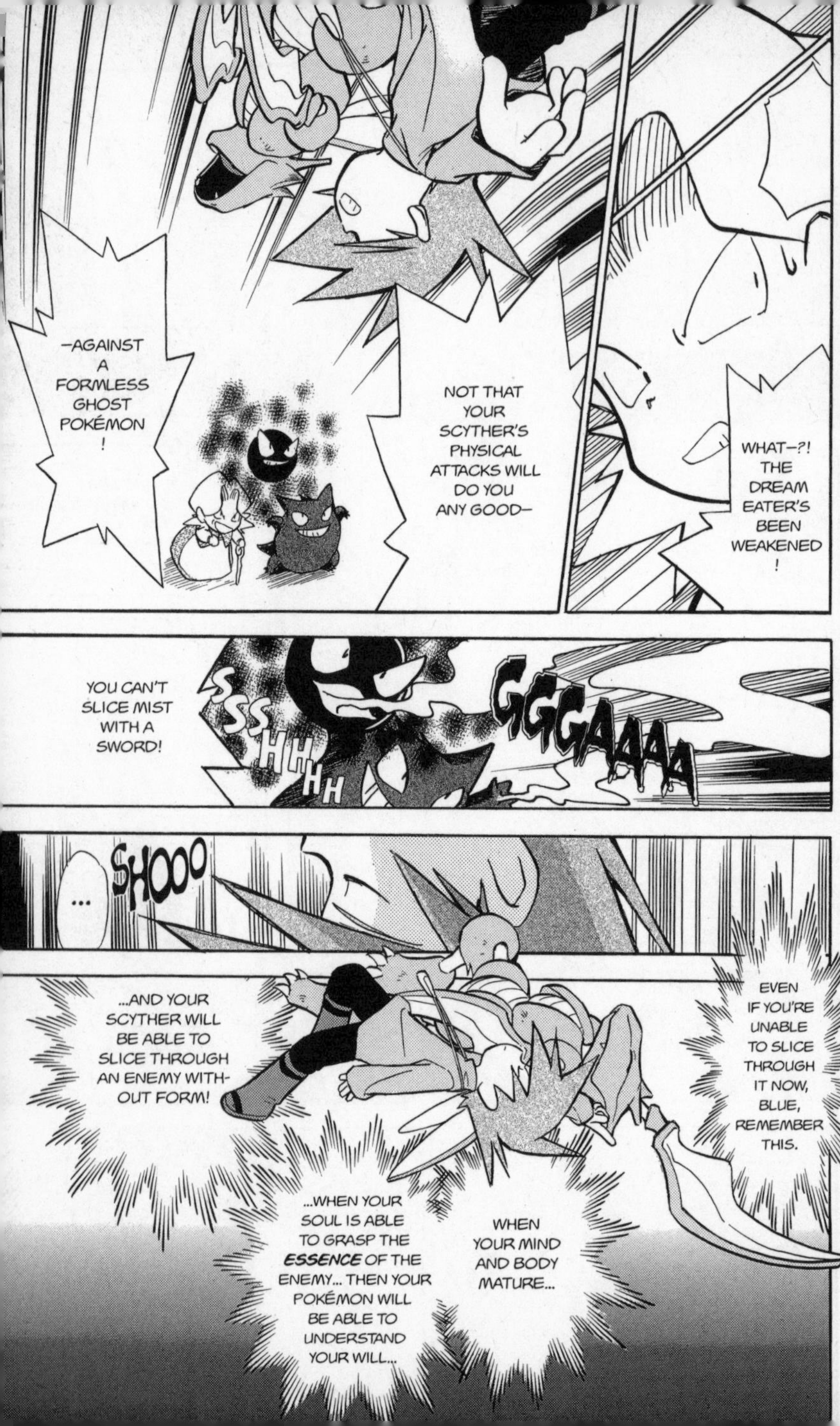
WHAT—?! THE DREAM EATER'S BEEN WEAKENED!
NOT THAT YOUR SCYTHER'S PHYSICAL ATTACKS WILL DO YOU ANY GOOD—
—AGAINST A FORMLESS GHOST POKÉMON!
GGGAAAA
SSSHHHHH
YOU CAN'T SLICE MIST WITH A SWORD!
SHOOO
...
EVEN IF YOU'RE UNABLE TO SLICE THROUGH IT NOW, BLUE, REMEMBER THIS.
...AND YOUR SCYTHER WILL BE ABLE TO SLICE THROUGH AN ENEMY WITH-OUT FORM!
WHEN YOUR MIND AND BODY MATURE...
...WHEN YOUR SOUL IS ABLE TO GRASP THE ESSENCE OF THE ENEMY... THEN YOUR POKÉMON WILL BE ABLE TO UNDERSTAND YOUR WILL...

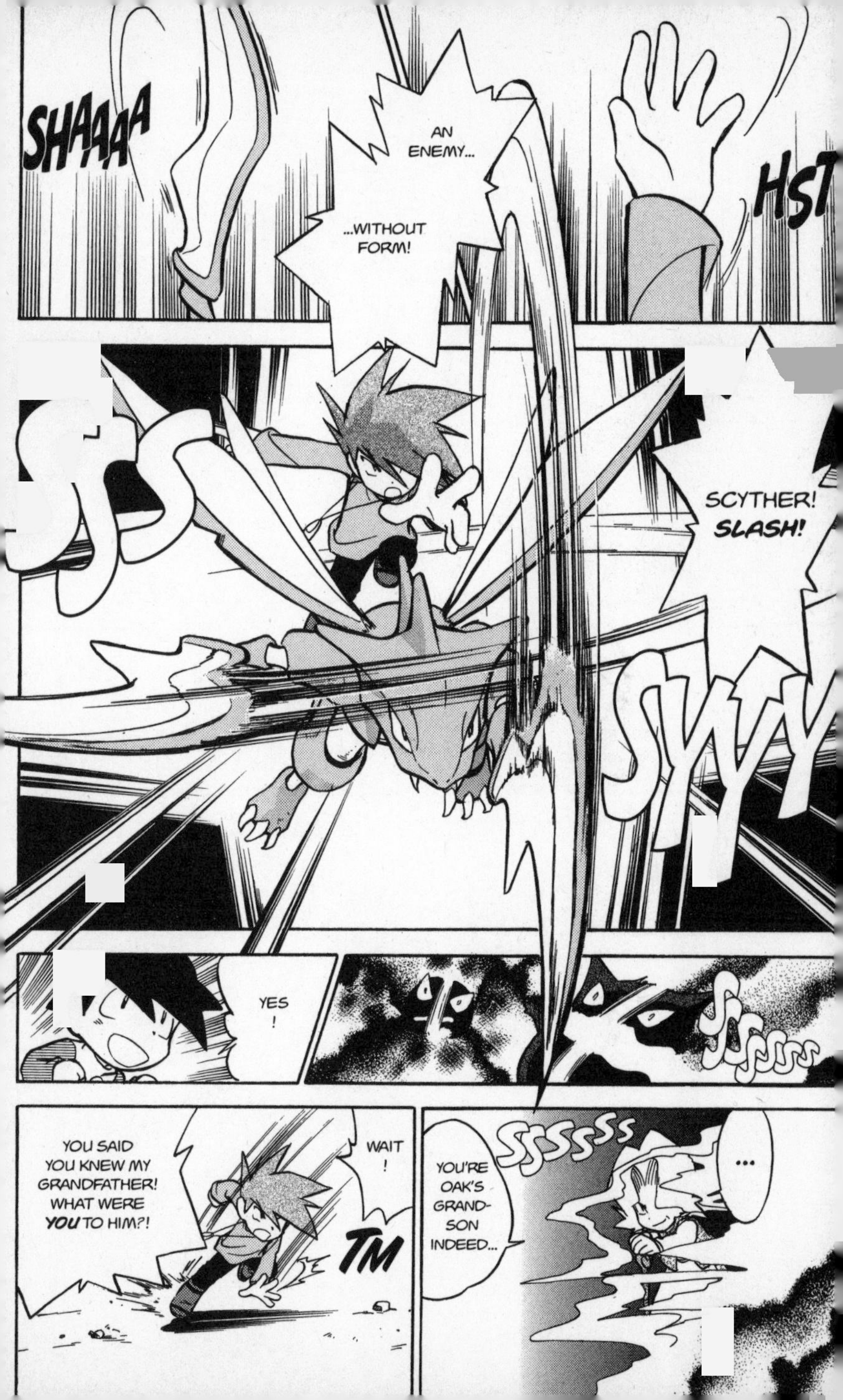
HST
AN ENEMY...
...WITHOUT FORM!
SHAAAA
SCYTHER! SLASH!
SSSSSS
YES!
SSSSSS
...
YOU'RE OAK'S GRAND-SON INDEED...
WAIT!
YOU SAID YOU KNEW MY GRANDFATHER! WHAT WERE YOU TO HIM?!
TM

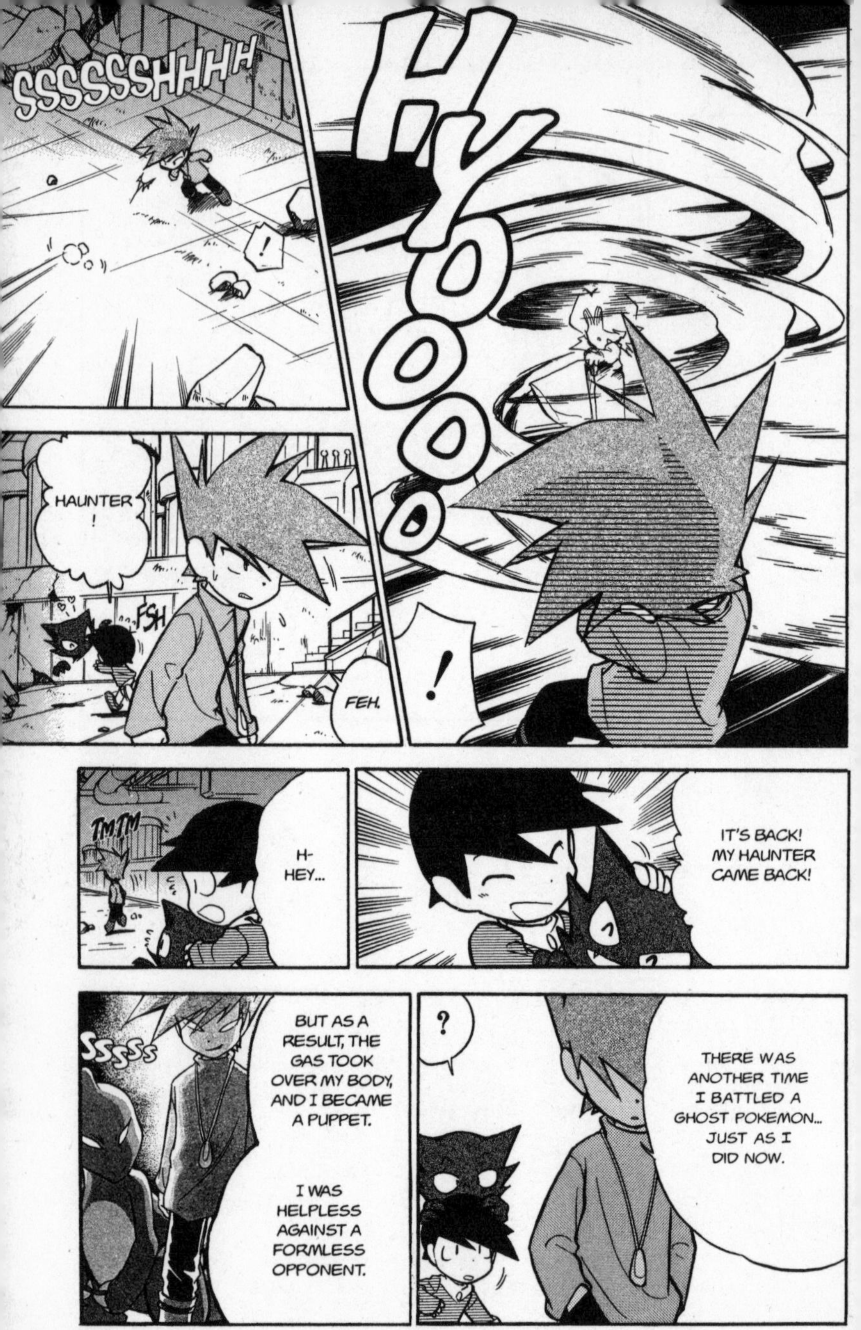
HYOOOOD
!
SSSSSSHHHH
!
HAUNTER!
FSH
FEH.
IT'S BACK! MY HAUNTER CAME BACK!
TMTM
H- HEY...
?
THERE WAS ANOTHER TIME I BATTLED A GHOST POKEMON... JUST AS I DID NOW.
SSSSS
BUT AS A RESULT, THE GAS TOOK OVER MY BODY, AND I BECAME A PUPPET.
I WAS HELPLESS AGAINST A FORMLESS OPPONENT.

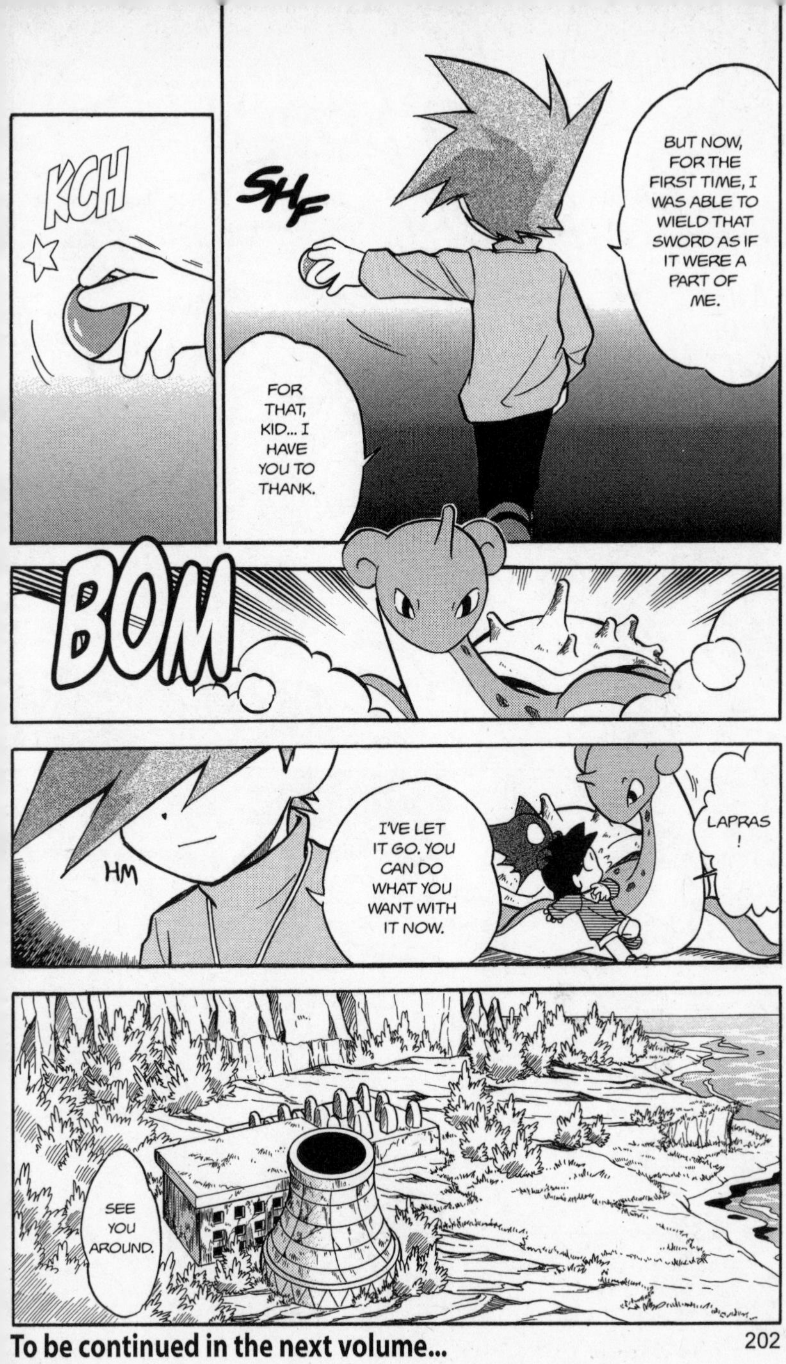
BUT NOW, FOR THE FIRST TIME, I WAS ABLE TO WIELD THAT SWORD AS IF IT WERE A PART OF ME.
SHF
FOR THAT, KID... I HAVE YOU TO THANK.
KCH
BOM
LAPRAS!
I'VE LET IT GO. YOU CAN DO WHAT YOU WANT WITH IT NOW.
HM
SEE YOU AROUND.

To be continued in the next volume...

NEXT VOLUME PREVIEW!

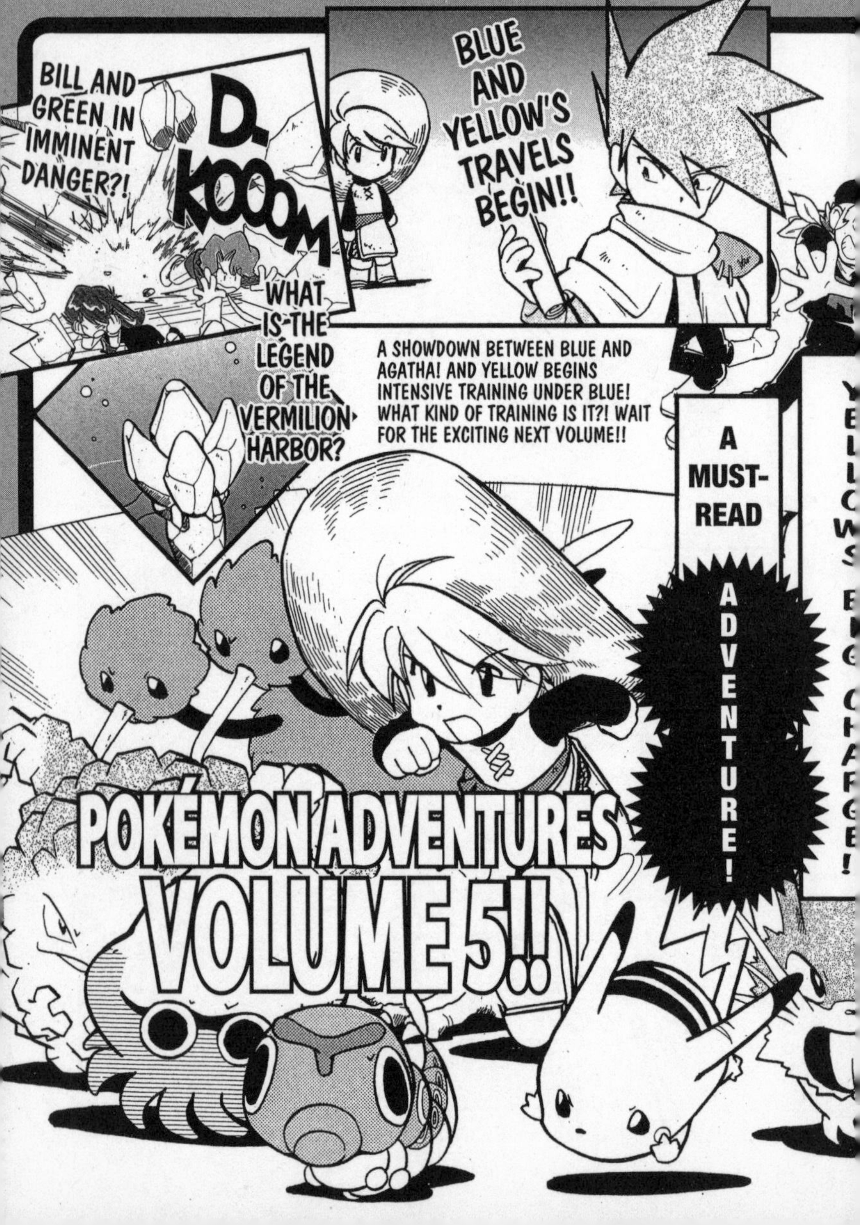
BLUE AND YELLOW'S TRAVELS BEGIN!!
BILL AND GREEN IN IMMINENT DANGER?!
D. KOOOM
WHAT IS THE LEGEND OF THE VERMILION HARBOR?
A SHOWDOWN BETWEEN BLUE AND AGATHA! AND YELLOW BEGINS INTENSIVE TRAINING UNDER BLUE! WHAT KIND OF TRAINING IS IT?! WAIT FOR THE EXCITING NEXT VOLUME!!
YELLOW'S BIG CHARGE!
A MUST-READ ADVENTURE!
POKÉMON ADVENTURES VOLUME 5!!

ADVENTURE ROUTE MAP 4

HEAD OUT OF PALLET TOWN WITH PIKA, TRAVEL THROUGH VIRIDIAN FOREST ALONG THE RIVER AND THEN MOVE ON TO CELADON CITY!! FOLLOW BLUE'S PAST ADVENTURE ROUTE AS WELL!!

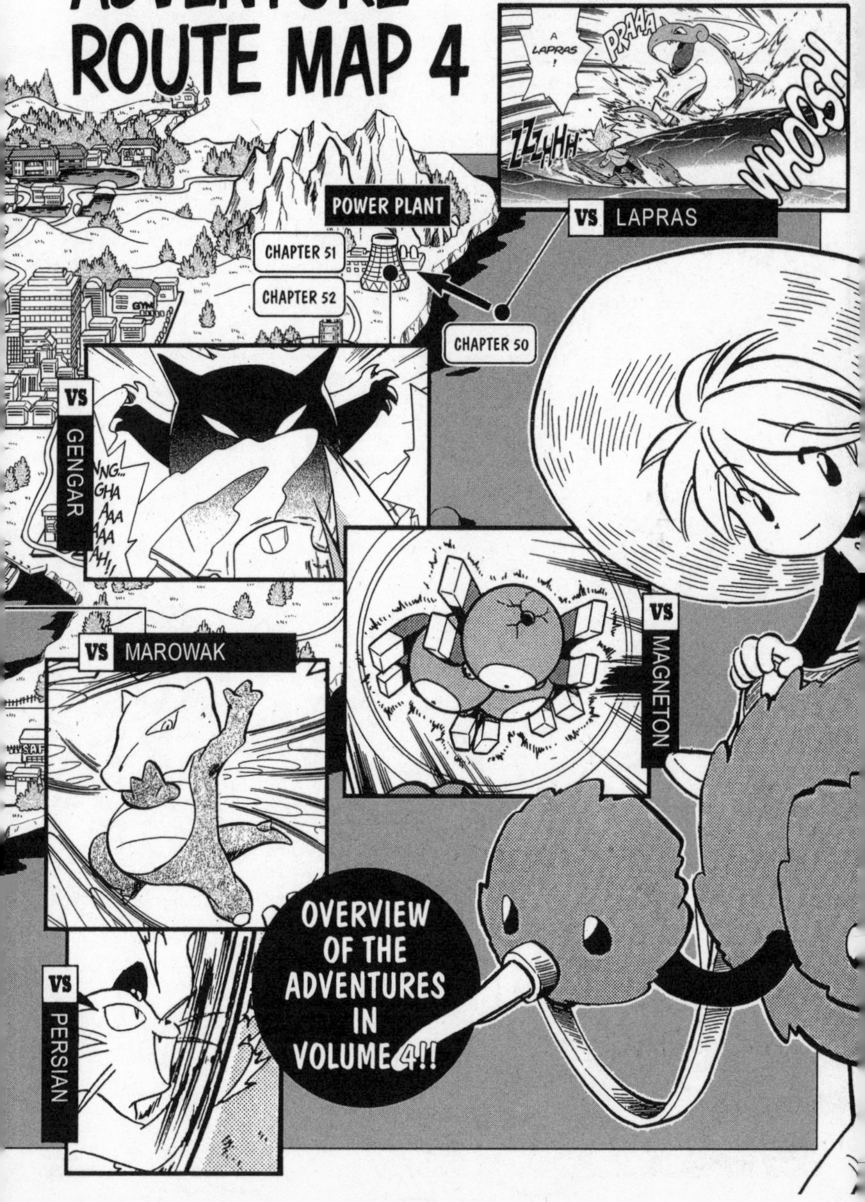
WHOOSH!!
PRAAA
A LAPRAS!
ZZZHHH
VS LAPRAS
POWER PLANT
CHAPTER 51
CHAPTER 52
CHAPTER 50
GYM
VS MAGNETON
VS GENGAR
NG... GHA AAA AAA AH!!
VS MAROWAK
VS PERSIAN
OVERVIEW OF THE ADVENTURES IN VOLUME 4!!

GOTTA CATCH 'EM ALL!!

ADVENTURE ROUTE MAP 4

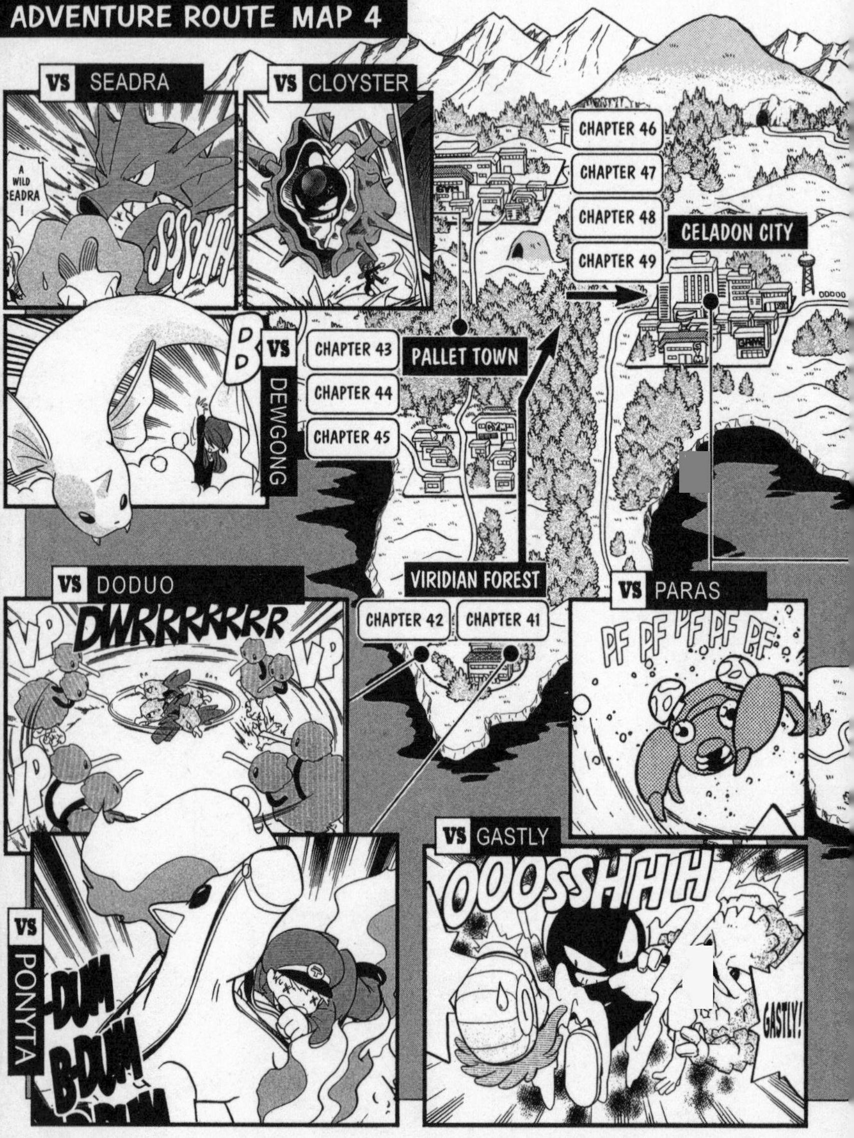

VS CLOYSTER
VS SEADRA
A WILD SEADRA!
SSSHH
CHAPTER 46
CHAPTER 47
CHAPTER 48
CHAPTER 49
CELADON CITY
PALLET TOWN
CHAPTER 43
CHAPTER 44
CHAPTER 45
VS DEWGONG
B
VIRIDIAN FOREST
CHAPTER 41
CHAPTER 42
VS PARAS
PF PF PF PF PF
VS DODUO
DWRRRRRRR
VP
VP
VP
VS GASTLY
OOOSSHHH
GASTLY!
VS PONYTA
B-DUM
B-DUM

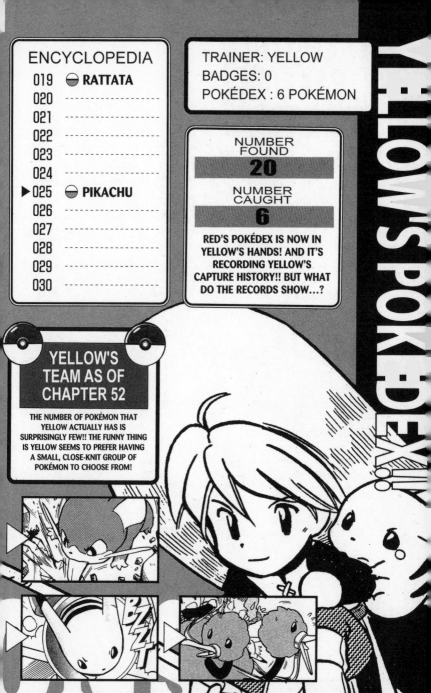

YELLOW'S POKÉDEX!!

ENCYCLOPEDIA

019 RATTATA
020 ---------------
021 ---------------
022 ---------------
023 ---------------
024 ---------------
▶025 PIKACHU
026 ---------------
027 ---------------
028 ---------------
029 ---------------
030 ---------------

TRAINER: YELLOW
BADGES: 0
POKÉDEX : 6 POKÉMON

NUMBER FOUND
20

NUMBER CAUGHT
6

RED'S POKÉDEX IS NOW IN YELLOW'S HANDS! AND IT'S RECORDING YELLOW'S CAPTURE HISTORY!! BUT WHAT DO THE RECORDS SHOW...?

YELLOW'S TEAM AS OF CHAPTER 52

THE NUMBER OF POKÉMON THAT YELLOW ACTUALLY HAS IS SURPRISINGLY FEW!! THE FUNNY THING IS YELLOW SEEMS TO PREFER HAVING A SMALL, CLOSE-KNIT GROUP OF POKÉMON TO CHOOSE FROM!

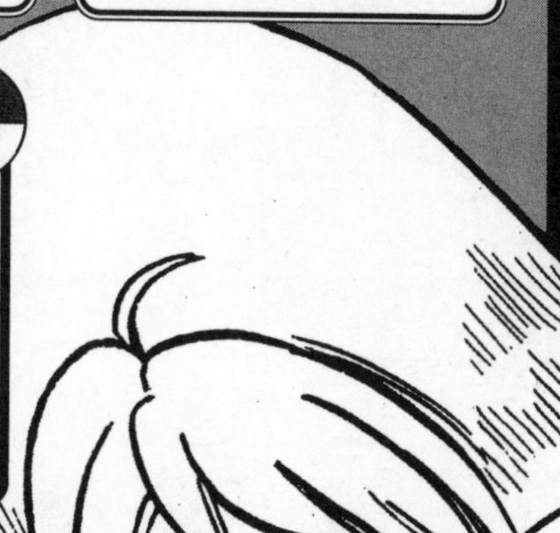

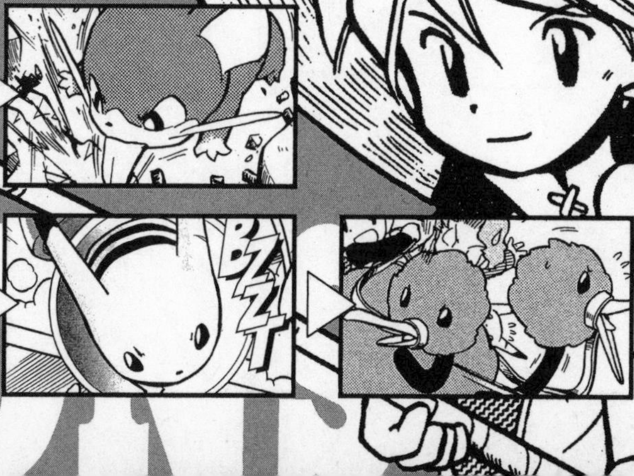
BZZZT

POCKE

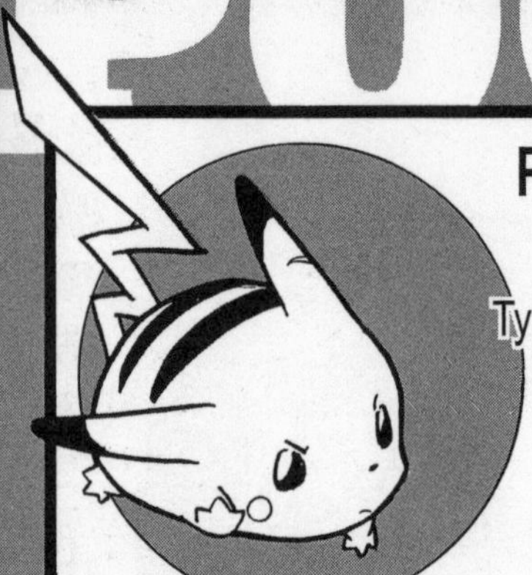

PIKACHU

LV: 56

Type 1/Electric

Trainer/Red

BEING THE POKÉMON THAT WON THE POKÉMON LEAGUE CHAMPIONSHIP ALONGSIDE RED, PIKA'S EXPERIENCE LEVELS ARE SKY-HIGH, AND ITS ELECTRIC ATTACKS HAVE GOTTEN EVEN MORE AMAZING!! NOW PIKA TRAVELS WITH YELLOW IN ORDER TO FIND RED, AND IT ISN'T LONG BEFORE PIKA BEGINS TO WARM UP TO ITS NEW TRAINER!

NO.025

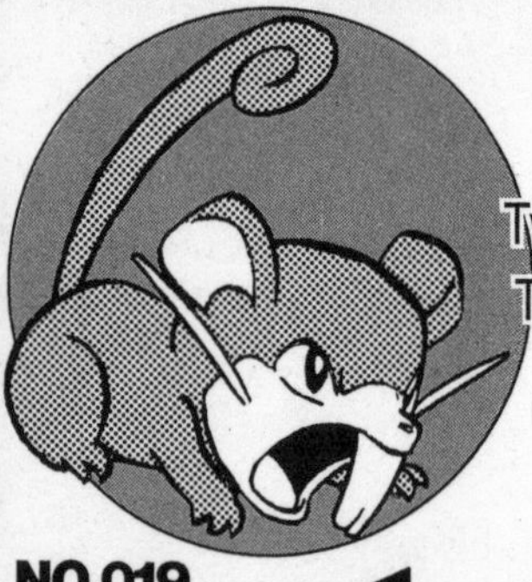

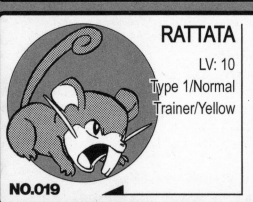

RATTATA

LV: 10

Type 1/Normal

Trainer/Yellow

"RATTY" THE RATTATA IS THE VERY FIRST POKÉMON THAT YELLOW BEFRIENDED. ITS FRONT TEETH ATTACKS ARE STRONG ENOUGH TO PULVERIZE CONCRETE!! WITH THAT KIND OF POWER, THIS SMALL BUT DEPENDABLE POKÉMON HAS SAVED YELLOW'S TEAM FROM MANY A TIGHT SPOT!!

NO.019

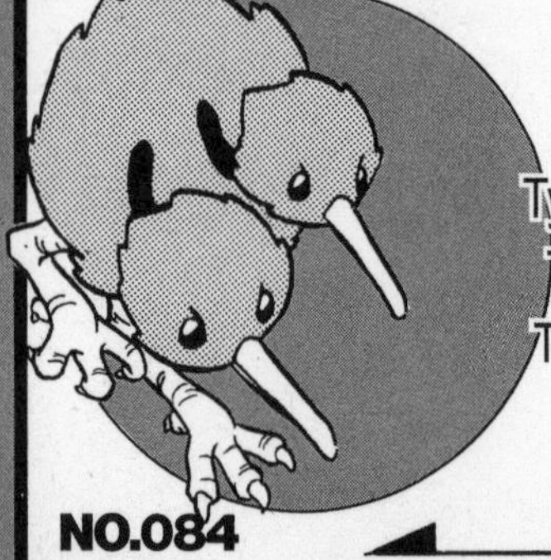

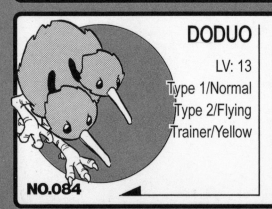

DODUO

LV: 13

Type 1/Normal

Type 2/Flying

Trainer/Yellow

WITH AMAZING SPEED AND A COMFORTABLE SADDLE, "DODY" THE DODUO IS A POKÉMON KNOWN FOR ITS POWERFUL LEGS! BUT THOSE LEGS ARE USED MORE FOR ESCAPING AND CONFUSING OPPONENTS THAN ATTACKING! COULD THAT BE BECAUSE YELLOW PREFERS TO INJURE NEITHER FRIEND NOR FOE...?!

NO.084

Message from
Hidenori Kusaka

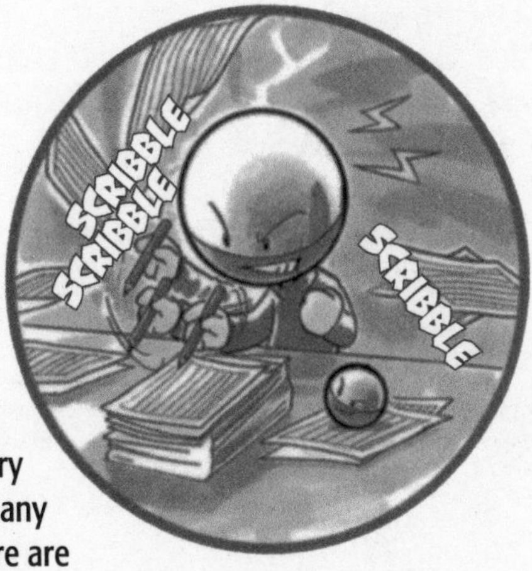
SCRIBBLE
SCRIBBLE
SCRIBBLE

In volume 4, the story heads off in a new direction, introducing new characters and brand-new adventures!! (Of course, your old friends are here too!) This second story arc proves that there are as many Pokémon stories to tell as there are Pokémon and Pokémon trainers... So enjoy!!

Message from
MATO

Fans of Yellow, your wait is over! Yellow makes his grand entrance in this special volume. I think you'll relate to Yellow's love of Pokémon. The Elite Four are a little scary... but I drew all the pictures with tender loving care anyway!

More Adventures Coming Soon...

Pokémon trainer Red has vanished... Trainer Yellow Caballero and Red's faithful Pikachu are off to rescue him. But it will take smarts, skills and a lot of help from friends and other Pokémon to find and rescue Red!

And watch out for the Elite Four, Yellow Caballero... Are you a strong enough Pokémon trainer to defeat all four of them?

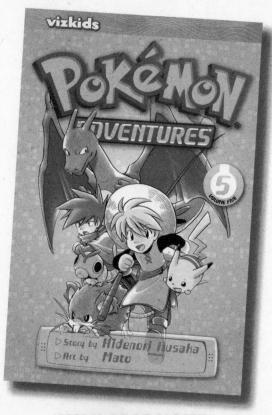

AVAILABLE NOW!

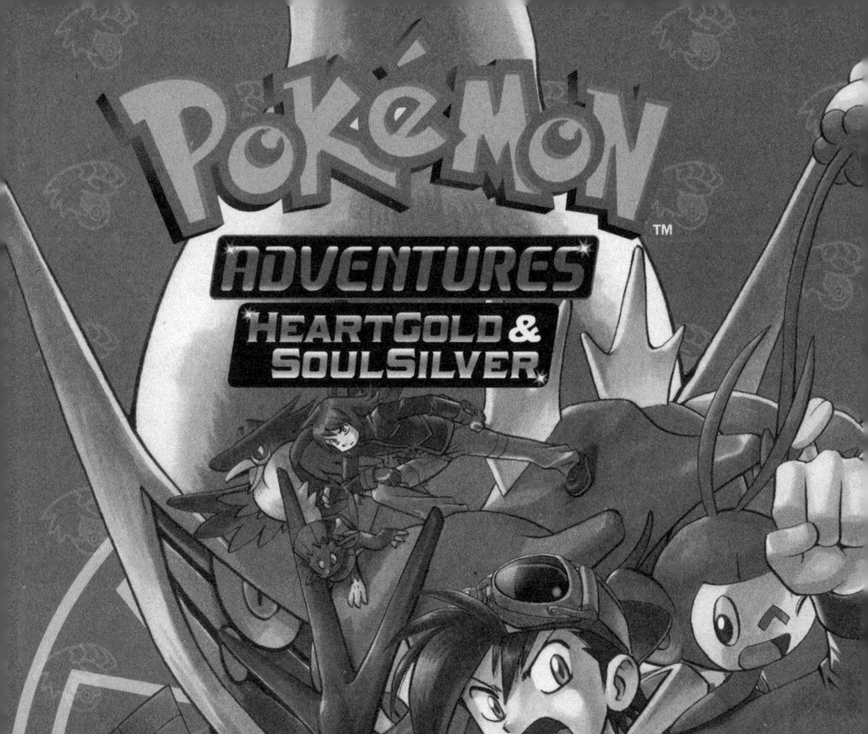
Pokémon™
ADVENTURES
HEARTGOLD & SOULSILVER
ory by HIDENORI KUSAKA
t by SATOSHI YAMAMOTO

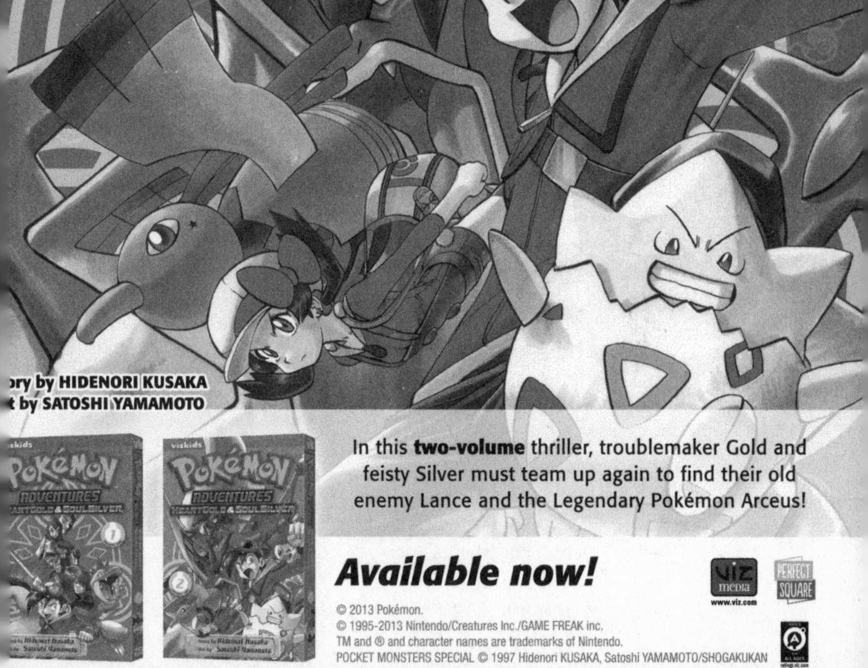

The adventure continues in the Johto region!

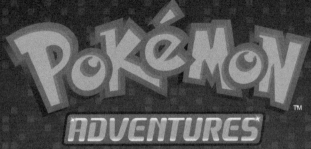

POKÉMON
ADVENTURES
GOLD & SILVER BOX SET

Includes **POKÉMON ADVENTURES** Vols. 8-14 and a collectible poster!

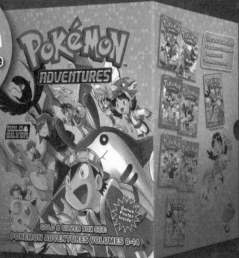

Story by
HIDENORI KUSAKA

Art by
MATO,

SATOSHI YAMAMOTO

More exciting Pokémon adventures starring Gold and his rival Silver! First someone steals Gold's backpack full of Poké Balls (and Pokémon!). Then someone steals Prof. Elm's Totodile. Can Gold catch the thief—or thieves?!

Keep an eye on Team Rocket, Gold... Could they be behind this crime wave?

www.viz.com

ISBN: 978-1-4215-8128-6

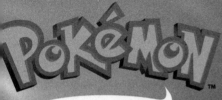

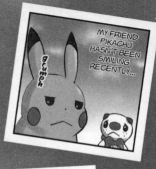

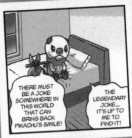

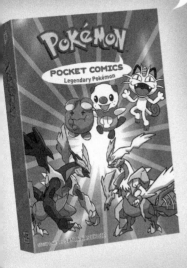

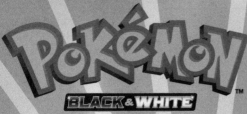
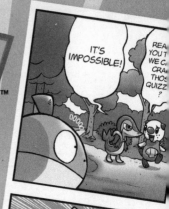
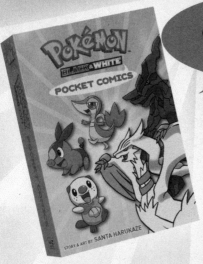

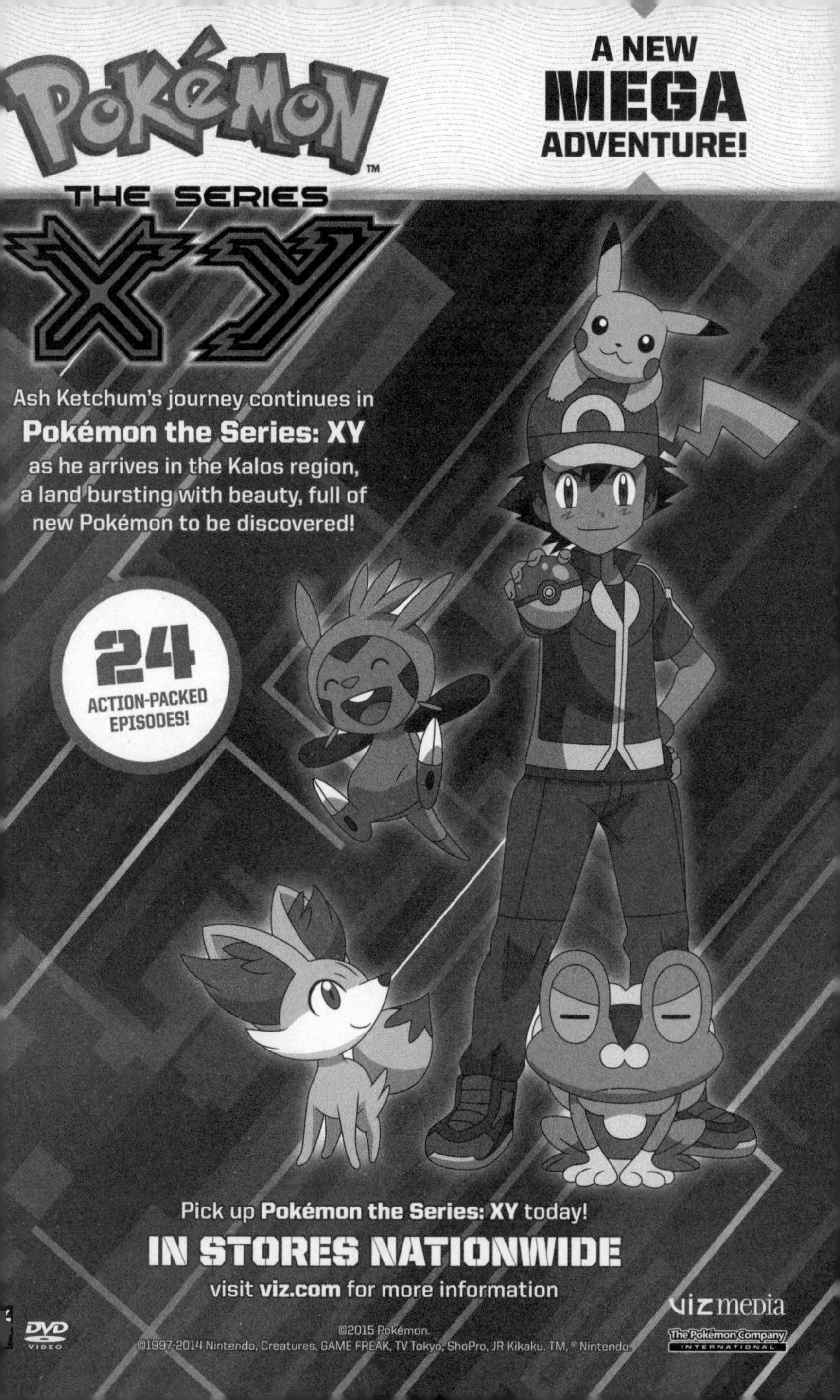

Pokémon™
THE SERIES
XY
A NEW
MEGA
ADVENTURE!
Ash Ketchum's journey continues in
Pokémon the Series: XY
as he arrives in the Kalos region, a land bursting with beauty, full of new Pokémon to be discovered!
24
ACTION-PACKED EPISODES!
Pick up Pokémon the Series: XY today!
IN STORES NATIONWIDE
visit viz.com for more information
viz media
The Pokémon Company INTERNATIONAL
DVD VIDEO
©2015 Pokémon.
©1997-2014 Nintendo, Creatures, GAME FREAK, TV Tokyo, ShoPro, JR Kikaku. TM, ® Nintendo.

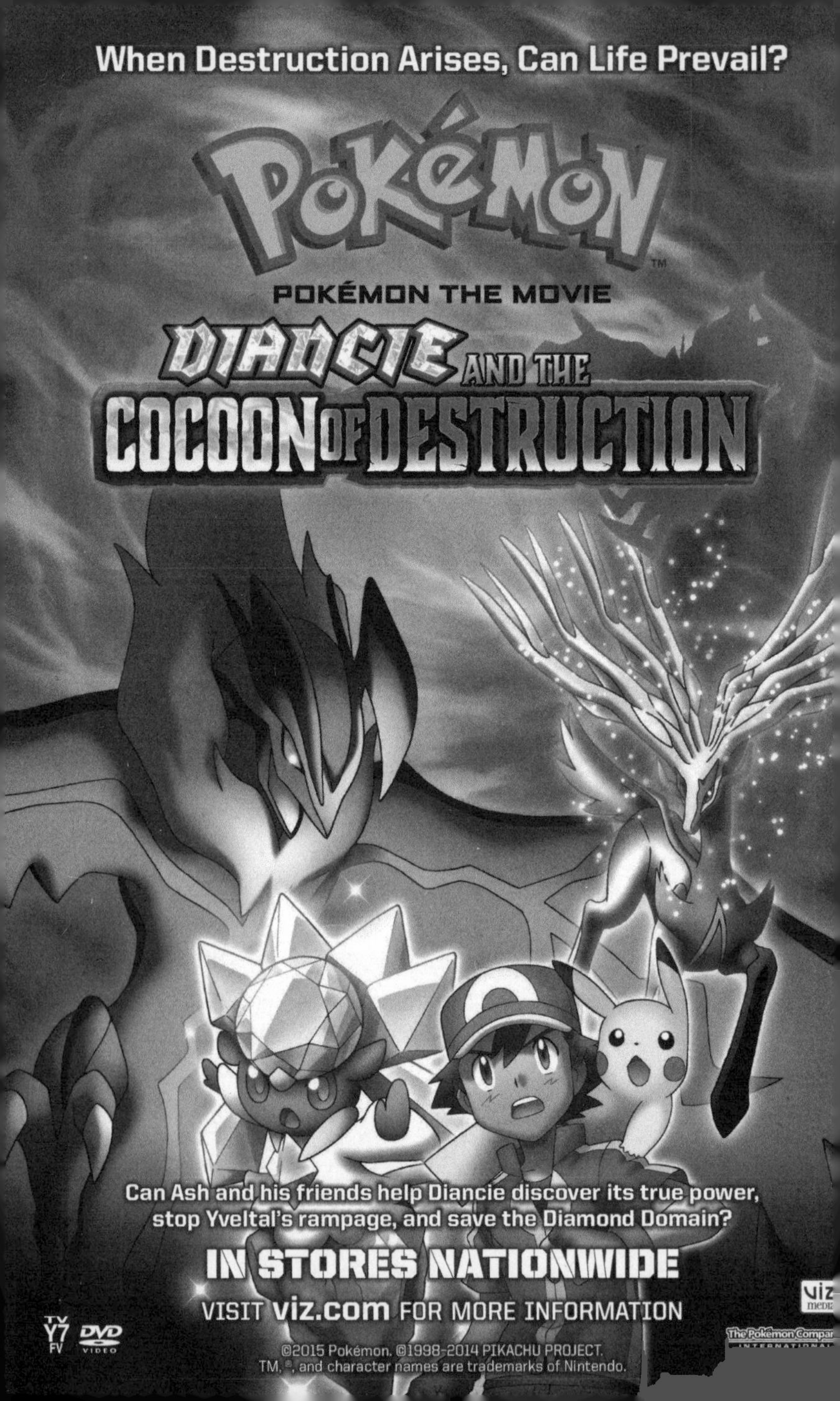
When Destruction Arises, Can Life Prevail?
POKÉMON
POKÉMON THE MOVIE
DIANCIE AND THE COCOON OF DESTRUCTION
Can Ash and his friends help Diancie discover its true power, stop Yveltal's rampage, and save the Diamond Domain?
IN STORES NATIONWIDE
VISIT viz.com FOR MORE INFORMATION
TV Y7 FV
DVD VIDEO
©2015 Pokémon. ©1998-2014 PIKACHU PROJECT.
TM, ®, and character names are trademarks of Nintendo.

Hey! You're Reading in the Wrong Direction!

This is the *end* of this graphic novel!

To properly enjoy this VIZ graphic novel, please turn it around and begin reading from **right to left.** Unlike English, Japanese is read right to left, so Japanese comics are read in reverse order from the way English comics are typically read.

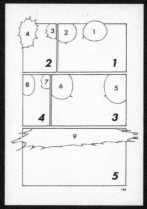

Follow the action this way

This book has been printed in the original Japanese format in order to preserve the orientation of the original artwork. Have fun with it!